KU-309-668

HOLLY GREEN

Workhouse Orphans

EBURY
PRESS

13 5 7 9 10 8 6 4 2

Ebury Press, an imprint of Ebury Publishing
20 Vauxhall Bridge Road,
London SW1V 2SA

Ebury Press is part of the Penguin Random House group of companies
whose addresses can be found at global.penguinrandomhouse.com

Copyright © Holly Green, 2017

Holly Green has asserted her right to be identified as the author of this work
in accordance with the Copyright, Designs and Patents Act 1988

This novel is a work of fiction. Names and characters are the product
of the author's imagination and any resemblance to actual persons,
living or dead, is entirely coincidental

First published in the UK in 2017 by Ebury Press

www.penguin.co.uk

A CIP catalogue record for this book is available from the British Library

ISBN 9781785039980

Printed and bound in Great Britain by Clays Ltd, St Ives PLC

Penguin Random House is committed to a sustainable future for our
business, our readers and our planet. This book is made from
Forest Stewardship Council® certified paper.

Prologue

'They've got to go! I've told you. We've got five of our own. We can't cope with any more. They'll have to go.'

May could hear Mr Johnson shouting from downstairs. Then she heard the door bang as he went off to his work on the docks. She shifted her position in the narrow, crowded bed. Jenny's elbow was sticking into her ribs and Maisie's foot was right by her nose.

A sound reached her, a sniff followed by a half-stifled whine, like the cry of an animal in pain. Gus was crying, and trying not to be heard. She eased herself out of the bed and wrapped her shawl round her shoulders. The boys' bed was close by and by the smell of it one of them had wet himself – not Gus, her little brother never did that. She bent down and scooped him up in her arms and he buried his face in her shoulder, snuffling. She moved over to the one rickety chair and sat down with him on her lap.

'Don't cry, Gus. It'll be all right. You'll see. We'll be all right.'

She wanted to believe it, but it was hard. She had been three when their father disappeared, 'lost at sea', and Gus just a baby. That was nearly three years ago. They had never seen much of him, because he was a sailor and away from home most of the time. She had got used to being without him; but she had seen her mother grow thin and tired, taking in washing to keep them from starving.

Then, just a few days ago, she had come in from playing out in the cobbled yard, with its smell from the two privies shared between eight families, to find Mrs Johnson waiting for her. 'Your mam's poorly,' she had said. 'You're going to stay with us for a while.' She had watched people going in and out of the house where she had grown up, and one day four men had come out carrying a big box and Percy, Mrs Johnson's eldest, had said, 'Your ma's dead. That's a coffin. They're taking her to be buried.'

As soon as they had eaten their breakfast, thin porridge made for six but shared out between eight, Mrs Johnson put on her cap and shawl and told Percy to keep an eye on the others and see they didn't get up to mischief while she was out. When she got back she took Gus on her lap and pulled May close to her.

'Now, listen to me. You understand your mam is dead, don't you?'

'What's dead?' Gus asked.

'It means she's gone to heaven to live with Jesus.'

'When's she coming back?'

'She can't come back, love. When people die they can't come back. But she'll be watching out for you, looking down from heaven, wanting you to be good and brave. But now, there's no one to look after you and you can't stay here, because there's too many of us already. You can see that, can't you?'

May nodded.

'So a nice man is coming today and he's going to take you to live in a big house at the top of the hill with lots of other children. That'll be good, won't it? You'll have your own beds again, and plenty to eat and friends to play with, so you must go along with him like good children. Understand?'

Gus just sniffed miserably but May nodded. Anything had to be better than sharing a bed with the other girls and hearing Mr Johnson shout at his wife.

The man arrived not long afterwards, a tall, thin man in a hat that made him look even taller and a coat that looked as if he had spilled something down it and not wiped it off properly. He and Mrs Johnson talked for a few minutes and then he said, 'Right, you two. You come along with me.'

Mrs Johnson came to the entry from the court into the road to see them off. 'Now, you be good children, and May, you look after your brother.'

'I will,' May promised.

They set off, almost running to keep up with the man's long strides. Gus began to grizzle and May took hold of his hand to help him along. She tried to ask the man about the place they were going to, but he did not seem to want to talk, so she kept quiet and let her imagination wander.

When her mother was alive and not too tired to talk, she used to tell them stories. They were always stories about poor little girls who somehow met a mysterious stranger who turned out to be a prince and took them to live in his beautiful palace. When May had asked what a palace was, her mother said it meant a big house full of lots of fine things. Perhaps, she thought, that was what Mrs Johnson had meant by the big house where they were going to live.

Perhaps this man was really a prince in disguise, or perhaps he was the prince's servant who had been sent to fetch them.

It seemed a long way, but at last they found themselves walking along the side of a high brick wall.

'Not far now,' the man said.

May thought the wall did not look much like the outside of a palace, but then perhaps it was just a wall round the palace gardens and the palace itself was inside. They came to a big gate and the man knocked. May held her breath, waiting to see what was on the other side. There was no palace, just a cobbled yard surrounded by more high brick walls. It was cold and the ground was damp, as if the walls stopped the sun from ever reaching it. Two men in shabby clothes were sweeping away dead leaves. As they crossed the space May heard a woman's voice, high pitched and cracked, yelling something unintelligible. The man led them down a narrow alley and up a flight of steps to a door, on which he knocked.

A gruff voice called, 'Come in.'

The man opened the door and he put one hand on May's shoulder and the other on Gus's to propel them inside. 'The two new orphans, Governor.'

A man with a bushy beard and side whiskers was sitting behind a desk. 'Very well. Ask Mrs Court and Mr Taylor to come here.'

The man left and the one he had called 'governor' opened a big book and picked up a pen.

'Name?'

May's legs were beginning to shake. 'May Lavender, sir.'

'Age?'

'Five and a half, sir. I'll be six in May.'

'And the boy?'

'He's Gus – Augustus, sir.'

'Age?'

'He was three last August.'

The governor peered at her as if he thought she might be telling fibs. 'You are May, and your birthday is in May. And he is Augustus, and his birthday is in August?'

'Yes, please, sir. It was our father's idea, I think. That's what my mam told me.'

The governor peered at his book and muttered as if he was talking to himself rather than her. 'Father lost at sea, mother deceased. No other relations.' There was a knock at the door. 'Come in.'

Two people entered: a woman in a black dress with a white cap and apron, and a man in a grey suit. The governor looked up.

'Ah, here you are. Two new inmates. May Lavender and her brother Augustus. I'll leave them in your charge.'

The woman held out her hand. 'Come along, May. You come with me.'

'And you come with me, boy,' the man said.

Gus looked at him and shrank back, grabbing May's hand.

'Please, sir,' May said, 'let him come with me. I always take care of him.'

'You may have done so,' the man said, 'but now he is in my care and he will come with me.'

'But why can't we go together?' May begged. 'He's my brother!'

'That's as may be. But boys and girls don't live together here. Gus will sleep in the boys' dormitory and be taught in the boys' classes, and you will sleep and be taught with the girls. That is how things are here.'

'But …' May began.

'Enough!' It was the governor's voice. 'You will learn not to argue, or you will regret it. Now, get along with you.'

Gus was still clinging to May's hand. She bent down to him. 'You must be a brave boy, Gus. Go along with the gentleman, like he asks.'

'No! No! I don't want to,' he wept, but the man stooped down and picked him up.

'You will have to learn to do as you are told, boy,' the man said. 'Now, shut your noise.'

He headed for the door and as he carried Gus down the stairs May could hear him crying, 'Let me go, let me go! I want May! May! May!'

The woman grabbed May's hand. 'Come along. There's nothing you can do. He'll get over it.'

As she was led down the stairs, May looked around her through eyes blurred with tears. 'Please, ma'am, where is this? It's not a palace, is it?'

'A palace?' The woman looked down at her and for a moment it seemed she was going to laugh. 'Whatever put that idea into your head? Don't you know what this place is?'

'No, ma'am. Mrs Johnson said a big house.'

'And you thought she meant a palace?' The woman's voice had softened. 'You poor mite. This is the workhouse.'

One

'Hold out your hand, girl!'

May bit her lip, scrunched her eyes closed and extended her hand, palm upwards. The ruler descended with a crack. There was a sharp sting, but May knew from experience that the worst pain would come a second later.

'That will teach you not to waste your time scribbling instead of getting on with your work. You are not a baby. You are thirteen years old. You should know better.'

'But ...' The word was out before May could stop it.

'But ... BUT!' Miss Bale's hollow cheeks flushed crimson. 'You dare "but" me, miss? Hold out the other hand.'

This time the blow was harder and tears forced themselves between May's closed lids. She opened her eyes and gazed up at the schoolmistress. It might mean further punishment, but the injustice was too great to be born.

'But I finished all the sums!'

For an instant Miss Bale's eyes flickered. 'Show me.'

May held up her slate. Down the centre was a neat column of sums, all worked out and all, she was sure, correct. Around them, the borders of the slate were decorated with an intricate pattern of leaves and flowers. May thought it looked rather beautiful.

'So you have time to waste!' Miss Bale's voice grated with anger. 'We shall have to make sure in future that you have enough to keep you occupied. Now, clean this mess off your slate and do the sums again. Go back to your seat.'

May returned to her place on the bench and reluctantly began to scrub her slate clean. Her friend Patty nudged her arm and gave her a quick look of sympathy, but neither of them dared to speak.

By the time May had redone the sums the bell had sounded for dinner, but as she rose to follow the other girls, Miss Bale's voice cut through the scraping of benches and the shuffling of feet. 'Not you, miss! You can sit back down and work these new sums, since you're so quick at it.'

She wrote six more sums on the blackboard and May's spirits sank. By the time she finished them dinner would be almost over. She would be lucky to get anything to eat before supper.

When at last she had finished and was dismissed, it occurred to her that Miss Bale had probably missed her meal as well. That was some comfort. In the dining hall, the children had finished eating. The boys were dismissed first, and May had to wait by the door as they filed out. From habit she searched the line for one bright ginger head. Poor Gus! Saddled with the double burden of red hair and a ridiculous name. She had been luckier. Her hair was darker, more like the colour of one of last year's conkers. She did not mind being called May, but she thought Augustus was a cruel infliction on a small boy.

As her brother drew closer she saw that his nose had been bleeding and his lip was cut. 'Gus!' she hissed. 'You've been fighting again!' He shrugged and made to pass by her. She caught his arm. 'Meet me outside the chapel door at the end of dinner break.'

'You there!' It was the schoolmaster's voice. 'Get on and stop talking!'

Gus twitched his arm out of her grasp and walked on.

The girls were dismissed next and May was about to join the line, her stomach grumbling with hunger, when one of the women who had been given the job of supervising the dining hall called out to her.

'May? Where've you been, ducks? You've missed your dinner.'

May looked across the room. It was Ruby, who always had a kind word for her. She was small, round-faced and cheerful, and how she had ended up in the workhouse, May did not know. It was not something you asked – not as a child to an adult, anyway. It was not hard to see why some of them were there. There was very little contact between the children and the adults, except for those like Ruby who were trusted to help in the running of the place, but she had seen them wandering the narrow lanes, dishevelled and muttering to themselves. But there were plenty of others, respectable-looking women, who were there for no reason May could understand. She went to Ruby.

'Miss Bale gave me extra work to do.'

'Oh, did she?! Yes, she doesn't like the clever ones. 'Fraid they'll show her up, I shouldn't wonder. Sit down there. There's still some broth in the kitchen.'

She bustled away and came back with a tin bowl full of soup, in which a few pieces of gristly beef floated, and a hunk of bread.

'Get that inside you, but be quick. I'll catch it if I'm not back in the kitchen soon.'

'Thank you, Ruby. I'm famished.' May ate rapidly, knowing that the dinner break was almost over and afraid that the bell might ring before she had time to swallow it all. The food they were given was wholesome enough but there was never quite enough of it and she could not afford to miss out completely. She just had time to wipe up the last of the gravy with her bread before Ruby whisked the plate away and hurried off to the kitchen.

Outside, she found Gus huddled into a corner of the porch in front of the chapel door.

'What do you want?' he demanded fretfully. 'We'll catch it if they find us nattering.'

'I can talk to my own brother, can't I?' May asked, knowing full well that the answer was 'no'. Any communication between the boys and the girls was strictly forbidden, even between brother and sister. 'You know what I want,' she went on, before he could contradict her. 'Why were you fighting?'

'What am I supposed to do?' he replied. 'Jackson was saying I never really had a father. He said I was a bas—'

'Hush! You are not to use that word. You don't need to fight him. You know quite well that we did have a father, and a mother. Just tell anyone who asks that our dad's dead, that he was lost at sea.'

'Lost at sea!' he repeated angrily. 'What's that mean anyway?'

'I suppose it means he drowned. I suppose his ship sank.'

'He might not be dead,' Gus said. 'Lost doesn't mean dead.'

'Yes, it does. If he was still alive he would have come home, wouldn't he?'

'Maybe he couldn't. Maybe he's marooned on a desert island. I've heard stories like that. Maybe he found buried treasure and he's living in a palace. Maybe he's forgotten all about us.'

May looked at her brother's small, fierce face and understood the pain behind it. 'Don't, Gus. He wouldn't forget. He's dead and gone. You have to get used to that.'

'I don't believe you. One day I'm going to go to sea and look for him.'

'Gus …' But he had turned and was already running back to the boys' yard on the far side of the chapel.

The bell on the roof of the chapel sounded and May moved away. It was time for work. From her first days in the workhouse, May had been made to understand that one day she would have to leave and make her own way in the world. It was her duty to make herself ready to perform some useful function, which would allow her to earn her own living.

That meant, almost certainly, going into domestic service. It had taken her some time to understand that her future life would be spent scrubbing and cooking and mending for some family that was not her own, but she had had to accept it. So every afternoon was devoted to learning a skill that would prepare her for that.

That day, it was her turn to work in the nursery, where the babies of some of the women were cared for, along with the foundlings who were left outside the workhouse door. She made her way along the narrow lane between the tall buildings, the brick walls rising on either side to shut out all but a small strip of sky. In the yard a few women still recovering from childbirth were sitting in a corner where the autumn sun still penetrated, and May walked by them to the door of the nursery. Patty was waiting for her.

'Where have you been? We're late.'

'I had to talk to Gus. He's been fighting again.'

'Oh, that brother of yours! Come on.'

They opened the door to be greeted by the sound of furious wails and the harassed voice of one of the workhouse women who had been given the job of caring for the infants. There were half a dozen of them, all inmates of the workhouse, and May had got to know them by now. Some had small children themselves and were, to some degree at least, patient with the little ones in their charge; but there were two who seemed to resent the job and who tried to impose order by fear. They were overseen by a paid matron, but she was too overloaded with work to supervise them effectively.

The noise was coming from an infant May had not seen before, a little girl with a mass of golden curls, her face red with the effort of screaming. One of the women, a hard-faced character who never used her first name and was always called Smithy, was holding the child up and shaking her, shouting at her to shut up. Instinctively May hurried across to her.

'Shall I take her, Smithy? I know you've got a lot of work to get on with.'

'Take her and welcome! I've had enough of the little devil.'

She thrust the child into May's arms and went to deal with another wailing infant. May cuddled the little mite close and rocked her, singing softly. It was a song she remembered her mother singing as she nursed Gus.

'Lavender's blue, dilly dilly, lavender's green. When I am king, dilly dilly, you shall be queen ...'

Since her name was May Lavender she had always believed that the song was specially written for her. She still cherished a few memories from those long ago days, when she still had a family, when 'home' meant love and security, not brick walls and regimented discipline.

Smithy returned. 'You seem to have a knack with her. You'd better look after her from now on.'

May looked down at the child in her arms. She had stopped screaming and was quiet except for occasional hiccupping sobs. Her hot little head was resting on May's shoulder and she was sucking her thumb.

'That's a habit you'll have to break her of,' Smithy commented.

'Where has she come from?' May asked.

'Who knows? The porter found her outside the main door when he opened up this morning. Dumped there, sometime in the night, without so much as a note or a change of clothes. Lucky she didn't freeze to death.'

'Poor little mite. What's her name?'

'She doesn't have one – or if she does, we've no way of knowing.'

'Can I give her a name?'

'I don't see why not. What are you going to call her?'

May looked down at the golden head on her shoulder. 'I shall call her Angel. Don't you think she looks like a little angel?'

'That's not a proper name and she's more like a little devil, if you ask me. What a temper! No wonder her mother wanted rid of her! Anyway, you can look after her while

13

you're here. You'd better see if you can get her to take some food. She's turned her nose up at everything I've offered her.' She reached over to a nearby table. 'You'd better have this – she seems very attached to it.'

'This' was a rag doll, stained and frayed but obviously once very beautiful and as soon as she saw it the child stretched her arms for it and clutched it to her with little grunts and murmurs of pleasure.

From then on Angel became May's special care. She bathed her and changed her clothes, and persuaded her to take milk from a feeding cup and gruel from a spoon. But she could only be with her in the afternoons and the women told her that when she was not present the child screamed and refused to eat. May longed to be able to look after her all the time, but she knew it would be useless to ask to miss her lessons. All she could do was hurry to the nursery every day as soon as she had swallowed her dinner.

May dreaded the time when her spell in the nursery would come to an end. Until then she had not enjoyed working there. It was messy and smelly and the wailing of the babies upset her, but now it was the only place she wanted to be.

The next lessons were in needlecraft, something she normally enjoyed, but the thought of leaving Angel to Smithy's mercy was almost unbearable As the end of the month approached, she plucked up her courage and knocked at the door of the matron's office.

'Well?' Matron was an angular woman who seemed permanently harassed.

'Please, ma'am.' May struggled to prevent her voice from trembling. 'I've been looking after little Angel ...'

'Looking after who?'

'Angel, ma'am.'

'You mean Angela? The child has been baptised Angela. Angel is not a proper name.'

'Beg pardon, ma'am. Angela then. I'm the only one who can get her to stop crying and eat, but next week I've got to go to my needlework classes instead of coming to the nursery …'

'Well, what do you want? Get to the point, girl.'

'Could I be excused from needlework and go on looking after Angel … Angela … instead?'

'Good heavens, girl! I've never heard such nonsense. Do you really imagine that you are so indispensable? The child will eat when she's hungry, or go without. We've no time here to pander to her whims. And you have your classes to attend. Now, get along and stop wasting my time.'

There was nothing for it but to submit. All May could do from then on was to spend every spare moment she could find in the nursery. To her great delight, as soon as she saw her, Angel would stretch out her arms and babble 'My-may'.

'She knows me! She's trying to say my name.'

'That's all very well for you,' was Smithy's response. 'She keeps it up even when you're not here. I'm sick of hearing My-may.'

Mrs Kelly, the needlework teacher, was a widow who had earned her living as a seamstress before her marriage. She was small and plump, with a sharp nose and small, bright eyes that made her look, May thought, a bit like one of the robins who hopped around the yard outside the bakehouse looking for crumbs. May admired her skill when she demonstrated new techniques, her nimble fingers flying over the fabric, creating tiny, almost invisible stitches. She was softly spoken and patient with the clumsy efforts of some of the girls, and they all loved her.

Much of the work involved patching and mending the clothes worn by the other inmates, or making shirts and shifts to replace those that were worn out; but girls who showed sufficient skill were sometimes set the task of making articles for sale to the general public, to bring money into the coffers of the workhouse. Occasionally, there would be a special commission from someone who knew that this was a way of getting very high-quality work at a lower price than they would have had to pay elsewhere. May was good with her needle, and was one of those chosen for this more highly skilled work.

Sometimes, when they were all quietly occupied, Mrs Kelly would read aloud to them from a large book of fairy tales. It was beautifully illustrated with pictures of ladies in flowing gowns and princes in cloaks and feathered hats, standing in front of castles with towers and battlements or houses with roses growing round the doors. May loved looking at these pictures, but what fascinated her most was the fact that each one was framed by an elaborate design of leaves and flowers. It was that which had inspired her to create the pattern that had gotten her into so much trouble with Miss Bale. While her attention was fully occupied with Angel, she had almost forgotten her desire to draw, but now it returned, stronger than ever.

An order had come in for a batch of gentlemen's white evening shirts and May had been given one of them to make up. She had finished the work and taken it out to the teacher's table for her approval, but Mrs Kelly was engaged in unpicking a botched seam from another girl's work and demonstrating how it should be done. Waiting for her attention, May's eyes wandered over the table. The fabric for the shirts had been delivered wrapped in sheets of fine white paper, which had been neatly folded and laid aside. When she lived at home her mother used to let her draw on the paper bags that groceries came in, but here the only materials on offer were slates and chalk. The sight of those clean, white sheets presented an irresistible temptation. May glanced at Mrs Kelly's back. It looked as though she would be busy for some time. Cautiously she drew the paper towards her. There were pencils in a pot on the desk. She lifted one out and began to draw on one corner. Very soon she was so absorbed that she was unaware that Mrs Kelly had returned to the table, until a voice said, 'Well, well. What's all this?'

May shot upright, her hands going instinctively behind her back. 'Sorry, ma'am. I didn't mean … I thought … I didn't think the paper was needed any more.'

'Quite, quite.' Mrs Kelly's response was absent-minded. She was scrutinising May's drawing. 'Is this your own design?'

'Yes, ma'am. I mean, I saw something like it in the book you showed us.'

'Ah, so you copied it?'

'No, ma'am, not exactly. It gave me the idea, but it's not the same.'

Mrs Kelly looked across the table to where the book lay. It was closed. 'So you did this from memory.'

'Sort of.'

'You have a talent, May. We must find a use for it. Now, what did you want?'

May gasped with relief. 'Oh, I've finished the shirt, ma'am. I hope it's all right.'

The work was approved and there was still some time left before the end of the class. Mrs Kelly pushed the wrapping paper across the desk. 'There you are. You may as well finish what you began.'

For the next half-hour, May drew with total concentration and when they bell sounded Mrs Kelly took the paper and carefully folded it. 'May I keep this?'

May swallowed. No one had ever asked her permission for anything before. 'Yes, ma'am. 'Course you can.'

On her next visit to the nursery, Smithy was looking more irritable than ever.

'Is something wrong?' May asked.

'That wretched child you call Angel. She's been keeping us all awake every night. Every hour or two she wakes up and cries, and that sets the others off. I'm worn out with it. If it goes on I'm going to shut her in the bathhouse at night. She can scream her heart out there without disturbing anyone else.'

May felt tears sting the backs of her eyes. The thought of the little girl she had grown to love so much howling and alone was unbearable.

'Why not let me take her?' She spoke impulsively. 'She can sleep with me in the girls' dormitory.'

'And keep all of you awake instead? Nurse Baker would thank me for that – I don't think.'

Nurse Baker was one of the women in charge of the dormitory. They were given the title of 'nurse', though none of them had ever studied medicine.

'She might not cry if she was with me,' May said desperately. 'She's always good with me.'

'Because you spoil her, cuddling her and singing to her. She's a right little madam and you let her rule you. It'll do her no good in the long run, mark my words.'

May tried a new tack. 'You look ever so tired, Smithy. You need a good night's sleep. Why not let me take her for one night and see how it goes.'

Smithy looked from her to the child in her arms, frowning in indecision. Then she said, 'Well, Baker owes me a good turn. It's against the rules, but she'll turn a blind eye if I ask her. Take her for one night, but if she causes mayhem – and she will – it's the bathhouse for her and no mistake.'

As soon as she had finished her supper of milksoup and bread, May hurried to the nursery. She wrapped Angel, who was grizzling fretfully, in a shawl, picked up the rag doll from which she hated being parted, and carried her up to the dormitory she shared with forty other girls. It was a long, narrow room lined on both sides with beds so closely packed together that they were almost touching. It was on the second floor, just under the roof beams, which were festooned with cobwebs. The two 'nurses' on duty slept at the far end, away from the draughts that came up the narrow staircase and often after the lamps had been extinguished they would sit gossiping in low voices by the light of a candle. Neither of them took any notice as May carried Angel to her own bed nearer to the door.

Some of the other girls gathered round, excited and curious. 'What have you got there, May? Who is she? Do they know in the nursery you've got her? Why have you brought her up here?'

'You're daft about that child,' Patty said grimly. 'If she keeps us all awake you can go and sleep on the stairs with her.'

May undressed quickly and got into bed, cuddling Angel close to her. The little girl stopped whimpering and gazed up at her with wide, blue eyes. 'My-may,' she mumbled. 'My-may.'

'Hush,' May whispered. 'Go to sleep now.'

Angel gurgled quietly to herself for a few minutes, then she put her thumb in her mouth and fell asleep.

May was woken sometime later, but not by Angel. She was aware of movement and low voices and, opening her eyes, she saw a thin figure in a white nightgown walking down the narrow aisle between the beds towards the door. Nurse Baker was behind her, repeating her name in a hoarse whisper.

'Jeanie! Jeanie! Come back to bed. Where do you think you're going?'

There was no response. Jeanie kept walking, her eyes fixed straight ahead. Baker caught up with her and grabbed her arm.

'Will you listen to me! Get back to bed this instant!'

Jeanie twisted in her grip with a cry of fear. 'Let go of me! What … how did I get here?'

'Sleepwalking. I thought so. Come on, back to bed.'

Baker marched the now-weeping girl back down the dormitory and shoved her unceremoniously onto her bed. 'Stay there, if you know what's good for you.'

The following evening there was no objection when May went to collect Angel from the nursery.

'That's the best night's sleep I've had since the little horror arrived,' Smithy said. 'I bet you're regretting your offer now, aren't you?'

'No, she was fine. No trouble at all.'

'You'd better carry on, then.'

As May undressed for bed she became aware of low sobs from the other end of the room.

'No, please! Please don't do this! I'll be good, I promise.'

It was Jeanie's voice. Then Baker's in reply. 'Can't have you wandering about at night. You might have fallen down the stairs and killed yourself, say nothing of disturbing the rest of us. Now be a good girl and lie still.'

Peering down the room, May saw that Baker had fastened a rope round each of Jeanie's wrists and was tying it to the metal bedstead.

'There! That'll stop your nonsense. Now shut that noise and go to sleep.'

Long after lights out May could hear Jeanie whimpering. She longed to go and set her free but she knew that if she drew attention to herself it would almost certainly result in Angel being sent back to the nursery.

The following day, at the beginning of the needlework class, Mrs Kelly placed a small pile of fine cambric squares in front of May.

'Lady wants a dozen handkerchiefs as a present for her husband. These will need to be hemstitched and then his initials embroidered in the corner: D. L. You can embellish them to your own design. Here's some paper to sketch out your ideas. See what you can make of it.'

May settled to the work with alacrity. The hemstitching was tedious but she was thrilled when Mrs Kelly placed a box containing embroidery silks in many colours in front of her and left her free to choose. For the next few days she sketched and stitched, happier than she could ever remember being since she came into the workhouse.

The month was almost over and all but one of the dozen handkerchiefs were finished when May woke in the middle of the night to some kind of uproar at the far end of the room. There were shouts of alarm and then a scream, and one of the girls came running past, heading for the stairs, followed by two others. Sitting up in bed, May saw smoke filling the end of the room and at the heart of the smoke a red glow. Someone shouted, 'Fire! Fire! Get out! Get out!' More figures raced towards her, screaming. They reached the door and there was a struggle as they all tried to be first out. Another girl appeared out of the smoke with her nightgown on fire, flames streaming behind her as she ran.

May was on her feet by now, about to grab Angel and join the scramble for the stairs. An image flashed into her mind – her own shawl ablaze from a spark from the fire, her mother flinging her to the ground and covering her with the rag rug, beating out the flames. Without conscious thought she seized the blanket from her bed, and as the girl reached her she grabbed hold of her and pushed her to the floor, then threw the blanket over her and fell on top of it, using her own weight to suppress the flames. Staggering to her feet, she dragged the now-naked girl up with her and shouted 'Out! Go!' Then she picked up Angel, who was screaming, and ran for the door.

As she reached it, she was suddenly stopped short by a piteous cry from behind her.

'Help me! Please, somebody help me!'

It was Jeanie's voice and May realized with horror that she was still tied to her bed. She looked back. The flames were roaring now and smoke filled the far end of the room. The roof timbers had begun to smoulder and the fire was creeping ever closer to the bed where Jeanie lay helpless. A few more figures emerged from the smoke and staggered towards her. There was no sign of either of the nurses and no one paused to heed Jeanie's desperate appeals. May looked round. Patty was waiting at the door, urging her to hurry. She thrust Angel into her arms.

'Get her downstairs. Keep her safe.'

'Where are you going?'

'Back – for Jeanie.'

Smoke stung her eyes and made her choke as she stumbled back towards Jeanie's bed. The heat scorched her skin and she saw that the roof beam immediately above the bed was on fire and could collapse at any moment. She pulled her nightgown up and held a fold of it over her mouth and nose and forced herself to go on. Jeanie was screaming now.

'It's all right!' May choked out. 'I'll get you undone.'

She dropped to her knees by the bed and fumbled with the knots holding the rope to the frame. Her hands were already burnt from her earlier efforts and Jeanie's struggles had pulled them tight. Try as she might, she could not prize them loose.

'Keep still!' she begged. 'You're making it worse.'

Jeanie subsided, sobbing, and at last the knot gave. Jeanie's right arm was free, but her left wrist was still fastened to the far side of the bed. May stretched herself across the other girls' body and wrestled with the knots on that side. Above her she could hear the beam creaking and the flames were only feet away. Her eyes were streaming so much that she could no longer see what she was doing and she had to work by touch alone. For a few desperate moments she thought that she might have to give up and leave Jeanie to her fate; then the knot gave way and Jeanie wrenched her arm loose.

The two of them rolled off the bed and May found that here, on the floor, it was a little easier to breathe.

'Stay down,' she croaked. 'Crawl.'

Half crawling, half crouching, pulling Jeanie with her, she headed towards the door. Smoke billowed round them and at moments May almost lost her sense of direction. Feeling her way from bed to bed, choking for breath, she struggled on, until suddenly the way ahead was clear and the cold night air filled her lungs. She staggered to her feet, reached the top of the narrow staircase, and fainted.

Two

May opened her eyes. Where was she? This was not the dormitory where she usually slept with the other girls, and this was not her bed. Her body felt stiff and bruised and her hands hurt. She tried to sit up, but a gentle hand was laid on her shoulder.

'Lie quiet, sweetheart. Everything's all right. Just you rest.'

A face appeared above her, a beautiful face, but strange to May's eyes. Large, lustrous black eyes were framed by curling hair as dark and shiny as the wings of the starlings that fluttered around the yards, and the skin around them was the colour of the strong tea that she had seen on Matron's desk.

'Who are you?' May whispered. Her throat was sore and it was hard to speak.

'My name's Dorinda, honey – but most people call me Dora. I'm here to look after you. Now, drink this. Let me help you.'

An arm was slipped under her shoulders and she was helped to sit up and a cup was held to her lips. She sipped the water gratefully and lay back.

'What happened? Why am I here?'

'You don't remember?'

'No ... wait ... there was a fire.' Suddenly the memory was vivid: flames approaching; the heat and crackle and the choking smoke; the struggle to undo stubborn knots. 'Jeannie! Is Jeannie safe?'

'Just here beside you. Look.'

May turned her head. Jeannie was lying in the next bed. Her back was towards her but she could see that her head and one arm were heavily bandaged.

'Is she all right?'

'Thanks to you. You saved her life, you know that?'

'Did I?'

'If you hadn't untied her she would have perished along with the others, that's for sure.'

'Others? Do you mean some were ... some didn't get away?'

'Twenty-two children dead. It's a tragedy.'

'Oh no!' May felt a sudden surge of panic. 'The boys' dormitory – my brother Gus ...'

'Don't worry. The fire didn't spread to that floor. Your brother will be fine. But you could have escaped easily, from what I hear. You were near the door. But you went back. You're a brave girl.'

May looked down at her hands, wondering why they hurt so much. They were swathed in bandages. 'My hands!'

'You got burnt undoing those knots. But the doctor says they will heal. You will still be able to use them.'

May gazed at the bandages. Suppose the doctor was wrong. How would she survive if she could not use her hands? Suddenly another memory surfaced.

'Angel? Is Angel all right?'

'The little girl you had with you? Back in the nursery, safe and sound. No need to worry about her. Now lie back and try to sleep. You need to rest.'

May was woken from a doze by a hoarse voice calling her name. 'May? May! Are you all right?'

She looked round and saw Jeannie leaning towards her from the next bed. Under the bandage her face was patched with red and black and her eyes were swollen. 'I'm all right,' she assured her. 'How about you?'

'I'll be all right soon, I expect. But I wouldn't be if it wasn't for you. You saved my life.'

'Oh well.' May dropped her eyes. 'I couldn't just leave you there, could I?'

'The others did,' Jeannie said. 'I kept yelling to them to untie me but they just ran.'

'What happened to Nurse Baker and Margery? Why didn't they untie you?'

Jeannie shrugged. 'Don't know. I didn't see them.'

Dora came in with bowls of soup.

'Well, now. I'll have to feed you both, till you get the bandages off your hands. Who's first?'

'Feed May. I can wait.'

Dora sat May up and put a pillow behind her, then she perched on the bed and began to spoon soup into her mouth.

'This is good!' May said.

'Special broth for our two wounded heroes.'

When May had finished, and Dora was feeding Jeannie, she asked, 'How did the fire start?'

'No one knows for sure. But they think the two nurses had a candle lit. Maybe they fell asleep without putting it out.'

'So they're to blame?'

'Well, if they are, they're well punished.'

'How do you mean?'

'It seems they died along with the children.'

'That's terrible.'

'I don't think so,' Jeannie said. 'If it was their fault they deserved it.'

May shook her head and said no more. She could see the justice of Jeannie's words, but the thought of all those children and the two women, all burnt to death, was too horrible to contemplate. To distract her thoughts she asked, 'Where are you from, Dora? You're ... well, different, from most people round here.'

'Different?' Dora looked at her with raised eyebrows. 'You must have seen others like me. There are plenty of black faces in Liverpool.'

May thought back, to the days before she came to the workhouse. 'You mean slaves?'

'Brought here as slaves, yes. Free now ... at least that's what we're told. Free to starve sometimes.'

'But ...' May wrestled with this new concept '... but you're not black.'

'Not a black as my mother was, that's true. But not as white as my father, either.'

'Your father was a white man? But then how ...?'

Dora patted her arm. 'That's enough questions. It's a long story, and I don't tell it 'less I'm forced to. Now, settle back and rest.'

Later on she came back, carrying the rag doll, somewhat singed but otherwise intact.

'This was found in your bed when they were clearing up after the fire. Is it something you were given as a little child?'

'Oh, no! It's not mine. It's Angel's. She'll be missing it. Can you take it to the nursery for her, please?'

Dora put the doll on May's bed. 'Best you give it to her yourself when you see her. I've got enough to do without trekking down to the nursery.' Dora's voice was firm but kindly.

May spent five days in the infirmary. On the fifth, the doctor came and took the bandages off her hands. May shuddered at the sight of them, but he said it could have been much worse.

'Can you move your fingers?'

She tried gingerly. It hurt, but she could move them.

'There you are,' the doctor said. 'You've been lucky. Just make sure you exercise them, even if it is painful.' He stood up. 'Right. No need for you to stay in bed. You can go back to your usual routine.'

As soon as she was released, May headed for the nursery, carrying Angel's rag doll. It was morning, and she should have been in the classroom under the chapel, working out sums or scratching the words of a spelling test on her slate, and she knew she would be punished if Miss Bale found out, but she had to see for herself that Angel was all right. She hurried in through the door and came to a standstill, casting her eyes around the room. There were the usual babes in arms, lying in their cots; the usual toddlers staggering around the room; the usual noise of crying babies and babbling children and the usual, all-pervading smell of wet nappies. But there was no sign of Angel. She searched the room for the beloved golden head, but in vain.

Smithy came towards her. 'What are you doing here? You're not supposed to be working here this month. Anyway, you're too early. It's not dinner time yet.'

'Angel!' May begged. 'Where is she?'

'Oh, her. Gone, and good riddance.'

'What do you mean, gone? She's not … not dead?'

'Dead? No, whatever put that idea into your head? She's been adopted.'

'Adopted?' May felt as if all the breath had been knocked out of her body. 'How … who … when?'

'Couple of days ago. Don't ask me who. Man and woman came here, her all dressed up in a fur coat. Governor brought them in, said they were looking for a baby to adopt.'

'Angel isn't a baby.'

'I know that! But the woman took one look at her and she said, "That's the one! That's the one I want," and nothing would persuade her different. I could have told them that golden curls don't make a child an angel, whatever you like to call her. But she'd made up her mind. She'll soon find out her mistake. Me, I'm glad to see the back of the little madam.'

'But I loved her, and she loved me.' May wept. 'How could they take her away?'

'You should be glad, if you really care for her. I told you, there's money there. That child will be brought up as a little princess, you mark my words.'

'But who was it? How will I ever find her again?'

'I told you. I don't know the name. You won't find her, and you shouldn't look. Do you think she'll want to be reminded where she came from?'

May turned away and wandered out of the room. Her chest ached and her eyes were stinging and a cold hand gripped her insides. One thought went round and round in her brain. How could this have happened? How could

Angel have been taken from her, when she cared for her so much? How would she ever find her again? She found she was still holding the rag doll, which she had intended to give back. She pressed it to her face and felt her tears soak into the fabric.

Her feet took her automatically back towards the chapel and the classroom beneath it, but as she reached it the bell rang for the end of the morning session and the other children came tumbling up the stairs, eager to get their dinner. May stood back, waiting for the line to pass her, intending to follow.

'May!'

The call came from the line of boys issuing from the room on the far side of the chapel. It was Gus. She waved at him, but he left the line and pushed his way through the girls to reach her.

'You all right? I heard you got burnt. They wouldn't let me come see you ...'

'I'm fine,' she assured him. 'It's just my hands. They'll be better soon.'

'You, boy!' It was Miss Bale's voice. 'Get back in your line – now!' Gus gave May a look of helpless appeal and turned away. 'Now, miss!' the teacher went on. 'What do you think you're doing?'

May swallowed and put her hands behind her. Surely even Miss Bale wouldn't use the ruler on her now – not with her hands as they were. 'Sorry, ma'am. I only got out of the infirmary a little while ago.'

'I know that. You should have come straight to your lessons. You have been looked for. The governor wants to see you.'

'The governor!' May stared at her. She had never spoken to the governor, had only seen him passing through the rooms, usually in the company of some important personage. Why would he want to see her? What had she done?

'Don't stand there with your mouth open like the village idiot!' Miss Bale said. 'Come along, we mustn't keep Mr Ferguson waiting any longer.'

There was something in her voice that made May look up at her. She was anxious, even nervous! Of course. She would have been expected to know where May was, and produce her without delay. No wonder she was angry. It was a revelation, that teachers could be afraid of authority too. But that thought was banished by other more urgent concerns as she followed Miss Bale between the tall buildings towards the governor's house. If he wanted to see her so urgently her transgression must be very serious. Had he found out that she had Angel with her in the dormitory? It was against the rules, but would such an important man bother with something as small as that. So what else could it be? She must have done something terrible, and the worst part of it was, she didn't even know what it was.

By the time they reached the door of the governor's office May's knees were shaking so much it was hard to walk straight. Miss Bale knocked and a gruff voice bade them enter.

'You wanted to see May Lavender, Governor.'

The governor's hair was grey and thinning, but his luxuriant whiskers and bushy eyebrows seemed to be trying to make up for it. He peered out from among them and raised a hand.

'Come here, girl.'

Miss Bale gave May a shove in the small of her back that almost made her stumble. Shaking, she stepped forward and stood in front of the big, shiny desk.

'May Lavender?'

'Yes, sir.' Her voice was little more than a squeak.

'Show me your hands.'

There was a big ruler on the desk. May stretched her hands forward but she was trembling so much it was hard to keep them still. The governor put on a pair of spectacles and peered at them.

'Hmm. The doctor was right.' He looked up. 'I'm told you exhibited considerable courage at the time of the fire.'

'I ... I just did what I had to do, sir. I couldn't leave Jeannie to burn.'

'No, quite, quite.' He took off the glasses and studied her face. 'You seem to me to be a young woman with a strong sense of duty. That is to be commended. How old are you?'

'Thirteen, sir. Fourteen next May.'

'Next May?' he repeated. 'So you will be leaving us soon.'

'Yes, sir.' May had always known that when she reached her fourteenth birthday she would be sent into service somewhere in the city, but it was something she tried not to think about, being sent away, separated from her brother. Life in the workhouse was hard but at least it was familiar. Who knew what waited for her outside these walls?

'A hard-working, reliable girl, a girl with a sense of duty, a girl who can be trusted, can find a position in a good household, and who knows, she might rise to become a chief parlourmaid if she behaves herself. We have a number of families who rely on us to provide them with suitable servants. Mrs Wilmot, the housekeeper at Speke Hall, is looking for someone now. What do you think, Miss Bale? You know the girl better than most.'

Miss Bale drew herself up, her lips tight. 'I am sorry to have to tell you, governor, that I do not think May is suitable for such a position. She is a dreamer. She prefers to waste her time drawing rather than getting on with her work.'

The governor turned his eyes back to May. 'If this is true, I shall have to reconsider my opinion.'

'I only draw after I've finished my work, sir,' May blurted out. 'And I always get the sums right.'

'Is this correct?' The governor looked at Miss Bale.

'Oh, the girl is intelligent enough. That is part of the trouble. Because the work comes easily she thinks she has a right to spend the rest of her time on frivolity.'

'On frivolity?' The governor frowned. 'So you do not regard her as a suitable candidate for a position of trust?'

'It is my opinion, sir, that once away from the close supervision she gets here, she will spend her time dreaming and doodling when she should be working.'

'I see. That changes the situation.' He picked up a pen and returned his gaze to the papers on his desk. 'Very well, you may go.'

Outside the door Miss Bale looked down at May with a gleam of triumph in her eyes. 'So, if you thought your little bit of heroics was going to get you special treatment, you can think again.'

May gazed back, puzzled. The whole conversation had left her confused. All she could be sure of was that something had been offered and then snatched away. 'I didn't ...' she mumbled.

'Well, get along with you. Do you want any dinner or not?'

Miss Bale swept away and May trudged back to find out what was left to eat.

The month of needlework lessons was over and May's group had moved on to general housework, which meant a month of washing pots and scrubbing floors, polishing furniture and black-leading grates. None of the girls enjoyed these sessions, although they were told that this was the sort of work they were most likely to find themselves doing once they left the workhouse May viewed the prospect with even less enthusiasm than usual. The work always left them all with hands reddened and cracked from constant immersion in water and she quailed at the prospect of what it might do to hers in their present condition. The teacher in charge was a Mrs Evans, who had once been housekeeper to a family that had fallen on hard times and been forced to let her go. She was a martinet, and any girl whose work did not come up to the standard she set got short shrift; but May had noticed that she had a softer side, which came to the fore if anyone was really struggling.

Mrs Evans looked across at her as she entered the room. 'Ah, here she comes, our little heroine. Come here, girl.'

May went to her.

'Show me your hands.' Her hands were held between another pair coarsened by years of hard work. 'Hmm. We're not going to get much scrubbing out of you for a week or two. There's a pile of silver over there wants polishing. You'd best get on with that.'

Gratefully, May retreated to a side table and took up the jar of hartshorn paste and a cloth. The spirit mixed with hartshorn stung her fingers but at least it was better than scrubbing. She began to coat the silver forks and spoons and rub them over with a polishing cloth.

Patty had been set to polishing the floor and managed to work her way over to where May was sitting.

'You all right? You look a bit down.'

'Angel's gone. She's been adopted.'

'Adopted? Lucky thing! Who's taken her?'

'I don't know. Some well-off couple.'

'Well, she'll be all right then. Wish someone with money had adopted me! But then I'm not a nipper with golden curls. Who wants an older kid with hair like rat tails and eyes like currants in a penny bun?'

'Your hair's not rat tails,' May protested. 'At least you're not a copper knob like me.'

Patty looked up at her. 'I wouldn't mind that. Yours looks lovely when you've just had your bath.'

Every inmate was allowed a bath once a week. Some of the girls hated the ritual, because it meant undressing in front of someone else. Bathing was strictly supervised, carried out one at a time behind locked doors. There were rules about the temperature of the water and never putting anyone's head under, but May had heard that some of the women put in charge did not always abide by them. She had been lucky and she looked forward to feeling clean, for at least an hour or two.

'Here,' Patty said, 'what happened to you at dinnertime? I thought you were going to miss it altogether.'

'The governor wanted to see me.'

'The governor? Why?'

'He wanted to look at my hands, and then he said I was obviously a girl with a sense of duty and started talking about some place that was looking for a maid, some big house somewhere. But Bale told him I wouldn't be suit-able. She said I'd spend all my time drawing instead of getting on with my work.'

'The old witch! I wouldn't mind a chance to work in one of them big houses – get a chance to see how the toffs live.'

'Do you think?' May sighed. 'I don't know. Anyway, Bale's stopped any chance I had of that.'

'That's quite enough gossiping over there!' Mrs Evans's voice cut across the room. 'Get on with your work.'

The weeks passed and May's hands healed. It was some time before Jeannie returned to the group and when she did people gasped and looked away. The skin on one side of her face was drawn tight and shiny, pulling the corner of her mouth up into a kind of sneer and showing one of her teeth. May couldn't help it but was as repelled by the sight as any of them, but Jeannie immediately made her way to her side and seemed to regard her as her protector, so May had to make an effort to treat her exactly as she had before the fire. It took a week or two, but little by little the other girls began to do the same.

The month of housework came to an end and May was allowed back to the nursery, but she could find no pleasure in the work. She tried to give the other babies the same care and attention she had lavished on Angel, but she could not love them in the same way. She found herself becoming more short-tempered and was frequently scolded for leav-ing jobs half done.

Christmas Day dawned and instead of classes there was a long service in the chapel, which was decorated with wreaths of holly. May gazed around her in delight. It was so good to see some colour instead of the unrelenting grey and brown of her surroundings. Everyone in the workhouse looked forward to Christmas dinner. On that day charitable ladies and gentlemen gave money to provide a feast, and came to watch the beneficiaries of their largesse eating it. There was roast beef and potatoes followed by suet pudding with raisins. Some of the children stuffed the food into their mouths as if they were afraid it might be snatched away, but May ate the pudding slowly, savouring the first sweetness she had tasted in months.

Back in the needlework class again, Mrs Kelly called May and Patty to her.

'You two will be leaving us soon, and no doubt going into service. You need to be getting things ready for your boxes. Employers will expect you to have your uniform. You will be given a dress, though you may need to alter it to fit. You will need two aprons, one for working in and one for best, in case you are required to appear in front of guests; also two caps and two shifts. I will give you the material and you can start sewing right away.'

As May began stitching, the reality of what was about to happen came home to her. In a few weeks she would have to leave the place she had thought of as home for half her lifetime. Where would she be sent? Not to a great house, presumably. She was not deemed suitable for that. What did it mean, anyway? What was a 'great house'? She could remember, just, the house where she had lived as a small child. She had an image of small, dark rooms leading onto the roughly cobbled courtyard, around which were eight identical houses. She remembered playing there in the mud with other children, but the memory was tainted by the stench from the two privies, which were shared by all the inhabitants of the court. She recalled walking with her mother past big buildings with pillared doorways and asking, 'Who lives there, Mam?' 'Rich people' was the answer. Perhaps one of those was going to be her home from now on.

When all the girls were busy with their tasks, Mrs Kelly came and sat beside May.

'Tell me something: have you ever been into the town, on the days when you are allowed out?'

Once in every month residents of the workhouse were permitted to go out for one afternoon. May had known that, but it had never occurred to her that it might apply to her.

'No, ma'am.'

'Why not?'

'Who would I go with? I couldn't go on my own.'

'Would you like to go?'

May thought. She had no idea what it was like 'outside'. The prospect of finding out was intriguing, but also terrifying; but she reminded herself that soon she would have no choice in the matter.

'Yes, I suppose so, ma'am. But who would come with me?'

'I would.'

'You?' May stared at the older woman.

'Yes. There is something I should like to show you. I think you would appreciate it. Now, next Thursday is the day. I will meet you at the main gate immediately after dinner.'

Mrs Kelly got up and moved away to deal with another girl, who had pricked her finger and was leaving blood stains on the fabric she was stitching. May stared after her. It seemed the matter was decided, but she could hardly believe that it would really happen.

As soon as she had finished eating on the following Thursday she put on her cap and her shawl and made her way to the main entrance. The big double doors stood open and the adult residents were pushing and shoving to get out of them as quickly as possible – and there, almost unbelievably, was Mrs Kelly, waiting for her.

'Good, you're very prompt. Come along. We've got a lot to fit in.'

May followed her out into the street. The first thing that struck her was the light. It was still winter, but the sun was shining from a sky bigger than she had ever seen from the narrow streets of the workhouse. The next thing was the noise. What seemed to her to be hundreds of people were walking along the street, chattering to each other, calling out to friends. Street sellers were shouting their wares. A cart pulled by two huge horses rumbled past. Then she heard the sound of a bell, not the tolling of the bell on the chapel but a sharp, urgent *ting-ting* and a strange shape came into sight, pulled by another horse. It was like a cart, but much taller and people were sitting on top of it and inside it.

May stopped dead. 'What is it?'

'That? It's an omnibus. Did you never see one before?'

'No, I don't think so. What are those people doing? Where are they being taken?'

'Wherever they want to go. It's a great deal quicker and easier than walking.'

'Can anyone go on it?'

'If they have the pennies to pay the fare, yes. If you like, we'll ride back on one instead of walking up the hill.'

As they began to walk, May exclaimed, 'Oh, ships! I can see ships.' Away below them was a forest of masts and sails and beyond them an expanse of grey water. 'Is that the sea?'

'No, that's the River Mersey. The sea is out there.' Mrs Kelly waved an arm to the right. 'But the river is deep enough for even the biggest ships. That's why Liverpool is the greatest port in the Empire. All the wealth of the city comes from those ships.'

May gazed at the scene below her. That must be where her father had sailed from, in a ship like one of those. 'Where do they go?' she asked.

'Everywhere. America, Australia, India, China. All over the world.'

'How do they find their way?'

'They have instruments, like compasses and sextants, which tell them exactly where they are.'

'So they don't get lost?'

'No, they don't get lost.'

May said no more. If that was the case, how could it be that her father was 'lost at sea'? It made no sense.

They reached the bottom of the hill and turned to their right along a broad street.

'Now,' said Mrs Kelly, 'look there, May.'

She pointed ahead and May stopped short in amazement. In front of them, on a vast stone platform, stood a building like no other she had ever seen or imagined. Huge, its front and side lined with massive stone pillars, it towered above the street.

'Is it a palace, or a castle?' she asked. 'Is that where the queen lives?'

'No, though I think it is fit for a queen. That is St George's Hall. It was built while you were just a baby. You would have been about four years old when it was finished.'

'So who does live there?'

'No one lives there. It is a civic building. It belongs to the people of Liverpool. They have concerts there, and grand balls and meetings. And at the back of it are the courts of justice and underneath are the cells where criminals are kept during their trials. Come along.'

Mrs Kelly led the way briskly along the street until they stood in front of the building. At her back, May suddenly heard a great snorting and puffing, like a gigantic horse.

'Oh, what's that?'

'Just a steam train. That's the station behind us. You can ride all the way to Manchester along the rails. Let's cross the road.'

She took May's arm and marched her across the broad street, weaving between coaches and traps and carts loaded with objects May could not identify, until they stood at the foot of the wide flight of steps leading up to the front of the building.

'Oh, are those supposed to be lions?'

'Yes. They are beautifully sculpted, don't you think? You could almost stroke their manes.'

'I wouldn't dare!'

They climbed the steps towards the great door in the centre of the pillared façade. May hung back.

'Are we allowed to go in there?'

'Yes, it's free for anyone to go in and out. Come along, there's more to see yet.'

She marched boldly to the entrance and May followed, glad to see that people were indeed going in and out without being challenged. They crossed a corridor and Mrs Kelly put her hand on May's shoulder and pushed her gently through another doorway.

May gasped and stood speechless. Before her was a room so splendid and so beautiful that it surpassed anything she had ever seen in Mrs Kelly's book of fairy tales. Above her head was a great, curved ceiling decorated with coloured panels; to either side, tall red columns, which glowed in the light of many lamps, rose to support the roof, and between them were sculpted figures of men. But it was the floor that held her entranced. Made up of hundreds of vividly coloured tiles, it had a border of intricately patterned squares, while in the centre was a design that looked like a many-pointed star surrounding a circle of bright blue.

'What is that, in the middle of the floor,' May asked, when she had got her breath back.

'That's the royal coat of arms, the queen's own special symbol.'

May's eyes wandered over the floor. There were flowers and sea creatures and geometric patterns. It was too much to take in at one go.

'Well?' Mrs Kelly asked quietly, after a few minutes.

'Oh, ma'am! It's the most beautiful thing I've ever seen. Thank you! Thank you for bringing me here.'

The teacher smiled. 'I thought you would appreciate it. I think it is a wonderful work of art.'

'But how was it made?' May asked. 'It's all such tiny pieces.'

'The design was drawn by a man called Charles Cockerell. The tiles were made in the Midlands by a company called Minton, but the actual laying of them was done by Italian craftsmen who were brought here specially because they were experts in this kind of work.'

'It must be wonderful to be able to design something like this,' May murmured.

'Yes, indeed. But it doesn't necessarily have to be done on such a huge scale. Small things can be beautiful too. Now, have you seen enough? I think we should be moving on.'

May turned away unwillingly, but as they made their way out of the entrance something else caught her eye.

'Oh, ma'am. Look at that lady's hat!'

Mrs Kelly laughed. 'You see? As I said, things don't have to be on a huge scale to be beautiful.'

'It's got a bird on it!'

'Not a live bird. Just a model made of bird's feathers. Look, over there. There's another one.'

'Oh, it's got flowers and ribbons, and there's another one with more feathers, but different. I wish I could have a hat like that!'

May caught herself up. In her excitement she had been presumptuous. Of course, someone like her could never wear a hat like that. Only ladies could do that. But to her relief Mrs Kelly did not seem annoyed.

'Well, maybe one day you will. Now come along. I want a cup of tea before we start back.'

May followed obediently, puzzled by this new development. They crossed the street and turned a corner and Mrs Kelly pushed open a door, which caused a little bell to ring. In front of them was a room where there were a number of little tables covered in white cloths. A woman in a black dress with a starched cap and apron came over to them and Mrs Kelly said, 'Tea for two, please, Mabel.'

May was aware of being scrutinised, as if there was some doubt as to whether she should be admitted. It was a doubt she shared, but Mrs Kelly headed for one of the tables and sat down, and the woman in the cap and apron stood aside so May could follow. Very soon a silver teapot arrived, with milk in a jug and a bowl of sugar lumps, and cups so delicate May was afraid to pick one up; and they were followed by an even more surprising object, a structure supporting three plates, one above the other, and on each one were things she thought must be cakes, though they were unlike any cake she had ever seen.

Mrs Kelly poured the tea. 'Help yourself to a cake, May.'

May looked down at her hands, aware suddenly that her fingernails were far from clean. She put her hands under the table.

'Can't you decide?' Mrs Kelly asked, smiling. 'How about the chocolate one?'

She was pointing to a black square with little violet shapes on top. It looked dirty, or perhaps burnt, May thought. Perhaps she should choose that one. Her fingernails would show up less against it.

Mrs Kelly was watching her face. 'You've never seen chocolate, have you?' she said, her voice softening. 'Here, tell you what. I'll have half and you can have the other half.

She put the black square on her own plate, cut it in half with a tiny fork and slid half onto May's plate. Then she cut a small portion from her own half and put it in her mouth.

'Mmm! It's really good. Try some.'

May took a corner and put it in her mouth. The flavour that burst on her tongue seemed to encapsulate all the wonders and beauties she had seen that afternoon. She swallowed and took another bite. It tasted even better than the first. Very soon her plate was empty.

'Did you enjoy that?' Mrs Kelly asked. She was laughing, but not unkindly.

'Oh, yes, ma'am. It was lovely.'

'Well, try one of the others. Go on. Take whichever one you fancy.'

May chose one with pink icing. It was good, but not quite as good as the chocolate one.

As she ate, Mrs Kelly said, 'Tell me something. You will be leaving the workhouse soon. Has anyone said anything about where you will be sent?'

May told her about her interview with the governor. 'He said a Mrs Wilmot wanted a girl at some big house, but Miss Bale said I wouldn't be suitable.'

'Why not?'

'She said I'd spend all my time drawing instead of getting on with my work. But I wouldn't ...' May found herself protesting angrily. 'I've always done my work first.'

'I'm sure you have,' Mrs Kelly responded soothingly. 'Mrs Wilmot, eh? That would be Speke Hall then. Well, don't be too downhearted. I think you may have had a lucky escape.'

May blinked. 'Why, ma'am?'

'Girls think that being in a great house would be exciting, but I can promise you it isn't. A house like that has a huge staff. There's a housekeeper and a butler, and a

46

head parlourmaid and at least one lady's maid and under parlourmaids and nursery maids and laundry maids, not to mention footmen and boot boys and the rest. You would have been the lowest of the low, at everyone's beck and call. No, you would be far better off in a small household, where at least your employer would recognise your face.'

'Mrs Evans told us that ladies and gentlemen don't want to know we are even there. If we were to meet one of them on the stairs we should turn our faces to the wall, so they wouldn't have to see us.'

'That may be the way of it in some of these big houses. But if your employer is expecting you to bring them their morning tea and answer the door to their guests, they can hardly pretend not to see you, can they? That's my point. If you go into a house where there are not a lot of servants, you may have to work hard but at least you have the chance of getting noticed. You're a bright girl, and nice looking. If you behave yourself you have a good chance of being promoted. Now, as it happens I know of a family that is looking for a girl like you. Mr Freeman owns a shop selling gentlemen's clothing, but he's looking to expand his business and open a department for ladies' dresses. I know Mrs Freeman. I used to make dresses for her before she was married. I know she's looking for a maid of all work who is handy with a needle and thread, to make alterations and repairs. If you were to go there I think you might find all sorts of opportunities opening up for you.' She took a purse from her reticule and laid some coins on the table. 'Now, we must go. I promised you a ride on an omnibus, didn't I?'

Three

Nothing more was said about May's future for several weeks, but she did not worry. Her head was full of wonderful pictures of all she had seen in that one magical afternoon. She did her lessons automatically and stitched away at her uniform in a dream, and it was only the fact that the work came easily to her that stopped her from being reprimanded or worse. Then one day Mr Baker, who was in charge of the boys, called her over as she left the dining hall.

'Your brother has made a decision which I think he should discuss with you. He's waiting for you in the classroom.'

He led the way down the stairs to the boys' classroom. May followed, her brain churning. What sort of decision could Gus have possibly made? The room smelt different, a smell of sweaty feet, somehow indefinably male. Gus was sitting on one of the benches. He jumped up as they entered and Mr Baker said, 'Now, Augustus. Tell your sister what you told me this morning.'

'I want to go to the Industrial School, to learn how to be a sailor.'

'To go where? Where is it?'

'It is in Kirkdale, not far away,' Mr Baker said.

'But I won't be able to see you …' May protested.

'You're going away, anyway, soon,' Gus said. 'We won't be able to see each other.'

'I'm sure, May,' Mr Baker said, 'that when you have a day off from wherever you are employed you will be able to go and see your brother.'

'Do you think so?' May struggled to make sense of this new development. 'But why do you want to go, Gus?'

'So I can learn to be a sailor. I told you.'

'But why?'

'You know why.'

'Oh, Gus, you're not still thinking you can find our dad!'

'I might.' Gus's face set obstinately.

'It is a good choice for a boy, anyway,' Mr Baker said. 'I have heard of a number of boys who have obtained good situations on board ship and made a good livelihood.'

'But people get … get lost at sea,' May protested, her throat constricting with tears. 'Like our father did.'

'But most of them come home safely,' Mr Baker said, quite kindly. 'I don't think you should prevent your brother from pursuing the career he has set his heart on.'

'I can't prevent him, can I?' May said miserably. 'When will you go, Gus?'

'That is still to be decided,' Mr Baker said. 'There are arrangements to be made. It is quite possible that you will have gone to your new position before Augustus leaves.'

May drew a deep breath. It was true, of course. Whatever Gus chose to do, they would be separated soon. She swallowed. 'All right, Gus. If that's what you really want.'

She looked at Mr Baker. 'Will we be able to say goodbye, whichever of us goes first?'

'I'm sure that will be allowed,' Mr Baker said. 'Now, you had better get along to your class or you will be late.'

May looked at her brother. She wanted to put her arms round him, but they had not hugged each other since they came to the workhouse and even if such displays of affection had been permitted, she feared he would push her away. She sniffed and forced a smile. 'Goodbye, Gus.'

'Goodbye.' He ducked his head and looked away.

May climbed the steps and set off for the needlework room.

A few days later, at the end of morning school, Miss Bale called her and Patty out to the front of the class. They stood uneasily, wondering what they had done wrong. In spite of herself, May's eyes kept flickering to the ruler on the teacher's table.

'Now, girls,' Miss Bale said, 'you are all aware that May and Patty will be leaving us soon. I have just learned where they will be going. Patty –' she nodded towards her '– has been very fortunate. She will go to work at Speke Hall, which is a great house not far from the city.' There was a murmur from the other girls, which expressed a combination of excitement and envy. 'May –' Miss Bale's voice changed tone '– is going to work for a Mr and Mrs Freeman in the city. Mr Freeman is, I believe, in trade.' There was no mistaking from the expression on the teacher's face that she regarded that as a very inferior position. Even the very word 'trade' was spoken as if it produced an unpleasant smell.

May shifted uncomfortably, aware of pitying looks from the other girls. Then she lifted her chin. Mrs Kelly had said it would be a better position, whatever Miss Bale thought. Perhaps she was the lucky one after all.

Outside the room Patty gripped her arm. 'May, I'm so sorry! It should have been you going to the big house. Do you mind very much?'

'No, I don't mind at all,' May told her, trying to convince herself as well as her friend. 'I expect I'll be fine with Mr and Mrs Freeman.'

Much sooner than she had expected, May found herself standing in the governor's office with her box at her feet. In the box were her few personal possessions – a grubby and almost bald toy monkey that her father had brought back from one of his voyages, a brooch that had belonged to her mother and the rag doll which had once been Angel's. On top of these were her black uniform dress with a wide white lace collar, two aprons, two caps, two shifts and two pairs of woollen stockings. She was already wearing the simple print frock that would be her daytime uniform. Patty stood beside her with her own box.

The governor cleared his throat. 'So, girls. You are about to start out on a new path. You have been brought up to be God-fearing and obedient, and to know your place. I want you to remember that whatever you do now will reflect on the upbringing you have received here. Your future employers will expect you to be diligent, hard-working and respectful. I trust that you will not disappoint them. Now, here are your letters testifying to your good character and your suitability for the roles you are about to undertake. Take great care of them. If at any time you should find it necessary to seek new employment, your current master or mistress will add a new one. Make sure that they have no reason to include anything but praise. Any girl leaving her position without a character reference will find it almost impossible to obtain a new situation. Do you understand me?'

'Yes, sir,' they mumbled in unison.

'Take them, then.'

The governor held out the two envelopes. May stepped forward and bobbed a curtsy. 'Thank you, sir.'

When Patty had taken hers the governor went on, 'And I have one final small gift for each of you.' He held out two small books. 'If ever you feel alone or troubled, or if ever you are faced with a difficult decision, turn to this book; you will find it a very present help.'

They were copies of the Bible, in cheap bindings. May took hers and murmured thanks. She knew the governor was right and she should be grateful; but she just wished it had been a book with pictures in it.

The governor turned to Mr Baker, who was waiting near the door. 'Send the boy in.'

Gus came in, looking uneasy and embarrassed, and the governor said, 'Say goodbye to your sister. She is about to embark on life as an independent woman. Wish her good fortune.'

Gus lowered his head and looked at the floor. 'Goodbye. Good luck.'

May stepped closer to him. The urge to put her arms round him was almost irresistible and it was hard to hold back tears. 'Take care of yourself, Gus – and try not to get into any more fights.'

He looked up at her, then, and for a moment their eyes met. 'I might have to – but I'll be all right. Don't worry about me.'

'I'll come to visit you, at the school, when I get a day off.'

'All right.'

'Now then,' the governor said, 'it's time you two girls were on your way. That will be all, Augustus.'

Gus turned away to the door and May called after him, 'Gus. I'm going to work for a Mr and Mrs Freeman. He owns a shop.' He looked at her, puzzled. 'Just in case you need to find me one day.'

'Oh.'

'Goodbye, Gus. I'll see you soon.'

'Bye.' He did not look round and the door closed behind him.

The governor wished them goodbye and they were escorted to the front gate and found themselves out in the street. Spring had come but it was a day of fitful sunshine and a chill wind was blowing up from the Mersey. A trap had been sent for Patty, since Speke Hall was some distance from the city. It was driven by a brown-faced boy not much older than May. He greeted them with a grin as they emerged from the workhouse gate.

'Right, then. Which of you lovely ladies is coming with me?'

'I am,' Patty said, smiling and blushing.

'I'm Bill, by the way. What's your name?'

'Patty.'

'Suits you! Pretty Patty!' He lifted Patty's box into the trap. 'Jump in, then. We'll get to know each other on the way.'

Patty turned to May and they hugged each other. 'We'll keep in touch, won't we?' Patty said. 'Speke Hall isn't far away ...'

'We can try,' May responded, but already she felt that their lives were going separate ways.

'I'll come and call for you on my day off, or send you a note,' Patty promised. 'I've got the address.'

'Yes, do,' May said. 'Goodbye. Good luck!'

Patty climbed aboard the trap and Bill cracked his whip and the pony set off at a smart trot. May watched them disappear round a bend in the road. She had never ridden in a pony and trap, but it might have been Cinderella's coach as far as she was concerned.

'Well, are you going to stand there gawping all day?' a voice demanded. 'They'll be expecting you.'

No one had been sent to collect May so, because she did not know her way around the city streets, one of the older women had been told to escort her to her new home. Her name was Ivy and she was a dour-faced character who rarely spoke. May knew she had lived in the workhouse for years, but no more than that. They set off side by side, heading downhill as she had done with Mrs Kelly, but soon Ivy turned left and led the way along a street lined with tall houses. These were the sort of homes she had asked her mother about. It was where rich people lived. She was tempted to ask Ivy if she knew anything about the sort of people who inhabited such grand homes, but the woman had remained silent all through their walk and May felt uneasy about being the first to speak.

Her heavy box was making her arms ache, so she was relieved when Ivy announced, 'Number twenty-four

Rodney Street. This is it. Right, you know where you are now. I'll be off.' And without further words she turned and stumped off back the way they had come.

May stood gazing at the front of the house. To begin with she was unsure where No. 24 began and ended, because the houses were built side by side, in a long row. Then she saw that each had a slightly different front door. Some had pillars at each side, others had a semi-circular fanlight above them. Some had windows on either side, while some front doors were next to each other with windows on only one side. All were tall, with three rows of windows rising from street level. No. 24 was one of those with windows on one side of the door only.

With shaking knees, May climbed the steps to the front door and pulled the doorbell. It was flung open more quickly than she had expected, to reveal a short woman with a red face and a flustered expression.

'Yes?'

'Please, ma'am, I'm the new maid.'

'Good heavens, girl! Didn't anyone tell you that servants don't come to the front door? Your entrance is down those steps, in the basement.'

May hung her head. She had not made a good beginning.

'Well, don't stand there gaping. Best come in, now you're here. The mistress wants to see you.'

May stepped into the hall and knew at once that she had entered a different world. It was the smell that struck her first, a sweet, floral odour with an undertone of something more astringent. Her first visual impression was of shine and gloss. The floorboards shone with polish, there were lamps and ornaments with brass fittings that glowed in the

light from the doorway. And there was colour. A richly
toned rug covered part of the floor and there were pictures on the walls. She longed to stand and look at them,
but already the red-faced woman was saying impatiently,
'Come along, come along!'

She led the way down the hallway and opened a door.
'The new maid is here, ma'am.'

She stood back and gestured to May to pass her into the
room. May moved a few paces forward and came to a standstill. This room was even grander and more brilliant than the
hallway. There was a carpet patterned in many colours on
the floor, and a table covered with a crimson velvet cloth on
which stood a variety of ornaments. The walls were papered
with a design of flowers and leaves which reminded her of
the patterns she had seen in Mrs Kelly's book of fairy tales.
A fire glowed in the hearth, and the warmth enveloped her
after the chill of outdoors.

May stood, dazzled and fascinated, until from somewhere in the middle of all this richness a voice said, 'Come
over here, girl. Don't stand in the doorway.'

May's eyes located the source of the voice. A woman
was standing by the window and she realised that this must
be Mrs Freeman, her new mistress. She was tall and very
slender, with the tiniest waist that May had ever seen. Her
dress was pale blue, made from a fabric May knew must
be silk, though she had never actually touched such material. It had a wide spreading skirt embellished with fringed
panels in a deeper blue and decorated on the front with
velvet ribbons, a high neck trimmed with lace and long,
close-fitting sleeves with lace cuffs. Her hair, which was so
fair that it was almost silver, was parted in the centre and

drawn back into a heavy coil at the nape of her neck, held in place with more blue ribbons. To May's eyes she looked like a princess.

Mrs Freeman moved away from the window and sat down on a chair near the fire. 'So you are May Lavender?'

May bobbed a curtsy. 'Yes, ma'am.'

'How old are you, May?'

'Thirteen, please, ma'am.'

'And this is your first position?'

'Yes, ma'am.'

'Do you have your letter of recommendation?'

'Yes, ma'am. Here.'

May produced the letter from the pocket of her shawl and held it out. Mrs Freeman took it and, as she did so, May was uncomfortably aware of the difference in their hands: her own reddened and slightly grubby; her mistress's pale with carefully manicured nails.

Mrs Freeman glanced at the letter briefly and said, 'Very well. Now, as to your duties … there are three members of the family in residence at the moment: myself and Mr Freeman and our daughter Isabella, plus Isabella's governess Miss Parsons. We also have two sons, but they are away at school and will only be here during the holidays. You will be required to keep the house clean and tidy, help Cook as required, and on Tuesdays and Thursdays, which are my at home days, you will be needed to open the door to visitors and to hand round tea. Over and above this, I may need you to undertake extra duties to help me. I understand from Mrs Kelly, who recommended you, that you are handy with your needle. I may want you to do some sewing for me.' She glanced over May's shoulder towards the red-faced woman and May sensed a tinge of uncertainty in the look. 'I think that is all. Cook will give you detailed instructions and show you where you will sleep.'

'Yes, ma'am. You can leave all that to me,' was the reassuring reply.

'Very good, that will be all. Thank you, Cook.' There was definitely a tone of relief in the voice, as of a slightly awkward task successfully accomplished.

'This way,' Cook ordered. 'Follow me.'

May curtsied again, and followed the little woman out into the hall, along a passageway and down a flight of stairs into a room that was obviously the kitchen. Here she turned to look at May.

'I'm Mrs Wilkins. I've cooked for Mr and Mrs Freeman for near on ten years. You'll find me fair to work for, provided you do as you're told and keep your lip buttoned. There's just one thing. The missus ... Mrs Freeman ... she's ....delicate, and she hasn't been used to managing a household with more than one servant. So you may find that sometimes she will give you an order, then a bit later she will forget and tell you to do something different. If you ever get confused, just ask me. I'll keep you straight. Understand?'

'Yes, ma'am,' May murmured, though it was very far from the truth.

'No need to ma'am me,' the cook said. 'Mrs Wilkins, or Cook, if that comes easier. Now, this is your room.'

She opened a door on the far side of the kitchen and stood back. May peered past her into a tiny space, just big enough for a narrow bed and a small table holding a chipped basin and a ewer. Like the kitchen, it was partially below ground level and the only light came from a small, barred window above the bed. A smell of damp wafted into May's nostrils.

'You can stow your box under the bed,' Wilkins said. 'Take off your shawl and get your apron on and I'll tell you exactly what you will be doing from here on.'

May did as she was told and when she turned back into the kitchen, Mrs Wilkins was bending over the big iron range on the far side, rearranging dishes inside it. She straightened up, puffing and pushing her hair back under her cap.

'Right! Now listen carefully. This will be your daily routine. You will need to be up early, five o'clock if you're going to get everything done. First job is rake out the ashes in the range and build the fire up. Then pump up water and fill this big kettle here, and put it on to heat. You need hot water for the master to shave with, and then later for the mistress and Miss Isabella to wash. And you need to keep that kettle filled at all times so there is always hot water. Then go to the morning room – I'll show you where that is in a minute – open the curtains, move the chairs to the centre and spread a sheet over the carpet in front of the fireplace. Rake out the ashes and put them in the fire bucket and black-lead the grate. Make sure you do a good job. The missus likes to see a nice shiny grate. Then lay the new fire and light it, gather up the sheet, pick up the rug and shake it out, sweep the floor, put the furniture back straight and dust the ornaments. Then you can lay the table for Mr Freeman's breakfast. Missus usually takes hers in bed. After that you take up the rug in the hall and shake that out, sweep the floor, dust the banisters and the lamps, and scrub the front step. Are you with me so far?'

'Yes, m— er – Cook. I think so.' In truth May felt as if she was already drowning in this list of tasks.

'After that come back to the kitchen and be ready to take Mr Freeman's breakfast up to him when he rings. If we're lucky, there will be time to swallow a quick cup of tea and a bite of bread before he does. When he's finished you clear away and bring the dishes down here and wash them up. Then it will be time to take hot water up to the nursery for Miss Isabella and Miss Parsons.'

'How old is Miss Isabella?' May asked.

''Bout your age, a month or two younger.'

'Oh, I see. It's just that you said to the nursery.'

'That's what I still call it. It's Miss Isabella's bedroom now. Miss Parsons has the room next door, where the nurse used to sleep, and there's the schoolroom up there too, where Miss Isabella has her lessons. Now, where was I? Miss Parsons usually comes down to fetch the breakfast for her and Miss, but if she doesn't you will have to take it up to them. Then you must sweep out the schoolroom and get it tidy for morning lessons. About that time, the missus usually rings for her morning tea, so you take that up, and hot water for her to wash, and make up the fire in the bedroom. Then her breakfast tray will be ready to go up. She usually gets up about nine. Before she's about, you need to sweep the stairs down and shake out the rugs on the upstairs landing, so she sees everything neat and clean when she comes out of her bedroom. Once she's up you can clean her room, empty the slops, air the bed and make it up, and after that you can do Miss Isabella's room and Miss Parson's. Bring down all the dirty laundry from all the bedrooms and sort it. Washing days are Monday and Thursday, so on those days you need to fill the copper and light the fire under it. Next job is sweep and clean the drawing room and the dining room and Mr Freeman's study. Mrs Freeman will be writing letters and giving her orders in the morning room, so you won't be in her way.'

Mrs Wilkins stopped for breath and May rubbed the back of her hand across her forehead. She had done all these various chores at the workhouse, but to do all that was required in one morning seemed impossible.

'Next job is get the lunch. Sometimes Mr Freeman comes home but mostly he eats out midday, and Miss Isabella and Miss Parsons have theirs in the schoolroom. So it's just one to lay for in the dining room. You carry up the missus's lunch, then while she is eating we can grab a bite for ourselves. After that, you fetch her dishes and wash them up. Then you change your dress and put on your better apron and cap and do some light work like cleaning silver or any sewing the mistress may want done until it's time to take in the tea. Once you've cleared that away, go upstairs and make up the fires in the bedrooms and turn down the beds. Then take up nursery supper for Miss Isabella and Miss Parsons and lay the table for the master and mistress's dinner. Help me with the dinner, and carrying up dishes, collect them when they're finished with and wash them up. Tidy the kitchen and make up the fire and then the last job is polish all the boots and shoes ready for morning. Now, is there anything you want to ask?'

'Why doesn't Miss Isabella have dinner with her mother and father?'

'She's too young to join the grown-ups for dinner. She won't do that for a year or two yet. Now, time is going by and I've already lost too much talking to you. Mrs Freeman will be ringing for her lunch and we'll have nothing ready. Get those potatoes peeled and then I'll show you the dining room and where everything is kept.'

Nursery lunch, as Mrs Wilkins persisted in calling it, consisted of soup and cottage pie, and when Miss Parsons came down to fetch it May had her first encounter with a woman to whom she immediately took a dislike. She was middle-aged, dressed entirely in black, her hair scraped back so tightly that it seemed to stretch the skin round her eyes, making them into slits. But it was her manner that May found offensive. When Mrs Wilkins introduced May as the new maid, she barely glanced in her direction and made no acknowledgement, continuing to speak to Mrs Wilkins as if May did not exist.

Mrs Freeman had soup for lunch, followed by roast beef with potatoes and cabbage, and an apple dumpling for pudding. May wondered how she could possibly eat it all and remain so slender. The answer was that there was a good deal left over and, looking at what remained of the joint, May began to hope that some might come her way. But it was taken away and closeted in the larder, which Mrs Wilkins kept locked. Instead, on the table for May's midday meal there was a bowl of watered-down soup, and a hunk of yesterday's bread. May looked to see what Mrs Wilkins was eating, but she said she would have hers later; and while May was washing up in the scullery she heard her unlock the larder door.

May changed into her black dress and the cap and apron with lace ruffles, and the rest of the day passed in a blur as Mrs Wilkins conducted her round the house and listed once again what she was expected to do in each room. The cook took up the tea tray herself, remarking that she was not sure yet that May could be trusted with the delicate bone china cups and saucers – but it was a different story when it came to the washing up. Then there were more potatoes to peel and carrots to scrape and onions to chop until at last dinner was ready to be carried up to the dining room. May tried to stop her hands from shaking as she lifted the tray. Mr and Mrs Freeman faced each other down a long table and May saw that Mrs Freeman had changed her dress and was now arrayed in violet and gold. It was her first sight of her employer's husband. Mr Freeman had thick brown hair, parted in the centre and slicked down with pomade, and neatly trimmed side whiskers and moustache. When he looked up at May she saw he had hazel eyes with creases at the corners that made him look as if he might laugh at any moment.

'You're the new girl, are you?'

May nearly dropped the soup tureen she was holding at the shock of being addressed. 'Yes, sir.'

'What's your name?'

'May, sir.'

'Are you settling in all right?'

'Of course she is!' Mrs Freeman cut in. 'Let the girl get on with her work, Charles.'

When May got back to the kitchen she was just in time to see Mrs Wilkins returning the lunchtime beef joint to the larder, and there was an empty plate on the table with a slick of mustard on it. May's supper was another piece of bread and a small portion of cheese. When she had finally polished the last boot and was able to crawl into her narrow bed, she was hungry, cold and exhausted. She missed the frowsty companionship of the dormitory, the murmur of voices, the sense of Patty's sleeping form close beside her. The food at the workhouse had been bland and uninteresting, and she had often wished there was more of it, but at least she had rarely gone to bed so hungry. Of all her lessons, the ones she least enjoyed had been the basic housework, and now it seemed that her life was going to be a long succession of tasks she hated. She leaned over and groped inside her box until she found Angel's rag doll. She held it against her cheek, breathing in the faint aroma that still clung to it, and gave way to the tears that had been building inside her all day.

She was woken next morning by Mrs Wilkins pounding on her door and shouting to her to get up. She staggered to her feet and splashed her face with icy water from the ewer, struggled into her dress and apron, pushed her hair under her cap and hurried into the kitchen.

'Well, this is a fine way to start!' was the cook's greeting. 'You'll need to do better than that if you're going to give satisfaction. Now get that fire going!'

It set the pattern for the day. No matter how much she hurried, May always seemed to be behind. The governess did not come down to fetch the breakfast tray, so May had to climb the three flights of stairs to the nursery floor with it. Then Miss Parsons complained that the schoolroom was not swept ready for her. It was at that point that May had her first sight of Isabella. She was a small replica of her mother, but the fairness that gleamed like silver in Mrs Freeman's hair was pale and dull in her daughter's, and where her mother's features were even and delicate, Isabella's nose and chin were too pronounced for beauty. Her eyes were small and she blinked continuously. She looked, May thought, like a small, frightened mouse.

May was late taking up Mrs Freeman's breakfast and she had rung for it twice, which earned her a reprimand from the mistress and another from Cook. It was not until she had swept out and dusted all the rooms that it occurred to her that she had had no breakfast herself, but lunch was more watery soup and dry bread. Supper was bread and cheese again and that night May was too hungry and weary even to cry.

Over the next weeks she slowly came to terms with the work and developed a routine that enabled her to get most of it done on time, but she was always tired. Her meagre diet did not vary and her hip bones and ribs began to stick out sharply under her shift. When she caught sight of herself as she dusted the big looking glass in the drawing room she was shocked to see how hollow her cheeks were and how sunken her eyes. One morning she was carrying in Mr Freeman's breakfast tray when she was suddenly seized by a fit of dizziness. She staggered forward and managed to set the tray down on the table and then her legs gave way under her and she collapsed onto a chair.

Mr Freeman looked up from his newspaper with a start and May felt a strong arm round her shoulders in support.

'May? What's wrong? Are you ill?'

May forced herself to sit up. 'No, no sir. I'm sorry, really I am. I just came over dizzy. I'll be all right in a moment.'

'Look at me!'

May timidly raised her eyes. She had been taught never to make direct eye contact with her superiors.

'Are you getting enough to eat? No, foolish question. It's obvious you are not. Here, drink this.'

A cup was held to her lips and she took a sip. It was milk, fresh and sweet. She swallowed eagerly and drained the cup.

'Now eat this.'

A piece of buttered toast was put into her hands. Nothing had ever tasted so good, but even as she chewed it she was thinking fearfully of the consequences. She was eating her master's breakfast. She would pay for it when Mrs Wilkins found out.

When she had finished the toast she glanced anxiously up at Mr Freeman. He was frowning.

'What have you had to eat this morning?'

'Tea, sir, and a bit of bread.'

'And last night for supper?'

'Bread, sir, and some cheese.'

'And for your dinner?'

'Soup and bread, sir.'

'And is this your usual diet?'

'Yes, sir. Please, sir, don't say anything to Mrs Wilkins. It's very kind of you to ask, but I'm not complaining, really!'

'I know you are not, but this state of affairs cannot be allowed to continue.' He touched her shoulder reassuringly. 'Don't worry. I shall not complain, either. You will not get into trouble. Just leave everything to me. Now, do you feel strong enough to go back to work?'

'Oh, yes, sir. Thank you, sir! And I'm ever so sorry about earlier.'

'There's nothing for you to be sorry about,' he said. 'Go along, and don't worry.'

All morning May expected to be scolded or worse, dismissed, but nothing happened. Then, when she was dusting the drawing room, she heard voices from the morning room, which was next door. Mr Freeman was in there, which was surprising as he usually spent all day at his shop.

'How can you expect the child to work, when she's half starved?' His voice was raised in what sounded like exasperation.

Mrs Freeman's reply was too quiet for May to hear, but then her husband replied, 'Really, Lydia, you amaze me sometimes. Are you in charge here, or is the cook? Oh, never mind! Leave it to me.'

Just before teatime, when May was busy polishing the knives and forks ready for dinner and Mrs Wilkins was sitting by the range with some knitting on her lap and her eyes closed, Mr Freeman came into the kitchen. It was an unheard of event and Mrs Wilkins jumped to her feet in a fluster and curtsied.

'Mr Freeman, sir! Is there something you want? Why didn't you ring? The girl could have brought you anything you need.'

'It is about the girl that I wish to speak.'

May dropped the knife she was polishing in alarm and Mrs Wilkins turned to her sharply. 'Take those things into the scullery and finish them there.'

'Yes, ma'am,' May mumbled and scuttled away. So it had come! Mr Freeman had promised not to say anything, but this showed what a gentleman's promise was worth. She knew Mrs Wilkins was already dissatisfied with her. A complaint from the master would be all that was needed to get her dismissed – and without a character, in all probability. She remembered the governor's warning and choked back a sob at the thought that she might be cast out onto the street with nothing.

Mr Freeman's voice carried through the half-open door. 'My wife tells me she leaves the ordering and management of food entirely in your hands. So I am asking you why it is that May is being kept on such a meagre regime.'

'She's been complaining to you, sir, has she? She's no right or reason to do that.'

'She has not complained, but I have eyes in my head. The girl is half-starved and I want to know why.'

'The food's there. It's not my fault if she doesn't eat it.'

'I do not think that is entirely true, Mrs Wilkins. Now, let us have no more evasions. What is behind all this?'

'Well, sir –' May could hear that the cook was desperately trying to find excuses '– it's like this: when Madam agreed that we needed more help in the house, she told me that it was her understanding that the feeding of an extra mouth should come out of the housekeeping, without any extra cost. I tried to tell her different, but she would have it so.'

'I have been through the household bills for the last month, Mrs Wilkins, and it seems to me that the sums spent on food are adequate, I might even say excessive, for the sustenance of the number of people in the house. I have no doubt that there is often food left over from our dinner, which could well be used to make nutritional dishes, without requiring any extra expenditure. So from now on, I expect May to be given adequate nourishment for the performance of her duties, which is clearly not happening at present – and I shall ask her, from time to time, what she has eaten. Is that clearly understood?'

'Yes, sir, of course. I was only trying to abide by the mistress's orders.'

Mr Freeman's voice took on a harder edge. 'You know as well as I do, Mrs Wilkins, that my wife has little interest or … competency … in household matters. She relies on you a great deal. I hope that confidence is not misplaced.'

'Oh no, sir! You can be sure of that. I'll make sure your orders are carried out.'

'It will be better for all of us if that is the case.'

When Mr Freeman had gone the cook called May back into the kitchen.

'Well, miss! This is a nice state of affairs you've brought about. To think of Mr Freeman having to trouble himself with such things! You'd better be sure he doesn't have any further occasion to come down here.'

'No, Mrs Wilkins,' May murmured dutifully. She knew that she had scored a small victory and had found an ally, but she understood too that at the same time she had acquired an enemy. It remained to be seen which of them would prove the more powerful.

That evening the Freemans had lamb chops for dinner and there were four left over. When May brought them back to the kitchen, Mrs Wilkins pushed two of them onto a plate and shoved it into her hands.

'Here, you better have these, I suppose. And there's mash left over. Help yourself.'

From then on, May never went to bed hungry.

Four

'Come here, boy.'

Gus made his way reluctantly to the front of the classroom.

'New, are you?'

'Yes, sir.'

'Name?'

Gus lowered his voice to just above a whisper. 'Lavender, sir.'

'What? Speak up!'

'Lavender, sir.'

'Is that your Christian name or your surname?'

Already he could hear the stifled sniggers from the boys behind him. 'Surname, sir.'

'Christian name?'

'Gus.'

'What?'

'Augustus, sir.'

'Augustus Lavender. Correct?'

The laughter broke out in snorts and yelps. 'Yes, sir.'

'Silence! Where do you think you are? The next boy to snigger will feel the weight of my hand. Very well, Lavender, you may sit down.'

As Gus made his way back to his seat he could feel eyes following him and saw covert nudges and kicks. He lowered his eyes to his slate and tried to ignore them.

It was his first morning at the Kirkdale Industrial School. He had been marched there at first light by one of the men employed as porters at the workhouse. He had felt excited, as if he was being set free from prison, but that sensation had rapidly faded as he entered the imposing gatehouse. The building was much bigger than he had imagined. Tall grey walls with rows of windows encircled a central courtyard that was crowded with boys, most of them older and bigger than he was. They were being marshalled into lines by masters wielding canes and there was a lot of shouting and scuffling. He had been taken to an office, where a clerk had taken his name and age, and then directed along a long passageway to the classroom where he now sat. The lesson was arithmetic, which he normally found quite easy, but whereas Mr Baker's manner had always been quiet and controlled, the master here was barking out mental arithmetic questions and picking on individual boys to answer. Any boy who failed to give the correct response received a sharp clip round the ear.

The class came to an end, without Gus being called upon, and the boys filed out into the courtyard. Gus gazed around, searching for a corner where he might escape notice, but before he could move away a hand grabbed his shoulder. He swung round to face a boy with a shock of straw-coloured hair and a face full of pimples. He was a good head taller than Gus but he had narrow shoulders to which his thin arms seemed only loosely attached. He was grinning broadly, exposing front teeth that were brown and chipped. A small crowd of other boys stood close behind him.

'Hey, girly, what you doin' here?' he demanded.

'I'm not a girl!' Gus responded furiously.

'Augustus Lavender!' He pronounced the name with a high-pitched giggle. 'That's a girl's name.'

'No, it isn't!'

'Where d'you get a name like that, then?'

'From my father.'

'Go 'way! You never had a father.'

'Yes I did.'

'Where is he then?'

'He was lost at sea.'

'That what your mother told you, is it?'

'Yes. He's a sailor. One day I'm going to find him.'

'Get on! You believe that, you'll believe anything. I bet you never saw him.'

'I did!'

'Garn, you never! I bet your mam never even knew his proper name. She made that one up so's you'd never know you was a little bastard.'

He staggered back as Gus's fist made contact with his nose. For a second it seemed he was too shocked to retaliate, then he lunged at Gus and they went down together, punching, kicking, biting, while the boys standing by joined in a joyful chant of 'Fight! Fight! Fight!'

It was the blow of a cane across his shoulders that brought Gus to his senses. A strong hand grabbed him by the scruff of the neck and he was hauled to his feet. Beside him, his tormentor was held in an equally ruthless grip. Their captor was a short, thickset man with shoulders like a bull's and arms that easily held the two struggling boys apart.

'Now then, you two little bilge rats, what's it all about?' The voice was deep and hoarse.

'He called me a bastard!' Gus panted.

'Did he, now?'

'And he said my name was a girl's name.'

'I see. And what is your name?'

'Gus Lavender.'

The man pursed his lips thoughtfully. 'Never come across a wench called Gus.' He turned to Gus's assailant. 'And you? What do they call you?'

'Murray.'

The man's brow creased, as if puzzled. 'Mary? Mary what?'

The boy wriggled violently but he was unable to break free. 'Not Mary! Murray, Jack Murray.'

'Oh, right, Murray it is,' the man said, but already the damage was done. All round the circle boys were tittering, and Gus could hear the whisper of 'Mary! Mary!' going round. The man caught Gus's eye and he was almost sure that he winked.

'Now then,' the man said, 'shake hands, and if I catch either of you scrapping again you'll be kissing the gunner's daughter. Know what that means?'

Gus shook his head and the man looked at Murray who nodded sulkily. 'Means getting a flogging.'

'Correct. Now, I'm going to let you go and I don't want any more trouble. Got it?'

'Yes, sir,' both boys muttered.

'Yes, Cap'n.'

'Yes, Cap'n,' they responded.

The heavy hand was lifted from Gus's shoulder. 'Shake!' came the order. Reluctantly Gus held out his hand and received the briefest of touches from his opponent.

'Now, clear off,' the captain ordered.

The boys began to disperse and someone began chanting 'Mary, Mary, quite contrary ...' until Murray rounded on him and spat out, 'Shut it, you!'

Gus made to move off too, but the captain detained him, swinging him round to face him. 'Not seen you before.'

'No, sir ... no, Cap'n. I only got here this morning.'

'You from the workhouse?'

Gus dropped his gaze. 'Yes.'

'No need to be ashamed of that. All the boys here are orphans – leastwise, that's what they claim. There's some parents as try to pass their kids off as orphans to get them in here.'

'Why?' Gus asked in astonishment.

'Because boys here get the best training there is for going into a trade. Cobbler, carpenter, tailor, you can learn all that here. So what are you aiming to do?'

'I want to learn to be a sailor, like my da,' Gus said eagerly.

'Do you indeed? Well, it's good we made each other's acquaintance then. I'm Captain Thomas and I'm in charge of the boys who want to be sailors.' He looked Gus up and down. 'How old are you?'

'Thirteen ... well, nearly.'

'That'll be eleven, then,' the captain said. 'Well, you're small but you've got guts, I'll give you that. But no more fighting. Keep that temper under control and you and me will get on famously.' He lifted his head as a bell began to ring. 'Time for dinner. Off you go. I'll see you later.'

He strode away, leaving Gus wondering which way the dining hall was. As he hesitated, a figure detached itself from the shadows under the cloister which ran round the courtyard.

'Lost?'

'Er, yes, a bit.'

'Come on, I'll show you. My name's Will, by the way.'

'I'm Gus.'

'Yes, I heard. I liked the way you stood up to that lout Murray. It's time someone took him down a peg or two.'

'I think the cap'n did that, not me,' Gus said honestly.

'Well, you gave him as good as you got. In here.'

The hall was crammed with boys, seated on long benches drawn up to trestle tables. Gus would have hesitated to push in, but Will slapped a boy on the shoulder and exclaimed, 'Shove up, will you? There's two more of us here.'

The boy addressed looked up as if to refuse, but when he saw who it was his expression changed. 'All right, Will. Come on, lads, move over.'

Will prodded Gus to sit in the space that opened up and squeezed himself onto the end of the bench. Bowls of broth and hunks of bread were passed from hand to hand down the table and a cheery conversation began over Gus's head between Will and some of the others. Munching his food, Gus cast surreptitious glances at his new friend. He reckoned he was probably two, maybe three years older and, though he was dressed in the same ragged shirt as everyone else, he somehow managed to look cleaner and tidier than the rest. His hair was dark and his eyes a very bright blue and there was something about his friendly, cheerful manner that made Gus feel lucky to be sitting next to him.

After a few moments he plucked up courage to ask, 'What trade have you chosen, Will?'

'Same as you,' Will replied. 'Who wants to be cooped up in a stuffy room making boots or sewing shirts when you could be at sea?'

Gus grinned delightedly. 'Yes, that's what I think too.'

'It's not easy, mind,' Will said. 'Cap'n Thomas reckons you've got to be ready to do anything you're asked and if he gives you an order you'd better jump to it, or you end up regretting it. But he's fair. He treats everyone the same – not like some.' On these last words his face clouded and Gus wondered if someone had treated him unfairly, and if so, how.

Another question came to his mind. 'What about Murray? Is he with us?'

'Him? No! You wouldn't catch Murray climbing the mast. He's happy to squat around with a needle and thread.'

The meal came to an end and Gus followed Will out to a patch of open ground behind the building. As they reached it he gave a gasp of amazement. There in the middle of the worn grass was a full-sized ship, its three masts towering above him.

'It's a real ship!' he exclaimed.

'Real enough,' Will agreed, 'except it isn't floating. Come on, the cap'n's waiting.'

Captain Thomas was standing at the bottom of three rope ladders, which led up onto the deck high above them, surrounded by a group of boys of all ages. He checked their names off on a register and this time there were no titters when he called out 'Gus Lavender?'

'Right then,' he said. 'Let's find out who is fastest today.' He called three names and three boys stepped forward and took hold of the bottoms of the ladders.

The captain blew a whistle and the three started to climb, swarming up the ladders in an effort to outdo each other. The boys on the ground cheered them on until one gained the deck and raised his arms in a triumphant salute. Three more followed, and then Will's name was called. Glancing at his face as he moved forward, Gus was surprised to see his usual cheerful grin replaced by a frown of grim determination. When the whistle blew the other two boys with him began to climb almost as fast as the first ones, but it was clear that Will was struggling. Halfway up he stopped and hung there, his head drooping; then he seemed to find a new reserve of energy and climbed on. He reached the deck safely, but well behind the others, and Gus felt a stab of disappointment, followed by another of shame at what felt like disloyalty.

Gus was one of the last three to attempt the climb. 'Now,' the captain said, 'you haven't done this before. Take your time, hold on tight and don't look down. Off you go.'

Gus grabbed the lower rungs of the ladder and hauled himself up. It was much harder than he had expected. The ladder swung and twisted, banging his knees and knuckles against the side of the ship. It seemed a very long way up and halfway up he, too, stopped, panting, and looked below him. His gut churned at the sight of the drop. Then a voice called, 'Don't look down, Gus. Look at me.' He tore his gaze away from the ground and looked up. Will was leaning over the side. 'Keep going! You're nearly there. Come on!'

Somehow he struggled on until he reached the ship's rails and Will grabbed his arm and pulled him aboard. Captain

Thomas swung himself over the rail a moment later and clapped Gus on the shoulder.

'You'll do, young 'un. We'll make a seaman of you yet.'

Gus was out of breath and all his muscles ached, but he felt triumphant. Then he noticed Will. He had sunk down onto his haunches, leaning against the side. He was pale and he seemed to be struggling to breathe. Gus bent over him.

'You all right, Will?'

Will nodded and wheezed. 'I'll be fine in a minute. Just a bit out of breath.'

'Gather round,' the captain ordered, and Will dragged himself to his feet. Gus turned to join the others.

The rest of the afternoon passed in a blur. There was so much to learn. While the rest practised complicated knots in bits of rope, Captain Thomas began teaching him the correct names for different parts of the ship. There were two others who were also fairly new and he had them running backwards and forwards to commands of 'Aft! For'ard! Port! Starboard!' until they were dizzy and breathless with laughter. When eventually he was able to rejoin the others, Gus was relieved to find that Will was surrounded by a heap of knotted rope and apparently breathing normally.

By the end of the day Gus was so weary that he felt his legs might give way under him. Will put a hand on his shoulder.

'Come on, I'll show you where we sleep.'

He led the way down a passage and opened a door. The smell hit Gus like a solid wall, a sharp ammonia reek that caught at the back of his throat.

'Stinks, don't it?' Will said.

'What is it?'

'Some of the lads wet the bed, and it never gets a chance to dry out.'

The long room was lined on both sides with iron bedsteads and Gus saw that some of them where wide enough to accommodate three mattresses. They were so close together that the only way to get onto them was by climbing over the foot and crawling up. Already boys were pulling off shirts and breeches and scrambling into their narrow places.

'There's room for you there,' Will said, indicating a bed where one of the three mattresses was unoccupied.

'Where are you?' Gus asked.

'Over here, next to the door. I had to bribe the fellow who slept there to swap, but it was worth it. It's draughty but at least there's a breath of fresh air.' He gave Gus a slightly twisted grin. 'Goodnight.'

''Night,' Gus murmured. He pulled off his outer clothing and crawled into bed. The mattress smelt, but at least it was dry and there was a thin blanket to cover himself with. The other occupants of the bed were either already asleep or pretending to be, because neither of them made any attempt to acknowledge his presence. Briefly Gus thought of the dormitory at the workhouse. It had been crowded, but at least it was clean and the other boys were friendly. But he was too tired to care about that and within minutes he was asleep.

In the weeks that followed Gus experienced the extremes of euphoric excitement and total exhaustion. He was excited because everything he was learning seemed to bring him closer to his dream of going to sea; but his body was ill-prepared for the demands he was making on it. The food at the workhouse had been adequate but not designed to build muscle and there had been little opportunity for any kind of vigorous physical activity. He had played with the other boys in the yard, kicking a makeshift ball or running races, but that was a long way from the effort required to follow Captain Thomas's orders. He fell into bed each night aching in every muscle. But slowly, as the weeks passed, he grew stronger. He was not as fast up the rope ladder as some of the older boys, but he could make it to the top without stopping, and the blisters that had developed on his hands hardened into callouses.

Morning lessons were much the same as he had been used to, concentrating on reading and writing and basic arithmetic, and, once he had got over his fear, he was able to answer the questions without incurring the wrath of the teacher. It was the afternoons on the ship that he lived for. There were so many new skills that he sometimes felt he would never be able to master them all, but the captain was a good teacher, demanding undivided attention but patient where he saw there was real difficulty. Gus learned the various knots and their uses; he learned to repair sails and splice ropes; he took his turn in the galley and swabbed the decks; but what he enjoyed most were the occasions when the captain spread out his maps and charts and began to teach them the basics of navigation. For the first time, Gus saw the outline of the places his father had sailed to, the places where he still might be; Africa, the West Indies, and the coast of America.

Best of all were the times when Captain Thomas could be persuaded to talk about his own days at sea. He knew all the places he pointed out on the maps, and could describe them, so that Gus was not the only one fired with longing to see them for himself.

'Mind you,' the captain said, 'things were very different in my day. We sailed what was called the triangular route. From Liverpool we'd sail south to the coast of Africa. We'd buy blackamoors there and load them into the holds; then we'd sail across the Atlantic – what they called the Middle Passage – to the West Indies or the coast of America and sell them as slaves to work on the plantations, and with the money from the sale we'd buy coffee and sugar and cotton for the mills in Lancashire and bring them back to Liverpool. Sometimes we'd bring some of the slaves back here to work as well.'

'But that was wrong, surely.' It was Will who voiced what was in all their minds. 'You can't buy and sell people. Isn't it against the law?'

'It is now,' Captain Thomas replied. 'Perhaps it should always have been, and I can't say but what there were times, when I saw the state those poor wretches were in, that my conscience troubled me. But I was just a midshipman and the captain said it was business and it had always been done that way, so who was I to argue?'

'But we don't have slaves any more, do we?' Gus asked.

'We don't. But there's places in America where they reckon they can't do without them. That's what the war's about.'

'What war?' someone asked and the question was repeated around the group.

Captain Thomas shook his head. 'What do they teach you in those classrooms? Scribbling on slates and adding up numbers is all very well, but you don't know what's going on under your noses. Well, not under your noses, but it might as well be, for it makes a big difference to the trade from this port.'

'So, who is fighting?' Will asked.

'The Yankees are fighting each other. Their president tried to bring in a law forbidding slavery but the big land-owners in the southern states weren't having it, so they set up their own Confederacy, as they call it, to fight the government. It's been going on for over a year now.'

'But what has that got to do with trade from here?' someone asked.

'Like I told you, we used to bring back cotton and other things from the southern states. They'd be happy to let us have them still, in exchange for guns and ammunition, but the northerners don't want that, so they're blockading the ports.'

'So no one can get in or out?'

'Some are trying, so I hear. They call them blockade runners, and ships are being built specially for the purpose, but if they're caught the ships are scuttled and the crew is made prisoner. Now then –' the captain got up from the barrel where he was sitting '– enough talking. Time to get back to work.'

There was one lesson that Gus was dreading. He had seen the older boys sent 'aloft' to climb the masts and inch out along the yards to untie the gaskets that kept the sails furled and allow them to drop down or to roll them up and stow them again. He remembered the feeling he had had when he looked down from the rope ladder, but this would be ten times worse. He was afraid that if it came to his turn he would not be able to summon up the courage. Even Will had gone up there, and he did not want to shame himself in front of his friend. Eventually he voiced his fears.

Will nodded. 'It's scary – I can't pretend it's not – but it's not as bad as it looks. You climb the ratlines like climbing a ladder. Just don't look down, and you'll be fine.'

Inevitably, the day came when Captain Thomas said, 'Time you went up aloft, young 'un. There's nothing to worry about. I'll send one of the others up with you to show you the ropes. Ready?'

Gus swallowed. He felt sick but he knew he must not refuse. 'Ready, Cap'n.'

The boy chosen to go with him was called Bob. He was the oldest in the group and would soon be leaving, hoping to find an apprenticeship on board a real ship. He grinned at Gus.

'Come on! It's easy.'

To begin with it was not as terrifying as Gus had feared. Bob climbed beside him, giving instructions.

'Hang onto the shrouds, and step up on the ratlines. Your right foot, now your left. That's good, keep going.' Gus gritted his teeth and kept his eyes on where his hands were gripping, and so he went on until they reached the lowest yard. 'Now step out sideways onto the foot line,' Bob instructed. 'Hang onto the yard and shuffle along.'

The foot line seemed very thin and as he moved out away from the mast he glanced down. Bile rose in his throat and he swallowed and clung on desperately. He knew he was supposed to go out further, towards the end of the yard, but he was unable to move. It was a huge relief when Captain Thomas called, 'That'll do for today. Bring him down.'

Once back on deck Gus breathed a huge sigh of relief. Bob chuckled. 'Easy, eh?'

'Not as bad as I thought it would be,' Gus lied, trying to look unconcerned.

'You think it's easy, Bob?' the captain said. 'Wait till you have to do it in a gale with a big swell running!'

Once he began to feel less exhausted at the end of every day, Gus had time to pay more attention to what was going on around him. He noticed, for one thing, that Jack Murray was often hanging around, not close enough to be a threat, but near enough to overhear his conversation with friends. It bothered him, but he put it to the back of his mind because he was far more concerned about Will. It had been obvious from the beginning that there was something wrong with his lungs. Most of the time, when they were doing things that did not require too much effort, he was all right, but more than once Gus saw him sink down, gasping for breath, if they had to run around. Sometimes at night he woke to the sound of Will coughing. He understood after a while that all the others were used to this and seemed to think nothing of it, and that even Captain Thomas made allowances, but it worried him just the same. And there was more. During the day Will was cheerful and easy-going, but when evening came his mood darkened. He grew tense and watchful, as if waiting for something unpleasant.

There was a short time between supper and bedtime when they were allowed some leisure. The courtyard was the only vacant area, since the buildings were so over-crowded that rooms which had been intended for recreation had been turned into dormitories, so it was difficult to find a comfortable place to sit; but Will and his closest friends, amongst whom Gus was happy to be included, had found a corner where brooms and mops and buckets were stored and they usually met there to talk and play knuckle bones. There were times, however, when Will was unaccountably absent and Gus did not see him until he was in bed. Then Will would slip into the dormitory, without speaking to anyone, and curl up on his mattress, and once or twice Gus thought, though he could not be sure, that he was crying.

One morning he asked him where he had been the previous evening and Will looked at him in a way that scared him. Then he shrugged and turned away. 'Had to do some extra work for Frobisher.'

Mr Frobisher was the teacher in charge of Will's class. At one time Gus thought Will was lucky, because Frobisher did not shout like Mr Soames, who was his teacher; but later he realised that he had his own way of keeping order. He had no need to intimidate, because it was well known that, if anyone did not come up to his exacting standards, the punishments he imposed were draconian. It surprised Gus, nevertheless, that Will should have fallen victim, because he knew from the others that he was one of the best pupils in his class.

After these unexplained disappearances had happened several times, Gus decided to ask one of the boys who had known Will longer. He chose Mickey, who seemed closest to him.

'Why does Frobisher keep sending for Will? I thought he always got his work right.'

'He does,' Mickey said, briefly. 'It's not that.'

'Then what is it?'

'Don't ask.'

'Why not?'

'Because Will doesn't want to talk about it.'

'But I'm not asking him, I'm asking you.'

'Look, it's none of our business. Leave it!'

'I don't understand. It makes Will miserable. Can't we do something to stop it – whatever it is?'

'No. Now shut it, will you?'

Reluctantly Gus had to give up, but as the days passed he grew more and more concerned. Will was becoming preoccupied and withdrawn, no longer the friendly character Gus had first known. Finally, he decided he must tackle him directly.

'What does Frobisher want with you? It isn't just extra work, is it?'

Will looked at him and for a moment Gus thought he was going to explain, but then he turned away. 'I can't talk about it.'

'Why not?'

'Because ... he makes me do things.'

'What things?'

Will turned back to him and Gus saw undisguised anguish in his eyes. 'You're too young, Gus. You wouldn't understand. Just forget it, please!'

Two days later, Will was missing from the seamanship class.

'Where's Will?' he asked Mickey.

'Frobisher's got him picking oakum for a week.'

'Why?'

'Punishment for something.'

'What?'

Mickey shrugged. 'How should I know?'

Gus knew very well what picking oakum meant. It had been a common punishment in the workhouse, too. Those being punished were given pieces of old, tarry rope that were no longer usable and they had to pull them apart into their separate twisted strands and then rub the strands in their hands or on their thighs until they straightened out and could be gathered into a rough mat. Oakum was used for caulking ships, being stuffed into the cracks between the planking to make them watertight. Gus had been forced to do it once or twice, and he knew that it was tedious and painful. Fingertips soon blistered and nails broke with the effort of pulling the tarred strands apart, and the whole process produced an atmosphere of tiny dust particles that caught in the throat and got into the lungs. It was that that most worried him. Will coughed enough as it was. This could only make it worse.

His fears were realised that night. Will began to cough and wheeze as soon as he lay down and soon Gus saw, in the faint light from the small lamp which was kept burning, that he was sitting up, struggling for breath. He wriggled out of bed and felt his way across to him.

'Will? Can I do anything?'

'No.' The word came out as a gasp. 'I'll be all right in a minute. Go back to bed.'

'There must be something that will help.'

For a moment Will did not reply. Then he said, 'I might be better in the open air. Can you help me out?'

Gus gripped his arm. 'Lean on me.'

Will staggered as he got to the floor. He was bigger and heavier then Gus, but somehow he managed to support him as they crept to the door. Summer was over and a small breeze rattled the first dead leaves across the courtyard. A low wall ran around the cloister and Will sank down on it, trying to stifle a cough. Gus sat beside him, not knowing what else to do. It was against the rules to be out of the dormitory, but he could only hope that no one would see them.

'You get back to bed,' Will wheezed.

Gus shook his head. 'No. I'll wait with you.'

Little by little Will's breathing eased and at last he was able to stand. 'I'll be all right now,' he assured Gus. 'Let's go back.'

Even so, Gus was aware of his friend's struggling breaths, until finally sleep overcame him.

Next afternoon Gus got down to the ship before the others and found Captain Thomas seated on a barrel, smoking his pipe.

'Cap'n, you know Will's been made to pick oakum instead of coming here?'

'Yes, I was told not to expect him this week.'

'It's making him ill. Last night he could hardly breathe. Can't you speak to Mr Frobisher and tell him to let Will go?'

The captain rubbed the side of his nose with his thumb. 'Wouldn't do no good, young 'un. Mr Frobisher's not going to listen to an old sea dog like me.'

So as soon as he was dismissed from the lesson Gus headed for the governor's office. He had never spoken to him and knew him only from church service on Sunday mornings in the school chapel, when he gave long, boring sermons, full of warnings about the consequences of disobedience and ingratitude. His heart was thumping as he knocked on the door.

A gruff voice bade him enter. The governor was sitting behind a big desk covered in papers and he looked up irritably. He had a long face, framed by dark side whiskers, and eyes partly hidden under drooping lids. As he took in Gus's small figure his expression changed to incredulity.

'What do you think you are doing, boy? How dare you come knocking on my door?'

'Please, sir,' Gus croaked, 'I wanted to ask you to do something.'

'Ask me to do something? Do you imagine I am at your beck and call, to do what you want?'

'No, sir. But there is someone who needs your help.'

'My help? What are you talking about, boy?'

Looking into those heavy-lidded eyes Gus saw no hint of compassion or interest, but he floundered on. 'It's a friend of mine; please, sir. His name's Will. He's got a bad chest and he's been sent to pick oakum instead of coming to the seamanship classes. It's making him ill, sir. Please can you ask Mr Frobisher to let him off?'

'Ask Mr Frobisher to let him off?' The governor repeated the words as if he could scarcely believe his ears. 'Listen to me, boy. If Mr Frobisher has seen fit to punish your friend, it will be because he richly deserves it. I have no intention of interfering. Now get out!'

'But please, sir ...'

The governor rose from his chair. 'You dare argue with me? You are impudent! Come here!

He seized Gus by the collar and dragged him across the room. 'Over the back of that chair! Get down there!'

He forced Gus's head down to the seat of the chair and held him while he reached across for a cane. Gus had been beaten before. Very few boys escaped one or two floggings during their time at the workhouse; but this was different. The governor had a strong right arm, and he was furious. Gus tried to remain silent, but at the third stroke a cry was forced out of him and when he was finally allowed to straighten up his face was streaked with tears.

'Perhaps that will teach you not to argue with your betters,' the governor said. 'Now you can go and stand in that corner until I dismiss you. There will be no supper for you tonight.'

Gus slept little that night, kept awake by the burning pain in his buttocks and the sound of Will's gasping breaths. Next day he found any movement difficult. Captain Thomas soon guessed what the trouble was, but he said nothing; simply found him jobs that required the minimum of effort.

That evening at bedtime Will came over to him and drew him into a corner. 'Mickey told me what you did. You mustn't get involved. It won't help. But thank you for trying.'

That should have been the end of Will's week of penance, but the next day he was still missing from the seamanship class. When Gus saw him at supper he asked why, and Will shook his head despairingly. 'Frobisher says I haven't learned my lesson. He's given me another week.'

'What lesson?' Gus demanded in frustration.

'Never mind,' Will said and turned away.

It was another three days later that he caught Gus's arm as they went into supper. His face was deadly pale and his eyes were red and swollen.

'Gus, I can't go on any longer. I've got to get away. Will you help me?'

'Of course,' Gus replied, 'but how? We'd be seen if we tried to leave during the day, and the gates are locked at night.'

'There's a place in the fence, near the ship, where it's partly broken. I can't manage it on my own, but if you can give me a leg up ... I shouldn't ask, but I don't know what else to do.'

'I'll do it,' Gus said.

'I don't know what the consequences might be for you, if it's found out that you helped me,' Will said unhappily.

'Don't worry about that. I'll come with you. We'll run away to sea, together. You'll be all right when you get away from here.'

'Perhaps …' Will murmured. 'I've got to try something.'

'When?' Gus asked.

'Tonight, when the others are all asleep.'

That night, Gus lay awake, tensely waiting for the signal from Will. After what seemed a very long time he made out the shape of Will's figure moving towards the door. Very cautiously, so as not to disturb the other two boys, he slid out of bed and crept to join him. Outside, they looked at each other.

'You're sure you want to do this?' Will whispered. Already he was out of breath.

'Yes. Come on,' Gus said.

They tiptoed along the cloister and then down the passage that led to the rear of the building. There was a door and Gus felt a sudden shudder of disappointment. The door would be locked for sure. But Will led him into a small room beside it, which had a window.

'I tried this earlier,' he whispered. 'It opens.'

He was right, but climbing out was a different matter. The sill was several feet off the ground and even with Gus's help, Will struggled to hoist himself up, and when he was through he almost toppled to the ground, gasping with the effort. When he had recovered slightly they set off across the open space towards the ship, but Will had to stop every few yards, bending over with his hands on his knees, trying to catch his breath. By the time they reached the spot where the fence was partly broken he was leaning heavily on Gus's shoulder and breathing in shallow gasps.

Undeterred, he reached up and gripped the top of the fence. 'Give me a push up.'

He bent one knee and Gus stooped and gripped his leg and tried to lift him, but he was a dead weight. For a moment he scrabbled with his other foot in a last desperate effort, but then he let go of the fence and fell back onto the ground. Gus bent over him.

'Come on, try again!'

Will only shook his head. In the moonlight his face was deathly white and Gus thought for a moment that he had stopped breathing altogether. 'Leave ...' he gasped. 'Leave me ....'

'No! I'll wait. You'll be all right in a minute.'

The sound of voices brought him to his feet. Lights were moving in the space between the buildings and the ship. The voices were coming closer; lanterns were held high. Gus cast around him for a way of escape. He might have scaled the fence, but that would mean leaving Will. Then a voice he recognised shouted, 'There they are! I told you! They're over there.'

The voice belonged to Jack Murray.

Within seconds Gus and Will were surrounded. Two of the school porters were there, carrying lanterns, and with them was Mr Frobisher. Murray hung back, watching.

'So!' Frobisher said. 'Trying to run away, were you? You'll wish you'd never thought of the idea. Come on, get up! It's no good pretending you're ill.'

'He is ill!' Gus cried out. 'And it's all your fault. You sent him to the oakum picking room. It's killing him. Please!'

He turned his gaze to the two porters. 'Take him to the infirmary. He needs a doctor.'

'You won't get no doctor out here at this time of night,' one of them said dourly.

'He will go where I decide to send him,' Frobisher said, 'which will be back to the oakum picking as soon as he can stand.' He bent over Will and Gus saw his expression change. There was a flicker of something that almost looked like fear, but it was gone when he straightened up. 'Take him to the infirmary. I'll deal with him in the morning.'

One of the porters lifted Will in his arms and began to move off. 'I'll see you soon, Will,' Gus called after him.

'As for you ...' Frobisher caught him by the scruff of the neck. 'You'll answer for all this in the morning, and you'll regret your disobedience, I promise you. Now get to bed!'

Gus lowered his head and plodded back towards the building. What punishment Frobisher had in store for him he could only guess at, but he had not forgotten the sting of the governor's cane. Could there be worse than that? He found Murray blocking his way.

'Got you this time, girly!' he crowed triumphantly.

Gus looked at him. There were no words that he knew to express his feelings. 'You ... you traitor,' he muttered eventually. Then he pushed past him and went inside.

In bed he lay rigid with fear. The events of the night had worn him out, but as soon as he closed his eyes he saw Will's ashen face; and if he drifted into a doze he was jerked out of it by terrifying images of what might happen to him when morning came. All too soon it grew light and the boys began to rouse. Gus did not have long to wait. One of the masters opened the door and shouted, 'Lavender?'

'Here, sir.'

'Governor's office, now!'

The governor was not alone. Mr Frobisher was with him. He caught Gus by the collar and dragged him forward. 'This is the boy, Governor.'

The governor peered at Gus. 'You again? Did I not punish you for presuming to interfere only a day or two ago? Mr Frobisher tells me you were caught last night in the grounds with another boy. He thinks you were attempting to run away. Do you not understand what an act of disobedience and downright ingratitude that is? Explain yourself.'

'Please, sir, we had to get away. Mr Frobisher sent Will to pick oakum. He's got something wrong with his chest and it was making him ill. I told you that. Please, sir, how is Will? Is he all right?'

The governor and Frobisher exchanged looks, then the governor said, 'Will is dead. He died during the night.'

'Dead?' Gus repeated. It was too much to take in.

'Yes!' Frobisher said. 'And it is all your fault. If you had not encouraged him to attempt such a foolish escape, if you had not taken him out in the night air, when you knew already that his lungs were affected ...'

'It's not! It's not!' Gus hurled himself across the room and beat at Frobisher's chest with his fists. 'It's you! You made him do things! He hated it and when he refused you sent him to the oakum room.'

'What? How dare you accuse me?' Frobisher fended him off and the governor grabbed his arms and held him still.

'What do you mean, boy, by "made him do things"?' he demanded. 'What "things"?'

'I don't know.' Gus was weeping now. 'He wouldn't tell me. Bad things, horrible things ...'

'Governor! Will you let this ragamuffin make such accusations against me?' Frobisher exclaimed breathlessly. 'He doesn't even know what he is saying.'

'No, he clearly does not, but he cannot be allowed to attack the good name of one of my staff,' the governor said. He turned Gus to face him. 'Do you not understand that by making such wild accusations you are only getting yourself into deeper trouble?'

'It's true!' Gus sobbed. 'It's true!'

'This has got to stop,' Frobisher said. 'Let me deal with him, governor.'

'We shall both deal with him,' the governor said grimly. He gave Gus a shake. 'Get your breeches down, boy, and get over the back of that chair.'

They both laid into him, until he was sobbing and screaming, begging them to stop. Finally they let him up, his face wet with tears and snot and burning with the humiliation of what had been done to him.

'It's oakum picking for you until I decide you have learned your lesson,' the governor said. 'And don't dare repeat accusations like that again, to anyone. Now get out!'

Shortly afterwards, in the oakum picking room, Gus sat automatically pulling at the unyielding strands of rope. He was conscious only of the throbbing of his wounds. Two thoughts hammered in his head in rhythm with the throbbing: Will was dead; and, whatever happened, he would never let them do that to him again.

Five

'Afternoon off! You'll get an afternoon off when I think you've earned it, miss. And not a moment before.'

'It's just that my brother is at the Industrial School and I haven't seen him since I left the workhouse. I really want to make sure he's all right.'

'Well, you'll just have to work extra hard to earn the time off, won't you.'

The look on Mrs Wilkins's face told May that there was no point in trying to appeal to her better nature. As far as May could make out, she didn't have one. She sighed and went on polishing the silver. It was no good trying to go over her head to Mrs Freeman. May had been in service long enough now to understand how the household worked. Mr Freeman left everything to his wife, unless something was forcibly brought to his attention, as it had been by May's collapse; and Mrs Freeman was completely in thrall to Mrs Wilkins. From little snippets of gossip, overheard while she was working, May had divined that she had married very young and had come from a family that was not particularly well off. Her husband's success in business had lifted her up the social scale, but she was uncertain exactly what was expected of her now. Mrs Wilkins had established early on that she understood these matters and could be relied on to prevent her mistress from making some social gaffe, and now Lydia Freeman was frightened to go against her advice. As the household did not run to a lady's maid, Mrs Wilkins took on some of her duties. She helped Mrs Freeman to dress in the mornings and was often closeted with her for some time, 'taking the daily orders' in her words; but May wondered who was giving the orders and who was receiving them. Later, Mrs Wilkins helped her mistress undress and prepare for bed, and once again she was often there for much longer than seemed necessary.

Mrs Freeman's anxiety about establishing her position in society was confirmed by her attitude to Isabella's education. One day, while May was sweeping the stairs leading up to the schoolroom, she heard Miss Parsons' voice raised in irritation.

'You know quite well that your mama wishes you to acquire all the attributes of an educated young lady. The programme she has devised for you will equip you to mix in society at any level and it is in your own best interests to fulfil it to the best of your ability.'

The 'programme' was a subject of great fascination for May. Apart from her usual lessons with Miss Parsons, Isabella had a regular timetable of classes from experts in other areas. On Monday afternoons a large lady with a flamboyant taste in dress, called Madame Clara, came to give her piano lessons. On Tuesdays she was taken for riding lessons, Friday was dancing classes, and on Wednesdays Signor Carlucci, in frock coat and bristling moustaches, came to teach her singing. But it was the lessons that took place on Thursdays that filled May with envy. Then Mr Lattimer came to teach Isabella to draw and paint. May had to prepare the room for the lessons, setting out sketchbooks and sheets of unblemished paper, pencils and charcoal and boxes of watercolour paints. She was tempted, more than once, to help herself to a sheet or two of paper, but she knew that Miss Parsons kept a close eye on all the supplies and they would soon be missed. Occasionally, when she was clearing up, she sneaked a look at the contents of Isabella's sketchbook. It was obvious that she had very little talent for art.

One afternoon in early autumn May was polishing the brasses in the main hallway when Mrs Wilkins appeared from upstairs.

'Missus wants you. She's in her bedroom.'

'What does she want me for?' May asked nervously.

'I expect she'll tell you when you get there – if she hasn't got tired of waiting for you,' was the terse response.

May climbed the stairs and knocked on the door of Mrs Freeman's bedroom.

'Come in.' There was a hint of impatience in the tone. May entered, with Mrs Wilkins hard on her heels.

A green silk dress was spread out on the bed and Lydia Freeman was standing beside it, holding one sleeve and looking anxious.

'Jane Kelly told me you are good with your needle and have an eye for design.'

'Yes, ma'am. I mean, yes, Mrs Kelly did think well of my work.' May felt a small quiver of excitement.

Mrs Freeman threw down the sleeve she was holding. 'This gown was good enough last season, but fashions have changed. It's too good to throw out. There is going to be a Grand Bazaar in St George's Hall on October 8th in aid of relief for Confederate Prisoners of War and their families. A great many high-born ladies have volunteered to provide stalls and I have been asked to help. I must have something suitable to wear. I want you to see what you can do to bring this up to date.'

May swallowed. 'I don't know what the latest fashions are, ma'am. I'll do my best but ...'

Mrs Freeman interrupted her. 'There's a magazine here, with pictures of the latest things from Paris. You can copy from that.'

May's mind was whirling. This was a chance she must not miss, but was it within her capabilities? Already she could imagine the consequences if her efforts were not good enough. 'May I look at the dress, ma'am?'

'Of course, here, take it.'

May held the garment up. She had never touched such rich fabric, or seen anything so elaborately structured. The very feel of it sent shivers down her spine.

'Can I look at the magazine, ma'am?'

'I said so, didn't I?'

May took the magazine carefully and held it to the light from the window. Page after page was illustrated with beautiful dresses.

'When do you want the dress by, ma'am?'

'Next week. The bazaar is scheduled to open on October 8th.'

'Is there anything here you particularly like, ma'am?'

'Oh, I don't know! It's all too confusing. That's why I want you to sort it out for me.'

An idea came to May. 'Perhaps, ma'am, if I could have some paper and a pencil, I could make some sketches of what might be done. Then you could see which you like best.'

'Oh yes! That sounds like a very good idea. Don't you think so, Mrs Wilkins?'

Mrs Wilkins looked as if she was being forced to swallow some very bitter medicine. 'If you say so, ma'am.'

'Yes, I think that would be very helpful.' She looked at May. 'Go up to the schoolroom and ask Miss Parsons to give you paper and pencils. There are plenty there for Isabella's art lessons. But remember, I need this dress ready for next week, so don't waste any time.' She turned away and went to her dressing table, then looked back. 'All right, thank you. You can go.'

Outside, Mrs Wilkins glared at May. 'You needn't think that this lets you off your proper work. You do this in your own time, understand?'

It was on the tip of May's tongue to say that, as Mrs Freeman wanted this done in a hurry, this was more important than the dusting, but she bit the words back, knowing it would only prompt the cook to find her extra work to do.

'I'd better go and ask for the paper, like madam told me,' she said hesitantly.

'Go on then. You won't get much change out of Miss Parsons. She's as tight as ... well, never mind.' If there was one person Mrs Wilkins disliked more than May, it was the governess.

She was right about the reception May's request received. Miss Parsons looked down her long nose and said, 'Mrs Freeman wants you to design a dress for her?'

'Only some extra bits to bring it up to the latest fashion.'

'And what makes her think you are capable of that – you, a maid of all work?'

May stood her ground, refusing to be intimidated. 'My teacher at the workhouse, Mrs Kelly, thought I had some talent.'

Miss Parsons sighed deeply. 'Well, I suppose if it is madam's wish ... Here, take this. I'm not giving you the best paper, but this should do.'

It was still the nicest paper May had ever got her hands on. She took two pencils from the box on the table and carried her trophies back to the little room off the kitchen where she slept and packed them carefully in her box. She did not want them to disappear, or get used 'accidentally' for wrapping a joint or lighting a lamp.

She was kept busy for the rest of the day, and it was not until the last boot had been polished to Mrs Wilkins's satisfaction that she was able to think of the task ahead. She fetched the paper and the magazine and spread them on the kitchen table. Mrs Wilkins watched with tightening lips.

'You are not proposing to start on that now, are you?'

'I have to,' May said. 'Mrs Freeman wants the pictures in a hurry.'

Defeated, Mrs Wilkins picked up the only lamp. 'Well, you'd better be sure you're up betimes in the morning. There's a stub of candle over there. When that burns down you'll have to give up. I'm not wasting oil on mad ideas.'

May lit the candle and opened the magazine. She was dead tired and her eyes were smarting, but within minutes she had forgotten all that. Here was a treasure trove richer than anything she could have imagined, and for an hour she gazed and sketched and crossed through her work and started again. When the candle finally guttered out, she had her ideas down on paper. All that remained was to make fair copies.

How she managed to wake on time next morning was as much a mystery to her as it was a surprise to Mrs Wilkins, but somehow she dragged herself out of bed and rinsed the sleep out of her eyes. She went through her daily routine like an automaton and at bedtime she was ready to make her final sketches. Next morning, when she took Mrs Freeman's breakfast tray up to her, she had the drawings, carefully folded, in her apron pocket.

Mrs Freeman sat up drowsily and waved in the direction of the window, where sunshine was streaming in. 'Close those curtains again. I think I have one of my headaches coming on.'

May did as she was bid, though she wondered how her mistress was going to look at her drawings in the semi-darkness. She placed the bed tray carefully across Mrs Freeman's knees and said, 'I've done the sketches you asked for, ma'am,' adding, as the older woman seemed not to understand, 'the drawings of how we might change that gown to make it more fashionable.'

'Ah,' Mrs Freeman murmured. 'Leave them on the dressing table. I'll look at them later.'

Deeply disappointed, May placed the sketches on the dressing table and weighted them down with a perfume bottle. She could only hope that her mistress would remember to look at them when she got up, but it worried her that it was Mrs Wilkins who helped her to dress. It would be so easy to spill something over them.

When she collected the tray Mrs Freeman had gone back
to sleep and there was nothing more she could do.

That afternoon was one of Mrs Freeman's 'at home'
days and May put on her best cap and apron ready to open
the door to guests. Two ladies who were regular callers
arrived and were ushered into the drawing room. When the
mistress rang, May wheeled in the tea trolley. It was loaded
with the best china, Mrs Wilkins having decided that it was
easier to trust May with it than to give herself the extra
work; and there were plates of tiny sandwiches, piles of
buttered crumpets and delicious-looking cakes. As always,
May was astonished at the quantity of food these wealthy
ladies were able to consume.

As she pushed the trolley into the drawing room Mrs
Freeman exclaimed, 'Ah, here she is. This is May, the girl
I've been telling you about.'

It was the first time May could remember that her mistress had used her name. Usually she was just 'the girl'.
With a start she saw that her sketches were spread out over
the tea table.

The two lady visitors turned to look at her and one said,
'So you are the young woman who has done these beautiful dress designs?'

May wriggled her shoulders in embarrassment. 'Madam
asked me to think of ways to bring one of her gowns up to
date, ma'am. That's all.'

'But they are lovely,' the lady said. 'You are so lucky,
Lydia, to have such a talented girl in your service. We have
been trying to decide which one to choose, haven't we?'

Mrs Freeman had gone quite pink with pleasure. 'Yes,
we have.' She indicated one of the sketches. 'This is the

one I like best but can you do it? Can you make my green gown look like this?'

'Oh, I think so, ma'am.' May leaned forward eagerly, tracing with one finger the embellishments she had designed. 'If I made up these big bows, and then caught the overskirt back and used them to fasten it, then it's just a matter of making the lace ruffles for the neck and the sleeves …' She realised abruptly that in her enthusiasm she was forgetting her station and drew back. 'Sorry, ma'am.'

'No, go on,' Mrs Freeman said. 'You think it is possible?'

'Yes, ma'am. That is … it's a questions of the materials …'

'What would you need?'

'Ribbon for the bows, ma'am, and lace, of course.'

'Well, that will be no problem, surely,' the other lady put in. 'All that will be available at the haberdashery counter in your husband's new shop.'

'Of course!' Mrs Freeman looked as if the idea had not occurred to her. 'Tell me what you need and I will ask my husband to bring it back from the shop tomorrow. How much ribbon, and what colour?'

May hesitated. She had not thought about quantities. 'I'd … have to think about how much, ma'am. For the colour, I thought perhaps a deep blue, the sort with a bit of green in it …'

'Peacock blue, you mean?' the first lady suggested.

'Oh, yes, that would be it,' May agreed gratefully. 'But how much …? I'd need to work it out.'

'Well, do that, and let me have a note of it by dinner time, so I can tell Mr Freeman.'

May bobbed a curtsy. 'I'll do my best, ma'am. Can I take the drawing with me?'

'Yes, yes. You get along and do your sums.'

Outside the room May hesitated for a moment. She should go straight back to the kitchen, where Mrs Wilkins would certainly have a job waiting for her. She glanced around, then ran quickly up the stairs. The top floor was quiet, as she had known it would be. Miss Parsons had taken Isabella for her riding lesson. May crept into the schoolroom and sat down. She gazed at her picture. Four huge bows decorated either side of the skirt; but how much ribbon would be needed to make them? How could she work it out? For a moment she sat with her head in her hands; then she had an idea. Her apron was tied in a bow at the back. She took it off and retied it on the table in front of her. Yes, that was nearly large enough. She untied it and straightened the pieces. How long were they? Every morning when she prepared the schoolroom she put out pencils and rubbers and a ruler. She knew exactly where to find it. She measured the two pieces. Eighteen inches each. Add a bit extra to make the bows larger ... twice that, and then enough for eight bows ... for the first time she was glad that Miss Bale had made her learn her tables. Then the lace ... how much to edge the neck of the gown? She wrapped the apron strings round her own neck, and then round her arms. Altogether, it seemed to come to a great deal of material. It would be costly. Would Mrs Freeman think it was too expensive? But it could not be done properly for less. She jotted the amounts she had come up with on the edge of the drawing, retied her apron and put the paper in her pocket.

It was not a moment too soon. She was descending the stairs when she heard the front doorbell ring. It was Miss

Parsons and Isabella, back from her riding lesson. May opened the door and Miss Parsons swept past her without acknowledgement, as usual. Isabella's nose was red and her eyes were swollen as if she had been crying.

'But I don't like it,' she was saying fretfully. 'I hate that pony. He tried to bite me.'

'Be quiet, Isabella,' the governess snapped. 'You are a most ungrateful little girl. Your mama and papa are spending a great deal of money on your education. Many other children would love to have the opportunities you have ...' Her voice faded as she marched Isabella up the stairs.

You don't know the half of it, May thought, but you can keep the riding lessons.

She went to the drawing room to collect the tea things.

'I've worked out what I need, ma'am. I hope you won't think it's too much.'

'If that is what is required, that is what you must have,' Mrs Freeman said. 'Thank you, May. I will give this to Mr Freeman when he comes home. You can take the tea things.'

May pushed the trolley out into the hall. There was one cake left, a chocolate one. She looked round. There was no one about. Mrs Wilkins would be in the kitchen with her feet up. And she deserved a treat, didn't she? She put the cake into her mouth and allowed herself to savour it for a few seconds before she swallowed it, then wiped her lips on the hem of her apron.

'And where have you been, may I ask?' Mrs Wilkins demanded tartly.

'The missus kept me, asking about my drawings,' May said. Well, it was almost true, she thought.

'Huh! And what is that, on your apron?'

May looked down at the telltale chocolate stains. 'One of the ladies dropped a cake, and my fingers got sticky picking it up.' She could tell from her expression that the cook did not believe her, but could not think of any way to disprove her story. 'I'll get these tea things washed, shall I?' she added meekly.

'You'd better. We're behind hand as it is. And mind you don't chip any of them. Any breakages will come out of your wages. And get that apron clean or you'll have nothing decent to serve dinner in.'

May said nothing but headed for the scullery. She had never received any wages, so she assumed Mrs Wilkins' threat was simply a form of words.

She was ladling soup from the tureen into Mr Freeman's bowl when he startled her by looking up. 'I hear you have been taking on a new role, May.'

'What, sir? Sorry, sir.'

'I mean as fashion advisor to my wife.'

May dithered. The soup tureen was hot and she was afraid of dropping it. Was the master cross because she had stepped beyond her usual duties?

'No ... no. sir. I wouldn't presume ...'

'But I have an order here for materials.' To May's surprise he reached into an inner pocket and withdrew her sketch and studied it. 'Nine yards of peacock-blue ribbon, three yards of white lace ... These are not for you, I imagine.'

'Oh, no, sir!'

'Really, David,' his wife said petulantly, 'I don't know why you are making such a fuss. After all, I am not asking for a new gown. Just a few bits and pieces to make the old one wearable.'

Mr Freeman raised his eyebrows. 'My dear, I am not making a fuss. I am merely interested in the origin of these designs.' He looked at May and this time she saw the corners of his eyes crinkle and the beginnings of a smile half hidden under his moustache. 'Don't look so alarmed, May. I like your design very much and of course you must have the materials you require. Now, this ribbon ... velvet or silk, and what width?'

'Oh, I don't know. I think in the magazine it said velvet ...'

'I tell you what,' Mr Freeman said. 'It seems to me that the best plan is for you to come to the shop with me tomorrow morning and choose what you need.'

'Come with you, sir?' May almost dropped the tureen. 'But ... but my work, sir ...'

'Oh, come.' He chuckled. 'I don't think the household will collapse into chaos if the drawing room is not swept and dusted for one morning.'

'But Mrs Wilkins ...' May said.

'Ah, yes.' He nodded. 'I see the difficulty. Go back to the kitchen, May, and ask Mrs Wilkins to step up to the dining room for a moment.'

May left the room in such a hurry that she forgot to leave the soup tureen on the sideboard. When she conveyed her message, Mrs Wilkins's nostrils flared in triumph.

'Now what have you done, you foolish girl? If the master has found fault ...' She left the sentence unfinished and marched up the stairs. In the dining room, Mr Freeman was on his feet, helping himself to vegetables from the sideboard.

'Now, sir,' the cook began before he had time to open his mouth, 'I'm real sorry you've had reason to complain, but the fact is the girl's mind has not been on her work these last two or three days. I've told her she's not giving satisfaction, but her head's in the clouds ....' May saw the cook fix Mrs Freeman with a look that said quite clearly, 'This is all your fault.' She took in Mr Freeman at the sideboard and clicked her tongue. 'And now she's come running down to the kitchen and left you to serve yourself.'

'She came running down to the kitchen because I sent her,' Mr Freeman said mildly. 'And I have not asked you to come up because I have a complaint, but because I have a request.'

'A request, sir? Of course, I'll get you anything you want if it's in the house.'

'No, you misunderstand me. My request is this. I want you to spare May to come with me tomorrow morning. I am going to take her to the shop to choose the ribbons she needs for my wife's dress.'

For the first time May saw the cook at a loss for words. She stood opening and closing her mouth like the goldfish Isabella kept in a bowl in the schoolroom.

'Go with you, sir ...?' she uttered at last. 'But she's just, just ...'

'She's a clever girl, and I think we have been wasting her talents,' Mr Freeman said. 'She will come with me tomorrow, and we shall see what she makes of my wife's gown. Thank you, Mrs Wilkins. That will be all.'

The cook sent a last, malevolent look at her mistress, who lowered her eyes to her plate. Then she bobbed a stiff curtsy. 'Very good, sir.' She turned and marched to the door and as she opened it, May heard her mutter, not quite loud enough for Mr Freeman to hear, 'But no good will come of it, you mark my words.'

Back in the kitchen May prepared herself for the back-lash, but Mrs Wilkins said only, 'Get those dishes washed. You needn't think because the master's got a soft spot for you that you can get away with skimping your work.'

Next morning May was up even earlier than usual and she managed to get most of her chores done before Mr Freeman came down to breakfast. By the time he was fin-ished she had changed her cap and apron for her shawl and the bonnet she had been given when she left the workhouse and was waiting in the hall to hand him his hat and stick, as she did every morning. He looked her up and down and for a terrible moment she thought he was going to say that he had changed his mind, that he couldn't be seen walking through the streets with her. But he only said, 'Ready?'

'Ready, sir,' she answered breathlessly.

He opened the door and stood back for her to pass him, just as if she had been a real lady. She had not set foot out-side the house since she first entered it, except to follow the family to the church on the corner every Sunday morning, and the onrush of new sights and sounds and smells almost overwhelmed her. Cooped up inside, she had hardly real-ised that summer was over and the leaves on the trees along the street were turning brown.

Her nose was filled with half-remembered smells from her childhood; horse dung and dust and smoke from chimneys. Mr Freeman was already heading down the hill and she almost had to run to catch up with him. The street was crowded with carriages and carts and costers pushing barrows piled with goods. Well-dressed gentlemen walked briskly past, heading, she supposed, for their places of work, and there were women with baskets on their arms and errand boys dodging through the crowd. Two gentlemen rode past on horses whose coats gleamed in the sunshine and a nursemaid pushed a baby in a perambulator.

Trotting to keep up with Mr Freeman's long strides, May absorbed all this colour and variety as a starving man takes in food.

Mr Freeman looked down at her. 'Tell me something, May. How long have you worked for us?'

May thought back. 'I came just before my birthday. The beginning of May, it would be.'

'And now it is October, so five months?'

'That would be about right, sir.'

'And what do we pay you?'

May glanced sideways up at him. 'Pay me, sir?'

'Yes. What are your wages?'

'Wages?' She struggled with this new concept. 'I don't rightly know, sir.'

'Don't know? But you must have been given some money.'

'No, sir.'

'You have been in the household for five months and you have never received any payment?'

'I get my board and lodging, sir. That's enough, isn't it?'

He paused in his stride and looked at her, and there was an expression in his eyes that puzzled her. 'No, May. It is not enough. But there's no need for you to worry. This is something I shall have to look into.'

They headed down the hill and for a moment she thought they were going towards St George's Hall, which remained one of her most vivid memories; but when they reached the bottom Mr Freeman led her across the street, where a crossing sweeper had cleared a path through the horse dung, and she saw straight ahead of them a shop window full of beautiful dresses, and over it a sign: FREEMAN'S LADIES OUTFITTER. A man in uniform opened the door and saluted. Mr Freeman wished him good morning as he stepped inside, but May hung back, convinced that this exalted personage would not allow someone like her into a shop like this.

Mr Freeman looked over his shoulder, then turned back to her. 'Come along, May. There's nothing to be afraid of.'

May followed him in and then stopped abruptly. Her eyes and nose were assailed with so many new sensations that it made her feel dizzy. It seemed to her that she smelt crimson velvet and green silk; a woman passed leaving behind her a perfume like sunshine on clean linen and all around her light sparkled off glass and silver with the sharpness of freshly cut lemon. Then her senses cleared and she was able to distinguish counters of polished mahogany and shining glass, bearing rolls of coloured ribbon and piles of gloves and silk scarves and lace collars; and beyond them what she thought at first were real women dressed in lovely gowns, until their stillness told her that they were simply models. It was like Mrs Kelly's picture book come to life.

Mr Freeman said, 'Well, how do you like my shop?'

'It ... it's like a fairy land, sir ...'

'Fairy land? That is exactly it. I want to create a place where people can come, not just to buy things, but to enjoy a new, delightful experience. I intend this to be what is being

called a department store. The idea is that people will be able
to obtain everything they require under one roof. So instead of
going to the dressmaker for a new gown, then to the milliner
for a hat, then to the shoemaker for shoes and then perhaps to
a different shop to buy a shirt for their husband or a toy for a
child, they will be able to get it all in the one shop.

Mr Freeman beckoned to a pretty young woman in a white
blouse and a dark-blue skirt. 'Elsie, this is May. She has a
commission from my wife to buy ribbons and lace to revive
an old gown. Will you show her what we can offer, please?'

Elsie bobbed a curtsy. 'Of course, Mr Freeman.'

He looked at May. 'I'll leave you with Elsie and come
back later. Get whatever you need.'

Elsie gave May a friendly smile. 'Let's see what we can
find you, shall we? Over here.'

For the next half-hour May was in heaven. Together, she
and Elsie compared colours and textures in a variety she
had never dreamed existed. When she explained what it
was that she wanted to do, Elsie entered into the spirit of
the enterprise and they unrolled ribbons and formed them
into bows of different sizes, until finally May was satisfied
that she could bring her design to life.

'What about sewing thread?' Elsie asked, and there were
further choices to make.

'And needles?'

'No, thank you. I have needles.' Nestling at the bottom
of May's box was a small wallet covered in blue silk and
containing a selection of sewing needles, a parting gift
from Mrs Kelly.

They had just made the final decisions and Elsie was
wrapping her purchases when Mr Freeman returned.

'Have you got all you need?'

'Oh, yes sir, thank you, sir.'

'Good. And I have a little gift for you, to thank you for the extra work you are doing.'

He held out a small package. May took it and was immediately enveloped in a waft of perfume. 'What is it?' she asked.

'Just some soap, but it's lavender scented. I thought it was appropriate.'

May lifted the parcel to her nose. 'Is this what lavender smells like?'

He gave her that look again, as if something was hurting him. 'You have never smelt lavender?'

'No, sir. Oh, it's lovely! Thank you so much.'

'Not at all. Now, can you find your own way back?'

'Oh yes, sir, I think so.'

'You'd better get along then. You'll have your work cut out to get that dress ready in time.'

Back at the house Mrs Wilkins greeted her with a grim look. 'You're back, then. You'd best get your apron on. There's still all the dishes from breakfast to be washed and then I need you to peel the potatoes for lunch.'

'Yes, Cook,' May said meekly and moved towards her little room. Mrs Wilkins sniffed. 'And what's that I can smell?'

'It's lavender soap.'

'Lavender soap! What does a girl like you want with lavender soap? You haven't got yourself a follower, have you?'

'A what?'

'A follower. You've not got some boy hanging round, hoping to walk out with you?'

May felt herself blush. 'No, Mrs Wilkins. I haven't.'

'No? So who gave you that soap, then?'

May lowered her eyes. 'Mr Freeman gave it to me.'

'Mr Freeman gave you soap?' The cook sounded incredulous. Then her tone changed. 'Oh, he did, did he? Well, don't just stand there. Get on with your work.'

As soon as lunch was over and the dishes washed, Mrs Wilkins decided that the scullery windows needed cleaning. May was about to start on them when one of the bells above the kitchen door jangled.

'That's the mistress, in her bedroom,' Mrs Wilkins said. 'What does she want up there at this time of day? Well, I'd better go, I suppose.'

She stomped off irritably. May knew why. She usually expected to put her feet up for an hour after lunch, and now she had to climb two flights of stairs to attend to her mistress's whims. Serves her right! May thought.

The cook was back in surprisingly short time. 'It's not me that's wanted. It's you. Missus wants to see what you brought back from the shop this morning.'

May pulled off her working apron and replaced it with her afternoon one. Then she collected the parcels from her box and carried them up to Mrs Freeman's room. The green dress was laid out on the bed as before.

'Show me what you have brought,' Mrs Freeman said eagerly. 'I want to be sure you can have the dress ready in time.'

May displayed her purchases and demonstrated how the ribbon could be formed into bows and attached to the skirt. Mrs Freeman clapped her hands.

'Yes, yes! That is perfect. It will look just like the picture in the magazine. You had better get started at once.'

May hesitated. 'It's difficult, ma'am. I can't take the dress down to the kitchen.'

'Of course you can't,' her mistress snapped. 'Whatever put that idea into your head? You must do it here.'

May wriggled her shoulders uncomfortably. 'The thing is, ma'am, I've my work to do for Mrs Wilkins and I don't finish till late. By the time I'm done, you will be in bed so I can't come in then.'

'Oh, what rubbish!' Mrs Freeman exclaimed. 'This is more important than whatever it is you would be doing downstairs. You must tell Mrs Wilkins that I want you up here every afternoon until the dress is ready.'

May imagined the cook's face when she heard that and felt a small shiver of triumph. She curtsied. 'Yes, ma'am. If you say so.'

'I do say so. And you can start now.'

'Very good, ma'am. I'll need to fetch my sewing needles.'

'Yes, yes. Go along, but be quick. I want to see this started.'

Informed of her mistress's orders, Mrs Wilkins drew a breath so deep that May thought she might explode; but in the end she just said, 'Very well. If the missus doesn't care if the house goes to rack and ruin, who am I to argue?'

For the next week May spent every afternoon happily stitching. It gave her pleasure just to handle the rich fabrics and it was an added delight to see her design becoming reality. When the dress was finished, she helped Mrs Freeman to try it on. She stood for some time, looking at herself in the long mirror from every angle, while a triumphant smile spread across her face.

'It's perfect! No one at the bazaar will be more à la mode than I shall.' She glanced round at May. 'That will be all, thank you. You can go back to your work now.'

May gazed at her and felt tears prick behind her eyelids. No word of praise for her efforts. No real thanks. The smile had not been for her. But then, she was only a servant; servants were not expected to have feelings.

From then on it was back to her usual routine, except that Mrs Wilkins made sure that she worked longer hours than ever. A deep gloom settled over her as she foresaw once again a life of unrelieved drudgery before her. It did little to lift her spirits when she saw Mrs Freeman sweep out of the house wearing the dress. She remembered her first sight of St George's Hall and wished passionately that she could go with her.

Later that evening, while May was serving dinner, Mrs Freeman was chattering excitedly.

'Such a wonderful display! Each stall is dedicated to the welfare of prisoners from one particular state and you would not believe the goods that have been donated. And the great ladies standing behind their tables like women at market! Do you know how many people paid the entrance fee today? Two thousand five hundred!'

'Well, let us hope the next two days are as successful,' her husband said. 'The blockade of the southern ports is starving our cotton mills and the price of finished fabric has gone through the roof. This war needs to be brought to an end as quickly as possible. Though I have to confess that I am disturbed by the idea that we are supporting people whose only reason for fighting is so that they can continue to own slaves.'

'Of course,' Mrs Freeman added, 'this is only to help the prisoners and their families – not to buy weapons or anything like that.'

'Of course,' her husband agreed, but to May's ears it sounded as though he thought differently. 'Well, if the fortunes of the Confederate army are reflected in the number of Confederate flags being flown all over the city, the war should be over very soon. '

One evening, May was about to enter the dining room to clear away the dishes when she heard raised voices.

'But David,' Mrs Freeman was saying plaintively, 'you always tell me that we must avoid all unnecessary expense, so that money can be ploughed back into the business. I am only trying to carry out your instructions.'

'I know that.' His voice was quieter, but there was an undertone of controlled impatience. 'But we are not slave owners, Lydia, and this is not the southern states of America. Remember what the Bible says: "The labourer is worthy of his hire".'

Mrs Freeman sighed and said submissively, 'Very well, my dear. Whatever you think best.'

That seemed a good moment to interrupt, so May pushed open the door and went in.

'Can I clear now, ma'am?'

Mr Freeman looked round from his chair. 'Ah! Just the girl we've been talking about, right on cue. Come here, May.'

May went to stand in front of him. A quick glance at his face told her that he was not angry, so presumably she had not done anything wrong.

'I'm told the dress was a great success, much admired by the other ladies. Well done!'

'Thank you, sir.'

He put his hand in his pocket and produced some coins. He held one up.

'Do you know what this is?'

'No, sir.'

'It's a sovereign. It is worth one pound, or twenty shillings. What about this one?'

'No, sir.'

'It is a half sovereign, worth ten shillings. If I add two more, that makes a total of …?

'Fifty shillings, sir.' Why was he testing her on her arithmetic?

'Now, I have been making some enquiries and I am told that the usual wage for a girl in your position, after deductions for board and lodging, is six pounds per annum. That works out, if I am not mistaken, at ten shillings per month. You have been with us now for five months, so that adds up to …?

'Fifty shillings, sir.'

'Precisely. So here you are.' He held out the coins.

May gazed at them, making no attempt to take them.

'Come along, don't be afraid. These are for you.'

She raised her eyes to his face. 'What … what should I do with them, sir?'

'What? Well, for a start you should put them away in a safe place. Then, well, why don't you buy yourself a nice cape to wear instead of that old shawl, and a pretty bonnet?'

'When would I do that, sir?'

'Why, when you go shopping.'

She searched his face. He might belong to a different order of beings, for all he understood of her life. 'I don't go shopping, sir.'

A frown crossed his brow and she saw again that pained, puzzled look. 'Well, perhaps you should, sometime soon. Meanwhile, take the money and look after it. It's yours, honestly earned, and there will be ten shillings every month from now on.'

May took the coins and slipped them into the pocket of her apron. 'Thank you, sir. Can I clear away now, please?'

'Yes, yes. Carry on as usual.'

Back in the kitchen May said nothing to Mrs Wilkins. As soon as she could, she went to her room and hid the money beside the bar of lavender soap in her box. In bed that night she lay awake for a few minutes, thinking about it. When she was a child, a penny had been a fortune. Now she owned ... twelve times fifty – six hundred of them. Could she really walk into a shop, a shop like Mr Freeman's, and buy things. He had said so, but when could she do it? The only time she left the house was on Sunday mornings for church and the shops were shut then. She closed her eyes and put the thought out of her head.

Next day Mrs Wilkins was summoned to speak to her mistress and returned with a grim expression that made May fear the worst.

'It seems you're to have a half day off every two weeks – every other Wednesday, starting tomorrow. What I am supposed to do with tea to serve and dinner to prepare I do not know, but the master insists, I'm told.' She eyed May narrowly. 'You've wormed your way in there, somehow, but don't get too cocksure. It won't last.'

Lying in bed, May tried to decide what she would do with her time off. She had never experienced a time when her activities were not prescribed for her, and the thought was daunting. She could go back to Mr Freeman's shop. She could ask Elsie if it was all right for her to buy a cape ... her mind drifted ... Then she came awake with a start. Of course, she knew what she must do tomorrow. She must go to the Industrial School and see Gus. That was far more important than any shopping.

The next day, it took May an hour to walk to Kirkdale and she had to ask the way several times. It was an unseasonably warm day, so by the time she arrived at the school at the top of the hill she was sweating and her feet hurt. She gazed up at the building in awe. It might have been a castle in a fairy tale, with its turrets and gables. At length she plucked up courage to walk up to the main gate and found the porter's lodge. She knocked and a window opened at the side of the door.

'Yes?' said a gruff voice above her head.

'Please, sir, I've come to visit my brother.'

'Name?'

'I'm May Lavender. He's Gus ... Augustus.'

'Lavender?' The tone was different. 'You are Augustus Lavender's sister?'

'Yes, sir. Can I see him, please?'

The window was closed abruptly and a moment later the door opened and a thickset man in uniform came out.

'You need to speak to the governor. This way.'

'Oh, no, sir! I don't want to bother the governor. I just want to make sure my brother is all right.'

'Like I said, you need to talk to the governor. Come along.'

He led her through the courtyard where boys were coming and going. She searched among them for the familiar ginger head, but did not find it. The porter tapped on a door and an irritable voice bade him enter.

'Girl here says she's Lavender's sister, sir.'

The governor removed his pince-nez and peered at May. 'No one said anything about a sister. Where have you come from?'

'I'm in service, please, sir. With Mr and Mrs Freeman in Rodney Street. But before that I was in the workhouse, with Gus ... Augustus. Please can I talk to him, just for a few minutes?'

'I am afraid that is not possible. Augustus is no longer with us.'

'No longer ...' May felt as if her stomach had turned inside out. 'You mean ...'

'I mean he has absconded.'

'Ab ... what?'

'Run away. He disappeared some days ago.'

'Where has he gone?' Even as she asked the question she knew it was stupid.

'If we knew that,' the governor said testily, 'he would be back here by now, doing penance for his ingratitude.' He looked away and shifted some papers on his desk. 'We have searched, and made extensive enquiries. No one seems to have seen the boy.'

'When?' May asked. 'When did he go?'

The governor shuffled some papers on his desk. 'October 8th. Now, I am extremely busy so ...'

'But what happens now?' May asked desperately. 'What can I do?'

'Do? Nothing. There is nothing to be done. He may turn up, in due course, or he may not. That will be all. Good day.'

The porter opened the door. 'This way, miss.'

Numbly, May followed him out and before she could order her thoughts she found herself back on the street. She stood still, looking back at the closed gates of the school. It looked more like a prison than a castle, now. She turned and began to plod back the way she had come. The governor's words went round and round in her head. 'He may turn up ... or he may not. There's nothing to be done.'

Six

Gus crouched behind a pile of crates and peered along the dock road. Escaping from the school had not been difficult. He had waited several days, to allow the wounds inflicted by his beating to heal, but all the time he had been planning to get away. The nights were longer and darker and one evening he had made the decision to try his luck. To his amazement and delight he found that the window he and Will had used was still unfastened and the fence had not been repaired. A spring and a scramble and he was free, scarcely able to believe how easy it had been. It had taken him all night to walk from the school to the docks and now dawn was breaking and there was only one thought in his mind. He must find a ship that was ready to sail and get on board before the authorities caught up with him.

A plume of smoke from beyond one of the dockyard gates caught his attention. Captain Thomas had been dismissive of the newfangled steam ships, declaring them to be a flash in the pan that could never replace sail, but he had said enough for Gus to understand that the smoke meant that a ship had fired up its furnaces to get up steam ready for departure. That this was imminent was born out by the activity around the gate.

A steady stream of wagons was arriving, carrying supplies or cargo to be loaded. Each one was stopped by a guard, who checked the driver's papers before allowing it through. It seemed odd to Gus that this should be happening so early, before it was properly light, and the careful checking added to the impression that something secret was in hand. What that might be did not concern him. If he could only get on board and be at sea before he was caught, he did not care what the purpose of the voyage might be; but what did worry him was the fact that these precautions made it hard, if not impossible, for him to get anywhere near the ship.

He watched as, one after another, the wagons rolled up and halted in front of the gates. If only he could get into one of them and hide he would have a chance. He had almost given up hope and decided to try his luck elsewhere when a possibility offered itself. The contents of most of the wagons were concealed under tarpaulins, which were tightly fastened to the sides, but on one he saw that at the rear the cover had come loose, exposing the back of a crate, which had a splintered hole in it. It looked as though whatever was in the crate had shifted and broken through, though he could not see what had done the damage. What excited him was the thought that the hole was just about big enough for him to crawl into. Each wagon was kept stationary while the papers were checked, and by chance this one seemed to be the last in the line, so there was no one to see him as he slipped out from his hiding place and ran to the back of it.

He caught hold of the tailboard and struggled under the tarpaulin. The jagged edges of the hole in the crate caught at his clothes and a splinter dug itself into his thigh, but he forced his way through and found himself in a small space between two large objects. It was almost dark inside the crate, except for a faint glimmer that came through the hole, but after a few moments his eyes adapted themselves and he made out their shapes. It took a moment to understand what he was seeing, but then he caught his breath in mingled shock and excitement. He was crouched between the barrels of two big guns. They rested on wooden cradles and were roped in place. Someone must have spotted the damage and fastened them more securely, but had apparently not been able to repair the crate, or had not had time to do so.

The wagon gave a jolt and moved forward. Gus crouched lower, praying the guard would not see the hole and decide to investigate. It seemed he did not, because the wagon continued to bump over the cobbles, and Gus turned his thought to the next problem. He was inside the dockyard, but soon the crate would be opened so the guns could be loaded on board and he would be exposed. Was there any chance he might be able to make a run for it? And even if he got away, where could he hide next? How was he going to get on board the ship? He was no nearer to finding an answer when the wagon came to a halt and he heard the voices of men calling instructions to each other. The light increased as the tarpaulin was dragged off, then the crate rocked and vibrated and suddenly jolted upwards.

Gus clung to the barrel of one of the guns as it tilted and then righted itself and he realised that the whole thing was being craned aboard. For a few seconds he swung in mid-air and then he felt himself descending. Darkness fell again as the crate was lowered into the hold, and there was another, harder jolt. It had reached the bottom and different voices echoed round him.

'Eh, Joe, this one's split.'

'Never mind that. Nowt to do with us. Get it unroped before they start yelling for the next one.'

Gus heard the ropes being pulled off and then the men's footsteps, sounding oddly metallic, as they moved away.

Someone shouted from above, 'That's the last one, boys. Come on up.'

Gus wriggled to the hole and cautiously put his head out. His crate was on top of another one, and all around him other crates were piled one on another. Above him was a square of light, the hatch through which he had descended, and hanging from it a rope ladder.

The stevedores who had manhandled the crates into position were climbing up it, one after another. Gus realised with a shock that once they were all out, the hatch covers would be replaced and he would be incarcerated in total darkness. After that, the hatches would not be opened until the ship reached its destination, which might be weeks, even months ahead. Panic seized him. Whatever happened, he could not stay where he was. He crawled through the hole and let himself down to the deck. Through his fear he registered the reason for the odd sound of the men's boots. The deck was metal. He had heard of steel ships, but never understood how they could float. He ran to the bottom of the ladder and grabbed hold of it and began to haul himself upwards, grateful for the first time for the past months of

Captain Thomas's discipline, which had developed in him the necessary muscles to do it.

Just below the level of the deck, he stopped and hung there, listening. Once he was over the rim he would be in full view. He was bound to be seen. All he could do was throw himself on the mercy of whoever caught him and beg to be allowed to sign on as one of the crew. There seemed to be no sound of voices close by, so he drew a deep breath and pulled himself onto the deck, keeping flat to make himself less obvious. There was no immediate shout to suggest he had been discovered. No rough hands seized him. He lifted his head cautiously. The stevedores were swinging themselves over the rail, heading for the dock; members of the crew were busy, hauling on ropes, carrying packages. It was still barely light. No one seemed to have noticed a small figure, half hidden by the housing of the hatch cover.

Gus looked around. Not far away was the refuge he had imagined when he first planned to stow away – a lifeboat hanging from its davits. He gathered himself and sprinted across the deck, climbed the rails, and clambered into the boat. He lay flat under the thwarts, panting and shaking, expecting the shout that would tell him he had been seen, but none came.

Slowly his breathing returned to normal and the trembling stopped. He heard orders being shouted, familiar from his training, 'Cast off aft! Cast off for'ard.' Then there was a sound like a loud snort and a puff of smoke issued from the funnel, which he could see above him. The whole ship began to shudder and vibrate and he saw the tall masts swing against the lightening sky. They were moving! He had done it! He was going to sea!

When the first sense of triumph had passed he began to consider his next move. It was crucial to remain hidden until the ship was far enough out at sea to make a return out of the question. He must be sure that any accompanying tugs had left and that there were no other vessels heading back into port within hailing distance, to which he could be transferred. That meant lying where he was for several hours, perhaps longer. Probably he should wait until tomorrow. Tied round his waist was a small bundle, wrapped in his only spare shirt. It contained a bottle he had scavenged from the school kitchen and filled with water and a few dried crusts preserved from his last meals. He knew from some of Captain Thomas's stories that it was possible to survive for many days without food as long as you had water, but already his stomach was growling and the thought of going without eating for a day and a night was daunting. He took a swallow of water and rationed himself to one crust.

His thoughts were interrupted by the sound of the bosun's whistle and the cessation of the thumping noise of the engine. Worse followed, with the unmistakable sound of the anchor chain being run out. They were stopping, but why? The thought came to him that perhaps the authorities had ordered that all ships leaving port should be searched in case he was on board; but surely, he told himself, they would not go to such lengths for one runaway boy.

There was a gentle thud as something came into contact with the side of the ship. Curiosity impelled him to raise his head and peer over the gunwale. A tug was tying up alongside and a ladder had been lowered from the deck of the ship.

As Gus watched, several men climbed it and swung themselves over the rail, where they were greeted by a man whom he took to be the captain. Passengers, presumably, but if so why had they not boarded while the ship was in dock? They were all in civilian dress, but there was something about the way they tackled the rope ladder that made him think they were all used to shipboard life. He lay back, pondering. Down in the hold there was at least one crate containing cannons. The ship had been loaded with great secrecy, in semi-darkness, and now there were these strangers who had boarded in that unconventional manner. With a quiver of excitement at the pit of his stomach he concluded that he had chosen to stow away on a vessel bound for some clandestine adventure.

Very soon, to Gus's relief, he heard the anchor being raised and the engine started again. It was not long before the movement of the ship told him that they had reached the open sea. His relief was short-lived. He had heard people talk of seasickness, but had never imagined that he would be affected. The lifeboat, hanging in its davits, swung from side to side, exaggerating the roll of the ship, and above his head the masts described wide arcs against the clouds. He shut his eyes, but that gave little respite. It would pass, he told himself; but now he had another source of discomfort. He desperately needed to piss. To stand up and piss over the side would be to reveal himself, and anyway he was no longer sure he could stand; but he had to do something. Reluctantly, he wriggled to the stern of the boat, undid his breeches and relieved himself. Soon after that he was sick for the first time. After that he lay in a fog of misery that wiped out any possibility of coherent thought. He had been taught to pray in the workhouse, but he had mouthed the words without really thinking what they meant. Now he prayed in earnest, begging God to still the waves, but no answering miracle occurred. Then he prayed for death to bring a quick end to his sufferings, but that prayer was not answered either. He was roused from his stupor once by the sound of feet running across the deck and, opening his eyes, he saw men swarming up the masts and soon the great square sails were unfurled and the engine stopped. The ship heeled over and after that, it seemed to Gus, the rolling was less severe. Hours passed. Darkness came again and he heard the watch being changed, and at last he sank into an exhausted sleep.

Voices and movement on deck woke him and he saw that it was dawn and the watch was being changed again. He was shivering with cold and his whole body ached as if he had had another beating. He was lying in a puddle of his own piss and vomit and he knew that he could not stay hidden any longer. What reception he would get he could not guess, but he no longer cared as long as someone gave him something to drink and some dry clothes. Shakily he hauled himself to his feet and clambered down to the deck, arriving with a bump almost at the feet of a tall, dark-bearded young man in civilian clothes.

'Great God Almighty!' the man said, in an accent that was unfamiliar to Gus. 'Where the devil have you sprung from?'

Gus got to his feet unsteadily and ran his tongue over his cracked lips. 'Up there, in the lifeboat. I was hiding.'

'A stowaway! Well, I'll be damned!'

'Please, sir,' Gus begged, 'don't send me back. I'll do anything. I can work. I know a bit about ships.'

'Send you back? Well, it's far too late for that. But what is to be done with you now is the question. You'd better come with me to the captain.' He paused. 'On second thoughts, we'd better clean you up a bit first. You stink to high heaven.' He turned to a passing sailor. 'Throw a bucket of water over him, that should help.'

A few minutes later, drenched and shivering, Gus found himself on the quarterdeck facing the man he had seen welcoming the newcomers on board the previous day.

'Good God! What have we here?' the captain demanded.

'A stowaway, Captain Ramsay, sir. Seems he was hiding out in one of the lifeboats.'

'A stowaway? How the hell did he get on board?' The captain fixed his eyes on Gus. 'What in God's name made you choose this ship, of all ships?'

Gus replied through chattering teeth. 'I saw you were getting up steam, sir. I needed to find a ship that was leaving soon.'

'Why?'

'I didn't want to be caught, sir.'

'Caught? By whom? Who are you running away from?'

'The masters at the Industrial School.'

'The what?'

'It's a school for boys like me, sir.'

'What do you mean, boys like you? Criminals? Thieves?'

'No, sir. Just boys with no mother or father.'

The captain's glare became slightly less fierce. 'I see. So, why are you running away?'

Gus hung his head. It was too difficult to explain and he was afraid he was going to throw up again at any minute. 'They beat me,' he mumbled.

'Beat you? Well, you probably deserved it. All boys get beaten from time to time.' There was a pause. Gus could only shake his head in silence. The captain grunted. 'What's your name, boy?'

'Gus, sir. Augustus Lavender.'

For the first time he could remember, no one seemed to find that funny.

'Well, you're here now and here you will have to stay for the duration of the voyage. But you'll work your passage, understand?'

'Yes, sir.' Gus looked up. 'Thank you, sir. I'll do whatever you want.'

'You'd better!' The captain turned his eyes to the man with the beard. 'Take him away, Mr Mason. Find him some dry clothes and get some food into him. He looks half starved. Give him to Boney in the galley. He can help out there for the time being.'

'Aye-aye, sir.' Mason saluted and put his hand on Gus's shoulder. 'Come on, Gus.'

He led Gus down to a cabin below the quarterdeck, where a small man with a face as lined as a prune looked up from a list on his table.

'Stokes is our purser. He'll fix you up.' Mason said. 'Open the slop chest, will you, Stokes, and see if you can find anything to fit this lad.'

'Fit him? Not a chance,' the little man responded. He got up and unlocked a large chest and rummaged through it, eventually coming up with a pair of cotton trousers, a shirt, a pair of woollen stockings and a jerkin.

'Right!' said Mason. 'Off with those wet clothes.'

Gus felt shy about stripping in front of strangers. Stokes had gone back to studying his papers but Mason was waiting, holding out the trousers, so there was no help for it. He pulled off his shirt and wriggled out of his breeches and reached for the trousers, but as he stepped into them Mason put a restraining hand on his shoulder and turned him round.

'Hold hard a minute.' Gus heard him draw in breath through his teeth. 'You said you'd been beaten, but this ...' He gave Gus's shoulder a squeeze and released him and he scrambled gratefully into the trousers.

Stokes had done his best, but the trousers were only wearable if he pulled them up to his armpits and the shirt hung down to his knees. Mason began to chuckle and Gus responded with giggles that threatened to turn into sobs. With the aid of a length of rope round his waist he was finally able to walk without tripping himself up. He was still shivering, so Mason took a blanket from the chest and threw it round his shoulders.

The next stop was the galley, where Mason declared cheerfully, 'Here you are, Boney. I've brought you an apprentice. He's an unexpected addition to the ship's complement and the captain says he's to help you until further notice.'

Boney's nickname obviously referred to his figure, which was the exact opposite. He was a thickset man with a large belly and a round face with heavy jowls. He regarded Gus without apparent surprise. 'Poor-looking specimen, isn't he? Turn him sideways in a good light and he'd disappear.'

'You can feed him up,' Mason said. 'A week or two of your cooking and you'll have him as plump as a capon.' He smiled at Gus. 'Boney'll look after you. I must get back to work.'

'When did you last eat?' Boney asked.

'Don't know, sir. Yesterday? No, the night before.'

'No need to "sir" me. Sit yourself down over there.' He gestured to a stool in the corner, then turned to ladle something into a tin bowl. 'Get that down you.'

Gus took the bowl. It was full of soup and he longed to wolf it down, but the smell of it turned his stomach. He pushed it away. 'I can't … sorry … I just …'

'Queasy, eh? It'll pass. Here, drink this.'

He poured something into a cup and added water. Gus sniffed it doubtfully. 'What is it?'

'Grog. That'll settle your stomach.'

Gus was thirsty. He took a long draft and choked. 'It burns!'

'Never had spirits before, eh? Sip it, don't guzzle it.'

Gus sipped and felt a pleasant warmth begin to radiate from the region of his stomach.

Boney handed him a flat biscuit. 'Try that.'

Gus tried to bite it, but it was like biting rock.

'Dip it in the broth. That way it'll soften,' Boney advised.

This worked better and Gus managed to keep it down. He ate most of it, but his head was going round from exhaustion and the effects of the alcohol and he almost fell off the stool. Boney took the blanket from his shoulders and spread it under the bench at which he was working.

'Get your head down there and have a sleep. You'll feel better after.'

Thankfully, Gus crawled under the bench, curled up and fell instantly asleep.

He was woken by Boney prodding him with his foot. 'Shake a leg, there. There's work to be done.'

Gus got to his feet and stretched. He was amazed to see through the galley door that the sun was low and casting long shadows across the deck. The day was almost over. He felt better, as Boney had prophesied. It suddenly occurred to him that he did not feel sick any more.

'What do you want me to do?' he asked.

'Onions over there need peeling and chopping. You can make a start on them. And there's fresh water in that pitcher. Get yourself a drink.'

Boney kept him busy until the evening meal had been served to the crew and, when presented with a plate of beef stew for himself, he wolfed it down without a second thought.

'Make the most of it,' Boney said. 'It's the last fresh meat you'll get till we put into port somewhere. From now on, it's salt pork and biscuits.'

When the dishes had been collected and washed, Boney set him free to get some fresh air and he went out onto the deck. The ship was scudding along under full sail. Darkness had fallen and the sky was clear, revealing more stars than Gus had ever seen through the smoky atmosphere of Liverpool. He leaned on the rail and took a deep breath. This was the life!

'Feeling better?' asked a voice from behind him.

He turned to find Mason watching him from a few feet away. 'Much better, thank you, sir.'

Mason moved over and leaned on the rail beside him. 'Fine night,' he commented.

'I didn't know there were so many stars,' Gus said.

'Guess it makes you marvel at the Lord's creation all over again,' Mason said.

Gus glanced up at him and realised for the first time that, underneath the heavy beard, he was much younger than he had first thought, perhaps no more than his early twenties. It puzzled him to work out what his position on the ship was. The captain had addressed him as 'Mister'. That could mean he was a passenger; but he had responded with a salute and 'aye-aye, sir'. Gus knew from Captain Thomas that a midshipman would also be addressed as 'mister'. Mason could be a midshipman, but in that case why was he wearing civilian dress?

His thoughts were interrupted by a question from Mason. 'Tell me something. How did you manage to get on board? The gates were guarded.'

Gus explained about the hole in the crate and Mason gave an admiring chuckle. 'Well, you sure are a resourceful kid. I'll give you that.' Then he said, in a much more serious tone, 'You have seen something that no one except a few senior officers is supposed to know about. As far as the authorities are concerned we are loaded with coal bound for Bombay. You must give me your word of honour that you will not speak to anyone about what you have seen. Will you do that?'

'Yes!' Gus said breathlessly. 'Yes, I promise.'

'I should tell you,' Mason continued, 'that if the captain knew what you have seen he might think twice about giving you the run of the ship. You don't want to spend the rest of the voyage in irons, do you?'

Gus felt a cold trickle of fear run through his stomach. 'No, I don't. I won't tell anyone. I swear.'

Mason was silent for a moment. Then he said, more gently, 'Tell me about that school you ran away from.'

It was difficult to sum up his experiences in words, but Gus managed to produce a reasonable sketch, laying heavy emphasis on what he had learned from Captain Thomas, and when he finished Mason said, 'It sounds as though you were quite happy there, so why did you run away?'

Hesitantly at first, but then in a flood that almost reduced him to tears again, Gus told him about Will's fear of Frobisher, about their attempted escape and Will's death and his own violent punishment. When he finished Mason did not speak for a moment. Then he said, quietly but vehemently, 'Men like that should be hung, drawn and quartered.'

'Captain Thomas told us he'd seen men flogged near to death when he served in the navy.'

'It's true, that used to happen. But our navy abolished flogging as a punishment more than ten years ago.' Mason looked down at him. 'Was there no one you could turn to, no one who would listen to your complaint?'

Gus shook his head. The idea that such a person might exist had never occurred to him.

'You said you were an orphan. What happened to your parents?'

'My ma died when I was just a nipper. She got ill. I never knew my da. He was a sailor. He went away soon after I was born and never came back. Ma said he was "lost at sea".' He looked up at Mason. 'That doesn't have to mean he's dead, does it? Lost isn't the same as drowned. I'm going to look for him one day. That's why I wanted to go to sea.'

Mason shook his head and sighed, but all he said was, 'Don't you have any family at all? Uncles, aunts …?'

'I've got a sister, May. We were in the workhouse together, but she had to go into service. I haven't seen her since.'

'That seems … cruel.'

Mason fell silent so Gus was emboldened to ask a question of his own. 'Beg pardon, sir, but your way of speaking's different from the folk round where I live.'

Mason smiled. 'That's because I'm from Texas.'

'Texas? Is that in America?'

'Sure is.'

'Is that where we're really going?'

'The only man on this ship who knows for certain where we're headed is the captain. But even if I knew, I couldn't tell you.'

'It's just, my da used to sail for the Americas. He might still be there. Maybe he can't get back because of the war.' Gus reached back in his memory for a conversation with Captain Thomas. 'Is Texas in the south or the north?'

'Texas is one of the southern Confederate states, and as far as I'm concerned, it's God's Own Country.'

Gus frowned. 'You still think it's right to keep slaves.' He remembered Will's shocked look as he said, 'But that's wrong, surely?'

Mason did not seem to be disturbed. 'Seems to us it's the natural way of things.' He yawned suddenly. 'I'm going to hit the hay. You'd better get your head down, too. Have you been given a berth?'

'Beg pardon?'

'Have you got a place to sleep?'

'Oh, no. Only in the galley.'

'Get down between decks. That's where the crew sleep. Someone will find you a hammock.' He turned away. 'Goodnight, Gus.'

'Goodnight, sir.'

Having slept most of the day, Gus did not feel ready for bed. Besides, he had a great deal to think about. He was on a ship loaded with guns and ammunition, under conditions of great secrecy, and carrying officers from the southern states of America, who hid their identity under civilian clothes. He recalled what Captain Thomas had said about ships being secretly built in the Liverpool docks. It seemed beyond doubt that this was one of them, a blockade runner. The notion filled him with a mixture of excitement and fear – and it left him with a dilemma. Surely, right was on the side of the northerners, who wanted to free the slaves. Then he remembered something else. The reason for running the blockade was to bring back the cotton that kept men and women in his own country employed. He eased his conscience with the thought that if the great men of his city allowed the building of ships for this purpose then it must be all right.

Sleep was beginning to catch up with him and with it came a thought that put the argument to rest. Captain Ramsay had said, 'You're here now, and here you will have to stay.' There was nothing he could do about that, and at least he was safe from Frobisher – and the people he had fallen in with were being kind to him – so far, at least.

To Gus's surprise and relief, that state of affairs persisted. The ordinary seamen, whose living quarters he shared, were sympathetic to the story of his upbringing and adopted him as a kind of mascot. They taught him the basics of life on board, showed him how to climb into a hammock without falling out, warned him if he was about to infringe any rules and included him in their games. He was even given a proper job.

Captain Ramsay sent for him.

'It's come to my attention that we do not have a cabin boy on board. You can take on those duties.'

Those duties included helping the cook, but also meant serving the captain in his stateroom and the senior officers in the wardroom at meal times, and looking after their cabins. He soon had confirmation of his guess that the men who seemed to be passengers were in fact officers, but not regular members of the crew. There were a dozen of them, and they were all Americans. There was a tall, broad-shouldered, moustachioed man who was referred to as Captain Waddell, though why the ship was carrying two captains was a mystery. There were Lieutenants Grimball and Bulloch, and a surgeon, Dr Lining. And, like Midshipman Mason, none of them were in uniform.

In between his duties he explored the ship and tried to learn as much as he could about its management. Mason continued to take a friendly interest in him. He seemed to feel a kind of proprietorial pride in 'his' stowaway. Finding that Gus was intelligent and eager to learn he was prepared to answer his many questions.

'She's called the *Laurel*, and she's what is known as an auxiliary steamer. That means that sail is her principal means of propulsion but she has steam engines to give her extra flexibility. They are very handy in tricky manoeuvres, like getting into and out of port, or when the wind falls too light – or to give us an extra turn of speed when necessary.'

Most of the senior officers had little time for his questions, but Mason was always patient. Finding that Gus could read, he offered to lend him a book. It was called *The Cruise of the Alabama* and had been published just before they sailed. A lot of the words were difficult and Gus skipped quite a few pages, but the story was exciting enough to make him persist. The *Alabama*, a Confederate ship, was what was known as a commerce raider, her purpose to capture or destroy merchant ships belonging to the Union, in order to disrupt trade and deny the enemy essential supplies.

In the course of a voyage lasting two years she had captured or burnt sixty-five ships and taken 2,000 prisoners, without any loss of life on either side. She was eventually sunk after a thrilling sea battle off the port of Cherbourg by a Union ship called the *Kearsage*. It was, in effect, a story of piracy on the high seas, and Gus could not dismiss the feeling that it must be illegal, but it was clear that Mason admired the ship's exploits, and if he thought it was all right, that was good enough for Gus. Besides, it was a story with enough adventure and daring to set any boy's pulse racing.

Gus had been on board the *Laurel* for six days, and was beginning to feel quite at home, when the lookout gave the cry, 'Land Ho!' All the crew who were not engaged in other duties crowded to the rails, searching the horizon and pointing ahead. Gus followed the direction of their gaze and eventually made out a small, grey hump that might easily have been a cloud. As the ship drew nearer, the hump solidified into a mountain and the grey became green and Gus found himself looking at a landscape of terraced hillsides rising to a sharp peak, with a settlement of white buildings fringing a bay at its foot. The *Laurel* glided into the harbour and dropped anchor and Gus gazed in fascination. He had never seen anywhere so green and lush and there were trees he could not name and flowers that belonged in storybooks. The sight awoke a long buried memory, of pictures from the Bible he had been shown by a teacher in the workhouse.

'Where are we?' he asked the man next to him.

'Madeira,' came the response. 'That's Funchal town.'

'I think it should be called Paradise,' Gus said.

The man laughed. 'Aye, well, I guess that's near enough.'

'Why have we stopped here?' Gus asked.

'Coaling,' was the reply. 'That's the thing with a steamer. You've got to take of coal whenever you can.'

'But ...' Gus stopped himself. He had been about to ask why they had to take on coal, when they were supposed to have a hold full of it.

Most of the crew had called at the island on earlier voyages and there was excited chatter about the delights of the taverns to be found ashore and the beauty of the girls who served in them. The mood rapidly soured when it was learned that there was to be no shore leave. Gus shared in the general disappointment. He longed to set foot on this strange and exotic land.

For two days the coal barges shuttled to and fro and their cargoes were hauled aboard, though in a leisurely manner that Gus found surprising. Usually the officers kept the men working hard at any task, but now they seemed happy to let them take it easy. By the end of the second day all the coal had been loaded, but still Captain Ramsay appeared in no hurry to resume the voyage. Gus heard mutterings among the crew.

'What we doing, hanging about here? If we can't go ashore we might as well be on our way.'

Serving in the wardroom, Gus had the impression that the officers were uneasy, too.

'If we're here much longer the port authorities are going to smell a rat. We're fully coaled, so they're going to wonder what we're waiting for.'

It was remarked also that ever since they anchored, the captain had kept a lookout posted in the crow's nest, with instructions to watch out for another vessel.

'She'll be a sloop, ship-rigged,' he heard the next man to take the watch instructed.

'What does "ship-rigged" mean?' he enquired of Midshipman Mason as soon as he had an opportunity.

Mason laughed. 'Don't you ever get tired of asking questions? Ship-rigged means having three masts, all carrying square sails, as opposed to a bark, which has two main masts with square sails and a third mast with triangular sails set fore and aft. Why do you want to know?'

'Oh, just something I heard the captain say.'

On the third day in port some official-looking men came out to the ship in a skiff and were ushered into the captain's cabin. Sometime later they reappeared, one of them carrying a heavy object wrapped in sailcloth.

'I'll have this repaired for you as soon as possible, captain,' the man in charge said. 'Don't worry. You'll have your engines ready to get up steam in a couple of days.'

Funny, thought Gus, there didn't seem to be anything wrong with the engines when we came into port.

Two more days dragged by, and then on the evening of the second the lookout in the crow's nest called down, 'Vessel fine on the port bow!'

All the officers gathered on the quarterdeck, with telescopes to their eyes. Gus, taking advantage of the fact that dinner time was approaching and the table had to be set in the wardroom, sidled closer.

'Looks like her,' Captain Ramsay said. 'About time, too.'

'What's she up to?' someone asked. 'Why doesn't she close with us?'

'Not sure who we are, perhaps? It's nearly dark. Perhaps she's waiting for morning.'

When morning came it brought a sudden bustle of activity. The new ship had been sighted again and signals were exchanged, though knowing nothing of the meaning of the flags that were hoisted, Gus had no idea what was happening, and no one had time to explain. A boat was sent ashore and its return awaited with impatience. Meanwhile, the engineer was ordered to get up steam. When the boat returned, carrying papers of some sort, the anchor was weighed and the *Laurel* left the harbour. But they did not head for the open sea.

Followed by the strange ship, they set a course that took them along the shores of some smaller, apparently deserted, islands, until they entered a sheltered cove and dropped anchor again. The other ship followed them in and dropped anchor close by, and, for the first time, Gus had a chance to see her properly. Long and slender, it was obvious even to his untrained eye that she was built for speed. Her hull was painted black and on her stern was the name *Sea King*.

Her appearance was a cause for considerable excitement among the officers.

'What a beauty!' Mason exclaimed. 'She's the finest ship I've ever seen.'

A boat was lowered, and those officers who were still masquerading as passengers in civilian dress were rowed over to the other ship and went aboard. To Gus's distress, they all carried their ship bags, which contained what he had learned to call their dunnage: their personal possessions. That meant they were not coming back, and the thought that Mason, his friend and mentor, had departed without so much as a goodbye was painful.

On the *Laurel*, there was some consternation among the ordinary sailors. This was an unexpected, and largely unwelcome, diversion from what they took to be the purpose of the voyage. They were given little time, however, to discuss this new development as orders were issued for the contents of the *Laurel*'s holds to be transferred to the *Sea King*. The crew of that vessel joined in the work, but even with their combined numbers it was hard going. Further anger was generated by what seemed unnecessary haste. After hanging about off Funchal for days, it now seemed that everything must be done at top speed. Tackles were rigged on the masts and by means of ropes and pulleys the crates and boxes from the hold were raised and swung overboard and lowered onto the deck of the *Sea King*.

Gus, scurrying backwards and forwards with smaller packages, saw that they were being deposited faster than they could be stowed, so that before long the *Sea King*'s deck was cluttered with unidentified boxes. He saw, too, to his surprise, that the officers who had transferred to the new ship had taken off their jackets, rolled up their sleeves and were labouring alongside the crew.

They worked until dark and were up again at dawn, and finally by mid-afternoon the work was completed. Looking at the chaos on the *Sea King*'s deck, Gus had to revise his guess about the purpose of the *Laurel* and the armaments she carried. Was this new ship to be fitted out as a blockade runner instead? And why was the transfer of the cargo so urgent?

For the rest of the day the feeling of discontent amongst the crew grew.

Next morning, unexpectedly, they were all summoned aboard the *Sea King* and told to assemble on the deck, together with her crew. There was a short wait, while the men fidgeted and muttered, and then Captain Waddell led the other officers onto the quarterdeck above them. Now their true identity was plain for all to see, for they were all dressed in the grey uniform of the Confederate navy, complete with badges of rank. There was a general murmur of surprise, but the mood was far from friendly.

Waddell stepped forward. 'Men, I have assembled you all here to give you some important news. As from today, this ship is the property of the Confederate States of America. I have here the papers which confirm the sale and as soon as Captain Corbett, who brought her out, gets back to Liverpool aboard the *Laurel*, that change of ownership will be duly registered. She will be renamed the CSS *Shenandoah* and her role is to be a commerce raider. You may have heard of the CSS *Alabama*, which did such valiant work before she was sunk last year. The *Shenandoah* is to be her replacement.'

The announcement was greeted with a hostile silence. Gus saw glances exchanged amongst the crew.

Waddell continued. 'I am offering all of you the chance to share in this great adventure. You will be fighting on behalf of a brave and oppressed people in defiance of those arrogant dictators in the north. Moreover, as a commerce raider we shall be taking prizes, and the value of these prizes will be shared out amongst you all, according to rank. You will have the chance to go home rich men. Now, who will be the first to sign up to ship with me?'

Instead of the enthusiastic response that he was obviously expecting, there was a growl of discontent and one or two voices were raised above the general muttering.

'This isn't what we signed up for!'

'I shipped for a voyage to Bombay, not a raider.'

'We've been had!'

More voices joined in and the mood grew increasingly angry.

Waddell raised his voice above the din. 'I am offering a monthly wage of four pounds. That's more than you'll get on any other ship. And on top of that I'll give a bounty of ten pounds to anyone who signs up today.'

There were still no takers. Gus looked at the officers lined up behind Waddell and saw them exchanging worried glances. He felt angry on their behalf and disappointed at what seemed to him the cowardice of the men who refused to sign, but he knew it would be worse than useless to speak up.

'Very well,' Waddell said, 'I'll raise my offer. Seven pounds a month and a fifteen-pound bounty for any sailor willing to ship for a six-month enlistment. Take it or leave it.'

At that a few men went, rather sheepishly, up onto the quarterdeck and signed the articles of enlistment, but the majority remained stubbornly opposed. Then there was a new development. Two of the officers began to circulate amongst them with pitchers full of grog, which was eagerly accepted, and the mood soon became less irritable. Another officer appeared on the quarterdeck, carrying a bucket.

'Look at this, men,' Waddell called out. 'A share in this can be yours if you sign on.'

He dipped his hand in the bucket and pulled out a handful of something that glittered gold in the sunlight.

'Gold sovereigns!' a man near Gus exclaimed. 'My God, I never saw that much money in one place.'

Slowly more men gave way and signed up, but only a proportion of both crews, and it was clear that Waddell would have liked more; but in the end he gave up trying to persuade the recalcitrants and the crew of the *Laurel* were ordered to return to their ship. Gus lingered, looking up at the officers gathered on the quarterdeck. He had been thrilled by the story of the *Alabama* and now it was going to be repeated in real life, and he was not going to be part of it. He longed to sign up, but he was not a seaman. He was just a stowaway and he was afraid of being laughed at if he offered himself. He turned away, ready to scramble back onto the deck of the *Laurel*.

A voice stopped him. 'Gus, come over here.' Mason was beckoning him.

He went over and the midshipman laid a hand on his shoulder. 'Well, Gus, what is it going to be? Go back to Liverpool on the *Laurel*, or ship with us aboard the *Shenandoah*?'

Gus looked up at him, radiantly. There was no hesitation. 'The *Shenandoah*!'

Seven

'Letter for Miss May.'

The butcher's boy stood in the kitchen, holding out a folded scrap of paper. Mrs Wilkins snatched it from him.

'What's this? A love note? What's going on between you two?'

'Nothing!' the boy protested, turning scarlet. 'A bloke outside asked me to hand it in.'

'What "bloke"?' the cook demanded.

'Cheeky little blighter, driving a trap. I dunno who he was.'

Mrs Wilkins turned on May. 'So I was right! You do have a follower. Who is he?'

'I don't know, Cook,' May said. 'I've no idea who it might be. I haven't got a follower. Please, can I see the letter? It might be from my brother.'

For a moment she thought Mrs Wilkins was going to open the note herself, but after a brief hesitation she handed it to May. 'Well?'

May unfolded the paper. 'Oh, it's from Patty! We were friends in the workhouse. She went into service at Speke Hall.'

'Speke Hall?' Mrs Wilkins was impressed. 'She's done well for herself, then. What does she want?'

'She's asking if we can meet. She's got some time off on Sunday afternoon.' She appealed to Mrs Wilkins. 'Can I? I'd really like to see her.'

She saw the cook struggling with contrary impulses. She did not want to favour May but Patty's connection with the aristocracy, however tenuous, made her unsure about denying the request. In the end she said, 'Well, if you want to take your afternoon off on Sunday instead of the usual day, I suppose I can make an exception.'

May turned to the butcher's boy. 'Is he waiting for a reply?'

'Said he's got errands to do in town and he'll come by later for the answer.'

May scribbled a note, agreeing to meet Patty outside St Barnabas's Church in Parliament Street the following Sunday afternoon. Sometime later there was a knock at the back door, but when May moved to answer it Mrs Wilkins took the note from her.

'Oh no you don't, miss. I'll see to this.'

May heard her say, 'Here, you can take this, and make sure you deliver it. And I don't expect to see you round here again. Understand?'

The following Sunday May put on her new bonnet and cape, bought with the wages Mr Freeman had given her, and set off for the church. It was November, the sky was grey and the familiar icy wind was scything up the Mersey estuary. She found Patty huddled up in the church porch, with her old shawl pulled tight around her throat. Her friend jumped up as soon as she appeared and flung her arms round her.

'Oh, May, am I glad to see you! I've been pining for the sight of a friendly face.'

May looked at her, horrified by her pallor and the thinness of her shoulders under the shawl. 'Patty, what's the matter? Are you ill?'

Patty shrugged. 'Not ill, as such. Just hungry and cold and fed up. But look at you! Don't you look smart! How did you come by that bonnet and that cape?'

'Bought them, out of my wages.'

'You get wages?'

'Don't you?'

'I'm supposed to, but I ain't seen none yet.'

'I didn't either, for a long time. But then Mr Freeman found out and he told madam that I'd got to be paid – and he gave me the back pay I was owed.'

'Lucky you!'

'I thought you would be doing all right, working in a fine house like that.'

'Fine it may be, for them as owns it. And for the top servants, maybe. They do all right. But not for the likes of me.' Tears came to her eyes. 'I'm the lowest of the low, May, at everyone's beck and call. It's Patty do this and Patty come here, from first light till bedtime, and if I make a mistake or drop something I'm punished.'

'Punished how?'

'Oh, sometimes it's "That'll come out of your wages", which is why I've never seen any, I suppose. Or being sent to bed without any supper, or given extra work to do. It depends who's saying it. Isn't it like that where you are?'

'Well, Mrs Wilkins, the cook, is a bit of a dragon and she's got Mrs Freeman wound round her little finger. But Mr Freeman's all right. He stands up for me. What are the people you work for like?'

'You mean the grand ladies and gentlemen? They don't know I exist. If I happen to meet any of them I have to turn my face to the wall, so they can pretend they don't see me. It's the others are worse. They treat me like dirt. The other girls, who've been there longer, look down on me and give me all the worst jobs, and the footmen play tricks on me.'

'What about that boy who picked you up in the trap? Was it him who delivered your letter? I never got to see who it was.'

'He's the worst of the lot, always trying to put his arms round me and touch me. I had to let him kiss me to get him to bring the letter, and now he says I owe him something more.'

May sighed. 'Oh, Patty, I'm so sorry! I thought you were the lucky one. Mrs Kelly warned me what it might be like, but I didn't really believe her. I wish I could do something to help.'

'Don't suppose there's a job for me where you work, is there?'

'I'm afraid not. Mrs Freeman's very keen on saving money. She doesn't like having to pay my wages, so there's no chance she'd take on someone else – least ways, not as things are now.'

'What do you mean?'

'Well, I did hear Mr Freeman telling Madam that the business was doing well and they might want to take on extra staff, but I think he meant in the shop.'

Patty's eyes took on a dreamy expression. 'Wouldn't it be wonderful to work in a shop? Regular hours to start, and finish, and in the warm all the time.'

May thought of her visits to Freeman's Ladies Fashions. 'Yes, it would be nice.'

'If you ever hear of your Mr Freeman looking for someone, you'll mention my name, won't you?'

'Yes, of course,' May agreed, but inwardly she could not help thinking that Patty was not the sort of girl he would want in his shop. Her hair was lank and dirty, her hands were red and she constantly wiped her nose on her sleeve. The thought made her feel disloyal and she wanted to do something to help. She felt in the little purse she kept in the pocket of her skirt. There was just enough.

'Come on. Fancy a cup of hot chocolate?'

'What? Where?'

'I know a little caff that does smashing hot chocolate. Come on.'

May had spent her afternoons off exploring the city and she had discovered the place down near the docks. It was not as posh as the one Mrs Kelly had taken her to, but that was good. It meant she did not feel intimidated about going in there. She led Patty down Parliament Street and through some narrow alleys until they came to it.

'Can we go in there?' Patty asked doubtfully.

'Yes, it's all right. Come on.'

'I ain't got no money.'

'I know that. I'll pay.'

They sat at a table in a warm corner near the fire and May ordered hot chocolate. When it came Patty sipped it cautiously. Then a smile of pure ecstasy spread across her face.

'Oh, that's lovely! That's the best thing I ever tasted.'

'Yes, it is, isn't it?' May agreed.

'Hey, May,' Patty said. 'I meant to ask you. What's happened to that brother of yours?'

May sighed. 'I don't know. He went to that Industrial School, but when I went up there a few weeks ago they told me he'd – what was the word? – absconded, that was it. Run away. I've no idea where he might be, but I think he may have tried to get on a ship. You know he was always dead keen to be a sailor.'

'Lord!' said Patty. 'Who'd have thought it. Have you tried to find out?'

'I went down to the docks a couple of times and asked round, but no one knew anything. I didn't like doing it. Some of the men thought I was ... well, you know.'

'I can guess.' Patty reached out and squeezed her hand. 'Don't worry. He's a tough lad. He'll be all right.'

'I hope so,' May said sadly. 'But I do worry.'

The clock above the shop counter chimed the three-quarter and Patty put down her cup with a clatter. 'Oh, my God! He's supposed to pick me up at the church at four o'clock. There'll be hell to pay if I'm not there!'

'Drink up,' May instructed. She swallowed the remains of her chocolate, paid, and they hurried out of the shop and up the hill. They reached the church as the hour struck and saw the trap waiting.

''Bout time!' said the boy holding the reins. 'I was just going to leave you to find your own way back.'

'You remember Bill, don't you?' Patty said.

'Yes, I do.' May looked at the boy. He had seemed such a nice lad when he picked Patty up from the workhouse, that first time. She wanted to say something, to tell him to leave Patty alone, but she knew that if she did he would probably take it out on Patty for telling her what he had done. So she just said, 'Bye, Patty. We'll keep in touch. You'll look after her, Bill, won't you? I reckon you're a good fellow, a real gent. I know you can be trusted.'

'Oh, aye, you can trust me, all right,' the boy said, but May noticed that he blushed.

She gave Patty a hug and she climbed into the trap, Bill whipped up the horse and they rattled away. May watched them for a few moments, then turned away. She remembered what Mrs Kelly had told her about working in a great house. It seemed that she was the lucky one, after all.

Christmas was approaching, and May found herself working harder than ever as Mrs Wilkins began preparing for the festivities. She stirred puddings and heated up the water in the copper to steam them, and chopped fruit for mincemeat. She had never tasted either delicacy and the smell of the puddings as she stirred made her mouth water; but there were compensations for the extra work – a raisin secretly popped into her own mouth instead of the pudding basin, or her fingers run round the empty bowl and licked.

At the beginning of December there was a disturbance in the household. Miss Parsons announced that she needed two weeks leave of absence to help her married sister, who had just had a baby. Sweeping the stairs outside the schoolroom, May heard her giving her instructions to Isabella.

'Your other lessons will continue as normal, except for the riding as there will be no one to take you to the stables. Mrs Fortescue, Silvia's mama, will take you to dancing class with Silvia. I shall leave you tasks to perform while I am away. I shall expect them to be completed by the time I return.'

May felt that a shadow had been lifted from the house by the governess's departure and suspected that Isabella felt the same. She was increasingly sorry for the other girl. She seemed to have no friends of her own age, and very little leisure. From time to time other girls were invited for tea, but the event was always supervised by Miss Parsons and there was no chance for any of them to exchange private confidences. May thought back to her own childhood in the workhouse. It had been hard, but there had always been other girls she could gossip and giggle with. She had never heard Isabella giggle.

One morning, cleaning up the schoolroom while Isabella was downstairs having her piano lesson, May found several sheets of paper screwed up and thrown in the fireplace. She smoothed them out, thinking that she might be able to reuse them for her own drawings, and saw that they were designs for a sampler. The text, 'Honour thy father and thy mother', was written out in various different scripts and various ideas had been tried out to embellish it, but none were very successful. May guessed that this was one of the tasks set by Miss Parsons, but clearly Isabella was not making much progress with it.

Friday was the day for Isabella's art lesson and after Mr Latimer had departed May went in to tidy the room. She found Isabella hunched over her desk, sobbing.

'Why, Miss Isabella, whatever's the matter?' she asked, putting a hand on her shaking shoulders.

Isabella looked up, her face wet with tears. 'I've got to make a sampler for Mama's Christmas present, but I'm no good at this sort of thing. Mr Latimer says a child of two could produce a better design.'

'That's very unkind of him,' May said. 'Not everyone can be a talented artist.'

'But you are, May,' the girl said. 'I saw the pictures you drew for Mama's gown. Could you help me? Please! I've only got another week before Miss Parsons comes back and she'll be so cross if I haven't done it.'

May sighed. 'I'd like to, miss, but I don't have the time. I'm busy every hour of the day for Mrs Wilkins.'

'Oh, please!' Isabella begged. 'It wouldn't take you long.' She caught a breath. 'I know! You come up here every morning to clean, don't you?'

'Before you're out of bed,' May agreed.

'But I could be! I could get up early and you could help me then.'

'And who is going to sweep the floor?'

'Oh, never mind that! No one comes up here except me and Miss Parsons, except on Fridays. I have my piano lessons and singing lessons downstairs. No one will notice if the floor's not swept. Please, May!'

May hesitated. The idea was tempting. She would much rather sketch out designs than sweep floors and Isabella's tears had touched her heart.

'All right. Tomorrow morning, if you're up and ready when I come to clean, I'll help you. But I warn you, I get up very early.'

'I'll be up! I promise you.' Isabella reached up and pulled May down to kiss her cheek. 'Thank you, May. Thank you so much.'

Next morning she was as good as her word and was waiting for May in the schoolroom when she arrived, with a clean sheet of paper and pencils at the ready. May sat down beside her.

'Now, this is supposed to be your idea. So what do you want to do?'

For the next half-hour they were both absorbed in the task of creating a suitable design. Then May heard a clock chime in the hallway below.

'I must go! I'll never get through my work if I stay any longer.'

'Will you come and help me again tomorrow?'

'Yes, all right. But you must promise never to tell anyone what we've been doing. I'll catch it if Mrs Wilkins finds out.'

'I promise.'

For the rest of the week May spent every morning working with Isabella. Very quickly they forgot the division between servant and mistress's daughter and began to treat each other as friends. For the first time, she heard Isabella laugh.

On Friday she insisted that she must clean the room instead. 'If Mr Latimer notices the dust and mentions it to your mama our secret will be out.'

Next day, Isabella greeted her with glowing eyes. 'Mr Latimer loves the design. He said I'd surprised him. He didn't know I had it in me.'

It was on the tip of May's tongue to point out that it was not Isabella's work the art teacher was praising, but the younger girl was so delighted to have been praised for once in her life that she did not have the heart to spoil her pleasure.

The next step was to execute the design in cross stitch, but here, too, Isabella's abilities fell short. She was clumsy and impatient and May spent a good deal of time unpicking her mistakes. On the day before Miss Parsons was due back, the sampler was still not finished and Isabella was distraught.

'She's going to be so cross! And I have tried, haven't I, May?'

May had to concede that she had, but that did not ease Isabella's fears. 'Give it to me,' she said eventually. 'I'll finish it off for you.'

'Oh, would you, May? But when will you find the time?'

'I don't know. I'll manage it somehow. I'll make sure you've got it before Miss Parsons gets back.'

It meant sitting up late into the night, sewing by the light of a candle, but the work was finished as May had promised and next morning she handed it over when she went to clean the schoolroom.

'It's beautiful!' Isabella said. 'You are clever, May. Miss P. will be so pleased.'

'She'd better be,' May said grimly. 'Now mind out of the way. I've got to get this room spick and span before she arrives.'

Later she slipped upstairs, knowing that the governess would be resting after her lunch.

'What did Miss Parsons say?'

Isabella giggled. 'I didn't show it to her. I suddenly thought, it's Mama's Christmas present. So I wrapped it up and told Miss P. I want it to be a surprise. She thinks I've done it because it's a mess. I can't wait to see her face when Mama unwraps it!'

May had her doubts about the wisdom of that course of action, but there was no point in saying so.

Christmas that year fell on a Sunday and the previous Wednesday was May's afternoon off. She had heard that St

George's Hall had been lavishly decorated for the season and was eager to see it. She was not disappointed. A huge fir tree, decorated with ribbons and paper chains, stood on the pediment outside, while inside the hall the walls were hung with swags of holly and ivy. But still nothing, in her estimation, could match the glory of the tiled floor. The image of it had stayed in her mind ever since Mrs Kelly had taken her there the first time and she had been back several times since. This time she had a purpose other than to admire it. Her efforts with Isabella had reawakened her interest in design and on the way she used some of her wages to buy a sketch pad and a pencil. She spent over an hour copying the patterns and images and then creating her own designs around them.

When she left the hall it was getting dark, and hurrying down the steps she almost bumped into a gentleman who was standing gazing up at the tree.

'May?' he said. 'What brings you here?'

May looked up into his face. 'Oh, Mr Freeman, sir, I didn't see you. I'm ever so sorry.'

'No need to apologise. I just wasn't expecting to see you. Have you been admiring the decorations?'

'Yes, sir. Aren't they beautiful?'

'Very impressive. I've been thinking I should do something similar, on a smaller scale, in the shop windows.' He glanced down. 'Is that a sketch pad you're carrying?'

May felt herself flush. 'Yes, sir. I've been drawing some of the designs on the floor of the hall. I think it's so wonderful!'

'I agree. Can I see your drawings?'

May held up the book and Mr Freeman opened a page and turned it to catch the light from a gas lamp. Then he shook his head. 'It's no good. I can't see in this light. I tell you what. Let's go and have a cup of tea in the Adelphi and then I can look at it properly.'

'Oh, sir! The Adelphi? I can't go in there!'

'Why not? It's not an exclusive club.'

'But with you, sir? It wouldn't be fitting. And I'm not dressed for it.'

Freeman looked at her. 'Well, you look perfectly respectable to me. That bonnet really suits you. But if you feel shy about the Adelphi, we can go to a more modest establishment. Come along.'

He took her arm and she had no option but to go with him. He took her to the same tea shop that Mrs Kelly had taken her to all those months ago, and when she said, 'Oh, I've been here before,' he wanted to hear how it had come about. When they were seated, and the waitress had taken his order for tea and cakes, he took the sketchbook from her and began to study the pages.

'You know, May, you have a real talent for this sort of thing. We must find some way of nurturing it.' He snapped his fingers. 'Tell you what! Why don't you come up with some ideas about how I might decorate the shop windows? I know there isn't much time, but if you could sketch something out tonight, I could get it put into practice tomorrow.'

'Tonight?' May said doubtfully.

'Oh, of course. I suppose you have to go back and help Mrs Wilkins with dinner. What do you do afterwards?'

'Well, sir, there are usually jobs to be done, boots to be cleaned, ironing, that sort of thing.'

'Tell Mrs Wilkins that I've given you a different job this evening. I'm sure she'll understand.'

I'm not! May thought. The prospect was daunting, but at the same time, she was excited about the new challenge.

As they left the tea shop, Freeman paused to greet a lady whom May recognised as one of Mrs Freeman's regular visitors. There was something about the expression on her face as she responded to his cheery 'Good evening' that May did not like.

Mrs Wilkins's reaction to May's announcement that she had work to do for Mr Freeman was predictable, but perhaps a little less violent than May expected. As she sat at the kitchen table sketching, she was aware that the cook was watching her with narrowed eyes. It was an uncomfortable feeling. She soon put it out of her mind, however, as she concentrated on the challenge of designing a suitably festive window display.

She handed the designs to her master at breakfast next morning. As usual Mrs Freeman was taking her breakfast in bed, so he was alone.

'Oh yes!' he said. 'I like it. That's very clever. We use the mannequins to create a picture of a family at Christmas, but in each window it is a different family and the room is decorated differently. It looks festive, and at the same time gives us a chance to display a range of the goods we have to offer. Well done, May!'

He delved into his pocket. 'Here, take this. A little Christmas box. You deserve it.'

May found herself holding a golden guinea. She put it in her apron pocket, and as soon as she got back to the kitchen she stowed it away in her box, under her bed. Next day, going to the box for a clean apron, she had the impression that her things had been moved. Anxiously, she hunted for the guinea. It was still there, but she was convinced her box had been searched; and there was only one person who could have done that.

For the next three days May was too busy to think much about what had happened, but she was aware that Mrs Wilkins was closeted longer than usual with the mistress next morning; and she was surprised when the lady they had met on the omnibus arrived at the front door, although it was not one of Mrs Freeman's 'at home' days.

Christmas morning was no different from any other, as far as May was concerned. There was still all the routine cleaning to be done, the fires to be stoked, tea to be taken up to the bedrooms, breakfast to prepare. The only unusual thing was that Mr Freeman did not go into the shop, so he spent longer over breakfast, and Mrs Freeman got up to have it with him. The whole family went to matins at eleven o'clock and, as they were expected to do every Sunday, May and Mrs Wilkins went with them. Then they had to hurry back to make sure that the goose, which Mrs Wilkins had put in the oven before they went out, was not burning. Dinner was served at three o'clock and for once Isabella and Miss Parsons, who usually took their meals in the schoolroom, joined the family.

May was amazed at the amount of food that was set on the table for just four people. Apart from the goose there was a joint of beef and a game pie and mounds of potato in different forms. After that there would be the pudding, and mince pies, and then the desert of nuts and dates and fresh fruit. When she remembered what a treat a few slices of beef and some suet pudding had been for her old companions in the workhouse, it made her feel that there was something very wrong with the world; but there was one consoling thought. Mrs Wilkins could not possibly eat up all the leftovers. There was a good chance she would get to taste goose and Christmas pudding.

When the time came for the pudding to be served there was another surprise. Mrs Wilkins poured brandy over it and then, to May's alarm, set light to it.

'Won't it burn the pudding?' she asked.

'Rubbish!' was the answer. 'Now bring that white sauce and the brandy butter. Quick sharp or the brandy will burn off before we get to the dining room.'

The arrival of the pudding was greeted with applause. Mr Freeman served it and Isabella gave a squeal of delight.

'I've got the silver sixpence! That means fortune, doesn't it, Papa?'

Her father smiled. 'So they say. But they don't say you don't have to work for it.'

Isabella put down her spoon. 'When can we open our presents, Papa?'

Miss Parsons frowned at her. 'Hush, child. You must be patient.'

'Don't chide her, Miss Parsons,' Mr Freeman said. 'Any child is allowed to be a little excited at Christmas. We'll open them soon, Isabella. When we are having our desert.'

Heading back to the kitchen, May felt pleased that today, at least, Isabella was permitted to have some fun.

She was right. There was a lot of food left over and she was given a wing from the goose and allowed to scrape out the dish containing the remains of the game pie. She even got a slice of Christmas pudding. She went to bed that night feeling that life with the Freeman family was not that bad after all.

She should have known that such contentment could not last. Going upstairs to collect the breakfast dishes next morning, she was horrified when Isabella rushed out of the morning room in floods of tears and almost bumped into her.

'Isabella, what's wrong?' May asked.

'Mama knows I didn't do the sampler! Miss Parsons took one look at it and said, "You didn't make this. Who did?" I had to tell her, May. And now I'm not allowed to have any of my own presents, and I've been sent to my room.'

'Oh, dear, I'm so sorry,' May began, but Isabella broke away and ran upstairs, still sobbing. May stood where she was. What reception awaited her in the morning room she could only guess. She would have liked to run away herself, but she knew that if she failed to carry out her duties it would only make things worse.

She was doubly disconcerted to find that Mr Freeman had left for the store. Mrs Freeman and Miss Parsons were there and greeted her appearance with stony faces.

Miss Parsons rose to her feet. 'I'll leave you to deal with this, madam. As you will recall, I was not present when this … deception was conceived.'

'Thank you, Miss Parsons,' Mrs Freeman responded. 'Would you mind asking Mrs Wilkins to step up here?'

'Of course.'

May's heart sank. Mrs Wilkins had been closeted with her employer even longer than usual that morning and had returned with a nasty, smug expression on her face. If she was going to be involved she had even less chance of talking herself out of trouble than before.

Mrs Freeman held up the sampler. 'This is your work, is it not? Don't try to deny it. Isabella has already confessed.'

'I did some of it,' May agreed. 'Isabella was finding it hard and she was upset. She really wanted to make something beautiful for you for Christmas.'

Well, that wasn't quite accurate, she thought, but in a case like this surely a little white lie was allowable.

'The design is almost entirely your work, is it not?'

'No, ma'am. We did it together.'

'Don't try to fool me. Isabella is incapable of anything as … as complicated as this.'

There was a knock and Mrs Wilkins bustled into the room. 'You sent for me, madam?'

May reckoned she must have been waiting outside the door, to be on hand so quickly.

'Yes, Mrs Wilkins. Were you aware that May was doing the work Miss Parsons had set for Isabella?'

'I was not, madam, or I should have put a stop to it.'

'When did you and Isabella concoct this … this piece of work?'

'I helped her first thing in the mornings, ma'am. She got up early especially.'

'You mean, at the time when you should have been cleaning the schoolroom?' Mrs Wilkins said.

'I did clean it.' Well, I did on the last day, she thought. 'I gave Isabella some ideas and she worked them out.'

'You're lying. This is your design and these are your stitches.'

'Only some of them, ma'am. Isabella was afraid she wouldn't finish in time, so I offered to do it for her.'

'And when did you do that?'

'After bedtime, ma'am.' May threw a defiant look at Mrs Wilkins. 'When I had finished all my work.'

'And burning candles unnecessarily and without permission,' was the grim response.

'Ma'am,' May appealed to her mistress, 'I was really only trying to help. Miss Isabella was in a right state and I felt sorry for her.'

'Sorry for her! It is not your place to feel sorry for your employer, or his family.'

May hung her head. It was clear that whatever she said was going to be turned against her.

'But that was not the end of your misdemeanours, was it?' Mrs Freeman pursued. 'You then encouraged Isabella to wrap the parcel, so that Miss Parsons would not see it and realise that she had failed to do the task she had been set.'

'No, ma'am. That was Isabella's idea. She wanted it to be a surprise.'

'It was certainly that! And my daughter is *Miss* Isabella to you.'

'Sorry, ma'am.'

'You should be. Because that is not all I have to find fault with in your behaviour. You were seen the other day taking tea with Mr Freeman.'

'He asked me!' May exclaimed.

'I have watched you, May, trying to ingratiate yourself with my husband. He is a kind man and that sometimes makes him less than careful to maintain the appropriate distance between himself and the lower classes. But you are not stupid. You knew quite well that it was unsuitable for you to be sitting in a tea shop with him. And I believe he has been giving you money.'

May felt herself blush and was angry with herself. She had nothing to be ashamed of, but the blush made it look as though she had. 'He gave me a guinea for the work I did on an idea for his shop window.'

'May, can you not understand? You are a servant, a maid of all work. It is not your place to be offering yourself for that sort of activity.'

'I didn't offer! He asked me to do it!'

'Don't answer back!' Mrs Freeman turned to the cook, who was standing a few feet behind May. 'What do you think, Mrs Wilkins? It seems to me that May has scanted her work in order to conspire with my daughter to deceive me, and has failed to behave in a suitable manner towards my husband.'

'Seems to me, madam, that this girl has ideas above her station. She's not the sort of girl I want working for me.'

'I quite agree,' Mrs Freeman said, and May heard the relief in her voice. 'May, you have failed to give satisfaction and you will leave first thing tomorrow. And do not expect me to give you a character.'

'You're giving me the sack!' May stared at her. In her mind she heard the governor's warning. *'Any girl who is dismissed without a character will find it very hard to get another position.'*

'I have no option. You are not the sort of girl I need as a servant. You will pack your box and leave immediately.'

May gasped. 'Immediately?'

'You heard me. I want you out of this house within the hour.'

In less than that time, May found herself standing on the pavement with her box at her feet and no idea where to go next. It was bitterly cold and a fine sleet was falling, soaking through the thin cloth of the coat she had bought herself. She looked around her. A short distance off a baker's boy was going from house to house, hoping to collect a Christmas box, but otherwise the street was empty. She wondered if there would be any point in knocking at a few doors to ask if they happened to be in need of a new serving girl, but she knew no one would give employment to a bedraggled creature who could not even produce the vital letter attesting to her good character. She picked up her box and began to walk towards the centre of the city. The thought went round and round in her head. 'Where can I go?' At the bottom of the hill she came to the front of Freeman's store and for a moment she considered going inside and asking to see Mr Freeman; but she felt sure that his wife would not have dismissed her without his consent and she shuddered at the idea of being ignominiously ejected. There was only one place she could go for shelter, and that was back to the workhouse, but the thought of returning there and the humiliation of having to admit that she had been dismissed was unbearable.

She went into St George's Hall. At least here she was out of the rain, but she knew people were looking at her oddly, taking in her dishevelled appearance, and after a while one of the stewards approached her and asked what her business was.

'Please, sir, I'm just taking shelter from the rain.'

'Well, we won't have any begging in here,' was the response. 'You'd better be on your way.'

For the rest of the day she wandered the streets, taking shelter where she could, getting colder and hungrier. As the early darkness began to fall she huddled down in a shop doorway and wondered if she would live to see the next day dawn.

A woman's voice from nearby jolted her out of a half doze.

'Nowhere to go, lovey?'

May looked up. A nice-looking, respectably dressed woman was bending towards her.

'Lost your job, have you?'

'How … how did you know?'

'Oh, I've seen plenty of other girls in your position. Why don't you come with me? I'll give you a job, and a nice warm room to sleep in.'

May roused herself. 'Would you? Really?'

'I just said so, didn't I? Come on, up you get. You'll freeze if you stay here much longer.'

She took hold of May's arm and helped her to her feet. 'This way. It's not far.'

May allowed herself to be led along, but something felt not quite right. 'This is very kind of you,' she murmured. 'What should I call you, ma'am?'

'I'm Mrs Feather. And what is your name?'

'May Lavender, ma'am.' She hesitated a moment. 'What sort of job would I be doing?'

'Oh, there are all sorts of possibilities. We can discuss that when you are warm and dry.'

They came to a house in one of the streets leading down towards the docks. The woman knocked and the front door opened and May's senses were struck by a waft of scent composed of a mixture of perfume and cigar smoke and rich food. Her stomach rumbled and she felt suddenly faint.

The woman took her arm again. 'Come along, upstairs. That's the way.'

They passed the open door of a room where smartly dressed gentlemen were drinking and smoking in the company of a number of young ladies in brightly coloured gowns, which to May's eyes exposed far too much of their bosoms. Never mind them,' said Mrs Feather, urging her up the stairs.

She opened a door and led May into a splendid bedroom. There was a carpet on the floor patterned in shades of red and rich velvet curtains in the same tones covered the windows. In the centre of the room was a huge bed piled with pillows and a fire burnt in the grate. Mrs Feather went to a closet and pulled out a nightgown in fine white cotton and a dark pink shawl.

'Let's get you out of those wet things before you catch your death.'

She pulled off May's coat and unfastened the buttons of her dress, so that it fell from her shoulder and left her standing in her shift. May thought she would leave the room or at least turn away at that point, but instead she took hold of the fabric and lifted it in one swift movement over her head, leaving her naked. She was holding out the nightgown but not quite close enough for May to reach it, and looking her up and down. Then she nodded.

'Pretty little thing, aren't you? Bit thin, but that's no matter. Here.'

She stepped closed and slipped the gown over May's head but then, while May's face was still obscured by the cloth, she felt a hand thrust between her legs, probing her secret places. May gasped and jumped back, the nightgown falling into place around her.

'What? Why? Why did you do that?'

Mrs Feather was completely undisturbed. 'Just checking you, lovey. Nothing to worry about. Now, you warm yourself by the fire and I'll have some supper sent up to you.'

She scooped up the pile of wet clothes and was gone before May could speak. Left to herself May sank down on a stool be the fire. Her legs were shaking. Her suspicions had been correct. There was something very wrong here and her instinct was to flee; but she had nothing to cover herself except the thin gown and the shawl. Even her shoes and her precious box had been removed. To go out into the street like this would be almost certain death, unless she could find sanctuary somewhere very quickly. She was racking her brains for a possible refuge when the door opened again and a girl came in carrying a tray on which was a plate with a silver cover and a steaming mug.

'Brought you some supper, miss.'

May jumped up and caught the girl's wrist. 'You don't have to call me miss. I'm a servant, like you – well, I was till this morning. What's your name?'

'Elsie.'

'I'm May. Elsie, what is this place?'

'You don't know?'

'No. I was just brought here by Mrs Feather.'

'Why, it's a brothel, that's what it is. Now, eat your supper. I've got to go.'

'No! Elsie, wait a minute, please. Where are my clothes?'

'Spread out to dry in the kitchen.'

'Bring them up to me, please!'

Elsie shook her head. 'Can't do that. Lose my job if I did.'

'But I can't stay here. It's all a mistake. Please help me!'

'Nothing I can do. Missus'd kill me if I let you get away. She sets great store by girls like you.'

'What do you mean, girls like me?'

'New, innocent. Worth a lot of money to the right gentleman. Did she touch you, down there?'

'Yes. Why did she do that?'

'Make sure you're still a virgin. That's what they pay for.'

'Who?'

'There's a lot of men want girls like that.'

May's legs gave way under her and she sank down on a chair. 'When?' She could hardly get the word out.

'Oh, not tonight. You needn't worry about that. She'll want to ask around, find the highest bidder.'

'Elsie, you've got to help me. Please! I can't let them do that to me.'

'Don't know what you're making a fuss about. You could have a good life. Fine clothes, plenty to eat, a warm bed to sleep in. Better than selling yourself on the street corner. You take my word for it.' She turned to the door. 'Get that food down you while it's still hot.'

The door closed behind her and to May's despair she heard the key turn in the lock. She put her head in her hands and sobbed.

After a while she sat up and wiped her eyes. Weeping was not going to help. She looked at the dish on the tray. She could refuse to eat, starve herself to death; but what would be the point of that? She was warm and dry and there was food in front of her. Whatever horror the next day held, she might as well make the most of what was on offer tonight. She lifted the cover and breathed in the smell. There was a slice of roast goose, the breast meat not a wing, with potatoes both roasted and mashed and plenty of gravy. She took a mouthful, then another, and did not stop until the plate was empty. The mug contained something warm and spicy and had a smell that reminded her of the brandy Mrs Wilkins had poured over the Christmas pudding. She drank it off and felt a delicious sense of ease take possession of her limbs. She was sleepy, so sleepy she could hardly keep her eyes open. There was a chamber pot under the bed. She pulled it out and relieved herself, then climbed into the big bed and pulled the covers over her.

The noise of a cart rumbling past the house woke her with a start. Her first thought was that she had overslept and Mrs Wilkins would be banging on the door at any moment. She was halfway out of bed before she woke up properly and remembered where she was. She cowered down again and hid her face in the pillow. Something terrible was going to happen to her and there was nothing she could do about it.

The sound of the key turning in the lock brought her to a sitting position with her heart thumping against her ribs, but it was only Elsie carrying a tray.

'Brought you some breakfast.' She dumped the tray on the table.

May slid her feet to the floor. 'Elsie, when ...' She could not finish the sentence.

'Told you. Missus is looking for the highest bidder. Could be soon, could be later. She picked up the dirty vessels from the night before and left the room, locking the door behind her.

May looked at the contents of the breakfast tray. There was a boiled egg with slices of white bread and real butter; the sort of meal she was used to taking up to Isabella every morning. She took up the spoon and cracked the top off the egg, but there was something about the smell that caused her stomach to contract with nausea. She just had time to pull out the chamber pot before she vomited.

There was a basin and a ewer of water on a side table. She rinsed her mouth and splashed her face. The fire had gone out and the room was getting chilly. She climbed back onto the bed and lay rigid, her arms at her side, waiting. A church clock somewhere struck nine, and the half-hour. The house was silent, no voices, no footsteps. The minutes ticked past. The clock struck ten. Then May heard Mrs Feather's voice, her breathing a little laboured as she climbed the stairs.

'This way, sir. Just up here. She's all ready for you.'

May was on her feet, shaking all over. Steps came closer and stopped outside the door.

A man's voice said, 'And you assure me that she is quite untouched?'

'Pure as the driven snow and innocent as a lamb,' the woman assured him.

May felt as though every drop of blood in her body had suddenly drained away, leaving her an empty shell. She knew that voice! 'Oh no!' she breathed. 'Not him! Not him of all people!'

The door opened. 'Here she is, sir,' Mrs Feather said and stepped aside.

David Freeman walked into the room.

May took a step back, clasping the flimsy nightgown at her throat, and found her path blocked by the bed.

Freeman turned to the door. 'Thank you, Mrs Feather.' His tone was dismissive and she retreated.

'I'll be here if you want me.'

He closed the door and crossed the room to where May was standing. She gasped aloud as his hands gripped her shoulders.

'May! Thank God I've found you! I looked for you half the night. I had no idea what my wife intended. I would never have permitted it.' He stopped and looked at her. 'Have they hurt you? If you've been harmed in any way ...'

She could only shake her head, unable to speak.

His voice softened. 'Don't worry. There's no need to be afraid any longer, you're safe now.'

It was enough to break the logjam of emotions and she burst into tears. He pulled her to him and let her sob against his chest. After a moment he held her off and put a clean handkerchief into her hand. 'There now. Dry your eyes. It's all over. Where are your clothes?'

'In the kitchen, drying.'

While she mopped her face he strode to the door and flung it opened, finding Mrs Feather half stooped to the level of the keyhole.

'Ha! I thought you would be here. Fetch this girl's clothes. I'm taking her home.'

'Oh no, sir! You can't do that. That wasn't the agreement at all.'

'I don't care a fig for your agreement. This girl belongs to me. She is a servant in my house. She should never have been here. Now, get her clothes, if you don't want me to report you to the authorities for kidnapping.'

Mrs Feather leaned over the banister and bawled, 'Elsie! Bring them clothes what was drying up here. Quick sharp!' She came into the room, her tone conciliatory now. 'See here, sir. I found the girl sheltering in a doorway last night. I saved her. She wouldn't have lasted the night if I hadn't brought her here. And she's had bed and board at my expense …'

'If that's what you are after,' Mr Freeman said, 'I'll give you half what you were going to charge me. Here!' He threw a handful of coins onto the table. 'Let that be an end to it.'

'Well, 'tis a poor reward for my trouble,' the woman began, but Mr Freeman took a sudden step towards her and she scuttled out of the room. Elsie came in with May's clothes and her box. She rolled her eyes from him to her, dumped them on the bed and left.

'Get dressed, May. I'll wait outside until you're ready.'

She scrambled into her clothes, trembling fingers struggling with buttons and shoelaces, afraid that when she opened the door he would not be there. But he was waiting for her, leaning on the banister, and as soon as he saw her he took her arm.

'Good girl! Come along, I've got a cab waiting.'

He held onto her going down the stairs and she was grateful for the support, feeling that at any moment her legs might give way. No one tried to stop them but Mrs Feather watched them with baleful eyes from the doorway of the sitting room. A hansom cab was waiting outside, the horses' breath misting in the cold air. Mr Freeman handed her in and gave the driver the Rodney Street address, then settled himself beside her.

'May, I can't begin to tell you how sorry I am that this has happened. When I came home last night and heard what my wife had done I was ... Well, let us say I made my disapproval very clear. And as for Mrs Wilkins's part in this ... I told her that it was only because Lydia depends on her so much that I did not put her out to share your fate. Though,' and she saw the beginnings of a smile hovering on his lips, 'I doubt whether Mrs Feather would have found her such a tempting proposition.'

She caught his eye and choked back a hysterical giggle. After a moment she said, 'How did you find me, sir?'

'I searched the streets for you late into the night, and then when I found no trace of you it struck me that you might have been picked up by someone like Mrs Feather.' He looked at her. 'I hope you don't imagine that I am in the habit of frequenting such establishments?'

'Oh no, sir! I could never think that.' But she had thought it, for a moment. As a form of amends she went on, 'You have always been so kind to me. I think you are the kindest man on earth.'

'Hardly that,' he said, 'but I do feel we have a responsibility to the people we employ, and to those less fortunate than ourselves. That is why I have joined with some other like-minded gentlemen to try to help women who have been lured into a life of prostitution. In that endeavour, we have made a friend in the police force, an inspector who also concerns himself with such matters. Last night, in desperation, I called on him and he agreed to help. He has eyes and ears all over the city and this morning he was able to tell me that Mrs Feather was putting the word around that she had a very special offer for a man who was prepared to pay her price, a girl she had picked up from the street the night before. I took a chance that it might be you and it was. Thank God I wasn't too late!'

'I'll never be able to thank you enough, sir,' she said.

'There is no need,' he replied. 'You should never have been there in the first place. But, May, you have seen the worst side of mankind today. You must not think that we are all so depraved.'

'I know that, sir.'

After a while she plucked up courage to ask the question uppermost in her mind. 'Am I to have my old job back, sir?'

He smiled at her. 'No, you are not. I have something else in mind.' He raised a hand to prevent her further questioning. 'Wait till we get home. I'll tell you everything then.'

When they arrived at the house, May would have gone down the steps to the servants' entrance but he took her arm and led her in through the front door. Lydia Freeman was waiting for them in the morning room. She was pale and May thought she had been crying. She got to her feet as they entered, twisting a tiny handkerchief in her fingers.

'You found her.'

'Yes, and unharmed, thank God,' her husband responded. 'You should be glad I did. If she had been dead in a ditch or … or worse, it would have been on your conscience. Now, please be so good as to ring for Mrs Wilkins.'

Mrs Freeman crossed the room and pulled the bell pull, and an awkward silence ensued. May wondered if she should try to apologise for her part in the events that had led up to her dismissal.

'Ma'am,' she began, 'I'm really sorry if I displeased you about that sampler ...'

It was Mr Freeman who cut in. 'There is no need for you to apologise, May. I have spoken to Isabella and it is clear that you acted with the best intentions – and in the process created something rather beautiful.'

There was a knock and Mrs Wilkins came in. She saw May and pursed her lips in disapproval. 'Oh, you're back, are you?'

'Yes, she is,' Mr Freeman said, 'and if I had not found her you would now be looking for another position.'

Mrs Wilkins shot May a look that said very clearly, 'Just wait till I get you downstairs!'

'However,' Mr Freeman went on, 'she is not staying. It has become apparent that May is totally unsuitable for her position as a maid of all work. She is far too good for that. You have failed to recognise her remarkable talents, Lydia, but I have not. So I am going to offer her a position more suited to her abilities.' He turned to May and gave her a reassuring smile. 'How do you like the idea of becoming a milliner's apprentice?'

'A milliner, sir? That's someone who makes hats for ladies, isn't it?'

'That's correct. As I think you know, my business is expanding rapidly. I intend to open a millinery department. I have employed a very talented milliner. Her name is Nancy Driscoll, but she is always known as Nan. As I said, she is very good at her job, but she is not a young woman and I have persuaded her that it would be a good idea to take on an apprentice. I think it is a job that would suit you very well. What do you say?'

May glanced at the two women. Lydia Freeman was sitting with her head bent, biting her lips. Mrs Wilkins was white-faced with fury and May could see she was stifling words of disapproval.

'Yes, please, sir!' May said. 'I think I should like that very much.' She hesitated. 'Where would I live? Would I still live here?'

He shook his head. 'No. We shall need your room for whoever takes your place. Nan has a room in her house that you can have. But you must understand one thing. An apprentice cannot expect wages. I shall have to pay Nan for your board and lodging out of the six pounds a year I have been paying you. But since you have been used to earning, it seems hardly fair to expect you to do without altogether, so I will make you an allowance of two pounds per year. But you will be learning a skill, and in a few years' time you should be able to command a good salary, or even go into business on your own account. So, what do you say?'

May did not have to pause for thought. 'Yes! Oh, yes, thank you, sir!'

'Good. You can start tomorrow. You can stay here tonight, until I have made other arrangements. Bring your box to the shop in the morning and I will introduce you to Nan.' He looked at his wife. 'I think that is a satisfactory solution to the situation, don't you, my dear?'

'Whatever you say, my love,' she mumbled meekly.

Next morning, packing her few possessions into her box, May came across something she had not thought of since her first days in service – the rag doll which had once belonged to Angel. She held it to her cheek for a moment and fancied that she could still smell that faint, indefinable scent of a baby's skin. Where was Angel now, she wondered. Living in some fine house, with all the toys she could want, probably. She packed the doll into her box, closed the lid and carried it out into the kitchen, where Mrs Wilkins was washing the breakfast dishes.

'You'll be off, then,' she remarked.

'Yes. Goodbye, Mrs Wilkins.'

'Goodbye – and good riddance,' the cook said. And with that kindly farewell ringing in her ears, May closed the door and climbed the area steps to the road.

'Service entrance is down the side, miss.'

May looked up at the doorman in his smart uniform and felt herself blush. Of course, seeing her arrive carrying her box, he would have known she was not a customer.

'Beg pardon, sir,' she mumbled, and turned quickly away.

She found her way down the alley at the side of the shop to a door marked 'Freemans – Staff Entrance'. Suddenly her embarrassment was transformed into a sense of pride. She was more than a customer. She belonged!

Inside, she was stopped by another doorman, less splendidly costumed.

'Please, sir. I'm supposed to see Mr Freeman. I'm coming to work here.'

'Right you are. Go down that passage to the far end, turn left and you'll see Mr Freeman's office at the end.'

May arrived outside an impressive door of solid oak. Her heart was thumping and her arms ached with the strain of carrying her box. She knocked timidly and was reassured by the familiar voice calling, 'Come in.'

Mr Freeman was seated behind a large desk, and next to him stood a small woman who seemed to May, at first sight, to be completely round: a round body, tightly swathed in a black dress, and a round, red face.

Mr Freeman looked across at her with a smile. 'Ah, you're here. Good. Nan, this is May Lavender, your new apprentice. May, this is Mrs Driscoll – but I'm sure she will be happy for you to call her Nan, like everyone else.'

'May Lavender,' the little woman said. 'Pretty name for a pretty girl.'

May felt herself blush again. She never thought of herself as pretty.

'Nan, can you see that May is provided with a suitable dress?' Freeman said. 'I'll leave her in your capable hands. I'm sure the two of you are going to get along famously.'

Nan led her along a warren of corridors to a room where several women were sitting at tables, stitching, and rolls of brightly coloured fabrics were stacked along the walls.

'New recruit,' she announced. 'Needs fitting out with a uniform dress.'

May had already seen that all the assistants on the shop floor wore coats and skirts in the same dark blue, with white blouses. It seemed that this uniform colour extended to those working behind the scenes, but in the form of a dress. She was more than happy to exchange her worn, black skirt and much-darned blouse for one of these.

'You're a skinny little thing, aren't you?' the seamstress who fitted her remarked. 'You'll have to feed her up, Nan.'

'Oh, you can leave that to me,' Nan responded with a chuckle. 'Now then, bring your box and I'll show you where we work.'

May followed her down another passage and into a room, which, to her eyes, resembled an Aladdin's cave. Hats in various stages of completion rested on hat blocks and stands on the tables, and surrounding them were boxes full of ribbons and coloured feathers and artificial flowers.

'Oh!' the exclamation escaped without her intention.

'Like what you see?' Nan asked.

'Oh yes!'

'Good. Put your box down under the table there and we can get started. Now, Mr Freeman tells me you have a good eye for colour and design. See that one there?' She pointed to an almost-completed hat. 'It wants something, just to finish it off. What would you suggest?'

May stared round the room. The question was so unexpected that for a moment she could not think of a response. Then she said, 'Is it a hat for a young lady, or someone older?'

'A young woman, quite a girl actually.'

'And what colour is her dress?'

'Aha!' Nan reached across and held up a swag of fabric and ribbon. 'You're asking the right questions. Now, what?'

May looked around again and alighted on the box of artificial flowers. 'These,' she said. 'Violets would be perfect with those colours.'

'Well done!' said Nan. 'Mr Freeman was right. I can see we are going to get along very well. Now, pull up that stool and we'll start from the beginning.'

Eight

Gus clung to the rail on the leeward side of the deckhouse with numbed hands and stared about him. In the two months since the *Shenandoah* had left Madeira, he thought he had encountered King Neptune in most of his moods, from storm to flat calm; but he had never imagined that the sea could be whipped up to such a fury as it was today. His shipmates had told him that they were now in what was called the 'roaring forties', a stretch of the ocean close to the Antarctic that was constantly swept by violent winds, and he understood how the name arose.

The sound of the wind drowned all others; but it seemed from what they said that even here such a storm as this was unusual. The sails were close reefed and in the wheelhouse behind him the steersman was clinging to the wheel as it bucked and twisted like a wild animal. Huge waves rushed towards them, towering above the tops of the masts, and the *Shenandoah* clawed her way up them and then pitched dizzily down the far side. Sometimes, increasingly often it seemed to Gus, she failed to reach the peak and a torrent of seawater swept over the deck, and almost before it had drained away through the scuppers the next wave was upon them.

As he watched, another such wave broke over the bows, but this one was bigger than any of the previous ones and in seconds the whole of the main deck was flooded, so that the men working there were up to their waists in water. The ship wallowed, weighed down by the extra weight of water, which was now sloshing from side to side as she rolled. Men scrambled to find handholds or to haul themselves up onto any part of the superstructure that rose clear of the flood. Gus twisted round at the sound of a shout from the wheelhouse and saw Lieutenant Whittle, the ship's executive officer, lowering himself into the maelstrom.

'Four men with me! We have to knock out one of the gun ports!'

Four men heeded his call. Half wading, half swimming, they struggled aft. Gus held his breath. One more big wave could sweep them into the sea – or send the whole ship to the bottom. He saw Whittle duck his head and disappear completely under the water, followed by two others. There was a pause that lasted so long that Gus was sure all three must have drowned and then Whittle surfaced, gasping, followed by the other two. In spite of the odds, they had succeeded. Water gushed from the open port and the ship was stabilised. Gus turned and clawed his way along the rail and round to the door of the galley.

Boney was stirring a huge pot on the range, legs spread wide to keep his balance, seemingly unconcerned.

'There you are! What kept you? We've got a Christmas dinner to prepare. Get those spuds on to cook.'

Gus staggered across the pitching deck and picked up a knife. Christmas! he thought. How could anyone think of celebrating Christmas under these conditions?

It seemed that the officers expected to do just that, and it was Boney's job, helped by Gus, to produce a suitable meal.

An hour later, the wardroom echoed to cheerful voices as Gus served goose, roast pork, fresh vegetables and mince pies.

That such a miracle was possible, on a ship that had not called at a port since leaving Madeira sixty-six days earlier, was due to the successful pursuit of the purpose of the voyage. The *Shenandoah* was a commerce raider, and her aim was to capture as many merchant vessels belonging to the Union states as possible. As they sailed south they had encountered several, and a blank cartridge fired across their bows quickly persuaded them to heave to and allow themselves to be boarded. Having once established that the ships were, in fact, registered to Yankee owners, the crew were taken prisoner, all useful goods were taken on board the *Shenandoah* and the ships were then set on fire or sunk. That was how they had acquired the delicacies on which the officers were now feasting.

When they first sailed, such an outcome had seemed unlikely. The *Shenandoah* had been built as a merchant ship, not as a ship of war, and any conversion had to be undertaken well out of the jurisdiction of any neutral power who might have impounded her. Also, there was the constant fear that a Union naval vessel might get wind of her position and attack her. Gus had overheard a number of vigorous arguments in the early days of the voyage. Some of the officers felt they should have remained at anchor off Las Desertas until necessary modifications had been completed, but Captain Waddell had insisted on sailing at once.

So gun ports had been cut in the ship's sides, and the guns mounted, while they were at sea.

Gus had begun the voyage full of enthusiasm for this great adventure, but now, with experience of what it meant in practice, he was not so sure. It was all very well to send the enemy ships to the bottom. It was the treatment of the prisoners that bothered him. They were severely under-manned, because so few of the crew that had brought the *Sea King* out from London had agreed to sign on under her new name, and Lieutenant Whittle was determined to make up the shortfall from amongst the prisoners.

The captain and officers were allowed to give their parole, promising to do nothing to hinder the *Shenandoah*'s purpose, or to reveal her existence once they were set ashore, and given the freedom of the ship. But the men were given a choice. Sign on, or spend the rest of the voyage in irons. Unsurprisingly, most of them chose to sign on. With the first one to refuse, Lieutenant Whittle adopted a different method.

'Trice him up,' he ordered.

The man in question was seized by two of the crew and dragged to a position close to the mast. His wrists were handcuffed and the chain between them passed over a spar above his head, so that his feet only just touched the ground. In this position he was left to contemplate his decision. Gus, moving around the ship on various errands, found his eyes inescapably drawn to the straining muscles in the man's arms and shoulders and the expression of agony on his face. After an hour Whittle returned and asked if he had changed his mind. The man shook his head obdurately.

'Trice him higher,' Whittle ordered, and the chain was shortened so that only the tips of the man's toes touched the deck. Half an hour of that convinced him that shipping with the *Shenandoah* was better than the alternative.

This happened not once but repeatedly, every time they took a prize, and in the end Gus could not keep silent any longer.

'It can't be right, treating prisoners like that!' he said to Boney as they worked together in the galley.

'Right or wrong,' Boney replied, 'it has to be done. We're undermanned and we can't go on like this much longer. Men are having to take double watches. Even the officers are having to turn to and do jobs that would rightfully be left to the men.'

'But it's ... it's torture!' Gus blurted.

'They bring it on themselves,' Boney said. 'If they had the sense to sign on in the first place it wouldn't be necessary. And if I were you, I'd button my lip. You don't want the same treatment.'

'Me?' Gus looked at him in horror. 'Do you mean they don't just do it to prisoners?'

Boney put down the knife with which he was chopping salt pork and looked at him. 'Discipline is discipline, and it has to be enforced somehow. When the navy abolished flogging, 'bout ten years back, they brought this in as an alternative. I've seen men flogged, and believe me, I'd rather be trieed.'

Gus turned away, with a sick feeling in his stomach. His first impression – that he was under an authority which imposed discipline through means that were basically benevolent – had been rudely dispelled. It seemed to him now that he had escaped one brutal regime only to fall into the hands of another.

The storm of Christmas day abated and by December 29th the *Shenandoah* was sailing under full canvas.

A few weeks later, rumours began to circulate that they were bound for Australia. The crew were delighted with the prospect, but Gus gathered from listening to the conversation in the wardroom over meals that the officers had doubts about the wisdom of the idea. The seas around them were a prime area for Union-owned whaling ships, which presented a very tempting target, and the officers felt that they should be pursuing them rather than heading for port. They were worried, too, that there might be Union ships already there and that their position would quickly become known to their enemies. The captain, however, had other ideas and, the winds having fallen light, ordered the engineers to get up steam. His hopes of a rapid passage were dashed, however, when the engine broke down and it was discovered that the propeller was also damaged. This made a stop in harbour all the more vital.

Gus forgot his doubts in his excitement at the thought of seeing one of the places he had only heard of from Captain Thomas's stories, and his sense of anticipation was fuelled by the tales told by crew members who had visited Australia before. None of them had been ashore since they set sail from Las Desertas, and Gus longed to feel solid ground under his feet again.

On January 29th they heard the welcome cry of 'Land Ho!', and soon afterwards the *Shenandoah* glided into Port Philip Bay and anchored off a busy dockyard.

'Where are we?' Gus asked one of the older crewmen.

'Melbourne,' was the answer.

They had scarcely dropped anchor before a whole flotilla of small boats put out from the shore and came to encircle them. Many of them carried bundles of newspapers, which were eagerly seized upon. In this way, they learned for the first time that Abraham Lincoln had been re-elected as president of the United States and that General Sherman had captured Atlanta. The war was not going well for the Confederates.

None of that concerned Gus particularly, though he was sorry to see his fellow crew members disappointed. All his thoughts were directed to the possibility of going ashore. Two days of frustrating waiting followed.

He managed to catch the attention of Midshipman Mason for a few minutes.

'Beg pardon, sir. What are we waiting for? When will we be able to go ashore?'

'When we have established that the state governor is prepared to let us stay.'

'Why wouldn't he?'

'Because Australia is a British colony, and Britain has signed a pact of neutrality in this war we are engaged in. If the governor lets us stay for repairs and resupply it might be taken as a violation of that pact.' He looked at Gus and smiled. 'Don't look so crestfallen. My bet is we'll be able to go ashore soon.'

Eventually the longed for permission was granted. The crew could go ashore, one watch at a time. Gus found himself at a loss. He was not officially a member of the crew and had not been allocated to any watch in particular, so he was unsure whether the permission included him. He decided to ask Boney, since most of his time was spent working for him. The cook shifted a chew of tobacco from one cheek to the other and regarded him thoughtfully.

'Well, seeing as how most of the officers are on shore and not in need of our assistance, I don't see why not. Off you go, lad, and enjoy yourself.'

There was another problem, which he had not considered in his initial excitement. Who would he go with? He got on well with most of the men, but he had never made any real friends. The disparity in age between himself and even the youngest crew members was too great. Mason, who had befriended him on board the *Laurel*, was an officer and would go ashore in the company of others of his kind. Gus faced the prospect of finding his way around a strange city all alone.

He was hovering on the fringes of a party of men preparing to board a tug which would take them to the dock when a tall, gangling young man, who was known to everyone as Lofty, clapped him on the shoulder.

'Hey up, lad! Coming ashore?'

'Yes. Yes, please.'

'On your own, are you?'

'Yes, I suppose so.'

'You come along of us.' Lofty grinned round at his mates. 'We'll show you how to have a good time.'

Having a good time, in Lofty's estimation, meant touring the waterfront from one tavern to another. Gus had got used to the effects of the daily ration of grog and learned to enjoy the sense of warmth and well-being that it engendered, but he had never drunk beer or any other spirits. The men he was with had money in their pockets and insisted on including him in every round of drinks. Very soon he was enveloped in a kind of miasma that made every place look the same and gave him trouble keeping his feet.

Finally, he found himself somewhere that looked rather different from the bars they had visited so far. There were chairs with brightly coloured cushions and a smell of perfume, and there were women. The women were sitting on his companions' knees, and there was a lot of whispering and giggling, and then some of them got up and led the way up a flight of stairs. Gus's drowsy lethargy disappeared and was replaced by a sense of panic. He had heard enough sailors' gossip to know what this place was and what went on there – or at least, he had a rough idea; but what might now be expected of him filled him with terror.

Lofty pushed a girl off his knee and grabbed the hand of another. 'Come on, Lil! You can take this lad in hand.' He stopped and guffawed. 'You know what I'm getting at. It's time he learned what's what.'

Dora was plump, with breasts that threatened to escape from the bodice of her dress, and a face elaborately rouged and powdered. Gus cowered as she bore down on him.

'Come along, sweetheart! There's nothing to be afraid of. Why don't you come upstairs with Dora, eh?'

'No!' Gus squirmed out of her grasp and got to his feet. 'I ... I don't feel well. I think I'm going to be ...'

He made it out of the door just in time and threw up in the gutter.

He was sitting on the kerb, sweating in the heat and longing for a drink of water, when a voice said, 'You all right, mister?'

A girl about his own age was standing a few feet away. She was neatly dressed in a blue pinafore and her hair was a mass of golden ringlets.

Gus passed his tongue over his lips and swallowed. 'I'm … I'm thirsty. Do you know where I can get a drink of water?'

'Come with me.' The girl held out her hand. 'I'll show you.'

Gus blinked at her. Was this another invitation, like Dora's? He couldn't believe that this girl was associated with the place he had just left. Could he trust her?

She began to move away, impatiently. 'Are you coming, or not?'

Gus got unsteadily to his feet. She seemed unthreatening, and he couldn't just sit where he was. The men from the ship would be out any minute, and he could not face them. She came back and took hold of his hand.

'My name's Victoria. You can call me Vicky. What's yours?

'Gus,' he mumbled.

She led him along the road and round a corner to the entrance of an imposing building. A sign above it read 'CROFT'S HOTEL'. He hung back.

'I can't go in there.'

'Why not?'

'I … I'm not smart enough. That's where the toffs go.'

'It's where I go,' she said. 'My dad owns it. Come on.'

He followed her into the cool shade of the vestibule and heard her say, 'It's all right, Georgy. This is one of the sailors from the steamer. I'm taking him to see Mama.'

She led him up a flight of stairs, along a corridor and into a room like no other he had ever seen. Large windows opened onto a veranda, overlooking a garden full of trees and flowers he could not name. There were easy chairs and pictures on the walls and carpet on the floor.

A woman rose from one of the chairs. 'Goodness me, Victoria. Who have you got here?'

'His name is Gus. He's from the steamer and he's not feeling very well.'

The woman came closer and bent her head towards Gus. She sniffed. 'I can see why. Who's been buying you drinks, Gus?'

Gus hung his head. 'Some of the fellows from the ship.'

'I thought as much. They ought to know better – but that's sailors for you.'

'He's thirsty. He wants a drink of water.'

'I bet he does! There's some lemonade on the table over there. Pour him a glass of that.'

The drink was cool, and sweet and sharp at the same time. Gus thought he had never tasted anything as good. He drank it off in one draft and wiped his lips on the back of his hand.

'Thank you, ma'am. I'm … much obliged.'

She looked at him with a mixture of amusement and curiosity. 'You're very welcome, Gus. Tell me something, how old are you?'

Gus frowned. He had all but lost count of time since he ran away from the school.

'Thirteen, ma'am … I think.'

'That's very young to be a sailor. How do you come to be on board that ship? Is your father one of the officers, perhaps?

Gus fidgeted. This was getting awkward. 'No, ma'am. I haven't got a father.'

'No father? So, were you apprenticed to someone on the ship?'

'No, ma'am.' It seemed there was no way to escape the inquisition, but if he told these people the truth, surely they could not send him back – not from here? 'I ... I stowed away, ma'am. But now I'm part of the crew,' he added quickly. 'I'm the cabin boy.'

'You stowed away? You must have quite a story to tell. When do you have to be back on board, Gus?'

'Ten o'clock tonight, ma'am.'

'Then you must have dinner with us. My husband would be interested to meet you. Now, I expect you would like a wash. Victoria, show Gus the bathroom and find him a towel.'

The bathroom frightened Gus. He had never seen anything like it. You pumped a handle and water flowed into a pristine white basin, which could be swivelled over to empty into a bucket underneath, and there was a zinc bathtub with some kind of strange contraption over it that reminded him of the boilers in the ship's engine room. He sluiced his face and hands quickly and went back into the hallway. Victoria was waiting for him.

'Come along. My papa is waiting to meet you.' She took him by the hand. 'Don't worry. He's not going to be angry with you.'

Far from being angry Mr Croft was a genial man, with abundant moustaches and twinkling eyes, and Gus quickly found himself recounting the story of how he had come to be aboard the *Shenandoah*. He skated over the reason why he had run away, but he was not pressed for any further explanation.

'You say your father and mother both died. So who brought you up?'

'I grew up in the workhouse.'

'You poor boy!' was Mrs Croft's reaction and Victoria looked at him with tears in her eyes.

'It must be horrible growing with no mother or father.'

Gus shrugged, and Mr Croft said, 'Under the circumstances, I think Gus is to be admired for having the courage and initiative to carve out a career for himself.'

Conversation turned to the *Shenandoah*, but when it came to explaining the ship's objective Gus found himself in difficulties.

'Beg pardon, sir, but I'm not supposed to talk about that.'

'Your discretion does you credit. But there's no need to worry. There have been plenty of reports in the papers, so we have a pretty good idea of what you've been up to. Now, that's the gong for dinner. I expect you're hungry, aren't you?'

Gus had never sat at a family dinner table, but he had watched the way the officers on board the ship behaved and he managed to get through the meal without disgracing himself.

Towards the end he felt able to ask a question himself.

'Have you always lived here, in Melbourne, sir?'

'No. We came over from Van Dieman's Land – what they are calling Tasmania now. I had a small hotel there, but when we heard about the gold rush here we thought there might be more opportunities in Melbourne. And we were proved right.'

'Gold rush, sir?'

'You didn't know? Near on fifteen years ago, gold was discovered near here at Clunes and then at Ballarat. It brought thousands of men here to dig. Most of the easily got stuff has gone now; it's all deep mining. But it made this city what it is today: one of the busiest and most prosperous places in Australia.'

'I wish I could have been here then,' Gus said.

'Oh, there were fortunes made and lost. But there were plenty who went home empty-handed too. Now, if you have to be back on board you had better get going. I'll get one of my people to walk you back to the docks.'

'Mama, can Gus come and visit us again?' Victoria asked.

'If he is allowed ashore, of course. We'll be glad to see you any time, Gus.'

Gus had been worried about the reception he might get from his shipmates and expected to be teased about his embarrassment in the brothel, but when he arrived to board the waiting liberty boat, they were far more interested in his new friends. He had 'fallen on his feet there, all right' was the consensus, and he seemed to have gone up in their estimation.

The *Shenandoah*'s stay in Melbourne was longer than anyone expected. She was taken into dry dock for repairs and it was discovered that more work was needed to make her seaworthy than previously thought. Her crew had no objection to the delay. Her officers, who had once been so doubtful about the wisdom of calling at the port, found themselves lionised and invited to balls and dinners at some of the most exclusive clubs and hotels. Gus, too, was more than happy to stay.

Whenever he was allowed ashore he headed straight for Croft's Hotel, where Victoria and her mother undertook to give him a thorough tour of the city. After the soot and cloudy skies of Liverpool, he relished the sunshine and was enchanted by the tree-lined banks of the Yarra River and the streets of pretty, clapboard-fronted houses with their elaborate wrought-iron balconies.

There were less attractive areas, too – streets of hastily built shacks and smoking factory chimneys – but his hosts avoided them. The high point of his explorations was a visit to Melbourne Zoo. He had seen very few animals in his life. There were cats in the workhouse to keep down the mice and the occasional stray dog that wandered in, and in his rare glimpses of the outside world he had seen horses pulling carts and traps. On board ship there had been pigs and live chickens. Now he saw creatures whose mere existence was almost beyond belief: kangaroos that bounced along as if they had springs in their feet; somnolent koalas and spiky echidnas. And birds in such vivid colours that at first he could hardly believe they were real. He wished that he had May's ability to draw, so he could keep a record of them.

The thought of his sister brought to the surface a sense of guilt that he had been trying to ignore. He mentioned it to Victoria, who said at once, 'Why don't you write her a letter?'

'Could I? How would it get there?'

'There's a mail boat that goes from here back to England with letters – and it's sailing in a couple of days' time.'

'I don't know,' Gus muttered. 'I've never written a letter. I wouldn't know how to begin.'

'I'll help you,' she offered.

Gus found Victoria's friendship disturbing. All his life had been spent in the company of his own sex and his only guide as to how to behave towards women had been the raunchy gossip of his shipmates. Victoria had two older brothers, one away at school and the other working somewhere 'up-country', and she also had a wide circle of friends of both sexes, which Gus found surprising.

She had a matter-of-fact, straightforward manner with all of them but Gus found it hard to hit the same tone. When he was close to her it set up all sorts of unfamiliar sensations, both in his body and his mind. At night in his hammock he could not stop thinking about her and had dreams that produced effects of which he was deeply ashamed. It was Lofty, who seemed to feel he had a responsibility towards him since their first excursion on shore, who took him off to a quiet corner of the deck and explained, in coarse sailors' terms, the facts of life.

Despite his hesitation, Gus accepted Victoria's offer of help and an hour spent with their heads together over a sheet of paper resulted in a letter that seemed acceptable.

'What's the address?' Victoria asked.

'Oh! I don't know.'

'You can't send a letter without an address.'

'No, I s'pose not.'

'You said she was in service somewhere.'

'Yes.'

'What was the name of the people she worked for?'

Gus racked his memory. 'Began with F ... Foster? No, Freeman. That was it.'

'Didn't she ever tell you where they lived?'

'No ... Just a minute ... No, I can't remember. I think she said he owned a shop.'

Victoria looked doubtful. 'I suppose if you addressed it to her at Freeman's shop it might get there.'

'Best I can do,' Gus said.

One day, when repairs to the ship were almost completed, a posse of policemen appeared at the dry dock. Gus was just finishing tidying the officers' cabins and preparing to go ashore. He went out on deck and heard the man in charge of them shout up to Lieutenant Grimble, who had been left in charge of the ship.

'We have reason to believe that you have on board men you have illegally recruited during your stay here. They have broken the law forbidding men to join foreign forces and the statement of neutrality proclaimed by Her Majesty's government. We wish to come on board to search for them and arrest them.'

'I am afraid,' Grimble replied, 'in the absence of Captain Waddell I do not have the authority to permit that.'

The policemen went away, but next morning they were back with the same demand. This time the captain was on the quarterdeck.

'According to maritime law,' he shouted back, 'the deck of a warship constitutes part of the country whose flag she flies. This means that you cannot exert any authority over this ship and you have no right to search her. However, as a gesture of goodwill, I will have my own master-at-arms search the ship to see if any men such as you describe have hidden themselves on board.'

The search was carried out and returned a negative response. The exchange gave Gus cause for thought. He was aware that some familiar faces had not been seen for some days, many of them belonging to prisoners who had been forced to sign on. And he had also seen a number of strangers around the ship, though he had heard Captain Waddell tell at least one of them that he could not take him on as crew without breaking the law. When he mentioned it to Mr Croft, next time he went ashore, he was not surprised.

'There's plenty of men around who came out here looking for gold and didn't strike it lucky. Now there's no work for them. I dare say a lot of them would be glad to get taken on for a sailor's wages and the chance of prize money.'

Back on board Gus sought the opinion of Boney. 'Is it true that some men have deserted?'

'Seems like it. Rumour has it that they are being put up in hotels at the expense of the American consul, and paid their wages by him too.'

'Why would he do that?'

'Anything to make life difficult for us. I guess he's pretty angry that we've been allowed to stay here.'

'And are we taking on other men? I've seen some new faces.'

Boney gave him a look. 'Know what, boy? You ask too many questions.'

The next day those on board were stunned to see a large force of police, backed by soldiers, taking up positions on both sides of the dock. When the workmen arrived to complete the repairs, they were turned away. No shore leave was possible and for a day and a night there was stalemate. Waddell steadfastly refused to let them come aboard and no more work was done. Gus, along with the rest of the crew, sat around, frustrated and bored, while the officers paced the deck in impotent fury.

How the impasse was resolved Gus never found out, but quite suddenly everything changed. The troops were withdrawn, the repairs were completed, and *Shenandoah* was towed out of the dry dock and dropped anchor again in the bay. As if by magic, a collier flying the British flag materialised and offloaded tons of much-needed coal; supplies were brought aboard and Gus realised to his dismay that they were preparing to sail. His urgent request to be allowed ashore to say goodbye to his friends was refused and at dawn next morning the *Shenandoah* weighed her anchor and headed for the open sea.

'Cheer up, lad!' said Boney. 'That's a sailor's life for you. It's full of goodbyes.'

'But I didn't get to say goodbye,' Gus protested.

'They'll understand.'

'I wonder.'

One further incident occurred before they settled down on the next leg of the voyage. As soon as they were in international waters, men Gus had never seen before began appearing from every corner of the ship. Some had been in the lower hold, some in empty water tanks and a few in the hollow bowsprit, and all had apparently eluded Captain Waddell's professed efforts to search for them. They were mustered on deck and the captain asked what nationality they belonged to. Every man declared that he was a native of the southern states and had stowed away with the express purpose of joining their fellow countrymen in their fight against the oppressors. Captain Waddell then had them all signed on as crew.

The *Shenandoah* was now fully manned, for the first time in the voyage.

Nine

Freeman's Wishes All Our Customers Health, Happiness and Prosperity in 1865

The notices were in all the windows of the shop. May hugged the idea to herself, feeling that it applied to her as well. A new life had opened up for her and she intended to grab the opportunities it offered with both hands.

From her first day working for Nan Driscoll she had known that she had found her proper place. Nan was an expert at her trade and seemed to enjoy imparting her skills, and, for May, the chance to spend her days surrounded by beautiful things was more than compensation for long hours and little pay. The shop opened at eight o'clock and she was expected to be there to prepare the equipment and materials for the day's work.

Nan usually arrived about nine, and they worked together until six, except for an hour's break for the midday meal. Then May had to stay and tidy up and sweep the scraps of fabric and threads of cotton off the floor before she went back to the house. But that was a vast improvement on what she had been used to. No more rising at the crack of dawn to scrub and dust; no more making up fires and pounding clothes in the copper and turning the mangle; no more being ordered about by Mrs Wilkins.

Nan owned a little terraced house ten minutes' walk from the shop and May had a room on the top floor. It was not large, but there was a comfortable bed and a cupboard for her things, and on the floor below there was one of the new water closets, so no more emptying chamber pots. The only thing that bothered her was the fact that Nan was far from house-proud. The sitting room, which May was welcome to share, was strewn with bits and pieces left over from her trade, together with old newspapers and knick-knacks of various sorts; no one ever swept the stairs and the kitchen needed a thorough clean. Coming from a household where a speck of dust or a dirty dish would be seen as a crime against the natural order of things, May found this initially disturbing, and then wonderfully liberating.

She soon understood why Nan spent little time in the kitchen. The shop had a canteen, where all the workers took their main meal of the day at twelve o'clock, and in the evening Nan's habit was to buy a pie or some fish and chips from a local shop. Cooking did not figure in her daily routine. May was happy to settle for that. She had spent long enough in a kitchen.

Usually, after they had eaten in the evening, Nan would declare that she was popping out for a 'constitutional'. May at first assumed that this meant a walk, and offered to accompany her; but the offer was politely refused. 'I'll be meeting up with some old friends. It wouldn't interest you.' She returned with a smell on her breath that May could not at first identify. It was one of the girls who worked in the seamstress's department who explained it. 'She goes to the pub, of course. Everyone knows Nan likes a drink.'

There was only one cloud on her happiness. The memory of that night in Mrs Feather's house still haunted her. Every night, when she said her prayers, she thanked God for sending Mr Freeman to save her; but even so there were many nights when she woke with a start, sweating and shivering, from a dream where she was back in that room and something unknown and terrible was about to come through the door.

Most of the other girls who worked in the shop – either on the shop floor or in the various departments making items for sale – lived in. There was a dormitory on the top floor and they took all their meals in the canteen. A few still lived at home, but both groups envied May her relative independence. The girls who lived in had to observe strict rules, up at six and in bed by ten, with very little freedom. They were supervised by a housekeeper, Mrs Stevens, who had the reputation of being a dragon. Nan's house had its drawbacks, but provided she did her work May was free to come and go as she pleased.

'Coming tonight, May?'

It was Maud, one of the apprentice seamstresses, who asked the question.

'Coming where?'

'Ain't nobody told you? Ma Stevens thinks we're going to Jenny's parents' place for a party. But we're really going to the pub.'

'A pub?'

'Yeah, the Eagle. It's a great little place. You must come.'

May shook her head. 'Oh no, I don't think so.'

'Come on! It's New Year's Eve. You can't go back to Nan's and sit there all by yourself.'

'I've never been in a pub before. Are we allowed?'

'Some of the boys are coming. The landlady won't mind as long as we've got men to escort us.'

'The boys' were the young men who worked in the menswear department, who were also accommodated in the building, though on a different floor and well separated from the girls. May had seen them in passing, but never spoken to any of them. Several other girls had gathered round and now added their encouragements, so in the end May yielded and agreed to meet them after work.

'You'll have to change your dress,' Maud said. 'You can't go out on the razz in your uniform.'

'I haven't got anything else,' May said. She had, of course, the simple print dress she had made in the workhouse, but she couldn't wear that. None of the girls knew about her early life there, or that she had been in service with the Freemans. Knowing that they would look down on her if they found out the truth, she had been forced to make up a story. In this version, her father had been a sea captain, not a simple sailor, and she had lived at home with her mother until a few months ago, when her mother had been taken ill and died. Shortly after that there had been a disastrous fire, in which she had lost almost all her possessions, and the Freemans, who had been friends of her father's, had taken her in and given her this job. 'All my decent clothes were burnt in the fire,' she explained.

'Right. We'll have to find you something. Maisie's about your size. She'll lend you something for the night.'

So it was that soon after the shop closed May found herself, arrayed in a borrowed dress and her own cape and bonnet, walking down Lime Street with four other girls and half a dozen young men. The streets were busy. Groups of people, many of them youngsters like the ones she was with, criss-crossed under the lights of the gas lamps. Some shops were still open, their windows lit with candles and gas lanterns. As they passed the Adelphi, horse-drawn cabs were pulling up, disgorging ladies and gentlemen in evening dress. May shivered with excitement. This was a world of life and colour she had never had a chance to enjoy.

The Eagle was a tiny pub, but that night it was crammed with people. Most of them were men and heads turned as the girls walked in, but no one commented. One of the boys, a good-looking, dark-haired lad called Fred, pushed his way through the crowd.

'Come on, girls. We'll go in the snug. You'll be more comfy in there.'

They huddled together on a bench against the wall and May gazed around. The ceiling was low and beamed, the plaster stained yellow by tobacco smoke, and it was hard to see across the room because of the fug, but a good fire burnt in the grate and in the gaslight faces took on a rosy glow. It was, she sought for the right word, cosy. The boys fought their way to the bar and came back with tankards of beer for themselves and glasses for the girls.

'Drink up, ladies,' Fred exhorted them. 'Here's to a happy New Year.'

May picked up her glass and took a sip. It tasted horrible! She put it down and looked round the table. The other girls seemed to be enjoying their drinks but she had no intention of trying it again. Paul, a slight, blond boy, caught her eye.

'Don't you like it?'

'Not much.'

He stood up. 'What are you thinking of, Fred? Beer's no drink for a young lady. Hold on, love. I'll get you something nicer.'

He came back with a smaller glass of pink liquid. 'Here you go! Port and lemon. That's a lady's drink.'

May sipped. He was right; it was much nicer. She took a big swallow.

Time slipped by. The other girls chattered and the boys talked to each other and laughed. Someone bought May another port and lemon. In the warmth she grew drowsy until she was jolted awake by a loud shout. 'Time, gentlemen, please! Off you go, before we have the coppers round.'

Everyone was getting up. May rose too. The room seemed to be swaying. Maud grabbed her arm. 'Come on. We've got to get back.'

Stumbling slightly, May followed the others out into the cold night air. One of the other girls was saying, 'Hurry up! If we're not back soon Ma Stevens will be on the war path.'

They all set off, almost trotting in their haste. May tried to keep up, but her legs refused to cooperate. A hand touched her shoulder.

'Come on, I'll help you along. You take my arm. I'll get you back.'

It was Paul. He drew her hand under his arm and she leaned on him, grateful for the sensation of a warm, steady presence. They walked on together, following the rest of the group. May saw Maud hanging on to Fred's arm and laughing at something he said. Then, quite suddenly, they both disappeared into a shop doorway. May hesitated, calling, 'Maud, are you all right?' but Paul squeezed her arm tighter and urged her forward.

'She'll be fine. Come along.'

As they passed the doorway May looked round and saw that the two of them were pressed against each other, faces together.

'He's kissing her!' she said, shocked.

'Well, I don't think she minds,' Paul said with a laugh. 'Don't worry about her. Fred will get her home all right.'

As they walked on May noticed two young women on the far side of the street, standing under a lamp post. They were flamboyantly dressed, with very low-cut bodices, and apparently alone.

'What are those two waiting for?' she asked.

Paul looked at her. 'You don't know?'

'No. Should I?'

He cleared his throat. 'Well, they're ... ahem ... how can I put it? They are ladies of the night. Come along. We'd better catch up with the others.'

He hurried her on, clearly embarrassed by the turn the conversation had taken and May bit her lip. She should have known, of course. The women she had glimpsed at Mrs Feather's had been dressed like that. They reached the shop and the other girls clattered down the side alley, while the boys lingered to stub out their cheroots. May stopped short.

'I don't live here.'

Paul looked down at her. 'I'd forgotten that. Where do you live?'

'With Nan Driscoll.'

'Where's that?'

'Needham Street. It's about ten minutes from here.'

'Want me to walk you home?'

May hesitated, remembering Mrs Watkins's strictures about 'walking out'. Did letting him walk her home constitute 'walking out'? And if it did, what were the likely consequences? On the other hand, the thought of walking back alone frightened her.

'Yes, if you don't mind,' she replied timidly.

''Course not. Can't let a lady walk the streets alone, at this time of night. Come on.' He took her arm again. 'Best foot forward.'

As they walked, he said, 'Do you live in Liverpool? I mean, where's home for you?'

May wriggled her shoulders. These were questions she did not want to answer. 'I s'pose it's here.'

'What about your family? Where do they live?'

'I haven't got any family. My ma and da are both dead. Well, I've got a brother but … but he's at sea. What about you? Do your family live near?'

'Over the water, in Birkenhead. Dad works in the shipyard.'

'Any brothers or sisters?'

'Yes, six of them …'

He seemed quite happy to talk about them, so she let him go on until they reached Nan's house. Just as they got there the church clock struck midnight and then all the bells in the city began to peal.

He turned to her. 'Happy New Year, May.'

'And the same to you.'

They looked at each other in silence for a moment, and May felt a sensation she had never experienced before, a quiver of the nerves that was both excitement and fear. She wondered if he was going to kiss her, and if so what she should do. Then he bent his head and kissed her very lightly on the cheek.

'Goodnight.'

'Goodnight, Paul. Thanks for walking me home.'

'It's no trouble. See you tomorrow.' He touched his hat and turned away.

It was a struggle to wake up next morning and she was late for work; but it did not matter because Nan was later still, and seemed out of sorts. Usually easy-going, she was irritable and complained of a headache; but later in the day she seemed better and apologised for snapping at May.

'Celebrated the New Year a bit too thoroughly. I ought to know better, at my age. Now, what did you do?'

May told her, guessing that she was in no position to tell her off for going to a pub.

'I hope you didn't have to walk home on your own. The streets are not safe for a girl on her own at that time of night.'

'No. One of the boys, a lad called Paul, walked me home.'

'That's good.'

In the dinner hour she found Dora and the others in the canteen, looking very crestfallen. Mrs Stevens, it turned out, was not as gullible as they had thought. She had called round at Jenny's home, on the pretext of seeing the girls home, and discovered that the family party was a fabrication. The girls had been hauled over the coals and threatened with dismissal; but to May's relief it seemed that her name had not been mentioned.

When the men came in for their dinner she looked for Paul. He came in with a group of others, and when she caught his eyes he smiled and nodded; but he did not come over to speak to her. The dinner hour was the only time in the day when there was any chance for the men and the girls to mix and there were some who always sat together, but although she looked out for him every day, Paul made no attempt to join her. After a week of so she heard in a chance conversation that he was engaged to a girl who lived on the other side of the water.

From that day onwards, as she walked back to Nan's, May began to notice other women, alone or in couples, hanging around street corners or shop doorways. She always averted her gaze and hurried on, as if by simply looking at them she might be infected with their shame. Then, one evening, she saw a single, slight figure, not brazen and garishly dressed but huddled into a dark cloak. There was something about it that seemed familiar and as she drew closer the girl lifted her face to the light of the street lamp and she knew why.

'Patty!'

The girl started, and then turned and began to hurry away down a side alley. May ran after her.

'Patty, stop! Wait! It's me, May.'

The girl stopped and swung round to face her. 'Leave me alone! Mind your own business!' The voice was husky, almost a growl.

'But Patty, what are you doing? What's happened to you?'

'Dismissed without a character, that's what.'

'Why? Why were you dismissed?'

The angry tone vanished and suddenly Patty's voice was the one May remembered, but cracking with tears. 'I took a pie from the larder. It was only a little one, left over from the gentlefolk's dinner. They said it was stealing. I was hungry, May. So hungry!'

May felt tears rising in her own throat. 'Oh, Patty, that's terrible. What can I do?'

'You? Nothing. There's nothing you can do.'

'Are you hungry now?'

'What do you think?'

May's brain was whirling. She could not leave her friend in this state, but what could she do to help? She remembered that, back at the house she had begun to think of as home, there would be a warm fire and hot food from the pie shop.

'Come with me,' she said. 'I'll get you something to eat.'

'How? Where? Back to the place you work? They won't let me in there.'

'I don't work there any longer. I'm apprenticed now and I live near here. I'll explain later. Just come with me now.'

She was pulling Patty back towards the lighted street. For a moment the other girl resisted, but then she gave way and followed May down the street to Nan's house. As they went, May's mind was in turmoil. She knew she could not just take Patty into the house. Nan was easy-going, but she would draw the line at that. But in a little while Nan would go out.

The house was at the end of a terrace and beside it an alley led to the back, where each house had a tiny garden and a shed, which had once – or in some cases still did – housed the privy. Nan's was exceptional in having installed a water closet. May led her friend to the back gate and took her through.

'Hide in there for now. It's not a privy any more and at least you'll be out of the wind. The woman I live with will go out in about an hour and then I'll come and get you. Can you wait that long?'

'Do I have a choice?' Patty reached out an icy hand and gripped May's. ''Course I'll wait. You're a good pal, May. But don't get yourself into trouble on my account.'

'Don't worry,' May said. But even as the words left her mouth she knew that she had embarked on a course of action that could lead to serious problems. She pushed the thought away. All that mattered now was to see Patty fed and warmed. 'I'll be back soon. You will wait, won't you?'

'I've said I will, haven't I?'

May hurried into the house. Nan was just unwrapping two steak pies and putting them on plates.

'Ah, there you are. You're late tonight. I was afraid the food would get cold.'

'I . . . I met an old friend. Sorry if you've been waiting.'

'No, no. I've only been in a few minutes. Here, sit down.'

She put a plate in front of May. Savoury steam rose to her nostrils and saliva welled up in her mouth. With an effort she put the plate aside.

'I'm not very hungry, Nan. Do you mind if I eat it later?'

Nan peered at her. 'You sickening for something?'

'No, I don't think so. I had a big meal at dinnertime. I'll have my pie later, if that's all right with you.'

'You do as you please,' Nan said. 'I'm not going to let mine spoil.'

'I'll put mine in the oven,' May said.

For what seemed a very long time she had to sit and watch Nan eating her pie, hoping the older woman would not hear her stomach rumbling. Eventually, Nan wiped up the last of the gravy on her plate with a piece of bread, stretched and got to her feet.

'Time for my little constitutional.'

As soon as she was sure Nan was well away, May ran down to the shed, where she found Patty shivering convulsively. She took her by the arm and led her into the kitchen, where she sank into a chair.

'Oh, it's warm! You don't know what it's like to be cold all the time. I thought I had it rough at the big house, but I know now I was in clover compared to what I've got now.'

May set the pie in front of her. 'Here you are. Get that down you.'

Patty looked up at her. 'Is this your supper?'

'No, no,' May lied. 'I've had mine. Nan always buys extra.'

Patty did not ask any further and neither of them spoke until the plate was empty. Then May could not resist asking the question that was nagging at the back of her mind. 'Patty, did you …? Have you …?'

'Done it, with a man? 'Course I have. It was that or starve. What choice did I have?'

'Where have you been living?'

'On the street, mostly. Sleeping in a doss house when I had enough pennies to pay for a bed. I'll have to get used to it, I suppose. This is nice …. ' She indicated the kitchen and her empty plate. 'But it can't last. I'll have to get back on the street soon.'

'No!' May exclaimed. 'You can't! I won't let you.'

'How you going to stop me?'

'You can stay here,' May said.

'Here?'

'Yes! You can share my bed. I'm out all day and so is Nan – she's the woman I work for. We're at the shop all day. You can stay here. Just keep quiet until you're sure she's gone and hide away in my room when she comes back – that's just after six. As long as you don't disturb anything she won't know you're here.'

'That might work for a bit,' Patty said doubtfully, 'but it can't go on for ever.'

'No, I know that. But it will give us time to think of something else. We'll have to find you a new situation.'

'How are we going to do that, when I haven't got a character?'

'There must be a way. Listen, it's late. I need to get to bed and I don't mind betting you do too. I'll think about it tomorrow.'

May had a restless night. Patty was so cold that even under the blankets she still seemed to radiate a chill that kept May awake. And if that was not enough, her mind was churning constantly over the problem of finding a permanent solution to their problem. She rose next day stiff and almost as weary as when she went to bed.

'Listen,' she whispered in Patty's ear. 'You must stay absolutely quiet until you hear Nan leave. Then you can go down to the kitchen. There will be tea in the pot still and the kettle on the hob and you can cut yourself one slice off the loaf. Nan will never notice that. Just remember, you must come back up here at six, before she gets home. I'll bring you some supper.'

Patty promised to do as she said, and May ran downstairs to grab some breakfast before leaving for the shop. It was hard to keep her mind on her work, and several times Nan reprimanded her for inattention. At dinner, she managed to hide a potato in her apron pocket and on the way home she bought two penny buns from the baker. She had not yet worked a full month, so she had not been paid the allowance Mr Freeman had promised, and the small amount of money she had saved from her previous job was all but gone. Patty was in her bedroom and gobbled up the food gratefully.

'I can't tell you how wonderful it is just to sit in a warm place and do nothing all day.'

'Is it?' May asked. 'I think I'd get bored. Now, stay quiet. I'll save some supper for you when Nan's gone out.'

This time Nan had bought fish and chips. May continued the deception that she was not hungry and forced herself to save some of the fish and most of the chips, but it was harder than the night before. It might have been pleasant to have company after Nan had gone out, but Patty seemed to be able to talk of nothing but how miserable she had been in her job at the great house, and May was on edge the whole time in case Nan came home unexpectedly. She was glad when bedtime came. That night she slept better, but she woke in the morning with an itching arm. Inspection revealed a row of small red bites and when she showed Patty she responded with, 'Oh yes. I get that all the time. Horrible, isn't it?'

The sleeve of her dress hid the bites but all day the itching nearly drove May mad and Nan wanted to know what had got into her.

'You're as fidgety as a cat on hot bricks. Sit still and get on with your work.'

For three more days May continued to save her food for her friend and struggle to hide the irritation from a growing number of bites. On the fourth day the bites had appeared on her face and there was no way of hiding them. Nan, coming into the workroom, gave a cry of horror.

'I knew you were sickening for something. It's the measles! Now we shall all have it. You need to be in the infirmary, in isolation.'

'No!' May exclaimed. 'It's not measles. They're just bites. Please don't send me to the infirmary.'

Nan came closer and scrutinised her face, then pushed up her sleeve and examined her red and swollen arm.

'Those look like bedbug bites to me. Where have you picked them up?' May could only shake her head and Nan went on, 'We'll have to check your room. It'll probably have to be fumigated. Why didn't you show me these before?'

'I ... I didn't know what it was,' May stammered. 'I'll check it when I get home this evening. Please, don't you worry about it. I'll wash all the sheets and everything.'

'Hmm.' Nan searched her face for a moment, then said, 'Well, get on with your work for now. But if you've brought those creatures in here ...'

She said nothing more and May spent the rest of the morning anxiously trying to work out how to deal with the bugs without revealing Patty's presence. Nan always went out for her midday meal, instead of eating in the canteen, and May had guessed some time ago that she went to the pub, so she thought nothing of it when she left. But when she returned to work after the dinner break Nan appeared at the door.

'Come with me, miss. Mr Freeman wants a word with you. I popped home in the dinner break and guess what I found!'

In Mr Freeman's office May found a shaking, tearful Patty.

'Oh May, I'm that sorry! I never meant to get you into trouble. I'm so sorry.'

'Never mind apologies,' Mr Freeman said. 'I want an explanation. May?'

In broken sentences May told him how she had found Patty and the lengths she had gone to keep her concealed.

'So that's why you've lost your appetite,' Nan said. 'You've been feeding her your own food.'

Mr Freeman sighed deeply. 'May, I am disappointed in you. I never thought you capable of deception. You have abused Nan's hospitality and my trust. Many employers would dismiss you on the spot.'

'Oh, please, sir, don't send me away!' May's voice broke. 'Where would I go? What would I do?'

'That is precisely why I am going to give you another chance,' Mr Freeman said. 'We have seen what lengths a young woman is forced to go to if she loses her position. I do not wish to be responsible for consigning you to that fate. You will stay, and Nan has agreed that you can continue to live with her. But the room will have to be fumigated and the bedding probably burnt, and the cost of that will come out of the money I was going to allow you. You need not expect to receive anything for several months at least.'

'Oh, I don't mind that, sir.' Tears of relief flooded May's cheeks. 'I'll do anything you ask. You've been so good to me. I never meant to do wrong by you.'

Mr Freeman's stern demeanour relaxed slightly. 'I believe you. And I understand why you felt you had to do something to save your friend; but you should have come straight to me with the problem. There are organisations that have been set up to deal with exactly this.'

He turned his attention to Patty, who was snivelling quietly.

'Which brings me to the question of what should be done with you. I do not propose to go into the rights and wrongs of why you were dismissed. If a lesson was required, I am sure you have learned it. You ought to have remembered, May, that I have been working with some gentlemen who are concerned about the fate of girls such as Patty, and I have agreed to contribute to a project they have in mind. There is a house intended for the accommodation of women who have been occupied in the trade you have been forced into. It offers a roof and regular, wholesome meals for those who are prepared to forsake the streets and learn some other way of supporting themselves.' He paused. 'I am in some doubt about the wisdom of sending you there, because you will inevitably come under the influence of women who are much more experienced in this shameful business than you are; but I trust that you will see the contrast between their way of life and what you are being offered and make the right choice. Do you have any skills to offer?'

'She was taught the same as me,' May put in before Patty could answer. 'She can clean and cook – Patty's a good cook. She always did well in those classes.'

'Would you be prepared to go into service again?' Mr Freeman asked.

Patty sniffed and nodded. 'I didn't know when I was well off. I won't make the same mistake again.'

'Very well. From time to time I learn from friends that they are seeking a girl to help in their houses. If you apply yourself and I get a good report of your conduct in the home, I might be prepared to recommend you, on a trial basis. But I need to be sure that you will not let me down.'

'I won't, sir. I swear. If I get a second chance I won't let it slip out of my hands.'

'Very well. I will take you to the home myself and I think the contribution I have made will ensure that a bed is found for you. After that, it is up to you to prove that you will live up to your promise. As to you, May,' he turned to her, 'you had better go back to the house now with Nan and see what needs to be done to cleanse your room – and I would recommend also that you pay a visit to the bathhouse. Nan will give you the money and I will recompense her. Is that agreeable to you, Nan?'

'Seems to me they are both getting off lightly,' Nan remarked. 'You should be thankful, both of you, that Mr Freeman is a man known for his philanthropy. Any other employer would have seen you both on the streets. Come along, May. We've a lot of work to do.'

Walking back to the house, May knew that she was going to have to work very hard to regain Nan's good opinion. It distressed her to think what she had lost, but she could not see what other course she might have taken. It was all very well for Mr Freeman to say she should have gone to him, but how was she to know that he would take such a generous approach to the problem? But she should have known, she told herself, remembering his kindness to her. She resolved to do all in her power to deserve the reprieve she had been given.

She was soon given the opportunity to put her resolve into action. Back at the house she was instructed to light the fire under the copper and then she had to carry all her bedding and spare clothing down to the kitchen and put it in the copper to boil. Then she and Nan carried the mattress down into the little garden and beat it energetically. While the clothes were boiling, under Nan's supervision, she pulled out the bed and the washstand and scrubbed every corner and crevice with an evil smelling liquid that Nan produced from a cupboard. That done, it was time to haul the clothes out of the copper, put them through the mangle and hang them out to dry. By the time she was finished she was as tired as she had ever been.

'Right,' Nan declared, when she was satisfied. 'Off to the bathhouse with you.'

The bathhouse was a luxury she had permitted herself on her afternoons off when she was still working under Mrs Wilkins. Since starting her new job she had not had the money to pay for it. A regular bath was something she had been used to at the workhouse, albeit under the supervision of an older woman, and she had missed it when she went into service. There, under Mrs Wilkins's orders, every Saturday night, she had filled a tin bath in the kitchen with water from the copper and then been banished to her tiny cubbyhole of a room while the cook enjoyed it. Afterwards, she had been permitted to use the now lukewarm, scummy water to wash herself. There was a zinc bath in the bathroom at Nan's, but hot water had to be heated in the kitchen and then carried upstairs, and, since moving in, May had confined her ablutions to a wash down in tepid water once a week. Now, to be allowed to wallow in steaming water was a luxury she hardly felt she deserved.

Back at the house, Nan put a steaming suet pudding in front of her. 'Now, I want to see you eat every scrap of that!

May required no second bidding.

Over the next weeks May worked doubly hard, determined to redeem herself. Nan's displeasure was short-lived and, finding May an apt pupil, she began to give her more responsibility. All the hats were made to order and the first step was to take down the client's measurements and discuss what fabric was required, whether felt or straw, and what style, perhaps a tiny bonnet to be tied under the chin with ribbons, or a high-crowned hat decorated with flowers or feathers. Was it to be worn every day, or for a special occasion? If the latter, what colour and style of dress was it to accompany? Making notes of all these facts became May's duty and increasingly the clients asked for her opinion. More and more often Nan left the actual construction of the hat in her hands and the clients were always well satisfied with the result.

Spring arrived, with a rush of new orders, and May found herself taking on increasing amounts of work. She did not mind. Creating a beautiful hat gave her enormous satisfaction and her happiness was increased when she was called into Mr Freeman's office and told that, as he had received several flattering comments about her work, she would now be given the allowance he had promised.

Towards the end of March she was called into his office again. She always went with some trepidation, afraid that someone might have had reason to complain, but he greeted her with a smile.

'May, who do you know who might be writing to you from Australia?'

'Australia?' She stared at him. 'No one, sir.'

'Well, I think this must be for you, though it's quite remarkable that it arrived safely given the brevity of the address.' He held up an envelope and read, 'May Lavender, Mr Freeman's shop, Liverpool, England.' He held it out to her. 'Here you are. See who it is from.'

May slit open the envelope and ran her eyes down the scrawled page. Then she let out a gasp. 'It's from Gus! My brother, Gus.'

He smiled. 'I thought it might be. Did you not tell me once that you thought he might have run away to sea?'

'Yes, I did. But Australia? How ever did he end up there?'

'Well, I dare say the letter will make that clear.' He got up from behind his desk. 'You will want some time to read it in peace. Stay here. I have business to attend to elsewhere in the shop, so you will not be disturbed.'

As soon as he had left the room May sank into a chair and stared at the paper in her hand. Gus, writing from Australia, after all this time. It was scarcely believable. She smoothed out the crumpled sheet and began to read.

January 22nd

Dear May,

*This is to let you know that I am safe and well and on board
the CSS* Shenandoah. *At present we are docked in Melbourne,
Australia, for repairs. I am sorry that I have not written to you
before, but this is the first port we have touched since leaving
Madeira last October. I cannot tell you what we have been
doing all that time, because it is a secret.*

*I like Melbourne very much. The sun shines every day and
I have seen plants and animals that I did not know existed –
even kangaroos which hop on their back legs and can get
along amazingly fast. The people here are very kind and I
have made friends. One of them is helping me to write this
letter. Her name is Victoria.*

*I do not know where we are going next or when I may
have a chance to get back to Liverpool but please don't
worry about me. I am doing fine. I hope you are well and the
people you work for are treating you well.*

Your brother,
Gus

May sat staring at the letter. There was so still so much
she did not understand. What did CSS stand for, and
how had Gus got to Madeira in the first place? Who
was this Victoria? It was hard to imagine her ferocious
little brother with a sweetheart. Or was she perhaps an
older woman, a motherly sort, who had taken pity on an
orphan boy? What was so secret about what he had been
doing?

When Mr Freeman came back she was still studying the letter, as if it might reveal some hidden secret.

'Well?' he asked. 'Good news, I hope?'

'Yes. Yes, he writes that he is safe and well, but I don't understand some of what he says. Please, sir, what does CSS stand for?'

'May I see the letter?' Mr Freeman asked. May handed it over and he glanced through it. 'CSS stands for Confederate States Ship, and from what I read in the papers it seems ships like that have been attacking American merchant ships and taking them as prizes.'

'Then Gus has been mixed up with fighting?'

'I don't think he will have been in any danger. The Confederate raiders are armed and the vessels they attack are not. But what will happen to them, and their crews, in the long run is more problematic. I gather the southerners are losing the war.'

May frowned, remembering the grand bazaar for which Mrs Freeman had needed a new dress. 'We are on the side of the South, aren't we?'

Mr Freeman sighed. 'Officially, we are neutral, according to the queen's proclamation. Our commercial interests dictated that we should prefer a Confederate victory, but I have to admit that, as a Christian, the idea of allying ourselves with slave owners distresses me. But the best thing for everyone concerned is that the fighting should come to an end, and it seems that that cannot be long in coming.'

'So when the war is over, Gus will be able to come home?' May said.

Mr Freeman's expression was grave. 'Certain…activities… have been seen as acceptable for belligerents in time of war;

228

but what attitudes will be when the war is over is another matter. As I understand it, what ships like the *Shenandoah* have been up to is tantamount to piracy. If they have to surrender to the Americans they may have to pay the price.'

'You mean ... prison, or ... or ...'

He laid a hand briefly on her shoulder. 'I shouldn't worry. Gus is only a boy and how he came to be on board is a matter of chance. I don't see how he could be held responsible. I'm sure the Americans will see that and send him home.'

May tried to comfort herself with that thought, but instead of relieving her vague general anxiety about her brother's whereabouts, the letter, or Mr Freeman's comments on it, had given her a much more concrete reason to worry. She had never before taken much interest in the news of what was happening in America but now she had good reason to follow developments in the conflict.

Nan regularly bought the *Liverpool Daily Post* and for the first time May made a point of reading it. Only two weeks after Gus's letter had reached her, she read that on April 9th Confederate General Robert E. Lee had surrendered to the Union General Ulysses S. Grant at somewhere called the Appomattox Courthouse. So, the war was over; but did that mean Gus would be free to come home?

A few days later there was another shocking headline: PRESIDENT ABRAHAM LINCOLN ASSASSINATED!

Ten

Gus wrapped his arms across his chest and tucked his icy hands into his armpits. He had never known it could be so cold! But the spectacle before him kept him on deck, rather than retreating to the warmth of the galley. Last night, when he had gone to bed, the ship had been enveloped in a thick fog; but he had woken to find her transformed into a fairyland. Every rope and spar was outlined in sparkling ice, and icicles feet long hung from the yards. Even the sails looked like sheets of ice. The sun, which never disappeared for more than an hour or so, hung low above the horizon and in its light everything about the ship glittered.

Voices from the quarterdeck above told him that the officers were equally enthralled and some of their comments brought home to him that for these southerners the sight of ice was even more remarkable than it was to him. He had memories of windows rimed with frost and games of snowballs in the yard at the workhouse, but he had never seen anything like this.

A shout from the lookout in the bow broke the enchantment.

'Ice, dead ahead.'

Gus went to the rail and peered forwards. Lying across their path, a few hundred yards distant, was a solid wall of ice and they were headed straight towards it.

Feet pounded the deck in response to shouts from the officer of the watch. 'Get those sails stowed. We need to get weigh off her, fast.'

Men laid hold of the icy ropes but, pull as they might, nothing moved. Blocks and lines were frozen solid and the breeze was still propelling the *Shenandoah* towards the ice. More shouts ordered the topgallant men aloft. Gus watched, holding his breath, as step by cautious step they crept upwards. He still remembered vividly how he had felt when Captain Thomas had made him climb the mast on the training ship – and that had been firmly set on the ground. Now, to see men climbing the swaying mast, when every surface was slippery with ice, seemed to him to ask almost more than human powers could accomplish. The men reached the point where the yards to which the sails were attached sprouted sideways from the mast and began to inch their way out along them. Each man carried a spanner or a wrench and with these they began to knock the ice off the frozen blocks. It took a long time and all the while the ice came closer.

At last the lines were freed and the sails stowed away against the yards, but it was too late. With a jolt and a crunch the *Shenandoah* ploughed her bow into the ice. Peering over the side, Gus saw that it was not a solid field, as it had appeared from a distance, but was made up of individual floes which jostled against each other, sending up showers of ice and debris. *Shenandoah* was no longer moving forward, but the ice threatened to encircle her. The only way out was backwards.

Captain Waddell was on deck by now and Gus heard the command to fire the boilers and get up steam. There was a wait, while everyone could hear the floes grinding against the hull, then the first smoke issued from the funnel amidships. A boat was lowered, with one of the lieutenants in charge and men armed with grappling hooks. The screw began to turn and they pushed and pulled the ice floes aside, so that they did not foul it. Inch by inch, the ship backed out of danger.

Gus, heaving a sigh of relief, retreated to the galley and the warmth of the big cooking range.

It was four months since the *Shenandoah* left Melbourne. In that time they had sailed steadily northwards through the Pacific. There had been an idyllic interlude on Ascension Island, where the king of the island had made his many wives and daughters available for the entertainment of the crew. Gus could have joined in, but the prospect still filled him with alarm. Instead, he taught himself to swim in the lagoon and saw shoals of vividly coloured fish beneath him. It seemed like paradise on earth and he wondered if perhaps his father had found himself on such an island and decided to stay there.

All too soon they were ordered back on board and the voyage resumed. From then on there had been days and weeks where they had not seen a sail and the monotony of shipboard life had begun to bite. There was much speculation among the crew about their final destination, but the general consensus was that their mission was to capture and destroy as much of the US whaling fleet as possible. That was what had brought them now to the Sea of Okhotsk, between the frozen waste of the Kamchatka peninsula and

Siberia. This much Gus had gleaned from peering at charts over Midshipman Mason's shoulder.

The near disaster in the ice field apparently made Captain Waddell decide not to pursue the whalers in the sea of Okhotsk and the ship took a more southerly course, before turning north again towards the Bering Sea. After the boredom of the long Pacific voyage, this was a land of wonders for Gus. It was almost midsummer and the sun barely dipped below the horizon. Even at midnight it hardly got dark. Mason tried to explain the phenomenon to him by the use of the globe, which stood in the wheelhouse, but even then it was hard to grasp.

He was much more excited by a cry of 'There she blows!' A plume of water rose above the surface of the sea and seconds later an enormous tail fin appeared and then smashed down with a resounding slap.

'What is it?' Gus demanded of the nearest sailor.

'That? That's a whale, lad. That's what all these ships are up here to catch.'

'How?' Gus had seen men fishing from the side of the ship and the fish they had caught. The idea that you might be able to hook a creature the size of a whale seemed ridiculous.

'Harpoon them,' his informant responded. 'You'll see. We're bound to come across one being cut.'

He was right. Their next prize had a whale lashed to its side and the crew were busy with long knives cutting the flesh into chunks. Most of the men were apparently unmoved by the sight, but it made Gus feel sick. The ship was flying the Yankee flag, which made it a legitimate target, but as they approached Captain Waddell ordered a Russian ensign to be raised on the *Shenandoah*. It was the sort of subterfuge he often employed but, although Gus could see the sense of it, he couldn't help thinking that it was not playing fair.

The crew of the whaler, suspecting nothing, allowed a party sent over in one of the ship's boats to come aboard and only realised their mistake when they were informed of the *Shenandoah*'s identity and told that they were now prisoners. A blank cartridge, fired from one of the *Shenandoah*'s guns, reinforced the message. The men were taken on board the raider and the transfer of anything of use from the captured ship began. The haul included several tanks of fresh water, a welcome bonus, since the only other way of getting drinking water was to burn their precious coal in order to distil seawater.

Once the work was complete a party was sent to spread any flammable materials around the ship and knock down bulkheads in order to create a good draft, and the vessel was then set on fire. The whale oil on board guaranteed a spectacular conflagration.

It was when the master of the captured ship and his mates were invited to join the officers in the wardroom for dinner that problems started.

'I must say I'm surprised,' the master said, 'to find you still operating in these latitudes. I understood the war was over.'

Gus, pouring wine, almost tipped it into the man's soup plate instead of his glass. There was a moment of stunned silence and then Lieutenant Whittle gave a light laugh. 'Whatever gave you that idea?'

'We touched in San Francisco, about two weeks back, and the papers were full of it. According to what I read,

Charleston and Richmond have fallen and General Lee is in full retreat.'

Gus saw glances exchanged around the table and then Lieutenant Bulloch said, 'I never believe anything I read in the papers. Most of the time it's just gossip, or downright lies.'

'Well, here's another bit of news for you, and I don't think you can call it either gossip or lies. President Lincoln has been assassinated.'

The concerted intake of breath and the repeated murmur of 'assassinated' reminded Gus of the sound of the surf on the beach on Ascension Island. Then Whittle said, 'How? Who by?'

'Shot in Ford's Theatre, in the middle of watching a play. And who by? One of your people, a fellow called Booth.'

'Not one of ours!' Whittle said. 'No man of honour would stoop to such a dastardly act.'

'Mebbe not,' the master replied. 'But he was a southerner, that's for sure.'

Later that night, Gus, on his way to his hammock, saw that Mason was on watch on the quarterdeck. 'Sir?' he said, craning his neck to look up at him. 'Do you think the South is really beaten?'

Mason did not answer at once. Then he said, 'If there is any truth in the report, it is a bad day for our cause. But I refuse to believe it is lost.'

Over the next days the rumour spread that the civil war was over, and an atmosphere of unease permeated the ship. Gus heard low-voiced conversations and the import of them all was the same. 'If it is over, where does that leave us? We've been operating outside the law since the peace was signed.'

Their next prize was a ship called the *Susan Abigail*, and when Captain Waddell had interviewed the master he appeared in the wardroom with a beaming smile.

'There we are, gentlemen. I told you those stories were exaggerated. Captain Redfield has brought newspapers with him that he picked up in San Francisco as recently as April 17th. Lee has not been defeated. There has been a setback, admittedly, but he has retreated to North Carolina and swears to continue the fight.'

The announcement was greeted with a cheer, but Gus could see that a shadow of doubt still hung over some faces. Whether the captain believed it or not, he was obviously determined to add to his tally of prizes. In the next few days the crew of the *Shenandoah* boarded and burnt seven more whaling ships.

'At this rate,' Lieutenant Whittle said, rubbing his hands, 'the Yankees won't have a whaling fleet left.'

A week later they heard the welcome shout from the lookout. 'A sail! Fine on the port bow.'

Officers turned out of the wardroom with spyglasses at the ready. 'Not one sail,' Bulloch said. 'I see three, four, maybe six.'

Captain Waddell was on the quarterdeck by now. 'This looks like our best haul yet! What flag are they flying?'

'Old Glory, sir,' was the reply.

'Then hoist the same. We don't want them taking fright before we get close.'

As he spoke there was a renewed flurry of activity on board the whaler and a voice hailed them.

'They think we're here to help,' Waddel said. 'We should have no problem getting on board.'

Boats were lowered and crews assembled, each under the direction of a uniformed officer.

Gus watched, longingly. It seemed to him that he always missed the really exciting parts of the action. He saw that Mason was in charge of one boat and edged over to him.

'Sir? Can I come with you, please?'

Mason hesitated a moment and then smiled. 'Why not? You can be coxswain. It's time you saw a bit of action.'

There were nine Yankee ships and the *Shenandoah* had only five whaling boats. 'Speed and secrecy,' Waddell ordered. 'The longer we can keep them in ignorance of our real purpose the better.'

The five boats shoved off, each heading for its designated target.

Mason chuckled. 'They're in for a bit of a shock when they recognise the uniform.'

From behind them came an explosion, which echoed off the ice floes surrounding them. Waddell had ordered a warning shot to be fired.

The first five whalers, taken by surprise, surrendered meekly, and their masters were ordered to take their papers to the *Shenandoah*. Of the remaining three, two raised their sails and tried to make off, but the breeze was almost non-existent and, finding themselves becalmed under the *Shenandoah*'s guns, they too submitted. Only one, the *Felicity*, furthest away and the target of Mason's boat, showed signs of resistance. Approaching, they saw that the crew and most of the officers were huddled together in the stern, while a single figure stood on the roof of the deckhouse, brandishing a pistol. With his long, unkempt hair and clothed in what looked like an assortment of animal skins, he made an intimidating sight. More alarming were the two guns, used for shooting harpoons at whales, which were now pointing directly at them.

'Come any closer,' he roared, 'and I'll blow you clean out of the water.'

'Don't be a fool, man,' Mason shouted back. 'You're outgunned, and you know it.'

'I can blow your head off and sink your little skiff, for a start,' was the response.

'Better pull back for now,' Mason said. 'Our guns won't bear at that angle.'

The crew backed water to a safe distance and heard a cry of triumph from the deck of the *Felicity*. But Gus, craning round, saw that the *Shenandoah* was already on the move.

'The captain's seen,' he called. 'He's moving up.'

In a few moments the *Shenandoah*, with the advantage of steam, was close enough to bring her guns to bear on the defiant whaler and Captain Waddell's voice boomed across the water.

'Surrender, or I'll send you to the bottom.'

'I'll see you damned first!' The wild-haired man leapt to one of his guns and pulled the trigger. There was a click, but nothing more. Swearing, he flung himself at the other, with the same effect. He raised his pistol, levelled it at Mason and fired. Once again, there was nothing but the click of metal on metal.

Mason began to laugh. 'Someone's had the sense to remove the charges. Thank God for that!'

For a moment the master of the *Felicity* dithered, then threw down his useless weapon and raised his hands. 'Sold down the river by my own crew! That's it. You win.'

They took him on board and the reason for his show of defiance immediately became clear.

'He's been on the rum,' Mason said. 'He's three sheets to the wind if ever I saw it.'

As usual each ship was ransacked for anything useful. By nightfall all had been stripped but a problem remained. There were far too many prisoners to be accommodated on the *Shenandoah*. Waddell solved it by ransoming two ships, making the masters sign an undertaking that the owners would pay to get them back and that they would say nothing about the *Shenandoah*'s current position. The prisoners were then transferred to those ships and they sailed away. Then the remaining ships were fired.

Gus, as usual, had found a position close to his mentor, Mason, and heard him say, 'It's a terrible thing, to see so many good ships go up in smoke – but you have to admit it's an unforgettable sight.'

It was true. The ships had been denuded of sails and ropes, so they drifted without direction on the currents and as the flames roared skywards every spar and yard was outlined in fire against the blue-grey of the ice.

Leaving the burning hulks of the whalers behind, the *Shenandoah* headed still further north, in search of what was rumoured to be a large fleet in the Bering Sea.

'Look at this, Gus,' Mason said one morning. 'We are now within the Arctic Circle. That's Russia on our starboard bow and Alaska to port. It's not often you can see two continents at the same time.'

The information meant little to Gus. He was much more interested in a flock of seals, basking on the ice floes that drifted past.

The ship forged onwards until they found their way blocked by what appeared to be an unbroken wall of ice, thirty feet high in places.

'She's not built for this,' Gus heard the captain say. 'I'll not risk her again in conditions like we found in the Okhotsk.'

They went about and headed south again. Gus could tell from the atmosphere in the wardroom that some of the officers were disappointed that they would not be able to add to their tally of prizes. There were even hints that they felt Waddell was too timid. But he himself was not sorry to leave the Arctic. It had been an amazing experience, and he knew that he had been luckier than most of the crew in that his job kept him in the galley, which was always warm, and the wardroom which was heated too, by a stove captured from one of their prizes; but he was tired of waking in his hammock stiff and chilled to the bone and feeling his face and hands flayed by the icy wind every time he stepped out on deck. As day followed day, the sun stood higher in the sky at midday, the weather grew warmer and everyone seemed more relaxed. The officers took to reading on deck when they were not on watch and Gus, growing bored with the unbroken routine, envied them.

Mason, seeing him hovering nearby, asked, 'What is it, Gus? Is something wrong?'

'I was just wondering what you were reading, sir. I liked that book you lent me about the *Alabama*.'

'Did you now?' Mason regarded him keenly. 'You're a bright lad, Gus. You deserve a better education than your circumstances allowed you. But I'm afraid this book would not be much use to you. It's in French.'

'Oh,' Gus said blankly.

Mason suddenly brightened. 'Tell you what. Lieutenant Chew has amassed quite a library from the ships we've taken and I think he might have something that would suit you. Do you want me to ask him?'

'Yes, please, if you don't think he'd mind.'

The next day he handed Gus a thick volume and he spent his leisure moments for some time ahead absorbed in the work of Edgar Allen Poe.

The crew, meanwhile, were not given so much chance to take it easy. Lieutenant Whittle saw this as a chance to spruce the ship up. Scaffolds were hung over the side and a fresh coat of black paint soon had the *Shenandoah*'s flanks gleaming, while decks darkened by coal dust were holy-stoned until white.

The men had their own ways of relaxing, however, and one morning the word went round that that evening there would be dancing.

Boney, hearing the news, reached into a cupboard and produced a frilly white apron. 'Here you are, Gus. You'll be needing this.'

'What on earth for?'

'You'll see.'

When evening came the men who were not on watch gathered on the main deck. Gus found a seat on an upturned barrel and settled down to watch. An accordion struck up a familiar dance tune and several of the men rose and took the floor. To Gus's amazement, those who were to act the woman's role had designated the fact by wearing at their waists either an apron or, failing that, a white handkerchief. Remembering what Boney had said, he hastily stuffed the pinny he had been given out of sight underneath him.

He had realised early on in the voyage that some of the men found consolation for the long separation from the female sex with each other. He had been shocked at first, but had come to understand that such behaviour was generally, if tacitly, tolerated. He had had several propositions himself and had responded initially with outrage and then later with a kind of resigned amusement. But this was different. This open display struck him as outrageous.

The dancing began and Gus saw that his reaction had been mistaken. There was nothing overtly sexual in the men's behaviour. It was, instead, a parody of what they had seen on any dance floor ashore. The men playing the female roles tried to ape the behaviour of ladies and put on all the feminine wiles they had observed, to hilarious effect. They minced and curtsied and fluttered their eyes, but at the same time, Gus noticed, some were quite good dancers. He looked up at the quarterdeck and saw that several of the officers were watching and that they were amused, not shocked.

The dance ended and Lofty came bounding over. 'Come on, Gus. Where's your pinny?'

'Haven't got one,' Gus mumbled.

'Yeah, you have. Boney told me. There it is! It's no good sitting on it. Come along.' He held out his hand and made a mocking bow. 'May I have the honour of this dance, ma'am?'

'I can't,' Gus protested. 'I don't know how.'

Lofty was implacable. 'I'll teach you.'

The music started again and Gus found himself pulled from his barrel and almost frogmarched onto the floor; but once there the rhythm of the music and the general air of goodwill took over and he started to try to match his steps to Lofty's.

'There you go!' Lofty cried. 'I knew you had it in you!'

He seized Gus round the waist and whirled him round and Gus began to laugh. He had never seen a real ball; had indeed hardly seen women in his strictly segregated life, so he copied the affectations of the other men and soon Lofty was laughing too.

When the dance was over another of the sailors came over and asked Gus to dance with him, but Lofty put a possessive hand on his arm.

'Oh no! This one's mine. You find your own gal.'

His response to anyone else during the course of the evening was the same.

Next morning, as Gus served breakfast in the wardroom, Mason caught his eye. 'Saw you dancing last night. You're pretty light on your feet.'

Gus felt irrationally pleased with himself.

The dancing went on for several nights and Gus found himself increasingly sought after. Occasionally Lofty made a concession and allowed one of the other men to partner him, but it was made clear that it was only for the space of one dance. Gus was relieved to find, however, that during the day he was treated no differently by any of them from before.

New rumours were circulating. The captain was not looking for any more merchant ships as prizes; instead he was going to attack San Francisco and possibly capture one of the treasure steamers which carried gold from there to the Atlantic seaboard of the United States. But as the weeks passed and they reached the same latitude as the city without altering course towards it, it became clear that if Waddell had ever intended to attack he had changed his mind. Gus was aware of growing tensions in the wardroom. Even the senior officers were kept in the dark about the captain's intentions and they resented it. Coupled with the lack of any firm news about the fate of the Confederacy, it made them uneasy and bad-tempered.

For the first time Gus began to think seriously about his own future. To begin with he had been so happy to escape from the school, and to find himself at sea, that he had not thought beyond the next day. Then there had been the excitement of taking prizes and the changing weather conditions from tropical to Antarctic and back to tropical and then to the wonders of the Arctic. There were days when he was bored, and others when he was exhausted by the heat or chilled to the marrow by the cold; but the whole ship had had such a sense of purpose, in which they were all united, that he had been swept along by it, almost without thinking. Now that sense of purpose was gone and he was beginning to think that, if the Confederate cause was really lost, they might all find themselves accused of piracy. And the punishment for that was death, was it not?

He had also had at the back of his mind the idea that one day the triumphant ship would put into port in one of those places he had heard so often mentioned – Charleston, Williamsburg. He was convinced that it must have been to ports like that that his father was bound when he was 'lost', and he had promised himself that if it was at all possible he would leave the *Shenandoah* there and start the search he had always spoken of. Now it seemed that if he was ever to reach any of those places it would be as a prisoner.

As they continued to sail south, the general conclusion was that the captain intended to round Cape Horn and take them back into the Atlantic.

'If you ask me,' Gus heard Mason say, 'he just wants to be able to say that we've circumnavigated the globe, which is more than any of the other raiders have done.'

'All I wish,' Lieutenant Chew said, 'is that we might come across another ship – not to take as a prize but just to get some firm news of how things stand at home.'

On July 24th he got his wish. They sighted a bark, the *Barracouta*, and gave chase. The ship was flying the British flag and a prize party going aboard was disappointed to discover that this was not merely a ruse to avoid being taken. Worse followed; the bark was carrying newspapers dated as recently as July 20th, which confirmed beyond doubt that the Confederates had been defeated and that their president, Jefferson Davis, and vice-president, Alexander Stephens, were prisoners of the Union government.

Gus could not help sharing the mood of despondency that gripped the ship. It was not his country that had been defeated, but he had lived with these people for almost a year and they were the nearest thing to a family he had ever known.

The first practical effect of the news came in an order from Captain Waddell. The guns were dismounted and stored away below decks and the gun ports, which had been cut into the hull nine months earlier as they sailed from Las

Desertas, were boarded over. And to further disguise her, the black funnel was painted white. By the end of the day the *Shenandoah* had been transformed from a ship of war into a harmless merchant vessel. But the same question hung over every member of her crew: 'Where, in this vast globe, are we going to find a port that will give us refuge?'

Eleven

May had been at Freeman's for almost nine months. In that time she had not only mastered the basic millinery techniques but had built up a reputation for her eye for colour and design and was beginning to acquire her own clientele.

It had started when she was assisting Nan with final adjustments, and her suggestions for a change of angle here or an added embellishment there had lifted a hat from being simply smart into the heights of the latest fashion. Nan bought magazines with drawings of the latest fashions from Paris, and May studied them avidly and saw ways of adapting them to the needs of particular clients.

Increasingly, Nan allowed her to take on the whole creation from the initial discussion with the client to the finished product. Nan herself was tending to return later and later from her dinner break and often fell asleep in her chair while May worked on her latest creation. It suited May very well and she was careful that no hint of the older woman's foibles reached the management. Mr Freeman, happy with compliments from satisfied customers, increased her salary to six pounds per annum. She spent her savings on a new wardrobe, choosing clothes that were smart without being too showy.

She had another reason for being happy with her life. One evening, when she was tidying up ready to leave, the door of her workroom opened and Patty stood there, no longer the wild-haired, pinch-faced waif she had last seen, but clean and neat and wearing the uniform provided for Freeman's staff who worked behind the scenes.

'Patty! What ... how ...?' May stared at her.

'Thought I'd give you a surprise,' Patty said with a grin.

'But I don't understand. What's happened?'

'Your Mr Freeman's only given me a job in the kitchen here, hasn't he?'

It turned out that Mr Freeman had formed the habit of visiting the Home for Fallen Women of which he had agreed to become a patron, on a fairly regular basis. There he had seen Patty progress from an inmate to someone trusted to help in the running of the place, particularly when it came to cooking. So when one of the cook's assistants in the canteen attached to the shop left to get married, he had remembered Patty and offered her the job.

'I won't let him down, I swear!' Patty said. 'I'm not going to mess up this chance.'

'Patty,' May said earnestly, 'there's just one thing. No one here knows about the workhouse. If anyone asks, say our families were friends and that is how we know each other.'

'Don't worry,' Patty responded. 'I'm not such a fool as to let on about where we grew up.'

May did not see a great deal of her. Patty lived in with the rest of the girls and during the dinner hour she was always hard at work; but on their Sunday afternoons off they explored the city together and May introduced her to some of her favourite places, beginning with St George's

Hall, whose splendour she never tired of. They went down to the pier head and watched the ferries come and go to Birkenhead, and saw the great ships gliding down the Mersey. And they went to tea rooms and indulged themselves with chocolate cakes.

One afternoon, as they watched the ships, Patty said, 'Did you ever find out what happened to that brother of yours?'

'I had a letter, back in the spring, from Australia of all places.'

'Australia? Whatever was he doing there?'

'I don't know. He said he couldn't tell me because it was a secret. But he did say he was on a Confederate ship.'

'A Confederate ship? What would that be doing in Australia?'

'Goodness knows.'

'Anyway, the war's been over for months now. Why hasn't he come home?'

'I don't know. Perhaps he can't. Perhaps he's ...' May left the sentence unfinished.

'I wonder how he got on that ship in the first place,' Patty mused.

'Well, you know he always wanted to go to sea. He had this mad idea of going to look for our dad. Maybe he thought that ship would take him to America. That was where he thought Dad might be.'

'And instead he ended up in Australia. Poor old Gus!'

'Oh, I don't know. He seemed to be enjoying himself. He liked Melbourne. Maybe he decided to stay there.'

'Yeah, well –' Patty squeezed her arm '– as long as he's happy, eh?'

One morning May was busy with a final fitting for one of her favourite customers. Mrs Breckenridge was a widow, left comfortably but not extravagantly off by her cotton-trader husband. She had no social pretensions but very good taste in clothes, and was very appreciative of May's efforts. There was a tap on the door and one of the girls who worked on the shop floor in the ladies' fashion department put her head round.

'Excuse me, madam. I'm sorry to interrupt. May, Mrs Connor McBride is here. She wants to collect her hat.'

'Today?' May queried. 'I told her it would be ready on Friday.'

'She says she needs it for some event tomorrow.'

May sighed. Mrs McBride was the very opposite of Mrs Breckenridge. She was hard to please, never satisfied with the final result, and expected her work to take precedence over everyone else's. Her husband was a wealthy tea merchant, a member of all the most exclusive clubs, and highly thought of, if his wife's account was to be believed, by the most influential burgesses of the city. She was a small, dark woman, with a flamboyant taste in dress, who tried to make up for her lack of height by wearing heeled shoes and extravagantly tall hats.

'All right, Julie. As it happens I have got the hat ready. Tell her I'll be with her in just a minute.'

Julie withdrew and May turned to Mrs Breckenridge, who was admiring the new hat in the mirror.

'Excuse me, ma'am. I think if you were to wear it slightly more angled ... like that ... do you see?'

'Of course. It makes all the difference. May, you are a clever girl.'

'Well? said a voice from behind them. 'Am I supposed to stand here waiting all day?'

Mrs McBride stood in the doorway. May turned to her.

'I'm sorry, ma'am. I'll just pack this hat away for Mrs Breckenridge to take with her. Your hat is ready.'

She turned back and started putting the hat in a hatbox, while Mrs Breckenridge was replacing her own ready to leave. Mrs McBride advanced into the room, ignoring the other woman.

'Is this what you call service? I shall have to have words with Mr Freeman. I—'

'Angel!'

Mrs McBride had been followed by a small girl about five or six years old; a girl with blonde ringlets and huge blue eyes. Despite the years that had past, May would have recognised her anywhere and was already on her knees, holding out her arms.

'Angel, it's me, May. Don't you remember? I'm so happy to see you again.'

The child looked at her uncertainly and took half a step forward, but before she was in May's arms she was roughly grasped and dragged back.

'Get up! What do you think you are doing?'

May got to her feet. 'I'm sorry, ma'am. I didn't mean to give offence. It's just that I used to look after Angel when we were ...'

'Angelina!' Mrs McBride's voice cut across hers. 'Wait outside.'

'Mama ...' the little girl looked up, her gaze full of confusion and entreaty.

'Outside, I said! Now!'

Tears welled up in the blue eyes but she backed reluctantly out of the door. Mrs McBride turned on May.

'How dare you presume acquaintance with my daughter? You have never seen her before.'

'I'm sorry,' May repeated. 'But she is so like a little mite I looked after in the—'

'That will do! I want to hear no more of your rambling. Now, where is my hat?'

'Here.' May fetched it and Mrs McBride jammed it onto her head and peered at herself in the mirror. There was another tap at the door and Julie put her head round.

'Mrs Breckenridge's son is here to collect her.'

A tall, fair-haired young man stood in the doorway, looking faintly embarrassed. May's attention was recalled to her original customer.

'Mrs Breckenridge, I'm so sorry! I didn't mean to ignore you. Here's your hat.'

Mrs McBride swung round from the mirror. 'Well, I suppose this will have to do, if it's the best you can manage. I may have to take my custom elsewhere in future.' She headed for the door, then stopped and turned around. 'But you can rest assured I shall be complaining to Mr Freeman about your overfamiliarity. My husband and he are on very good terms. They sit on several committees together. I do not think you will keep your position here much longer.'

With this final barb, she swept past the bewildered young man in the doorway and May heard her imperiously commanding, 'Angelina! Come here at once!'

Mrs Breckenridge laid a gentle hand on May's arm. 'Don't take it to heart, my dear. Mrs McBride is known for her quick temper. It's the Irish strain coming to the fore.

I'm sure Mr Freeman knows what a splendid worker he has in you.' She gave her a smile and went to the door. 'James, I'm sorry you had to wait, dear. I'm ready now.'

'That's quite all right, mama,' he responded. 'Let me carry that.' Just for a moment his eyes met May's and he smiled.

For the rest of the morning May could not get the encounter with Mrs McBride's little girl out of her mind. She was convinced that it was Angel and almost sure that the child had recognised her, before she was so abruptly banished. She remembered being told that she had been adopted by a wealthy couple and reasoned that it must be the McBrides. She wondered how they had explained Angel's background to their friends. Surely they could not have pretended that she was their natural daughter, because she had been almost two years old when she was adopted. She told herself that it was really none of her business; but the expression on Angel's face when her mother shouted at her haunted her. She was afraid of her. May was sure of that, and she couldn't bear it.

May had just returned to her workroom after the dinner break when a messenger boy appeared at the door.

'Mr Freeman wants you.'

A chill went through May's stomach. There could be only one explanation. Mrs McBride had carried out her threat.

She was glad to see that her boss was alone in the office. That meant that at least she would have the chance to put her own point of view without being overridden by that McBride harridan, as she termed her in her own mind. But Mr Freeman's expression was bleak.

'May, whatever came over you, to behave like that to one of our best customers?'

'I didn't mean to offend her, sir,' May said. 'It was just such a shock. You see, I looked after Angel when she was left at the workhouse. The poor little mite didn't know what was happening to her and we sort of ... I don't know ... we grew fond of each other. I was the only one who could get her to stop crying and eat something.'

Mr Freeman shook his head. 'That's a very touching story, but it can't possibly refer to the McBride's child. I understand that she is the daughter of Mr McBride's sister-in-law, who lived in Ireland and sadly died when Angelina was less than two years old. The McBrides adopted her and brought her to live with them here.'

'That may be what they want people to think,' May said, shaken out of her usual deferential manner, 'but I'd know her anywhere. She doesn't even look like them. And why is she called Angelina? I gave her the name of Angel, because that's what she looked like – still does.'

Mr Freeman looked at her closely for a moment. Then he said, 'I can see that you feel strongly about this, so I will excuse your behaviour to me. But I'm afraid Mrs McBride will not be so easily mollified. Does it not occur to you that a family like that, with a position in society here, would not wish people to know that their adopted daughter was a doorstep baby, left at the workhouse for reasons we can only guess at?'

May lowered her eyes. 'I'm, sorry, sir. I meant no disrespect, to you or Mrs McBride. I was taken by surprise, that's all.'

'I understand that, but apologising to me is not going to be sufficient. Mrs McBride wants you dismissed.'

'Oh no, please sir!' May begged. 'Don't send me away. I love my work here and I'm good at it. You know that.'

'I do know it. But the McBrides are among my best customers, and they have a lot of influential friends. I can't afford to let them ruin the reputation of the business.'

'What can I do?' May asked, swallowing back tears. I'll do anything. Please, sir, don't sack me!'

Mr Freeman frowned and seemed undecided. 'All right. There's one chance. You can write a letter to the McBrides, apologising for any offence you may have caused and saying that you realise now that you must have been mistaken and that, of course, their daughter cannot be the child you cared for in the workhouse. I will give you the address.' He looked in a ledger on his desk and wrote something on a notepad. 'Here you are, and here is a piece of our headed notepaper and an envelope. Don't seal it, and bring it to me as soon as you have finished. I will have one of our messengers deliver it. Then we can only hope for the best.'

Back in her room May sat and stared at the blank sheet of paper. Nan was dozing in her usual chair, oblivious to what had taken place. May was glad of that. It meant that at least she didn't have to explain herself again. Her difficulty with the letter was not the need to apologise. She seemed to have been apologising for one thing or another for most of her life. It was not that she was required to lie. She had not been mistaken. Mrs McBride's adopted daughter was Angel. She was convinced of that; but she had told small lies before, to escape punishment or help a friend. That was not what stopped her from putting pen to paper. Angel was not happy; she was sure of it. The child had trusted her, and the denial seemed like treachery.

May sighed and shook herself. If she wanted to keep her job the letter had to be written. How would it help Angel if she got the sack? Nothing she could do was going to alter the position. She dipped her pen and wrote as Mr Freeman had required, signed the letter, addressed the envelope and took it back to his office. He glanced through and nodded.

'Very well. I'll see that Mrs McBride gets this at once. Meanwhile, I think for the time being it will be best if Nan deals with the customers and you keep to the back room.'

It was a slap, if not in the face, at least on the wrist. Biting her lip, May bobbed a curtsy and left. As soon as she got back to the house at the end of the day's work she went to her room and opened the box containing all the bits and pieces she had used in her life as a maid of all work. Underneath her best fancy apron she found the rag doll that Angel had left behind at the workhouse and which she had kept as a memento. She held it to her face and wept softly, unable to banish the image of those tear-filled blue eyes. That night, for the first time in many months, she took the doll to bed with her.

The next day was Saturday. May tried hard to keep her mind on her work but she kept imagining what Angel's life might be like. She remembered Isabella's unvarying regime of classes and closely supervised tea parties. She had felt sorry for her; but at least her parents were not unkind. Her mother tended to ignore her, but she had seen her father pull her onto his lap and kiss her. Perhaps Mr McBride did the same with Angel. Perhaps her mother was not always so short with her. Maybe, she told herself, Angel really had the wonderful life she had always imagined for her; but try as she might she could not convince herself. On her work table there was still the scrap of paper on which Mr Freeman had written the McBride's address and May's eyes kept returning to it: 14, Devonshire Road, Toxteth. If only she could go there and catch a glimpse of Angel. She would know then if her imagination was running away with her.

That night she told Patty that she was feeling unwell and planned to stay at home next day instead of going out after church as they usually did. As soon as the service was over she slipped away from the others and caught an omnibus to Princes Road in Toxteth. She had never been this far from the city centre and it might have been a foreign country. As the omnibus rattled along with Princes Road on one side and Princes Avenue on the other, she gazed in wonder at the terraces of grand houses with their gables and towers. She had thought Rodney Street was fine, but this, she realised, was where the really rich people lived. She got off the omnibus towards the end of the avenue and asked a nursemaid pushing a perambulator for directions. Turning into Devonshire Road she found herself in an even more breathtaking area. Here many of the houses were not in terraces but stood alone, their frontages covered in white stucco with pillared porches and bay windows. No. 14 was no exception. May strolled past, staring into the windows, but all she could see was her own distant reflection. This was stupid, she told herself. All she had learned was that Angel lived in a grand house. What went on inside she had no way of finding out.

She walked back, turning over various ploys in her mind. She could go to the service entrance and pretend she was looking for work. But suppose there was actually a job on offer? She would have to give her name and be asked for her references. She wondered if any of the staff had the afternoon off. If she could somehow get into conversation with a chambermaid or a ladies' maid ... As she was racking her brains she saw the front door open and a nursemaid in a smart uniform came out, leading Angel by the hand. May caught her breath, and then forced herself to turn her back. If Angel recognised her, the nursemaid would almost certainly take her back into the house and report the incident to her mistress. She reminded herself that all she intended to do was watch and try to make out if the little girl was happy.

The pair were walking away from her, back towards Princes Road. May followed, keeping her distance. A few houses further along they were joined by another nursemaid with two more little girls, one about Angel's age and one a little older. At the junction they turned right and crossed the broad avenue towards an imposing gateway, beyond which May could see tall trees in their golden autumn plumage. To her amazement, the little party walked straight in through the gates. Surely, May reasoned, this must be the private estate of some great aristocrat and anyone not invited in would be trespassing. But the two nursemaids and their charges were not the only ones going in. Four ladies and gentlemen out for a Sunday afternoon stroll followed; a boy bowling a hoop ran ahead of his mother and two more appeared carrying model yachts.

Emboldened, May followed in their wake. Inside was a landscape she had never expected to see outside the pictures in a storybook. There were gravel walks between flower beds still bright with the last blooms of summer and glossy-leaved shrubs and more different kinds of trees than she had ever known existed, some still green, others the colour of firelight, red and amber and gold. Further on she caught the glimmer of sunlight on water and found herself skirting a lake, where the colours were reflected. She was so enchanted by the sights that opened up before her that she almost forgot the purpose of her expedition, but the two nursemaids and their charges were still ahead of her.

They came to a place where there were benches and sat down. One of them produced a ball and the children began throwing it to each other, but none of them could catch and they soon tired of the game and began to play hide and seek among the shrubs. The two nursemaids were absorbed in conversation and paid little attention. May saw the chance she had been hoping for. In her bag she had the rag doll. She took it out and slipped in among the bushes, waiting for a chance to catch Angel on her own. It was not long before the little girl, seeking a hiding place, strayed close to where she crouched, half hidden by the branches of an evergreen.

'Angel! Over here!' May spoke in a voice just above a whisper.

The child stopped and looked around, puzzled.

'Angel, it's me, May. Do you remember?' She held out the rag doll. 'Look what I've got. It's Raggy. You used to love Raggy.'

Slowly Angel moved closer, a finger in her mouth, eyes wide.

'Here you are,' May encouraged her. 'You can have her.'

Angel stretched out a hand and at that moment a voice, sharp with anxiety, called, 'Angelina, where are you? Come back here.'

The child snatched the doll from May's hand, turned and ran back to her nurse. May straightened up slowly, aware suddenly that she had done something very foolish. She could hear the nurse questioning Angel, but not the child's replies. 'Who? Where? What lady? Did you find it? Where did you find it? Give it to me,' and then a scream of protest that went on and on and would not be silenced. 'Oh, very well! Keep it then. Only stop your noise. Come along, we're going home.'

May waited until the sound of their voices had died away and then she stepped out of her hiding place and made her way back to the omnibus stop.

She had hardly set foot in Freeman's Ladies Fashions next morning before she was ordered to go to her employer's office. This time Mr Freeman was not alone. Mrs McBride was standing between his desk and the door and as soon as May entered she let loose a diatribe.

'How dare you? How dare you spy on my daughter and frighten her? What gives you the right to meddle in the affairs of my family? And what possessed you to give her that filthy doll? Do you think a child of mine does not have a hundred better, more suitable toys? You wrote me a letter of apology, saying you accepted that Angelina was not the child you mistook her for – but you lied. You are impertinent, disobedient and thoroughly untrustworthy. Well, what do you have to say for yourself?'

May hung her head but anger was slowly boiling up inside her. What right had this woman to speak to her like that? What had she done that was so wrong? She looked up and met the older woman's gaze squarely.

'I'm not the one who is lying. You know quite well that Angel is the baby I cared for in the workhouse. You just don't want your friends to know where she came from. I loved that little mite. She was left on the doorstep with nothing except that rag doll and it meant the world to her. It was left behind when you ... when you took her away, so I kept it as a memento. I didn't intend any harm to her. I just wanted to give it back to her. I can see now that she has got a wonderful life and a beautiful home and I'm glad for her. I don't want to spoil anything for her, and if you want to keep it a secret where she came from that's your business. I will never tell anyone. I'll swear it if you want me to. I just ...' Her anger was ebbing and being replaced by misery. 'I just wanted to see that she was happy ...'

Tears stopped her voice and she turned an appealing gaze to Mr Freeman. His expression was grave but she saw signs that her words had made an impression. Not so with Mrs McBride. She swung round to face him, her lips drawn into a thin line.

'I don't want to hear any more excuses. I have given you my ultimatum. Either this girl goes, or neither I nor any of my family will ever set foot in your shop again. And we have influence in this city. Bear that in mind.'

Mr Freeman looked from her to May and slowly shook his head. 'If that is your last word ... I'm sorry, May. I must give you a week's notice. You can go.'

May looked from him to Mrs McBride, her vision blurred with tears. She wanted to appeal, to beg for a reprieve, but she saw that it would be useless. She turned away and stumbled blindly out of the room.

Back in the workroom she found Nan setting up for the day's orders. She took one look at May's face and put her arms round her.

'Why, love, whatever's happened? Tell me.'

In broken sentences May sobbed out the whole story. Nan patted her shoulder and sat her down.

'Don't take on so. This isn't the end of the story. You're the best little milliner in Liverpool, though I says it as shouldn't, and Mr Freeman knows that. He won't want to lose you.'

'But he can't afford to lose Mrs McBride's custom. He can't afford the damage to the shop's reputation. I can understand that. Oh, I wish I hadn't been such a fool!'

'Well, you've certainly blotted your copybook as far as he's concerned, but he's not stupid. He knows you bring custom into the shop. It's a question of weighing up profit and loss. Now, dry your eyes and get down to work. Leave things to me. Trust me, it is going to be all right.'

Two days later May was dispiritedly stitching a bunch of artificial flowers when Julie looked in.

'You're wanted in the fitting room.'

'Me?'

'Yes, you. Mrs Breckenridge wants a new hat.'

'Mrs Breckenridge? She only had one last week.'

'Well, a lady's allowed more than one hat, isn't she? Go on, you'd better get up there.'

'I'm not allowed. Get Nan to deal with her.'

'Nan's with her now, but she doesn't want Nan, she wants you. Hurry up! Mustn't keep a customer waiting.'

As soon as May entered the room Mrs Breckenridge came to her and took her rough, reddened hand between her own kid-glove-covered ones.

'You poor dear, you look as if you haven't slept all night.'

May made an effort to pull herself together. 'I'm sorry, ma'am. I'm ... I'm not very well, that's all. Now, what can I do for you? Is that hat not satisfactory?'

'It's perfect, as you well know. I'm not here to order a hat. I know a bit about what is going on. I was here, you remember, when there was that nasty little scene with Mrs McBride.'

'Oh, that ...' May murmured.

'Yes, that. To be honest with you, I've never believed the story that that beautiful child is the offspring of Connor McBride's brother's wife. I don't believe there's a drop of McBride blood in her veins. But that's beside the point. I don't know where you've seen her before, and I don't want to know. But I don't want to lose the only girl who makes hats that don't make my face look like a potato. So, I've written to Mr Freeman ...'

'Oh, that is so kind of you,' May exclaimed, 'but I really don't think he will change his mind.'

'Wait. I haven't finished yet.' Mrs Breckenridge fished in her bag and brought out an envelope. She extracted a sheet of notepaper and held it out to May. 'I knew Mr Freeman wouldn't be worried about losing my custom, so I called on several of my friends, people I know you have made hats for, and they have all signed.'

May glanced down the list of signatures and recognised several who, she knew, were very well-off ladies who were regular patrons.

'What do you think?' Mrs Breckenridge took back the letter and replaced it in the envelope. 'I'm going to take it to Mr Freeman in person, so he can see how well valued you are.'

May scanned her homely face. 'It's really good of you to take so much trouble, ma'am. But I don't know if it will work. I don't think Mr Freeman likes going back on his word.'

'Mr Freeman knows which side his bread's buttered.' Nan had listened to the conversation until then without comment. 'I told you, it's a matter of weighing up profit and loss.'

May looked from one woman to the other and felt her spirits lifting. 'Do you think so? Oh, Mrs Breckenridge, I can't tell you how grateful I am! What a clever idea!'

Mrs Breckenridge responded with a smile. 'Ah, well, I can't really claim the credit. It was my son, James, who suggested it. He's a very clever boy. He's an articled clerk to a solicitor, you know, hoping to qualify for the law himself one day. He was here, if you remember, that first day? He took quite a dislike to Mrs McBride and when I told him what Nan told me, he reckoned you were badly treated and he wanted to help. So he came up with this idea. Now, I must get on. I want to get this letter to Mr Freeman as soon as I can. And don't worry, dear. I'm sure he will see our point of view.'

The expected summons came an hour later. May stood just inside the door, her eyes meekly lowered but there was such a long silence that finally she looked up. Mr Freeman was studying her and she thought she caught a fleeting smile.

'Well, May. It seems you have more loyal customers than I realised.'

'People are very kind, sir.'

'Hmm. So I have a choice. Keep you, and lose one valued customer, or lose you and lose a dozen others. There appears to be only one sensible answer.' May searched his face, poised between hope and doubt. He wagged a finger at her. 'But no more escapades like last Sunday. Promise me.'

'I promise, sir. I'm really sorry I caused you all this trouble. It won't happen again, I swear.'

Mr Freeman raised an eyebrow. 'I seem to have heard that before, somewhere. All right. You have one last chance – and don't think that you are so valuable that you can get away with anything. There are limits to my patience. All right, off you go, back to work.'

'Oh, sir, thank you. Thank you so much!'

Mr Freeman had risen and moved to the door. 'I have a meeting to attend. Just remember, no more excuses.'

May followed him and felt a sudden rush of gratitude and affection. 'Please, sir, can I give you a kiss?' The words were out before she had a chance to think.

He stopped, with his hand on the door handle, and looked down at her. 'Between employer and employee, that would be completely irregular.' But he bent his head and allowed her to plant a kiss on his cheek. Then he opened the door and went out and May, dizzy with relief, made her way back to her workroom.

October gave way to November, and the streets rang to the cry of 'Penny for the guy!' The fifth was a Sunday and May joined Patty and a group of young men and girls from the shop to watch the procession and the fireworks along the dock road. As they waited they became aware of some excitement on the river frontage, which did not seem to be connected to the Guy Fawkes celebrations. Moving closer, they found a small crowd surrounding the crew of a tug that had just tied up at the pier.

'What's going on?' Patty asked a bystander.

'They say there's a ship in the offing flying the Confederate flag. Seems she's stuck on the sandbar. Won't be able to get off until the tide turns.'

'Can't be a Confederate ship,' someone said. 'They must have all surrendered months ago.'

Patty looked at May. 'What was the name of the ship Gus was on? Do you remember?'

'No, I ... wait a mo. Sh ... Shen something.'

'*Shenandoah*. That's the one,' the man from the tug said. 'That's her out there in the river.'

Twelve

The fireworks had little attraction for May that night. All she could think of was that Gus might be out there on that ship, waiting for the tide to turn. When she woke next morning her first impulse was to head down to the river to see if the ship had come in; but she knew that she must go to work as usual. She had come close to being dismissed and she could not afford to take any chances.

As soon as she had finished for the day she hurried down to the pier head. It was almost dark and there was a mist over the river, but she could just make out the outline of a slender, three-masted vessel anchored in the middle of the flood, astern of a British warship, which had been in the port for some weeks.

A policeman was on duty on the pier. May approached him timidly.

'Excuse me, sir. Can you tell me if any of the crew of that ship have come ashore yet?'

'That Confederate ship? No, and they're not likely to for a while yet. Sweetheart of yours on board, is there?'

'No. But I think my brother might be.'

'Brother, eh? He'll be an Englishman then.'

'Yes, of course.'

'In that case I wouldn't reckon on seeing him for a good long while.'

May felt a chill run through her nerves. 'Why not?'

'Broken the law, hasn't he? British citizens were expressly forbidden to sign up with either side in the American war.'

'But he didn't sign up!' May protested. 'At least, I don't think so. I think he stowed away.'

'Stowaway or not,' the policeman answered stolidly, 'he's been on board a privateer attacking harmless merchant ships. If you ask me, they are all no better than pirates, and deserve to be treated as such.'

The sound of marching feet behind her made May draw back into the shadows. As if to confirm the policeman's opinion, a detachment of Royal Marines embarked on a small boat, which transported them to the *Shenandoah*. The men on board were now, it seemed to her, prisoners on their own ship. Despondently, she turned away and plodded homewards.

When she went down to the docks the next evening there had been no change in the situation. Another British warship was now made fast alongside the *Shenandoah*, just in case, she supposed, the captain changed his mind and tried to head out to sea.

On Wednesday the shop closed at midday and all the staff had a half-day off. This was an innovation introduced by Mr Freeman six months earlier and it was regarded by other businessmen as tantamount to commercial suicide; but it was the envy of all other shop workers in the city. As soon as the midday meal was over, May joined Patty and a group of others and headed down to the dockside. The first thing she noticed was that a small flotilla of tugs and yachts and other craft were circling the *Shenandoah*, packed with sightseers all craning their necks to get a glimpse of the crew.

'Do you think we could get on one of those boats?' she asked Patty.

'Not a chance. They are full of ladies and gentlemen. They aren't interested in the likes of us.'

After a while the sightseeing boats returned to shore and for some time it seemed nothing else was going to happen. Then they saw a customs boat go out to the ship and several men in uniform climbed aboard. A tug followed and went alongside.

'Maybe they are going to let them come ashore now,' May said.

'Or maybe they are all going to be arrested,' one of the young men in the group added.

* * *

Gus stood on the deck of the *Shenandoah*, crowded with the rest of the crew onto the starboard side. Up on the quarter-deck he could see all the officers, together with a stranger in naval uniform. They had existed in a kind of limbo for the last two days. First there had been rumours that they were all going to be allowed ashore. Then these had been dispelled and the marines had come aboard. From that time on they had been relieved of all duties and there had been nothing to do but sit around and speculate about the future.

'You'll be all right,' Lofty had said. 'This is your home port. You'll have a home to go to.'

Gus shook his head. 'I've got no home, except the workhouse where I grew up.' But the exchange prompted another, terrifying thought. What if the people from the Industrial School were still looking for him? Could he be forcible dragged back there, to face whatever punishment the governor chose to inflict on him?

There had been one bright spot in the gloom. Fresh provisions had been sent out to the ship and for the first time in months Gus tasted meat that was not salted and fresh vegetables. But it did little to allay his fears for the future.

There was an emotional moment when the Confederate flag was lowered for the last time. Gus saw it carefully folded and handed to Lieutenant Whittle and he was almost sure he saw tears in Whittle's eyes as he turned and handed it ceremonially to Captain Waddell.

Now Lieutenant Whittle stood forward and raised his voice. 'Men, the authorities require to know what nationality each of you belongs to. I shall call your names one by one and when you hear that you must step forward and answer the question which Captain Painter here will put to you.'

He called the first name and a man stepped forward.

'What is your nationality?' Painter asked.

'American, sir. Born in the Confederate state of Texas.'

'The Confederacy no longer exists, as I am sure you know. Whether you were born north or south of the Mason Dixon line is irrelevant. You are an American. Stand over there.'

He indicated the port side of the deck and the man moved over. The next name was called and this man affirmed his American nationality and was sent to join the first. The same thing happened with the next and the next, until a name was called that belonged to a man Gus knew to be English, one who had been on board the *Laurel* and had then signed up to ship on the *Shenandoah*. To Gus's surprise, when asked the question he, too, replied that he was an American.

'He's lying!' Gus muttered to Boney who stood next to him. 'He's as English as I am.'

Boney looked at him. 'If you've any sense you'll forget that. For present purposes you're American.'

'I don't understand,' Gus said.

'Do you want to spend the next ten years in an English jail? The Americans are belligerents in someone else's war, so the British authorities have no jurisdiction over them. But we broke the law when we signed up. Get it?'

'I suppose so,' Gus murmured uneasily.

The roll-call continued. Amongst the polyglot crew, those who belonged to other nationalities admitted it and were sent to join the Americans. The English, the Scots and the Irish, in a variety of accents, all claimed American citizenship. When Gus's name was called, Boney grabbed him by the ear.

'You are an American, born and bred in South Carolina if anyone asks. Go!'

Gus's knees were shaking so hard as he stood before Captain Painter that he felt sure his lie would be detected, but the captain merely sighed wearily and waved him over to the port side with the others.

By the time the roll-call was complete the entire crew had moved from one side of the ship to the other. Gus saw Painter exchange looks with Captain Waddell, who merely raised his eyebrows and shrugged. For a few seconds Painter seemed to hesitate, then he shook his head and shrugged in his turn.

'Very well. You are all free to disembark. The ferry alongside will take you ashore.'

There was a muted cheer and men turned away to pick up their dunnage and head for the tug alongside.

* * *

'Oh, come on, May!' Patty's tone was exasperated. 'There's no point in hanging around here all afternoon. Nothing's happening.'

'No, wait!' May was straining her eyes through the gathering mist. 'Something is happening. I can see men climbing down into that tugboat.'

There was a tense wait while the tug filled up and then cast off and headed for the Albert Pier. Finally, it was made fast and the men on board began to file up the gangplank, carrying their bags and shouldering sea chests. A small crowd had gathered to watch and May had to dodge between the bodies to see their faces. One after another they passed and headed away along the dock and she began to believe that Gus had not been on board after all. Then she saw a bright ginger head coming towards her. For a moment she was gripped by uncertainty. Could that be Gus? He was so much taller, his shoulders were broader; even the way he walked was different. This was not the scrawny, defensive boy she remembered. He was almost past before she found her voice.

'Gus!'

He checked his stride and glanced round, looking for the source of the voice.

'Gus, it's me! May! Over here!'

His eyes found her and for a second he stood still, staring. Then he broke away from the column of men and came towards her. She hurried to meet him, but an arm's length apart they both came to a standstill, unable to find words.

'I didn't expect you to be so tall,' she managed eventually.

She saw his Adam's apple work as he swallowed. 'I didn't expect you to be so pretty.'

'Oh, Gus!' She stepped forward and put her arms round him and stretched up to kiss his cheek. He had to bend his head for her to reach, but he let her do it, something he would never have tolerated before he went away. 'I'm so glad to see you! I've thought about you such a lot, and wondered where you were.'

'Did you get my letter?'

'Yes, I did – and thank you for writing. But that was such a long time ago. I didn't know what had happened to you since.'

'Hello, Gus. Remember me?' Patty could not wait to be included in the conversation.

He looked past May and frowned.

'May and me were friends, back at the workhouse. Remember?'

'Oh, aye. How do?' he said, though May could see that he did not remember.

Three of the young men from the shop had come down to the pier with them and they now crowded forward.

'This your brother, then, May?'

'Introduce us, won't you?'

May turned to them. She wished they would all go away and leave her to talk to Gus, but good manners required otherwise. 'Gus, this is Jimmy and this is Paul and the other one is Alfie. This is my brother, Gus.'

He regarded the men suspiciously. 'Who are these then?'

'They all work at the store.'

'What store?'

'Freeman's. Oh, I'll explain later. That's where I work too.'

'You're not in service any more?'

'No. Not for nearly a year.' She looked around. 'There's so much to tell you and so much to ask, but we can't do it standing here in the street. Where can we go?'

'Pub?' he suggested.

'Oh, I don't know. I don't go into pubs often. A tea room?'

'Tea room? What's a tea room when it's at home.'

'Somewhere you can have a cup of tea and a cake.' She looked him up and down. 'No, perhaps not.'

'Tell you what,' Jimmy put in. 'How about the Baltic Fleet? It's only just across the street and they won't mind a couple of ladies as long as you're with us.'

'Do you think so? All right, then.' She looked at her brother. 'All right with you, Gus?'

He was shifting uneasily from foot to foot and looking at the disappearing backs of his fellow crew members. 'S'pose so. But if I lose the others I won't have anywhere to sleep tonight – less you can put me up.'

'Oh, Gus, I wish I could. But I only have a little room in someone else's house.'

'Are the rest of them heading for the Sailors' Home?' Paul asked.

'That's what they said.'

'We can show you where that is later, if you like.'

'I dunno. They may not have a bed left for me if I wait too long.'

'Couldn't one of your mates keep a place for you?'

'I s'pose they might. Tell you what. I'll run and catch them up and ask.'

'Yes, do that!' May said. 'But you will come back, won't you? We'll wait here.'

'Drinks are on me,' Paul said. 'That good enough?'

Gus gave a sudden grin. 'Hang on. I'll be back.'

They watched him sprint away, on a slightly erratic course.

'Is he drunk?' Patty asked.

'Hasn't got his land legs yet,' Alfie said. 'My da used to be like that when he came home from a long voyage.'

May saw Gus catch up with the others and speak urgently to a very tall man. Then he turned and trotted back.

'Lofty'll see there's a bed for me. Let's go.'

The Baltic Fleet was a handsome, whitewashed building facing onto the docks. It had only been built a few years earlier and inside they found wooden settles and scrubbed deal tables set around roaring fires. As they seated themselves in a quiet corner, Alfie said, 'This place used to be called Turner's Vaults. My da told me you had to watch yourself drinking here, 'cos it was a favourite place for the press gang to hang out. Not any more, of course.'

Paul and Jimmy came over with pints of beer for the men and a port and lemon each for May and Patty. May sighed.

She would have much preferred to talk to Gus alone, but she did not see how it could be managed.

'Now,' Jimmy said, 'tell us all about it. How come you ended up on a Confederate ship in the first place.'

Finding himself the centre of attention, Gus was embarrassed at first and the story came out in broken sentences; but as he went on he was encouraged by his audience's eager attention and began to relax. Without explaining his reasons, he told them he had always wanted to go to sea and had stowed away on the *Laurel*, only to be forced to choose between returning to Liverpool and shipping on the *Shenandoah*, and how the ship had been converted from a merchantman to a warship.

'But what for?' May asked.

Gus paused a moment. 'Well, we was all sworn to secrecy; but it's all over now so I guess I can tell you.' He went on to describe how Yankee ships had been stopped and stripped of their cargoes and then burnt to the waterline. 'But we never harmed any of the people on board,' he added. 'No one was ever killed. We took them prisoner, and then when there were more than we could keep on board they were put off on one of the ships we captured and sent to the nearest port. That is ...' He stopped, remembering the tricing up of recalcitrant recruits. 'That is except the men who agreed to sign up as crew.'

'I know you went to Australia, because you wrote to me from Melbourne,' May said. 'Where did you go after that?'

'All the way to the Arctic Circle,' he replied, suddenly aware of the vast scope of his experience. 'We were after the Yankee whaling fleet.'

'Did you see whales?'

'Oh yes. And seals, sitting on ice floes like they was a feather bed. I seen dolphins and albatrosses and flying fish – not all in the same place, or course. And in Melbourne I saw kangaroos and little furry bears they call koalas.'

'You are so lucky!' Patty said. 'I wish I could go to sea.'

He shook his head. 'It's not all it's cracked up to be. Days and days you don't see anything except the sea. Sometimes you're so hot you think you're being fried alive and then sometimes it's so cold you can't feel your fingers, or it's blowing a gale and the old ship's pitching and rolling till you're black and blue all over. I'm glad to be back on shore, I can tell you.'

'One thing I don't understand,' Paul said. 'The war has been over for months. Where have you been all this time?'

'We didn't know it was over for a long time. See, we never called in at any ports. The only time we got news was if we took a prize and they happened to have newspapers that weren't too out of date. But then, when we did get the first news, we didn't want to believe it.'

'Hold on a minute,' Jimmy put in. 'Who's this "we" you keep talking about? Anyone would think you were the captain.'

Gus dropped his eyes and flushed. 'I didn't mean it like that. But fact is, part of my job as cabin boy was to serve the officers their meals, so I got to hear them talking among themselves. They didn't want to believe the war was lost. You can understand why.'

'So what did they do, when they found out it really was over?' May asked.

'Nobody knew what to do. First thing, we stowed all the guns below and boarded up the gun ports, so we didn't look like a raider any more. After that there were all sorts of rumours and it seemed like the captain couldn't make up his mind. First we thought we was heading back to Australia. Then some of the officers were all for going to Cape Town and surrendering the ship there, but the rest wanted to come to Liverpool 'cos they didn't see how they was going to get home from Cape Town. In the end, it was Liverpool but it took months.'

'How many months?'

'It was July when we finally made sure the war was over, and it's November now.'

'And you sailed all that time without calling at another port?'

'We didn't dare put in anywhere, in case the ship was seized. But it was hard going. One time, it didn't rain for days on end and we were running out of fresh water, just a cupful a day for each man. When it did rain, you should have seen us, out on deck with every pot and jar we could find and standing there with our arms held out, just letting the rain wash through our clothes. You don't know how uncomfortable your clothes get when they're stiff with salt. Then we had storms going round the Horn and came close to being capsized by the weight of the water she was shipping. After that, coming up through the Atlantic we started to run short of food. Nothing but salt pork and biscuits full of weevils for weeks. And we were short of coal, so we couldn't make steam to get us along a bit faster. The worst of it was, because we'd used up so much of our supplies, the ship was very light. No ballast, you see. So every time the sea got up she bobbed around like a cork. I tell you, we were right glad to see Cape Clear, on the tip of Ireland, loom up out of the mist. We'd been all the way round the world, the only Confederate ship to do that – and we fired the very last shots in the war. So I guess it's something to be proud of – for the southerners, a least.'

Gus fell silent and took a gulp of beer. He was not sure whether to be proud of his sudden burst of eloquence or embarrassed by it. One thing he did know – he didn't really like beer.

'Well,' Jimmy said, 'that's quite a story. It's more excitement than any of us are likely to see in our lifetimes. Here's to you, Gus. Welcome home.'

'Yes, welcome home, Gus,' May said softly. 'I'm so proud of you.'

He looked at her. 'Proud? I don't know why. I haven't done anything special.'

Her response was drowned in a gale of laughter.

The men began an animated discussion of the rights and wrongs of the southerners' cause and under cover of that Gus turned to his sister.

'You haven't told me what you've been up to. How come you're not in service any more? What's this store you were talking about?'

As briefly as possible May told him about Mr Freeman's offer of an apprenticeship and the different direction it had given to her life, omitting to mention that twice she'd nearly lost her job.

'You're doing all right, then,' he commented when she finished.

'Yes, I've been lucky. But what about you? What will you do now? Will you go back to sea?'

He shook his head. 'Not if I can help it. I've had enough of that life.'

'And you've given up that silly idea of looking for our dad?'

He gave a rueful shrug. 'I've seen how big the world is – and how dangerous the sea is. If he is out there somewhere the chances of finding one man are so small. "Lost at sea" means just that – lost. Dead or alive makes no difference.'

'So what will you do?'

'Dunno. I expect something will turn up.'

* * *

Gus woke early next morning, disturbed by the unfamiliar stability of his narrow bed. He looked along the line of beds in the dormitory of the Sailors' Home and saw that no one else was stirring.

He stretched and put his hands behind his head and lay looking up at the cracks in the ceiling. He was in a situation that he had never experienced before. All his life, from his childhood in the workhouse, through his time at the Industrial School and then on board the *Shenandoah*, his time and energies had been directed by some higher authority. Now he was a completely free agent, and he had no idea how to employ his liberty. He needed to find a job. That was obvious. But how did one go about it?

Over breakfast of thin porridge and dry bread he listened to the others discussing the same problem. They all had money in their pockets for the time being, having been paid off by the purser aboard the *Shenandoah* before she docked, though the amount had been less than they were due. It seemed that there was simply not enough cash on board to pay everyone in full. There had been vague promises that the sum would be made up in due course, but no one set much store by that. It was clear that all of them would have to find work soon.

The Americans were all keen to sign on with a new ship; but there was disagreement about its destination. Most of them were anxious to discover how family and friends had fared after the defeat of the South, but many were worried that if they set foot on American soil they might be arrested and accused of piracy. Better, they suggested, to find a ship that was headed for China, or South America. Other members of the polyglot crew were eager to find ships heading for their own countries, or simply to get taken on by anyone who would give them a job.

Among the British, some had homes and families to return to in different parts of the country. Others, like Boney, had made seafaring their life and just wanted a berth in a new ship. That left four of them, including Gus, who had no homes to go to but were determined not to go back to sea.

'Snowy' White was a lean, agile man in middle age with muscles like whipcord. Pete Peterson was broad of shoulder and slow of speech, an ox of a man. Mick Macgregor was the nearest to Gus in age with a mop of blond hair and a cherubic expression that hid a fiery temper.

'There's always work on the docks,' Snowy said.

'Yeah, if you happen to have a mate who's a gangmaster,' Pete agreed. 'Otherwise you can stand at the dock gate every day and not get taken on. I know. I tried it before I signed up to my first ship.'

'It's worth a try,' Mick said. 'What else are we going to do?'

They agreed that the four of them would scour the docks that day to find out where ships were expected which would require unloading, and which others were ready to be loaded with a new cargo. By evening, they had located three possibilities and it was agreed that they would each take one, with Gus, who had no experience, joining Pete.

That settled, they proposed to spend the rest of the evening in the pub. Gus declined, using the excuse that he had promised to meet his sister. It was true. They had agreed that he would wait for her outside Freeman's when she finished work; but he was glad of the excuse. He had never forgotten his experience in Melbourne and had no wish to repeat it.

He found Freeman's without difficulty. The store now occupied three adjacent shops on Lime Street and the windows, brightly lit by gas lamps and full of all sorts of merchandise, were a welcome splash of colour in the growing gloom.

Gus stood outside, waiting for May to appear, and looked around him. To the left was the great bulk of St George's Hall on its raised platform and in front of it the broad expanse of the street was busy with carriages and carts and well-dressed ladies and gentlemen. It occurred to him that, although he had grown up in the city, he had never seen its heart. His image was of narrow, filthy alleyways or the tall, light-excluding walls of the workhouse. He experienced a sense of loss and growing anger. All this had been here but he had been shut away and excluded from it, through no fault of his own.

Voices behind him broke into his thoughts. A door had opened down a side street and a crowd of men and women issued from it, all in the dark-blue uniform of Freeman's employees. They streamed past him, calling goodnights, heading for omnibus stops or down to the pier head for the ferry, going home. He imagined them arriving at neat houses where a warm fire and a smell of cooking waited; where their families would welcome them – a mother, perhaps, or a wife. The sense of loss grew stronger. This, too, was something he had never known.

'Gus! I'm sorry. Have you been waiting long?'

May was hurrying up the street towards him. She was wearing her blue Freeman's skirt but over it she had a warm, well-fitting coat and on her head was a little hat with a feather.

She tucked her hand under his arm. 'Come on. Let's get out of the cold.'

He drew back, aware of his patched and stained trousers and fraying shirt. He had grown into the clothes he had been given aboard the *Laurel* and they had been supplemented from time to time from the slop chest on board the *Shenandoah* but they were still shabby and worn. 'You don't want to be seen walking with the likes of me.'

'Whatever do you mean? You're my brother.'

'Just look at you and look at me. You're smart, a real lady. I'm just a scruff.'

'Oh, rubbish! You look like what you are, a sailor who has just come back after a long voyage. And I'm certainly no lady! Come on.'

'Where are we going?'

283

'Back to Nan's. Her name's Mrs Driscoll, but everyone calls her Nan. She's the milliner I'm apprenticed to and I have a room in her house. She's a dear soul and she's been ever so kind to me. She's longing to meet you.'

'Are you sure?'

''Course I'm sure. It's this way, only ten minutes' walk.'

'You talk different from what I remember.'

'So do you. You've got an American accent – well, a bit of one.'

'No, I mean you sound more ... more ladylike. Posh.'

'Do I?' She thought about it. 'I suppose when you mix with people who speak differently you sort of pick it up. I'm not trying to put something on, Gus. But when you deal with customers who are real ladies you can't speak to them the way we did when we were kids. They wouldn't understand, for one thing. Do you see?'

He looked down at her, aware for the first time that he was taller than she was. He remembered his first reaction on seeing her. It had been right. She was pretty. Her hair, which he remembered as a mud-coloured tangle, now shone under the gas lamps with colours that reminded him of the polished mahogany table in the wardroom, and was coiled into a complicated knot behind the little hat. Her eyes were fringed with thick lashes and her skin glowed in the chilly air. He felt a small flush of pride in the fact that she was his sister.

'You're all right,' he said. 'You done well for yourself. I'm glad.'

Nan had bought steak pies for all three of them and a bottle of porter. She was eager to hear all about Gus's adventures, so he had to tell the story again. It was pleasant to be the centre of attention, and to eat food that was not salt pork in a room that did not sway and tip with the rhythm of the waves; but as he looked around him Gus experienced the same sense of dislocation he had felt when he was waiting for May. There was a good fire in the grate, brightly coloured cushions on the chairs, rag rugs on the floor and a clutter of newspapers and books and half-finished bits of embroidery. This, he thought, was what a home looked like; and the same bitterness rose in his throat.

May was very much 'at home' here, even if it did not belong to her. She had her job, and good prospects and a life that had changed out of all recognition since they last met. And what did he have? Stories to tell. Nothing else.

As he walked back to the Sailors' Home and his narrow bed in the dormitory, he resolved not to visit Nan's again.

At first light next day he was waiting with Pete outside the dock gates where a tea clipper had tied up during the night. The gate opened and a man appeared, gazing round at the eager faces.

'Twenty men needed today,' he said, raising his voice above the clamour of appeals. 'I'll take you, and you ...'

Pete shoved himself forward. 'Hey, master! Remember me?'

The gangmaster looked round. 'Yeah, right. Good worker. All right, you're on.'

Pete pushed Gus forward. 'My mate, too?'

The master cast a brief look over Gus. 'Too small. Not strong enough. Wouldn't be up to the job.'

It was to be a refrain Gus heard repeated over the next days. The other two had also found work and, when they suggested going to the pub that evening to celebrate, Gus went with them. He found that after a shot or two of rum he could enjoy beer after all. He looked round. This was where he belonged. Not in the softness of cushioned seats and the company of women. This was a man's place, in the company of his mates. He finished the evening in a pleasant, alcohol-induced daze.

In twos and threes his old shipmates were disappearing. Lofty and some of the other Americans had shipped with a vessel heading for Valparaíso, and one morning Boney sought him out.

'I've got a berth on a clipper heading for India, leaving tomorrow. Why don't you come with me? I'm sure I could get you a place as my assistant.'

Gus shook his head. 'I don't want to go to sea again. Thanks all the same.'

Boney looked at him with his lips pursed. 'What are you going to do with yourself then, lad? You're not having much luck on the docks, are you?'

'No, not so far,' Gus admitted.

'Do they know you can read and write and figure?'

'They? Who?'

'The gangmasters. There's a chance you might get work as a tally clerk, checking the cargo. Worth a try, don't you think?'

Next day Gus persuaded Snowy, who had struck up a good relationship with one of the gangmasters, to put the idea forward and from then on he was given occasional work helping the regular tally clerks. It was dirty and sometimes dangerous, as he clambered around in the holds of ships or stood on the dockside watching crates being lowered, but it put money in his pocket. There was no reason for any of the four of them to stay in the Sailor's Home, since they were no longer seamen, so they found cheap lodgings in Mersey Street, just off the dock road.

* * *

It worried May that she had not seen Gus again. She had told him that he could meet her any day after work and come back to Nan's with her, but the days passed with no sign of him. Eventually, she plucked up her courage on her afternoon off and found her way to the Sailor's Home, but there they disclaimed all knowledge of his whereabouts. 'Moved out days ago. No idea where he went. May have gone back to sea.'

She wandered away, disconsolate. She could not understand why Gus had wished to cut off all communication. They had enjoyed each other's company on that one evening. What had she done wrong? Was it because she had changed, become more 'ladylike'? Had he felt she was putting on airs?

To distract her thoughts she went, as she often did, to St George's Hall. She had an ongoing project to sketch all the different motifs in the tiles on the floor and she never tired of studying them. The hall was being prepared for the Christmas celebrations, now only three weeks away, and workmen were busy all round it, making sketching difficult. After a little she gave up and settled for watching the work.

In one corner a man was crouching, doing something to the tiles. May wandered over to see what it was and, aware of her presence, he looked up. She saw that he was young,

probably only a few years older than herself. His complex-
ion was golden, as if he spent a lot of time in the sun, his
nose straight, his hair very dark, cut so that it fell forward
over his brow to shade eyes of a deep brown. He stood up.

'Can I be of service, miss?'

His accent was not Liverpudlian but she could not
place it.

'No, no! I'm sorry, I didn't mean to disturb you. I just
wondered what you were doing.'

He looked down at the floor. 'Some of the tiles here had
been damaged. I was replacing them. It's done now.'

May bent closer. 'You would never know. You must be
very skilled.'

He gave a brief, deprecating laugh. 'Not yet, but I hope
to be one day, as skilled as my father who laid this floor in
the first place.'

'Your father made this wonderful floor?'

'Him and others, too. My family have been skilled in the
art of terrazzo for generations, so when the architect who
designed this building wanted people to lay the tiles he sent
for us.'

'Sent for you? From where?'

'From Atina. It's a tiny village in Italy.'

'So you're Italian.'

'I was born there, yes. But I have lived here since I was
five years old.'

'Do you like it here?'

'Oh yes. There is so much more life, so much more
opportunity here.' He paused and held out his hand. 'I
should have introduced myself. Armando Capaldi, at your
service.'

She put her cold hand into his warm one. 'May Lavender. How do you do?'

Their eyes met and for a moment neither of them spoke. Then he said, nodding at the sketchbook under her arm, 'You are an artist?'

'Oh no. I just like to copy designs. It helps with my work.'

'What do you do?'

'I'm a milliner, well, a milliner's apprentice. I make hats at Freeman's Department Store.'

'You are interested in terrazzo?'

'I love this floor. It must be wonderful to help create something that is going to last, to give people pleasure for years to come.'

'But you make things that give people pleasure too.'

'For a few months, perhaps. But at the end of the season my hats will be thrown away, or put in a cupboard and forgotten.'

'Would you like to see some more work like this?'

'Very much.'

'We are laying a floor in the Exchange Flags building. I could show you, if you like.'

She hesitated, unsure if it would be proper for her to agree.

He said, 'My father will be there, and my cousins.'

'They won't mind?'

'Not at all.'

'All right, then. When?'

'When are you free?'

'Not until this time next week.'

'Then I shall look forward to seeing you then. I will wait at the main entrance for you. About two o'clock?'

'That would be lovely.'

Walking back to Nan's, it occurred to her that she had not thought about Gus for several hours.

* * *

The following Wednesday she found Armando waiting as he had promised. He led her into the grand courtyard and up a flight of stairs to where several men were at work on a half-completed floor. He introduced her to his father, who took her hand with one so rough and calloused it felt like shaking hands with a rock, and then turned back to his work. Armando showed her how the tiny pieces of coloured tiles could be fitted together to form the design the architect had drawn up, and she spent the afternoon watching and copying the designs.

When the work was over Armando said, 'Can I ask you something? Do you like ice cream?'

'Ice cream? I don't know. I've never tasted it.'

'Never tasted ice cream? Then you must try some of my Uncle Giovanni's. He makes the best ice cream in the city – perhaps the best in the world.'

'Really? I'd love to try some.'

'Then you shall, on Sunday. If you will allow me, I will take you to my uncle's shop and we will have ice cream. Will you come?'

May hesitated for a moment, unsure if she should accept, but there was something in Armando's brown eyes, and the way they sparkled, that was irresistible. She nodded. 'Thank you. I should like that very much.'

She had agreed on the spur of the moment but, as the time approached she began to have doubts. She had heard enough dark hints from the other shop girls about the fact that men were only ever after 'one thing', and she wondered if there would be a price to pay for her ice cream. In the event, it was one of the most enjoyable afternoons she had ever spent. Armando's uncle's shop had a counter on the ground floor where people could buy ice cream to take away, and upstairs there were tables and chairs for those who wanted to eat on the premises. This room was crowded the whole time with friends and relations who came and went amid a babble of talk and laughter in a mix of Italian and English. Much of it was incomprehensible to May and it worried her to begin with that some of the conversations seemed to be violently argumentative, but Armando assured her that they were simply animated discussions between good friends.

He introduced her to cousins and aunts, who greeted her charmingly and then reverted to their native Italian; but she didn't mind. It was the lack of restraint, the bubbling animation of everyone around her that she found delightful. It was very different from any other gathering she had been in and she wondered why. She thought that it might be because these people were their own masters. Some were skilled tradesmen, others owned small shops or other businesses, but they worked for themselves and had no need to worry that if they overstepped some barely defined mark or showed a lack of respect for authority they might find themselves out of a job. It was an attitude of mind very different from the way she had been brought up and she found it invigorating.

And then, of course, there was the ice cream itself. She tried chocolate and strawberry and pistachio and could have had more but her stomach rebelled. Until then she had thought chocolate cake was the most delicious thing in the world; now she decided that chocolate ice cream was even better.

There was only one incident that made her feel uneasy. Towards the end of the afternoon a large woman in a black dress came in and Armando introduced her as his mother. She was perfectly affable and showed a keen interest in May's work, but her enquiries into her background were a little too pointed and there was something in her expression as she looked from her to Armando that made her uncomfortable. Walking home she said to Armando, 'I'm afraid your mother doesn't approve of me.'

He laughed. 'Take no notice of her. Italian mamas are like lionesses with cubs, ready to pounce on anyone who might lure them away from the den.'

'Is that what she thinks I am doing?'

'Not just you. It would be the same with any girl. I think she wants to be the only woman in my life. But forget about her. Did you enjoy yourself this afternoon?'

'Yes, I did, very much.'

'So I can see you again?'

'If you like.'

'I can't get Wednesday afternoon off. But perhaps next week you will come to Exchange Flags again?'

'Yes. I should like that.'

'Good. And afterwards we will go and eat ice cream.'

At the door of Nan's house he took her hand. 'Thank you for coming with me this afternoon.'

'No, I should thank you.'

He leaned closer and kissed her on the lips. It was the lightest of touches and as he stepped back she saw that he was blushing and guessed that it was the first time for him, too.

They smiled at each other and then he turned and walked swiftly away.

May had to suppress an impulse to skip like a child as she went into the house. She had a boyfriend, and she had had her first kiss!

Thirteen

With Christmas almost upon them, May made a determined effort to track Gus down and eventually succeeded in running him to earth in his Mersey Street lodgings. When she asked him tearfully why he had cut off all contact with her, he shifted from foot to foot and mumbled something about not belonging in her world.

'Gus, that's rubbish,' she protested, 'and you know it! We're brother and sister. We both came from the same place. Our lives have been different lately but that doesn't mean we can't still see each other. We've had so little time together. Even in the workhouse we weren't allowed to mix. Now we're both free we have a chance to get to know each other properly. Please, let's at least try.'

'All right' he muttered. 'What do you want me to do?'

'Come and spend Christmas afternoon with me. There's going to be a special Christmas dinner at the store for all the staff but after that I'm free. We can go back to Nan's. I don't mind betting she'll be off to spend the afternoon in a pub with her friends, so we'll have the place to ourselves.'

He agreed, but the afternoon was not as pleasant as May had expected. Gus seemed to have withdrawn into himself and their conversation proceeded by stops and starts. It came as a relief when it was time to say goodnight.

Christmas passed and Freeman's Department Store was festooned with banners wishing all its customers a happy, healthy and prosperous 1866. In recognition of the fact that she had worked there for a year, May was given a pay rise.

With the arrival of spring, most of her customers came to order new hats and Mrs Breckenridge was among them. May noticed with concern that she looked pale, but she passed it off with an airy, 'Just a nasty winter cold. I'll soon be better now the weather is warmer.' She had made the appointment for late afternoon and, as May was finishing the necessary discussion about style and colour, Julie put her head round the door.

'Mrs Breckenridge's son is here.'

May looked up as he came in and felt a sudden tremor of excitement. She put it down to her sense of gratitude to the man who had saved her job; but she could not deny that the sight of his tall figure and golden blond hair had something to do with it.

'Oh, really, James,' his mother said, 'there was no need for you to go out of your way to escort me. I'm quite capable of taking the omnibus on my own, you know.'

'Of course you are,' he agreed with a smile, 'but I finished work a bit early so I thought I would come and collect you.'

'Mr Breckenridge,' May said, 'I just want to thank you for what you did. Your idea saved me from the sack. I can't tell you how grateful I am.'

He turned to her with the same warm smile. 'I was very happy to help. I thought you were being very badly treated.'

His mother collected her parasol and her fur tippet. 'I'm ready now, dear. Shall we go?'

'Of course.' He nodded to May. 'Nice to meet you again.'

May cherished the words. Her customers were always pleasant to her, but they never treated her as an equal. Something about the way James Breckenridge had spoken gave her the feeling that he was seeing her as a person, not just a particularly useful servant.

Other concerns soon banished such thoughts. She was spending more and more time with Armando. On Wednesdays she often went to watch him at work, taking her sketchbook with her, and then they would go to his uncle's shop to eat ice cream. She had got to know most of his family and they were always friendly, but she sometimes felt an outsider. Partly, she told herself, it was just because she didn't speak Italian but that did not entirely explain it. Although she met his sisters and his two younger brothers and numerous cousins, she did not see his mother again, and although his father was almost always present when she went to see him at work, he had little to say to her.

On Sundays Armando quite often had family commitments and they could not meet; but when he was free he usually suggested that they should go for a walk. The weather was changeable and they very often had to take shelter in shop doorways from a downpour; but it was the only way they could be alone and it gave an opportunity for stolen kisses, which grew more passionate with every meeting.

They set May's nerves on fire and turned her insides to liquid, but when Armando's caresses grew more urgent and she felt his hands move over her body she always drew back. He accepted her restraint, but she could sense his frustration and she began to wonder where their relationship could go from here. Sometimes he would mutter consolingly, 'One day when ...' but he never finished the sentence. She thought he meant 'when we are married', but thinking about it rationally when she was no longer in his arms, she knew that that could not happen for many years. His apprenticeship had four years to run and he would not be in a position to support a wife for some time after that.

On summer Sundays, when they were not able to meet, she often went with some of the other girls to listen to the band that played in the bandstand overlooking the Mersey.

One afternoon, as they were leaving after the concert, she was arrested by a man's voice.

'Miss Lavender! It is you, isn't it?'

James Breckenridge was coming towards her. He took off his hat and looked round the group. 'Good afternoon, ladies.'

There was a giggle and a mumbled, 'Good afternoon, sir.'

May blushed with vexation at her companions' lack of manners but Breckenridge did not seem put out. 'Did you enjoy the concert?' he asked. The question was quite obviously addressed to her.

'Yes, very much,' she replied.

'So did I,' he said. 'Music raises the spirits, don't you agree?'

'Yes, I do.'

He nodded, and seemed about to speak again but thought better of it. 'I mustn't intrude. I'll say good afternoon.' He gave a little bow, put on his hat and walked away.

'Ooh, May! Who was that? How do you know him?' The questions came in a chorus.

'He's the son of one of my customers, that's all,' May said.

'Fancy him stopping to talk like that! I reckon he fancies you! Are you sweet on him?'

'Don't be silly! I've just seen him when he comes to collect his mother from the store. He was being polite, that's all.'

* * *

Gus was lost. Without the comradeship and the discipline of life on the *Shenandoah* he felt like a ship without a rudder, adrift in choppy seas. All through his childhood he had had one aim in life, to go to sea. Now he had done that and found it was not, after all, what he wanted. He no longer knew what he wanted, or where his life was going.

His contact with men like Mason and the other officers, educated men, had given him a glimpse of another kind of existence, where you could read books and have interesting discussions. He had seen the way Victoria and her family lived in Melbourne. Even his sister's new life was nearer to what he felt, however dimly, he wanted. But his lack of education and his poverty seemed to be an insuperable barrier and he could not see a way forward.

As the weeks and months passed he drifted from one job to another. He worked for a spell in the kitchens of the Sailor's Home, using the skills he had learned from Boney. But that came to an end when he lost his temper with a fellow worker and punched him on the nose. Then he got a job as a pot-boy in a dockside pub, but lost that after an altercation with a customer. He drifted back to working casually as a tally clerk, filling in when someone fell ill or was injured.

Now that they were all more or less solvent, the other three men he shared lodgings with began to look beyond the pub for entertainment. The streets around the docks were the haunt of prostitutes and Snowy, Pete and Mick all made use of their services. They tried to persuade Gus to join them, but he had not forgotten the brothel in Melbourne. The women with their painted faces and brazen manners reminded him too vividly of his humiliation then. The thought of paying for services, which so many other men had enjoyed before him, revolted him.

There was one girl, Lily, who attracted him, because she was pale and vulnerable and awoke in him a desire, not to sleep with her, but to protect her. But she had become Mick's particular favourite. She waited for him every evening and sometimes Gus watched covertly and saw how anxious she became if he was late and how pathetically eager she was to please when he appeared. His manner to her, on the other hand, was casual and offhand. Gus felt she deserved better.

May did her best to keep in touch with him and to encourage him, but it was hard work and she sometimes felt so exasperated with his lack of purpose that she almost gave up.

One Tuesday evening in early summer, as she left the store, two men stepped forward out of the shadows.

'Miss Lavender?'

She drew back involuntarily, glancing round to see if any of her colleagues were still within earshot in case she needed to call for help. 'Yes. What do you want?'

The older of the two took off his cap. 'My name's Arthur White, miss, but everyone calls me Snowy. This here is Mick MacGregor. We were shipmates of your brother's.'

'Oh!' May caught her breath in relief. 'I'm so pleased to meet you. I haven't seen Gus for weeks.' She looked from one face to the other. 'Is he all right?'

They exchanged glances. 'That's the thing, you see,' Snowy said. 'He's got himself in a bit of trouble.'

'Trouble? Where is he?'

'In the Bridewell.'

'The Bridewell? You mean in prison?'

'Yes, that's about the size of it.'

'But why? What has he done?'

'Drunk and disorderly. That's the charge.'

The younger man spoke. 'He got into a fight over a street girl.'

'A street girl? You mean a … a prostitute? What would he have to do with a woman like that?'

'Thought she was being pestered by some gent, it seems. He was a customer, like, but Gus took exception for some reason.'

'I must talk to him! Will they let me see him, do you think?'

'Might do. Do you want us to show you the way?' Snowy offered.

'Yes, yes, please. I can't believe he's done anything wrong. There must be a mistake.

'No mistake, miss, I'm afraid. But it'll be best if he tells you himself. It's this way.'

The Bridewell prison in Campbell Street was a forbidding structure of soot-blackened bricks dominated by a tall chimney. Snowy led May into a small office on the ground floor and explained what she had come for.

The officer behind the desk looked at her disapprovingly. 'Nice young woman like you shouldn't be in a place like this. Don't know what you want with a reprobate like Lavender.'

'He is my brother,' May said, her voice trembling. 'Please, sir, let me see him.'

A turnkey led her along a narrow passageway and unlocked a heavy oak door. 'Lady here claims to be your sister.' He turned to May. 'You've got ten minutes.'

Gus was slumped on a narrow bench. His face was pale and there was a smell of vomit in the air. He looked up. 'What are you doing here? Who told you where I was?'

'Your friends, Snowy and Mick. They came to find me. Oh, Gus, what have you been doing? How did you get into this state?'

'It doesn't matter. You don't want to know. Go away and leave me to it.'

'No! I want to help. What can I do?'

'Nothing.'

'What will happen to you?'

'Up before the beak at the next assizes. I'll probably get two weeks' hard labour – more maybe.'

He looked up and she saw that behind the bravado he was terrified. She sat on the bench beside him and took his hand. 'Tell me what happened.'

He hesitated, then began, his voice thick with anguish. 'There's this girl. Lily's her name. She's Mick's girl, not mine, but he doesn't treat her right. He doesn't look after her. She's only a kid, not much older than me. I try to look out for her. I was going back to the lodgings. I'd had a few drinks; I admit that. I saw her there, on the corner, waiting for Mick, and this bloke came up to her. Big fat bloke in a posh suit. He wanted her to come with him, but she didn't want to. She kept telling him she was waiting for someone else. He was pulling at her, calling her a whore, saying she had to go with anyone who asked her. I went over and asked him to leave her alone and he turned round and asked was I her pimp. Then he laughed and said he wanted her and he could pay for it, so what was I going to do about it. He'd been drinking too, I could smell it, and I could see Lily was really afraid of him. So I hit him.'

'What happened then?'

'He started shouting for the watch and a peeler came round the corner and the bloke told him he was just walking past and I went for him and hit him for no reason. 'Course I tried to tell them what really happened but they didn't want to listen to me. He was upper class, a gent, so they took his word against mine.'

'What about the girl? Didn't she stick up for you?'

'Lily? No, she scarpered as soon as she saw the policeman. Can't blame her. She'd have ended up in the cells for soliciting.'

May shook her head. 'Oh, Gus. I don't know what to do.'

'I told you. There's nothing you can do.'

The turnkey looked in. 'Time's up, miss. You'll have to go now.'

May rose. 'Don't worry, Gus. I'll think of something. There must be someone who can help.'

He made no reply, just sunk his head in his hands, and the turnkey slammed the door shut.

Outside, May discovered that Snowy and Mick had vanished and she was on her own. She began to walk back towards home, racking her brains. Gus had been at fault, but he didn't deserve to be sent to prison. The man he had punched had lied. It was unjust. Someone must be able to help.

Her first thought was of Mr Freeman, but he had helped her so often already she felt she could not ask him again. Then she had an inspiration. James Breckenridge had helped her before and he was some kind of lawyer, wasn't he? If anyone could help it would be him. She knew she should not presume upon their slight acquaintance, but she also remembered the look they had exchanged when she thanked him for his earlier intervention. She knew his mother's address, from having sent finished hats to her. It was against all the rules to go barging in at this time of night, but she was desperate. She turned her steps in that direction.

The Breckenridges' house was part of a neat terrace just off Parliament Street. May paused on the doorstep. She knew that what she was about to do could get her into trouble but she could see no alternative. She rang the doorbell and waited, her heart beating fast. A maid opened the door and May asked if Mr Breckenridge was at home.

The girl looked at her doubtfully. 'Who shall I say wants him?'

'May Lavender.'

'Wait there. I'll see.'

A few moments later it was Mrs Breckenridge who appeared in the hallway.

'May? Whatever are you doing here at this time of night? What do you want with James?'

'I'm really sorry to disturb you, ma'am,' May said. 'I know it's being presumptuous, but my brother's in real trouble and I thought Mr Breckenridge might be able to help.'

'Your brother?' Mrs Breckenridge frowned. 'I really don't understand why you think we should concern ourselves with your brother's affairs.'

'It's just that Mr Breckenridge was so good helping me when I was in trouble. I really need some advice and I don't know who else to turn to. Please!'

Mrs Breckenridge did not respond immediately. Then she stepped back and nodded. 'You'd better come in.'

May followed her into a comfortable drawing room, where James Breckenridge was reclining in an armchair with a book in his hand. He jumped to his feet when she entered.

'Miss Lavender! Well, this is an unexpected pleasure!'

'It's all highly irregular and most inconvenient.' His mother's tone was very different from the kindly manner May associated with her. 'You'd better explain what you have come for as quickly as you can. My son works very hard and he should not have his precious leisure moments interrupted.'

'Oh, come now, Mama,' her son responded. 'I'm not tired and I'm more than happy to help if there's anything I can do. Won't you sit down, Miss Lavender? You look exhausted. Mama, could we offer Miss Lavender some refreshment? A cup of tea perhaps?'

May said, 'Please, don't call me Miss Lavender. I'm just May.'

He smiled at her. 'Very well. I'll make a bargain with you. I'll call you May as long as you agree to call me James.'

Behind her May heard Mrs Breckenridge's snort of disapproval; but she rang the bell and told the maid to bring tea. James put a hand on her arm and led her to a chair next to a small table draped in a cloth of purple plush, on which was a collection of china ornaments. He took a seat opposite her and said, 'Now, what is the problem? I assume you are in some sort of difficulty and this is not just a social call.'

'Oh no!' she said. 'I mean, I wouldn't presume ... I need some advice and I thought you might be able to give it.'

'Advice about what?'

Finding the words with difficulty, and blushing with the shame of it, she told him what had happened to Gus. He listened without interrupting, only nodding occasional encouragement, and when she finished he said, 'I didn't know you had a brother. But then, why should I? We've only met a couple of times. Tell me about him. Has he been in trouble before?'

May hesitated. Neither Mrs Breckenridge or James knew anything about her childhood in the workhouse and she felt instinctively that if they found out they would think less of her. That meant that she could not go into detail about Gus's life, either. In the end she said, 'He's been at sea for over a year. He always wanted to be a sailor, like our father.'

'Do you have any other family? Are your parents still living?'

'No. They are both dead.'

'I'm sorry. How did they die?'

'My father was lost at sea. He was ... a sea captain.' The lie came to her lips unbidden. 'My mother got sick.'

'So you and Gus are orphans. Who brought you up?'

May floundered for a moment. Then she said, 'Oh, we lived with our mother until ... until quite recently.'

'You say Gus has been at sea. What ship was he on? If we could get the captain or one of the officers to speak on his behalf it might help.'

She shook her head. 'I don't think so. He was on the *Shenandoah*.'

'On the *Shenandoah*! How did he come to sign up aboard her?'

'He didn't mean to. He ... he stowed away. He didn't know which ship he was on until too late.'

James sat back and looked at her, his expression grave. 'I'm afraid the less the magistrate knows about that the better. It may not have been intentional but Gus broke the law by shipping on board the *Shenandoah*.'

May hung her head. 'I know.'

'And what has he been doing since the ship returned?'

'Just casual work on the docks. He's been helping to tally, when he had the chance.'

'Tallying? That requires a degree of education.'

'Oh, Gus can read and write and do figures. He's quite clever.'

'It's a pity he hasn't turned that to better advantage.' James shook his head slowly. 'It seems to me that the less the magistrate enquires into his background the better. My advice is that he should plead guilty and take the consequences.'

'But that means prison!'

'I'm afraid so, unless the magistrate can be persuaded to commute the sentence to a fine.'

'He's not a bad boy! If he goes to prison there's no knowing what will become of him.' She looked appealingly at James. 'Couldn't you speak up for him, sir? I'll willingly pay the fine, if you can persuade the judge.'

James shook his head. 'I can't. I don't have the right of audience in a criminal court. Only a qualified solicitor can do that and I'm not qualified yet. I'm sorry, May.'

Slowly May got to her feet. She felt as if all her limbs had turned to lead. 'I see. I'm sorry to have bothered you.' She turned to Mrs Breckenridge. 'I beg your pardon for intruding, ma'am. I hope you'll overlook my presumption.' She saw that Mrs Breckenridge was pressing a hand to her side as if she was in pain. 'Are you all right, ma'am?'

The older woman waved her enquiry aside. 'Flossie will see you out.'

May turned to James. 'Thank you for listening to me, sir. I hope I haven't taken up too much of your time.'

She was halfway to the door when he said, 'Wait!' She turned back and he went on, 'Sit down again for a moment. Let me think about this. Perhaps there is something that can be done.'

'James, really,' his mother protested. 'You should not be getting yourself involved.'

'It's all right, Mama. It won't hurt to consider all the possibilities. Come and sit down, May.'

May did as he bade her and he sat silent for a moment, frowning in thought.

'Our only chance would be to persuade the magistrate that Gus would be able to live a sober, responsible life if he escapes a prison sentence. To do that, he needs to have a job – a regular job – and a respectable place to live. Where is he living now?'

'He's sharing a room with three of his shipmates in a rooming house in Mersey Street.'

'Hmm. That's not going to impress His Honour. Is there any chance he could move in with you?'

'I don't know. I could ask Nan.'

'If we could tell the magistrate that he will be staying in a respectable home, with a sister who will undoubtedly be a good influence, that might help. But he really needs the offer of a proper job. That's something we shall have to work on. Now, the court doesn't sit until next Monday, so the first thing we need to do is apply for bail. Once he's out we can start to work out the best way forward.'

'Bail,' May said. 'Does that mean he'll be able to come home?'

'If we can assure the authorities that he will be in the care of a responsible person and unlikely to commit a further offence.' He looked at the clock. 'It's too late to do anything tonight. Can you be free tomorrow morning?'

Hope surged up in May's chest. 'I'll manage it somehow. Nan will let me off, if I explain to her.'

'You need to persuade her to let Gus stay with you, as well, even if it is only temporarily.'

'Yes, I'm sure I can do that.'

'Good. Then I will meet you outside the jail at ten o'clock tomorrow morning. Now, you had better get home and talk to Nan. Don't bother to ring for Flossie, Mama. I'll see May out.'

He rose and accompanied her to the door.

As she left she glanced back and saw Mrs Breckenridge sink into a chair, her hand still pressed to her side. In the hallway she said, 'Is your mama all right? She seemed to be in pain.'

A shadow crossed his face. 'She says it's just indigestion, but I am beginning to wonder … Anyway, nothing you need to concern yourself with. Try to get some sleep. I'll see you in the morning.'

'Yes.' She looked up into his face. 'I don't know how to thank you, sir.'

'You can start by calling me James. Goodnight.'

Nan was waiting for her when she got back.

'Where have you been? I've been worried.'

'I'm sorry, Nan.' May pulled off her hat and sank into a chair, feeling suddenly faint. 'I'll explain in a minute.'

'Have you eaten?'

'No.' It occurred to her for the first time that she had missed her evening meal. 'No, I haven't.'

'There's a pie here if you want it. It'll be cold now, but better than nothing.'

Nan fetched the pie from the kitchen, and as she ate May explained where she had been.

'You went round to Mrs Breckeridge's house, uninvited, at this time of night?' Nan looked shocked.

'I didn't know who else to turn to.'

'It's not right, May. Mr Freeman would be furious if he knew.'

'Don't tell him, please Nan!' May begged.

'Well, I won't say anything. But if Mrs Breckenridge decides to make a complaint ...'

'Oh, I pray she won't. I don't think James – young Mr Breckenridge – would want that.'

'Hmm.' Nan put her hands on her hips and contemplated May. 'I don't know what it is with you, girl. Ever since I took you on it's been one thing after another. First you're hiding Patty in your room and we had all that business with the bedbugs. Then there's the business with Mrs McBride's daughter. Now this!'

May put her head in her hands. 'I know! I don't mean to be a trouble, and this time it really isn't my fault. Don't be angry with me, Nan.'

Nan relaxed and patted her shoulder. 'I'm not angry, child. I just don't want to see you losing your position. You're too good at your job for that.'

May looked up. 'There's something else. Mr Breckenridge is going to apply for bail for Gus tomorrow. He wants me to meet him at ten o'clock.'

'Ten o'clock tomorrow morning you'll be at work.'

'I know I should be, but couldn't you let me off for once? We haven't got any fittings tomorrow. Things are quite slack right now. I'll work extra hours to make up if need be, but please let me off tomorrow.'

'Oh, very well. I suppose under the circumstances ...'

May jumped up and threw her arms round the portly figure. 'Oh, Nan, you are a dear! Thank you so much.'

Nan fended her off, saying, 'Now then, there's no need for a fuss,' but May could see that she was touched.

'There's one more thing,' she said. 'Gus has to have somewhere to stay, somewhere respectable, or they won't let him out. Please, Nan, can he come here – just until the trial is over? I'll sleep on the couch and he can have my room.'

Nan sighed and shook her head. 'The things you have me doing! All right. There's a truckle bed in the little box room. He can sleep there for the time being.'

After an uneasy night, May was early for her appointment with James Breckenridge next morning but she felt a quickening thump in her heart when she saw him approaching.

He lifted his hat and shook her hand. 'Good morning. Did you manage to get some rest?'

'A little.'

'Well, let's go inside and see if we can get your brother out, shall we?'

As soon as they entered the warder's office, May knew she had made the right decision to apply for James's help. At first sight of him, in his smart clothes, the man behind the desk got to his feet and greeted him politely. James's manner was courteous but businesslike. A senior officer was summoned; there was a conversation, much of which May did not understand; James signed a paper and Gus was produced, pale and dishevelled, his eyes red from lack of sleep – or perhaps from weeping. He seemed shocked by the turn of events and could hardly believe that he was free to go.

'You need to understand,' James said, 'that you are only being released temporarily, until you appear before the magistrates on Monday. And one condition of your release is that you stay with your sister at her address.'

Gus looked at May. 'Can I?'

'Yes. Nan says you can sleep in the box room.'

'Shall we go?' James asked.

Gus turned his eyes on him. 'I don't understand. Who is this?'

'This is Mr Breckenridge, Gus. He's …' she floundered. How should she describe James?

'A friend,' James said. 'Now, young man, we need to get you cleaned up. Come along.'

'Where are we going?' Gus asked.

'To my house. You can have a bath and some breakfast and then we can talk.'

'James, what about your mama? She won't want us barging in again,' May said. It still seemed odd to call him by his first name.

'Don't worry about that. I'll explain everything to her.'

Just the same, May was relieved when they arrived at the house to be told by Flossie that Mrs Breckenridge had taken breakfast in bed and did not wish to be disturbed.

'Is there plenty of hot water, Flossie?' James asked.

'Yes, sir. I stoked the boiler up this morning.'

'Good. I need some clean towels. This young man is in need of a good hot bath. Come upstairs, Gus. Oh, and make Miss Lavender a cup of coffee while she is waiting and prepare a good breakfast for our guest.'

'Shall I help carry up the water?' May remembered only too well the backbreaking work of lugging buckets of hot water upstairs.

James looked back over his shoulder with a laugh. 'No need. We have the very latest in piped water from the boiler in the kitchen.'

May sat awkwardly in the drawing room, sipping her coffee, and heard the sound of movements above her and running water. Half an hour later the two men reappeared, Gus pink and scrubbed, his hair a flaming halo, and wearing a pair of quite respectable grey trousers, a white shirt and a waistcoat.

'There! What a transformation, eh?' James had the air of a conjurer who has successfully produced a white rabbit. 'I knew there would be some clothes I grew out of years ago somewhere. My mother never throws anything away. It took a bit of a rummage in the attic, but I found these, and they are not a bad fit. Don't you agree?'

'You look very smart, Gus,' May said.

Flossie looked in. 'I've set breakfast in the morning room, sir.'

'Good. Let's go through, shall we? We can talk while Gus eats.'

While Gus set to demolishing a plate of eggs and bacon, James took a seat opposite him with pen and paper at the ready. May sat between them, looking from one to the other. James seemed transformed from the previous evening. Then his interest had been purely a matter of courtesy and his outlook had been fatalistic. Now, having decided to take on the challenge of saving Gus from prison, he was energised, almost excited.

'Now,' he said, 'we need a plan of action. I have explained to your sister, Gus, that if we are to persuade the magistrate to commute your prison sentence to a fine, we have to convince him that you will keep out of trouble in the future. We need to present you as a young man with prospects that will enable you to become a useful member of society. We've taken the first steps. You need a haircut but once that is done you will look quite respectable, and May has arranged for you to live with her for the time being.'

Gus looked across at May. There was egg yolk on his lips. 'You sure that's all right?'

'Yes. The box room's only small but at least you will have an address.'

'Now,' James resumed, 'the most important thing is that you should have the prospect of a proper job. Do you have any ideas that might help?'

Gus shook his head. 'All I know is the sea – and being a tallyman, but that's only casual.'

James rubbed his forehead. 'I've racked my brains for someone who might help, but I just don't have the right contacts. May, do you think Mr Freeman might suggest something?'

May's heart sank. 'I don't like to ask him. He's already been so good to me. Well, you know I nearly lost my job over that business with Mrs McBride. He kept me on then, on condition I didn't cause any more trouble.'

'But you wouldn't be asking for yourself,' James said. 'I've heard that Mr Freeman is of a philanthropic disposition.' Seeing that they both looked puzzled, he expanded. 'He wants to do good for other people, for society as a whole. Surely it would be better for society for Gus to be gainfully employed instead of going to prison. Could you not put it to him like that?'

'I suppose I could try,' May said dubiously.

'Do you want me to come with you, to put the case?'

May straightened her back. 'No. It's very kind of you but we've already asked a lot. This is something we should do for ourselves.'

'Well said.' He nodded approvingly. 'Now, Gus. If May does this for you, and if Mr Freeman can find you a job, you must promise on your honour to play your part. You must stick to the job and keep away from your old friends and your old drinking habits. Do you promise?'

Gus put down his knife and fork. He felt as if he was living in some dream world. He had spent all the previous night reconciling himself to the idea of going to prison and trying to formulate some plan for what he might do when he came out. Then he had been whisked out, bathed, dressed in clothes that were not his own, and asked to commit himself to a future that was not of his own choosing. Something in him rebelled at having his life organised by this stranger, however good his intentions. But he could see that the alternative was prison followed by a hand-to-mouth existence that might well see him back in jail before too long. He nodded his head. 'Yes, I promise. I'll do my best.'

'Good,' James said. 'Now, I should get back to my work and you need to go to see Mr Freeman. Take Gus to the barber's on the way, May, and get his hair cut. After that, all I can do is wish you luck.'

May stood up. 'There's just one thing I don't quite understand. If we do all this, how is the magistrate going to know? You said you couldn't speak for him in court.'

'You're right, I can't,' James said. 'But my principal, Mr Weaver, can because he's a qualified solicitor. I'm pretty sure I can persuade him to put Gus's case, after we've done all the spade work.'

May frowned. 'We would have to pay him, wouldn't we? I don't know where I'd find the money.'

James smiled reassuringly. 'Not necessarily. There's a concept we have in law, *pro bono publico*. It means for the public good, and sometimes lawyers act without a fee, if they feel it fits that category. I think Mr Weaver will see that it is better for society for Gus to follow the path we have set out rather than go to prison. Now, I must go. Come tomorrow and tell me how you have got on.'

An hour later May and Gus, his hair now trimmed and plastered to his head with pomade, stood outside Mr Freeman's office. May had sent a message in, asking for a few minutes of his time, and they had been told to wait.

A clerk came out carrying a ledger. 'You can go in now.'

Mr Freeman leaned back in his chair and regarded them testily. 'What is it this time, May? And who is this?'

'This is my brother Gus, sir.'

'Your brother? I thought he was at sea.'

'Not since the *Shenandoah* surrendered, sir,' Gus said. 'I didn't want to go back to sea after that.'

'I see. So what can I do for you?'

In as few words as she could manage, May explained the situation.

Mr Freeman heaved a deep sigh. 'What did I do when I took you out of my house and gave you a position here? You have caused me more trouble than anyone else on my staff.' He looked at her with his head on one side. 'Well, you certainly make life interesting. I never know what you are going to come up with next. So, you want me to find your brother a job.' He turned his gaze to Gus. 'What can you do, young man? What skills can you offer?'

'He can write sir,' May said.

'Let him speak for himself.'

'I can write a good hand, sir, and I'm good with numbers.'

'Anything else?'

'I know about ships, and the sea. I've been all round the world. And I've seen the cargoes that come into the port and where they go from there.' He hesitated and ploughed on. 'I like to think about where they came from, what they're used for.'

'In other words, trade between nations, import and export.'

'Yes, I suppose that is it.'

Mr Freeman passed a sheet of paper and an inkstand across the desk. Then he swung round in his seat and reached up to a shelf of books. He ran a finger along the spines and selected a copy of the Bible, which he opened. 'Copy out those two verses in your best hand,' he said, pointing.

Gus drew his chair up to the desk, flexed his fingers and took up the pen. He was reminded of his lessons in the workhouse school and could still feel the sting of the ruler across his knuckles when he made a blot or a mistake. He had resented the time spent on what seemed a pointless activity but he had learned in spite of himself. He bent his head and copied the verses in his best copperplate hand. When he finished he passed the sheet of paper back to Mr Freeman, who glanced at it.

'Good. That's quite ...' His expression changed. 'These are the verses I pointed out to you?'

'Yes, sir.'

'May, you saw that I opened the book at random?'

'Yes, sir,' she replied, puzzled.

'Gus, read out what you have written there.'

Gus took back the sheet of paper and read: 'And in the same house remain, eating and drinking such things as they give: for the labourer is worthy of his hire ...'

'Stop there. I have heard people say that when you have a dilemma you should open the Bible at random and read the first words your eye falls on and you will find the answer. I believe that is true in this case. Someone who is willing to work should receive his just reward. Are you willing to work, Gus?'

'Yes, sir.'

Mr Freeman passed him a ledger. 'Add those figures for me.'

Gus bent to the work again. He felt more confident here. He had always been good with figures. He calculated, checked and wrote down the answer and handed the ledger back to Mr Freeman, who cast his eye down the column and nodded.

'Good.' He leant back in his chair, his elbows on the arms, fingers steepled to touch his lips. 'So, where do we go from here? I have no vacancies for a clerk here, but I know a number of men who run shipping companies and who might be prepared to give a willing lad a fresh start in life. Come back tomorrow morning and I'll tell you if I have found anything for you.'

May and Gus spent the afternoon wandering the streets, visiting some of her favourite places. As they walked they talked and she heard for the first time the full story of why he had run away from the Industrial School. She looked at him with tears in her eyes.

'I never knew! And I've been thinking what a fool you were to run away from a place where you were getting a good education. You poor boy!'

He shrugged. 'Water under the bridge now.'

Next morning they were both waiting outside when the porter opened the staff entrance, but they had to wait longer until a messenger came to tell them that Mr Freeman had arrived and wanted to see them. May's heart was thumping as they entered his office.

He was standing by the window and turned as they came in. 'Ah, you are prompt. Well, I have good news. Mr Pilkinton of the White Star Line will take you on as a clerk, on a trial basis, starting next week. I have explained the circumstances and he has agreed that you can start on Tuesday, provided that you escape a prison sentence. If you are sent to jail, then I am afraid that his offer will be withdrawn. I know that is not ideal, but it is the best I can do. I hope, most sincerely, that the magistrate will be persuaded that a fine is the best solution.'

Monday was a long time coming. James Breckenridge expressed himself delighted with the news and assured them that Mr Weaver would speak on Gus's behalf, and after that there was nothing to do but wait. On Sunday afternoon they wandered down to the pier head and watched the great ships coming and going. May looked at her brother's face.

'Don't you sometimes wish you were on board one of those, heading for some far off place?'

Gus shook his head. 'I wouldn't mind being in one of those places, but I don't fancy weeks and weeks of being thrown around in a storm or stewing in the heat to get there.' He paused, frowning. 'It's funny. I've been round the world. I've seen the Arctic Ocean and the tropics. I've seen whales and dolphins and coral reefs, but the only port I've been in is Melbourne. I used to listen to the other fellows talking about places they had visited on other voyages and wish I could see them too; but we never called anywhere in all those months. I suppose that is what has put me off.'

May was given Monday morning off to attend the trial and they both arrived early, Gus smart in James Breckenridge's hand-me-downs, May in her best coat and a new bonnet she had been keeping for a special occasion. Outside the court they were introduced to Mr Weaver, a small man with pince-nez and a sharp nose that twitched when he spoke, giving him the appearance, May thought, of a particularly intelligent mouse.

There were two other cases before Gus's and both were summarily dismissed with sentences of two weeks' hard labour. May's spirits sank.

Gus's turn came and he pleaded 'guilty' as instructed. The chairman of the magistrates peered down from the bench.

'Mr Weaver. You wish to speak on behalf of your client before I pass sentence?'

Weaver rose. 'If it pleases, Your Honour, you see before you a young man with a bright future, who has fallen in with bad company but is now determined to change his life and seize the opportunities offered to him. He now resides with his sister, a respectable young woman employed by Freeman's Department Store. He has been offered a position with the White Star company as a clerk, but that offer will be withdrawn if he is sent to prison. I put it to Your Honour that society will be better served if he is gainfully employed, rather than being thrown into jail where he will inevitably come under the influence of bad men. He does not expect to escape punishment, but if Your Honours can find it in your hearts to commute the sentence to a fine, I believe he can become a useful member of society, rather than a danger to himself and others.'

Weaver sat down and the magistrates conferred amongst themselves. Then the chairman turned his attention to Gus.

'Are you determined in future to lead a godly, sober and righteous life, as the scriptures enjoin us?'

'I am, Your Honour,' Gus responded.

'Very well. Fined twenty-four shillings. You may stand down.'

The fine took most of May's savings, but she resolutely refused to accept James's offer to pay it. Outside the court, while Gus was expressing his thanks to Mr Weaver, James drew her slightly aside.

'You told me you like music. There is a concert next Sunday afternoon, in St George's Hall. I wondered if you would care to accompany me?'

May's heart, which had just begun to regain its normal rhythm, gave a sudden thump. For a moment she was lost for words. What could this unexpected invitation mean? Dare she accept? She looked up at him and saw that his blue eyes had an intensity that surprised her. He really wanted her to agree and after all, she owed him a great deal ...

She swallowed. 'Thank you very much. I should like that.'

The warmth of his smile rewarded her. 'Good. The concert begins at three. I'll meet you outside the hall ten minutes before, if that is all right with you?'

'Yes, thank you. I'll be there.'

Fourteen

Next morning Gus presented himself at the White Star offices and was put into the charge of Leonard Lloyd, the chief clerk. He regarded Gus with barely disguised distaste.

'You realise you are here on approbation? Mr Pilkington has taken you on as an act of charity and it's up to you whether you stay or not. Well, I suppose we had better see what we can make of you.'

Gus clenched his jaw. A desire to punch the man's supercilious face rose in him, but he forced it back and determined instead to prove that he was worth his hire and not an object of charity.

He was slightly disappointed to discover that White Star was not engaged in trade but was a passenger line, concentrating mainly on transporting emigrants to Australia; but the connection with that country was a consolation. He had had many long conversations with the crew members who had shipped on the *Shenandoah* from Melbourne and found their accounts of the gold rush fascinating, in spite of the fact that none of them had 'struck lucky'.

He was given a desk and set to work checking the records of passengers who had booked their places for the next voyage, with the payments they had made or were due to make. The work was undemanding and he had time to wonder who these people were and why they were willing to submit themselves to the uncertainties and discomforts of such a long voyage.

In the midday break he got talking to some of the other clerks and soon found himself something of a celebrity when they heard he had been on board the *Shenandoah*. He got on particularly well with a young man some four or five years his senior. He was called Jack Watts and he had a cheerful manner and a lively sense of humour that made up to some extent for the dour influence of Leonard Lloyd.

* * *

Next day, being Wednesday, May had her usual date with Armando and as always he walked her back to Nan's afterwards. She had told him not to kiss her goodbye there, in case Nan saw, and it was just as well. She waved him goodbye and turned back to find Gus watching her from the doorway.

'Who was that?' he demanded.

'Just a friend. His name is Armando.'

'An Italian?'

'Yes. He works in terrazzo, with his father. You remember I showed you the floor in St George's? His father helped to lay that.'

'So what does he want with you?'

'We're … friends. I've been to his uncle's shop to eat ice cream.'

'Huh!' Gus turned away.

She caught his arm. 'Gus, you mustn't be jealous. I've been all alone most of my life, since we left the workhouse anyway. We both need to have friends.'

He looked back at her and his face softened. 'Yes, I know. But you need to be careful going around with men. You don't want to lose your reputation.'

She gazed at him for a moment, then burst out laughing. 'You sound just like Mrs Wilkins, the horrible old cook I used to work for. She was always accusing me of having "followers".' Then she added more soberly, 'Don't worry. I do know what you mean. I'll be careful.'

Then she remembered that she had another assignation on Sunday and sobered up. Should she tell James about Armando? She decided not to.

She was uneasy, too, about telling Gus about it, bearing in mind his reaction to his first encounter with Armando; and she felt rather guilty about leaving him to his own devices on the only afternoon they both had off. He solved both problems by informing her on the Friday evening that he had been invited to play football with Jack Watts and some other friends on Sunday.

'You don't know how to play football,' she said.

'Anyone can kick a ball about,' he responded airily.

She made no other objection and said nothing about her forthcoming meeting with James. She had bought herself a good dress but she was nervous in case she was not sufficiently elegant for such a gathering. Her worries were dispelled, however, as she stood waiting for James. People of all sorts were making their way into the hall. There were ladies and gentlemen, but also ordinary working people in their Sunday best, all apparently quite at ease and confident of their right to be there. James hurried along Lime Street towards her and arrived slightly out of breath.

'May, I am so sorry to keep you waiting! Mama was feeling a little unwell after church and I had to go to a neighbour for a particular herbal tincture she finds helpful. I hope you haven't got cold.'

'No, I'm perfectly all right,' she assured him. 'I'm sorry your mother is unwell.'

'I'm sure it's nothing serious,' he said. 'She suffers from indigestion. Shall we go in?'

The concert opened a window for May onto a different life. She had never heard much music. In the workhouse chapel they had sung hymns, to the accompaniment of a tinny piano; and when she worked for Mrs Freeman she had listened to Isabella's piano lessons. Isabella had little more talent for music than she had for art, but sometimes her teacher took over and played a piece as it should have sounded and May had stopped in her sweeping and dusting to listen. And she had enjoyed the military marches of the brass band. But nothing had prepared her for this. When the orchestra played she was almost dazed by the glitter of the brass instruments and the variety of different tones from the strings and the woodwind, which seemed to her to weave together in a complex design of many colours.

Outside afterwards James looked down at her. 'Did you enjoy that?'

'I think it was the most wonderful thing I have ever heard, or seen.'

His look was almost tender. 'I'm so glad. 'Then he seemed to gather himself, as if remembering some secret obligation. 'Well, we must do it again some time. Now, can I walk you home?'

Something made her say, 'No, there's really no need. You should go back to see if your mama is feeling better.'

She caught the fleeting look of relief as he took her hand and pressed it. 'I'm glad you liked the concert. Until we meet again ...'

She watched him hurry away down the street and tried to suppress a sense of disappointment. She shook herself mentally. What had she imagined might follow from this meeting? She knew very well that there could never be any real relationship between her and James Breckenridge. He had been very kind and given her a real treat. She had no right to expect anything more. Anyway, she had Armando and that was a much more practical proposition.

You are a stupid, ungrateful girl, she told herself. You have so much to be thankful for. Gus is free and settled in a proper job. You have a job you love, and a boyfriend. What more could you want?

* * *

Life settled into a comfortable routine to which Gus introduced a surprising variation. Nan had taken a liking to him and agreed that he could stay with them until he had saved enough to find a decent place of his own.

One evening he said, 'Why do we always buy pies or chips for supper instead of cooking our own?'

'Because I'm no cook,' Nan said.

'And I had enough of scullery work when I was in service,' May added.

'There's a difference between scullery work and cooking,' he said. 'And you should stop eating pies. You're getting fat. Too much ice cream.'

It was true, May realised. Her skirt was beginning to feel uncomfortably tight round the waist.

'Well, what do you want me to do about it?' she asked.

'You could eat better in the evening.'

'I'm not going to start shopping and cooking on top of my day's work.'

'All right. I'll cook.'

'You? Don't make me laugh.'

'I can cook. I was the cook's assistant on the *Shenandoah*. His name was Boney. He taught me a lot. Most of the time it was salt pork or tinned bully beef but sometimes, when we'd taken a prize that had fresh produce on board, he used to make special dishes for the officers, especially if it was a birthday or some such.'

Gus examined the kitchen and declared it only fit for pigs, then set to and cleaned it from top to bottom. He started going to the market on his way home and found he could buy vegetables and fruit that were past their best but perfectly edible, and cheap offcuts of meat. Soon he was producing tasty stews and even the occasional roast, and he insisted that they should all eat fresh fruit.

'You don't want to end up with scurvy, do you?'

May still enjoyed her ice cream, but as the weeks passed she found her skirt getting looser again.

In the evenings Nan still went out for her 'constitutional', leaving brother and sister alone. For the first time in their lives they came to know each other properly. May was surprised to discover that Gus liked to read, and he told her about the influence that Mason had had on him.

He started buying little books called 'penny dreadfuls', which told stories of pirates and highwaymen; then one day he came home with an armful of magazines called *All the Year Round*. They were the previous year's editions, passed on to him by one of the clerks at White Star.

'They're produced by Charles Dickens,' he said. 'I've heard of him. He's famous for his novels. Mr Mason said I should try to get hold of one.'

May preferred to sketch during her free time but sometimes Gus read aloud to her, and in this way they both followed the serialisation of *Our Mutual Friend*. It was a lot harder going than *Black Bess*, or *Knights of the Road*, but Gus was determined to persevere to the conclusion.

May was very happy with these domestic evenings, but as the weeks passed she detected an increasing restlessness in her brother. Sometimes he would break off in the middle of a sentence and wander round the room, aimlessly picking things up and putting them down. Then he would yawn and stretch and go back to his reading.

Gus continued to play football on Sunday afternoons and May continued to meet Armando.

One Sunday he surprised her by saying, 'My mother asks if you will come to tea this afternoon. She would like to meet you properly.'

May accepted, with some trepidation, but she was received cordially enough. It was after tea that the purpose of the invitation became clear.

'So, May. Tell me, are you devout?'

'I'm sorry. I'm not sure what you mean.'

'Are you a good Christian?'

'Yes, I hope so.' It was not something to which she had ever given much thought. She had been taught her prayers and the Bible stories in the workhouse, but it had been a matter of routine, like learning to read.

'Do you go to church?'

'Oh yes, every Sunday.' That was routine too, expected of any employee of Freeman's.

'And which church do you go to?'

'St Barnabus, in Parliament Street.'

'Ah. You are not a Catholic, then.'

'Er, no. I'm afraid not.'

'I see.' It was said quite lightly and that was the end of the inquisition but she could tell from Armando's expression that it had made him uneasy.

* * *

Gus was trying to dispel an increasing sense of dissatisfaction with his current situation. He found most of the work at the White Star office boring and it was not helped by the sense that Mr Lloyd was constantly looking over his shoulder, waiting for him to make a mistake.

Initially he had enjoyed being at Nan's house with May. It offered a warmth and security and a sense of belonging that he had never had before. Nan had got used to his presence and never suggested that he should move out. But as the weeks became months he found himself asking, 'Is this all? There must be more to life than this'. He could not see any possibilities of advancement in the work he did, and the cosy evenings at home made him feel like an old man.

A slight change in his duties brought a new interest into his life. The main business of the White Star Line, as he knew, was transporting passengers to Australia and most of those passengers were Irish emigrants, desperate to escape famine in their own country. They arrived at intervals, singly or as families, with just enough money scraped together to pay for their passage; but quite often they had to wait for several days or even weeks before there was a ship to take them.

White Star had contracts with a number of lodging houses around the docks, where these people were accommodated, and Gus was given the job of conducting them to the appointed place and making sure that they had the bare minimum for survival until they were able to board their ship.

He found meeting these people at once intriguing and heartbreaking. Many of them were so thin and worn down by their privations that he wondered if they would ever survive the voyage; but he was impressed by their faith that a better life awaited them and their determination to succeed. He spent time talking to them and sharing what little he knew of Australia, and it fostered his own sense that there should be a better future in prospect somewhere.

* * *

May occasionally thought wistfully of the evening she had spent with James Breckenridge at the concert, but she pushed the memory firmly to the back of her mind. It had been a kind thought on James's part but that was all. She had not seen or heard from him since, and Mrs Breckenridge had not ordered a new hat, so even that connection seemed to be severed. Then one day, when the winter evenings were closing in again, a letter arrived.

Dear May,

There is to be a carol concert at the Philharmonic on Dec 10th. I think you would find it very enjoyable. If I can obtain tickets, will you come with me?

Yours sincerely,
James Breckenridge

This time May did not hesitate. She wrote back at once accepting the invitation.

She used the money she had saved from her pay rise to buy a length of jade-green silk, some velvet ribbon in a deeper shade and some pale-cream lace.

The dressmaking department at Freeman's had just acquired some of the new sewing machines and she persuaded one of the girls to show her how to use one and spent the evenings for the rest of the week cutting and stitching. She chose the new Princess style, which she had seen in Nan's latest fashion magazines, where the material was cut in panels from neck to hem and moulded to fit the body, with most of the fullness at the back of the skirt. It needed a framework to support the heavy fabric, so she made a hooped petticoat to go underneath. She also, mindful of Gus's comment about her figure, bought a corset, which could be laced tightly to give her a fashionably tiny waist.

When it was finished she tried it on to show Nan and Gus. Gus looked her up and down and made an elaborate mock bow.

'Blimey, if it ain't the Queen of Sheba come to visit. What is your pleasure, Your Majesty?'

'I think we should like a cup of tea,' she responded with suitable hauteur.

'What's this in aid of anyway?' he asked. 'Is it for this Armando fellow?'

'No, as it happens it isn't. James Breckenridge has asked me to go to a concert with him.'

'Breckenridge? The lawyer? What does he want with you?'

May put her chin in the air. 'Perhaps he just wants the pleasure of my company.'

Gus replied with his characteristic 'Huh!' and turned away. It was left for Nan, next time they were alone, to sit May down and say, 'We need to have a serious talk.'

'What about?' May feigned innocence.

'You know what. What is going on between you and James Breckenridge?'

'Nothing. He has asked me to go to a concert, that's all.'

'That may be all at the moment, but where is all this leading? You do realise it can never come to anything? Why would a man in his station in life be walking out with a girl in yours?'

May dropped her eyes. 'I know nothing can come of it, Nan. I think he is only being kind, because he knows I've never had a chance to go to places like that. And he does seem to enjoy being with me.'

'That's all very well,' Nan said, 'but we've all heard stories about young men with a bit of money taking up girls and ruining them.' She leaned forward and fixed May with a stern gaze. 'You haven't been to bed with him, have you?'

'Of course not!' May was scandalised. 'I wouldn't dream of it, and he wouldn't ask me. He's never so much as touched me, except to shake hands.'

'Well, you make sure it stays like that.'

As the evening approached May veered between wild anticipation and uneasy suspicions. It had never occurred to her not to trust James, but Nan had sewn seeds of doubt in her mind. When the day came, however, she banished those thoughts and made up her mind to enjoy that one occasion, knowing that it was unlikely to be repeated.

She had never been inside the Philharmonic Hall, though she had often walked past its imposing façade. The interior left her breathless. Down each side of the auditorium was a row of boxes, separated by gilded pillars, while the main body of the hall was furnished with comfortable, plush-covered chairs. The ceiling was covered in stucco and ornamented with elaborate designs, and swags of holly and ivy decorated with coloured ribbons hung along the balconies.

She had learned most of the carols in the workhouse, so that much was familiar, and when the congregation was invited to join in she sang along with the rest, hearing James's warm baritone beside her. But she was happiest when she could just sit and listen and let the music weave its magical patterns of colour in her mind. To add to her enjoyment, James was suitably impressed with the new gown and remarked how well it suited her.

Afterwards, instead of hurrying off as she expected, James insisted on walking her home. He gave her his arm and she felt a shiver of pleasure run through her nerves at the closeness of his body. As they neared the house she exclaimed, 'Oh, look! Isn't that beautiful?'

A gas lamp illuminated the frosted branches of a small tree, making them sparkle.

He looked. 'Yes, it is, but do you know? I would never have noticed it; you have such a sharp eye for beauty.'

'I love it when it's frosty. It makes these drab old streets look clean and bright.'

'It is even better in the country,' he said, 'when every blade of grass is encrusted with diamonds and the branches of the trees look like the skeletons of giants. Don't you agree?'

She glanced up at him, surprised by this poetic turn of phrase. 'I don't know,' she said. 'I've never been in the country.'

He looked at her, and there was a fleeting expression of pain in his eyes. 'Never?'

'No. I suppose the nearest I've seen is that place off Princes Street.'

'Oh, you mean Princes Park? It's quite small.'

'I've never seen so many trees.'

'Have you ever been to Birkenhead Park?'

'No. I've never heard of it.'

'It's huge. The city fathers in Birkenhead decided to set aside some land for the recreation of the general public. The land was a bit swampy, no good for building on, but they had it drained and fenced off and got a man called Joseph Paxton to design a park. There are trees and shrubs and flower beds, and a lake. You'd think yourself miles from the city.'

'You've been there?'

'My mother used to take me as a small boy. The trees were quite small then, of course, but I imagine they've grown a good deal now. You should go, sometime.'

'Maybe I will.'

At the door of Nan's house he took her hand, and she said, 'Thank you so much for inviting me. It's been a wonderful evening.'

'I'm glad you enjoyed it. So did I.'

For a moment she thought he might kiss her; but in the end he just squeezed her fingers and murmured, 'Goodnight.'

Armando told her that he could not meet her on Christmas Day because he had to be with his family. Gus had been invited to spend the day with Jack Watts and his family, so, after the Christmas dinner at the store, May spent the afternoon doing some mending, while Nan dozed in her armchair. When the banners went up in the store welcoming 1887, she began to wonder if the new year would bring a different direction to her life, or whether this was to be the pattern it would always follow.

It was a bad winter. January was cold and wet, not suitable for walking, so she and Armando had little time alone together.

She still met him at his uncle's shop, in the company of his many relations, but the passionate encounters they had enjoyed in the summer were much less frequent. Rather to her surprise, May found this a relief. Armando's kisses had set up a turmoil in her body that she did not know how to control.

* * *

There was one family in his care that Gus was particularly drawn to. They were in a slightly better state than many of the people he had to deal with and full of optimistic plans.

Patrick O'Dowd was a cobbler and shoemaker by trade and had had a good business, until the increasing poverty of those around him had meant that fewer and fewer people could afford to have their shoes mended, let alone buy new ones. He was determined to set up again in Melbourne, or if not there, in one of the new settlements that were growing up all over the country. With him were his wife Deirdre, his eldest son Liam, who was also his apprentice, two daughters, Katherine, always known as Kitty, who was about the same age as Gus, and Maeve, who was eight, and little Michael, aged four. Gus gathered that there had been at least two others who had not survived.

Gus struck up a friendship with Liam, which gave him an excuse for prolonging his visits; but it was Kitty who drew him back again and again. She had long dark hair, which she wore simply drawn back from her face into a long plait that hung almost to her waist, and very dark, blue eyes. Her figure was slender, but without the gauntness he had seen in so many of the other girls and boys waiting for their ship.

Patrick could play the fiddle and often in the evening he would take it out and play for the pleasure of the other residents in the boarding house. Sometimes Kitty could be persuaded to dance to his accompaniment. Gus watched in fascination as, while keeping her upper body still, her feet performed intricate steps so fast that he could not follow them.

When she was not dancing and he had a chance to sit beside her and talk, he found her different from most other girls he had met. His recent experience had been limited to the brash attractions of prostitutes or the timid fragility of a girl like Lily, or else the giggles and arch flirtatious looks he received from May's friends at the shop. With

Kitty he could hold a sensible conversation. She did not put on airs or pretend to be coy, and if an argument arose between her and her siblings she could more than hold her own. In many ways she reminded him of Victoria, who had befriended him in Melbourne. He thought she would do very well in Australia.

May was worried by his late homecomings and one evening she faced him and demanded to know if he had started drinking again. To set her mind at rest he took her to meet the O'Dowds. To his relief she got on well with Kitty and remarked that it was a pity they were leaving so soon, as they might have been friends.

* * *

The first daffodils were beginning to open in Nan's tiny garden when May received another note from James.

Dear May,

You told me at Christmas that you had never been to Birkenhead Park. Would you like to go? We could go next Sunday. I will meet you at the ferry at two o'clock. Let me know if that suits you.

Kind regards,
James

Her answer, dispatched immediately, was yes. He replied, 'I look forward to it. But don't come if it is raining. We need a fine day for it.'

That night she said her prayers, as she always did, repeating the words without really thinking, but she ended with an urgent plea for fine weather on Sunday.

Her prayers were answered. Sunday was a perfect April day, with clear blue skies and small white clouds chased along by a brisk breeze, which whipped up little waves on the surface of the Mersey so that the usually muddy waters sparkled in the sunshine.

James was waiting for her at the pier with the ferry tickets in his hand and took her arm as they negotiated the floating dock that gave access to the ferry. The little steamer was called the *Cheshire* and was the first, he told her, to boast a saloon.

He suggested that she might like to sit inside, but she refused and stood on deck watching the skyline of Liverpool retreat. The wind whipped colour into her cheeks and she longed to undo her hair and let it blow free. James was worried that she would get cold, but she told him that she found it exhilarating.

From the landing stage on the Birkenhead side of the river they took a horse-drawn tram, which put them down in front of an imposing gateway, a huge arch surmounted by an elaborate pediment and flanked by pillars. Men and women were going through it, some with children, others with dogs on leashes, but May was glad that she was with James. She would have been afraid to go in alone in case she got lost.

Once inside she forgot her nervousness. Princes Park had been a source of wonder, but then her attention had been on following Angel and her nurse. Now, able to give her whole mind to her surroundings, she found herself in what seemed to her an earthly paradise. There were flower beds full of spring flowers, set out in patterns that made her itch for her sketchbook. There were bushes bright with exotic blooms and a lake that reflected the vivid colours of a quaint covered bridge. There were swans and ducks with strings of ducklings in tow and everywhere the sound of birdsong. They walked and walked and every turn brought into view a new wonder.

'Aren't you tired?' James asked, but she shook her head.

'I could walk for ever here,' she said.

He laughed. 'Well, I can't and we shall have to go back soon. Once the sun goes down it will be cold.'

Reluctantly she allowed him to lead her back towards the tram and the ferry. As they boarded, James raised his hat to a middle-aged couple standing on the deck, but he did not introduce her.

'Who was that?' she asked.

'Oh, just an extremely tedious couple who are acquaintances of my mother. We don't want to be saddled with their company.'

He was right about the temperature, and she was glad to accept his suggestion that they sit in the saloon.

'I don't think I need to ask if you enjoyed yourself,' he said.

She met his eyes and there was a warmth in their blue depths that made her heart swell. 'You have shown me so many lovely things – the concert, the Christmas carols – but I think this was the best of all. Thank you.'

'It's my pleasure,' he responded. 'And that is not just a form of words. I have enjoyed all these outings with you far more than I ever would have done on my own.' He thought for a moment. 'Maybe one Sunday we could go into the real countryside. Would you like that?'

'I'll be happy to go anywhere with you.' The words were out before she had time to think how they would sound to him and she blushed furiously; but he smiled and squeezed her hand.

At the door of Nan's house she wondered if she should invite him in, but she remembered how untidy and dusty the room was and felt embarrassed. He solved the problem by taking her hand and saying, 'It's been a lovely afternoon. I'll get in touch when I have thought out where we should go next. Goodbye for now.'

May was busy in her workroom when a messenger came to say that Mrs Breckenridge was in the fitting room and wanted to see her.

She went up gladly because it was many months since she had last ordered a hat, and she had begun to think that she had never forgiven her presumption in turning up on her doorstep unannounced.

She found Mrs Breckenridge standing in the centre of the room, with her hands folded in front of her, instead of sitting in one of the comfortable chairs intended for customers. Something about her appearance worried May. Her features seemed sharper and for a moment May thought she had rouged her cheeks. Then she saw that the hectic colour had nothing to do with paint.

'Good morning, ma'am.' May bobbed a curtsy. 'I hope you are well.'

Mrs Breckenridge did not respond to her greeting. Instead she said, 'I have not come to order a new hat. I have come to speak to you about my son.'

May felt a jolt of anxiety. 'Is James all right?'

'He is in perfect health, but I fear he is about to be led into a situation which could have grave repercussions for his career.'

'I'm sorry. I don't understand.'

'Oh, I think you do. You have wheedled your way into his good books and taken advantage of his good nature. And it has got to stop.'

'I haven't …' May began.

Mrs Breckenridge overrode her. 'I don't know what you think might come of your relationship, but whatever it is you are going to be disappointed. James has a good career ahead of him, and when it comes to choosing a wife he will want someone of his own class, someone who can act as hostess for him and know how to conduct herself in good society.'

May felt the colour rising in her face. 'Mrs Breckenridge, I never expected anything like that. I know I'm not good enough for him.'

'Then what are you after? Do you think he is going to take a mistress? Is that what you want?'

'No! I wouldn't agree to that even if he asked me – which he won't. It's not like that. He is just a very kind man, and I suppose he sees that I haven't had the chances in life that some girls have and he likes to give me the occasional treat. That's all.'

Mrs Breckenridge studied her for a moment and then her attitude softened a little.

'May, you are a good girl at heart. I believe that. But you must understand. James has conceived a fondness for you, but if it were to go beyond that it would be very detrimental to his future prospects. He cannot afford to be involved in any kind of scandal, and I am afraid that that is what your relationship will result in. If you really care for him, the best thing you can do is put an end to it now. You do understand that, don't you?'

May lowered her eyes. She wanted to protest, to ask why, if they cared for each other, they should not be allowed to be together. But she knew that Mrs Breckenridge was speaking the truth. If people began to gossip about their friendship it would be harmful to James's career. It was unfair, but it was the way society worked. She drew a long breath and looked up.

'Very well, ma'am. I understand. I'll send James a note saying I can't see him again.'

'Thank you. I knew you would do the right thing when it was explained to you. I'll wish you good day.'

May returned to her workroom and took a sheet of paper and a pen. Nan was fiddling with a straw hat for another customer and took no notice of what she was doing. May wrote:

Dear James,

This is a very difficult letter to write. Your mother has just been to see me and pointed out to me that our friendship might be misunderstood and that it could damage your career. I should have seen that for myself. I have always known that our friendship could not last, but I have so much enjoyed our outings together that I never thought that it might cause you problems. You have been so kind to me and I shall always be grateful, but I see now that we must stop seeing each other. Please forgive me if this causes you any distress, but I know it is for the best.

Yours ever,
May

342

She found an envelope, addressed it and posted it on her way home.

Over supper Gus wanted to know what was the matter with her, but she made the excuse that she was not feeling well and escaped to her bedroom, where she wept bitterly but silently until she fell asleep from exhaustion.

The following Wednesday she found Armando waiting for her when she left work and saw at once from his face that something was wrong.

'I need to talk to you. Where can we go?'

It was a sunny afternoon. She led him to the pediment of St George's and they sat on the steps.

'What is it, Armando?' she asked. 'What's wrong?'

'They're sending me away.'

'Who are? Sending you where?'

'My parents. They're sending me to Italy, to live with my great uncle.'

'Why?'

'They say it will improve my skills. He is famous as a terrazzo artist. But I know it's not that.'

'What then?'

'They don't want me to see you any more. They are afraid that we are getting too fond of each other.'

'Is that so bad?'

'They think so. They want me to marry an Italian girl, and a Catholic.'

'I see.' May absorbed this in silence for a moment. Then she said, 'How long will you be gone for?'

'A year, two years? I don't know.' His head drooped. 'I'm sorry, May.'

'It isn't your fault. But did your parents really think we were going to marry?'

'Didn't you?'

'I don't know. We never spoke about it. But it would have been so far off, Armando. We are both too young to even think of marriage.'

'But I love you.'

'I know and I love you.' Even as she said it she was not sure it was true. 'But let's be realistic. We couldn't have gone on the way we were for much longer. I know what you wanted. I suppose I did too. But it couldn't happen. Perhaps it will actually be better for us to spend some time apart.'

He looked at her. 'Do you really believe that?'

'Yes. I shall miss you, Armando, terribly. But I think it is for the best.'

'I shall come back, in a year or two. Will you wait for me?'

'You shouldn't feel that you are bound to me. Your parents are probably right. You should marry an Italian girl. If you married me your parents would never accept me, and that would make us both miserable.'

'I don't want to marry an Italian girl! I want you!'

'You do now. But you may feel different in a year or two. I may feel different, too.'

'Is there someone else? Are you seeing someone else?'

'No. No, there's no one else.' At least she could be honest about that.

He got up. 'If that's what you want ...'

'It isn't what I want, Armando. But it is what has to happen. Can't you see that?'

He frowned at her. 'I won't change my mind. I shall come back for you.'

She sighed. 'You say that now, but things change. People change. Go to Italy. Improve your skills, like your parents want you to. When you come back, if you still feel the same we'll see . . .'She left the sentence unfinished and got to her feet. 'Good luck, Armando. Take care of yourself. I'll never forget the good times we had together.'

'You are cold!' He spat the words at her. 'You don't feel things like I do. Perhaps my mother was right. You are not the girl for me.'

'Perhaps she is,' May agreed sadly. 'Goodbye, dear Armando. I hope you find someone else.'

She reached up and kissed his cheek but he shrugged her off and walked away without looking back. She began to make her way home. They had planned to spend the afternoon together. Now there was nothing to do. She wondered at herself. She felt sad, but quite calm. In a way, it was a relief. Their relationship had become so intense, their physical passion so hard to control, that it had been a source of anxiety to her for some time. She had spoken the truth when she told him that she thought the separation was for the best. What she did feel was empty. She would not see James again, and now Armando was going. There was a vacuum at the centre of her life that she had no idea how to fill.

On Friday evening she could see that Gus was more on edge than usual. When Nan had gone out for her usual 'constitutional', he said, 'Come and sit down. I need to tell you something.'

He sat at the table instead of in his usual easy chair and she sat opposite him. 'What is it?'

'I'm going away. I've shipped aboard the *Royal Standard* bound for Melbourne as assistant purser.'

'Oh, you're going back to sea? Somehow I always thought you would.'

'No, not really. Only for this one voyage. When I get to Melbourne I'm staying there.'

'Staying there? For how long?'

'Always, probably. I'll find a job and settle down.' He leaned forward. 'They call it the New World, May, and it really is. It's a different life altogether. It doesn't matter who your father was or where you were born or educated. You can be whatever you want to be, as long as you're prepared to work hard. I've talked to the people who are emigrating, and they are full of such hope and optimism, and I remember what it was like when I was in Melbourne. There are so many opportunities. A man can get rich if he works hard.'

She reached across the table and grabbed his hands. 'Oh no, Gus! Please don't go. Don't leave me all alone.'

'You won't be alone. You've got Armando for one thing.'

'No, I haven't. Armando's parents are sending him back to Italy because they are afraid he's falling in love with me and they want him to marry an Italian girl.'

'Well, you seem to have been seeing a lot of James Breckenridge.'

'That's finished too. His mother came to see me and told me I'm damaging his career prospects. I've got no one now except you. Please, please Gus. Don't go!'

'Then come with me. Why not? We could set up home together and you could start your own millinery business.

Ladies in Melbourne need hats, just like they do here. I could still get you on board.'

'I can't!' The words came out as a sob. 'Don't you see? I've still got a year of my apprenticeship to run. I agreed to the terms and I can't go back on them now.'

'Ask Mr Freeman. He'll probably let you off.'

'No, I couldn't do that. He relies on me. I know I'm the apprentice, but Nan doesn't do much of the work now. You've seen how she is these days. Mr Freeman has been so good to me; I can't let him down. And Nan needs me too. She's been as good as a mother to me but now – well she needs looking after. I can't leave her.'

'Well, that's it, then.'

'Why don't you wait a year? I'll be free then and we could go together. You could hang on for a year, couldn't you?'

'No, I can't. I've signed on for this voyage. I'm committed.'

A thought struck May. 'It's this Kitty that's put the idea into your head, isn't it?'

He blushed slightly. 'Partly. I do like her, and I don't want to lose touch. But it's not just that. I can't see any prospects for me here, May. I don't want to be a clerk all my life. I've been thinking of going to Australia for a while now.'

She sat back and rubbed her tear-stained face. 'Then I suppose that's it. I'll have to cope on my own. I've done it before, so I can do it again.'

'You could come out and join me in a year, when your apprenticeship is up. How about that?'

'I don't know. Maybe. I'll have to think about it.'

'Yes, do that! It's the perfect answer. You'll love Australia, May. Please say you'll come.'

'I've said I'll think about it.' She got up from the table. 'I'm tired. I think I'll go up to bed.' Then as an afterthought, 'When are you sailing?'

'Sunday.'

'This Sunday?'

'Yes. Half an hour after noon.'

She leaned wearily on the banisters. 'I suppose I'd better come and see you off.'

On Sunday morning she missed church and went down to the docks with Gus. Her heart felt like a lead weight in her chest, but she was touched by his obvious excitement as he showed her round the White Star Line's only steamship. When the O'Dowd family came aboard she went with him to greet them and see them settled, and managed to behave politely to Kitty. Seeing the accommodation they had in steerage, the long rows of beds without privacy or comfort, she felt pity and was thankful that she was not travelling with them. She retained her dignity until the call went out – 'All ashore that's going ashore' – but then she clung to Gus and burst into tears.

'I don't know what I'm going to do without you.'

He shook her gently by the shoulders. 'Come on. I've only been around for just over a year. You coped all right before. You'll be fine.'

She drew back and stifled her sobs. 'Yes, of course I will. Do take care of yourself, Gus. And write as soon as you can. I hope you find what you are looking for.'

'I don't know what it is yet, but I'm sure I'll find it some-where. And you take care of yourself. Remember, it's only for a year. We'll see each other again then.'

The *Royal Standard* sailed with the tide and May stood on the dockside and waved her off. Then she turned and trudged miserably back towards Nan's house.

As she came in sight of it, she saw a familiar figure standing outside the door. She caught her breath and hur-ried forward.

'James! What are you doing here?'

'Where have you been? I looked for you at St Barnabus's and when you weren't there I thought perhaps you were ill, so I came to see.' He looked at her more closely. 'What's wrong? You've been crying. Whatever's happened?'

'Gus has gone to Australia. I've just seen him off. He … he's not coming back.' And suddenly she was in his arms, sobbing into his chest.

He held her tightly, rubbing his cheek into her hair and murmuring, 'Oh, poor girl! Poor girl! I'm so sorry.'

After a few minutes she collected herself and drew back to look at him. 'Why are you here? I told you it was all over.'

'I got your letter. That's why I came. Can we go inside?'

She opened the door and led him into the cluttered sit-ting room. She went to remove a pile of sewing from an easy chair so that he could sit, but he caught her arm and turned her to face him.

'May, don't be angry with me. I can't accept what you said in your letter. I have had a long talk with my mother. I've told her that you are a perfectly respectable young woman, the daughter of a sea captain. You can't be blamed for the fact that your family fell on hard times and you had to earn your own living. I said that I believe you could hold your own in any company and conduct yourself so that any man would be happy to have you for his wife. And finally I said point-blank that I am not prepared to give you up. So, can we forget all that silly business about damaging my career and go back to the way we were?'

She blinked at him, unable for the moment to find words. She had completely forgotten the lie she had told about her parentage. She had done it so that he would not look down on her, and now it seemed her deception had come home to roost. Her thoughts churned wildly. Was it too late, now, to tell him the truth? And if she did, would it change the way he felt about her? Perhaps it would be better to live with the lie ...

He put an end to her internal turmoil by taking her in his arms and kissing her properly for the first time.

Fifteen

For May, the summer of 1867 was replete with new experiences and new discoveries. She met James every Sunday afternoon and he decided that they should use the time to explore the surrounding areas by any means possible. On the first Sunday he met her with the greeting, 'Put on your hat. We're going on a train ride.'

'A train?' she said. 'I don't know ... I've never been on a train.'

'You'll love it, I promise,' he responded.

'Where are we going?'

'There are lots of possibilities. I've been looking at the schedules for the Crosby and Southport line. We might go as far as Southport one day, but today I thought we would just go as far as Bootle. Do you fancy an afternoon at the seaside?'

'Yes, I suppose so.' She had very little idea of what that term implied but if James thought it a good idea that was enough for her.

The train frightened her and when the locomotive came chuffing into the platform, breathing fire and smoke, it was all she could do not to turn and run. But once they were on board and moving she gave herself up to the thrill of speed.

'We're going so fast! I didn't know anything could go so fast.'

'It's exciting, isn't it?' he agreed, lifting his face to the wind rushing through the window.

May watched the city streets give way to fields of young wheat and meadows full of wild flowers. 'Oh, look! What are those animals? They don't look like horses.'

'That's because they're cows. Haven't you ever seen a cow before?'

'You don't see many cows in the city,' she pointed out.

The journey came to an end all too soon, but James promised that next time they would go further afield. They got out at the little station and walked downhill towards the sea. May was used to the broad expanse of the Mersey but the vastness of the open sea was almost overwhelming.

'What happens if you take a boat and just keep going straight out?' she asked.

'You fall off the edge,' he said.

She looked at him, for a moment thinking he was serious; then she laughed and punched him in the side. 'I'm not that stupid!'

'No, I know you're not. I suppose if you keep going you get to Ireland.'

It was a beautiful late-spring afternoon and the long beach was dotted with families enjoying the sunshine. Children were splashing in the shallows and a few hardy souls were swimming.

May stood on one leg and shook the other foot. 'The sand is getting inside my boots.'

'Take them off,' he suggested. 'We could paddle.'

They sat on the sea wall and he pulled off his boots and socks, then knelt in the sand and helped her to remove her shoes. She stood and turned her back to lift the hem of her skirt and pull off her stockings and then he took her hand and led her down to the edge of the sea. The sand was hot and dry under her feet at first, then cool and ridged and squeezed up between her toes.

'Ah, it's cold,' she gasped as the first small wave covered her ankles.

'No, it's not,' he said. 'Not when you get used to it. Let's walk along a bit.'

They strolled further up the beach, to where there were fewer people, and after a while he admitted that the water was cold and they moved to dryer land. Suddenly a ball whistled over their heads and landed on the sand a few yards in front of them. There was an excited bark and a scamper of running feet and a large brown dog galloped past them and seized the ball in its mouth.

'Oh dear, I must apologise,' said a breathless voice from behind them, and they turned to see an elderly lady hurrying in their direction. 'I do hope I didn't give you too much of a shock. I'm afraid my aim is not as good as it might be.'

'That's quite all right,' James said. He nodded towards the dog, which was trotting back towards them. 'He seems to enjoy the game.'

'Oh, he loves it, but I'm afraid he likes to play it his way,' she replied. 'Rascal! Here! Bring the ball.'

Rascal came to within a few feet and dropped the ball on the sand, but as his owner bent to pick it up he seized it and ran off again, then stopped to look back, his tail wagging furiously.

'You see! He just likes to tease me. He knows I can't run after him as I once would have done.'

'Allow me,' James said. He ran forwards, made a sharp lunge and grabbed the dog by the collar.

'Oh, be careful!' May called.

'Don't worry,' the lady said. 'He won't bite. He just loves a game.'

James and the dog wrestled playfully for the ball and James won. He straightened up and threw it again, far ahead of them, and Rascal pelted after it with a yelp of glee. He brought it back and dropped it at James's feet and the wrestling match was repeated, but this time instead of throwing it up the beach James spun round and called, 'May! Catch!'

The ball hurtled towards her and she instinctively raised her hands and caught it. Rascal was running towards her, but she threw the ball back to James. For several minutes they threw the ball backwards and forwards, while Rascal ran between them, yelping in hysterical excitement. Then May missed a catch and the dog had the ball and raced away with it. James went after him, fleeter of foot then she had ever imagined, retrieved the ball and brought it back to present it to the dog's owner with a small bow.

'Yours, I think. I hope you didn't mind us joining in the fun.'

'Not at all. Rascal hasn't had so much exercise for years. He'll be quite docile now till we get home. Now, I really must be getting back. Rascal! Heel boy!'

To May's surprise, the dog obeyed and the pair turned back towards the village. She looked at James. He had pulled off his tie and his shirt was open at the neck. His face was flushed and a lock of blond hair had fallen over his forehead. He saw her looking.

'What? Why are you looking at me like that?'

'It's just I've never seen you like this before. You look like a young boy.'

He laughed. 'Well, I'm not quite in my dotage yet.'

'I didn't mean that. But you always seemed so ... well, so grown up.'

'Oh dear! Am I such a dried-up old stick? I suppose it's working in the law. One is expected to exhibit a certain gravitas.' In response to her look of enquiry he explained, 'It means being sober and sensible. But it's only a pretence. How old do you think I am?'

'I ... I don't know.'

'All right. You tell me how old you are, and I'll tell you how old I am.'

'I shall be seventeen in about three weeks.'

'And I'll be twenty-one in August.'

'Is that all?'

'I'm sorry if it's a disappointment. I'm not the wise, old, elder statesman you imagined.'

'It's not a disappointment. I'm glad.' She reached for his hand. 'I like to see you like this.'

'Good.' He glanced round quickly to see if anyone was watching and swept her into his arms to kiss her.

The next Sunday they took the train further, to Freshfields, and walked through pine woods where tiny red squirrels scampered through the branches above their heads. Following that they took the ferry to the recently established resort of New Brighton, at the tip of the Wirral peninsula, where, in the woods that ran down almost to the edge of the sea, May saw wild primroses and bluebells for the first time.

At the edge of a little stream, daffodils flaunted their gold, and James said, 'Beside the lake, beneath the trees, fluttering and dancing in the breeze.'

'What?'

'You know, Wordsworth's "Daffodils". You don't know it?'

'I'm afraid not.'

'Don't you like poetry?'

'I ... don't know many poems.' How could she tell him that the only poetry she had ever heard was nursery rhymes?

'I love poetry. Not what you'd expect from a lawyer, perhaps, but I'm a romantic at heart. I was lucky. At school we had a teacher who was very keen on Wordsworth and Tennyson and Shelley. He made us learn whole chunks by heart. Some of the fellows were put off poetry for good but I found it easy. I still remember a lot of it.'

'Where did you go to school?'

'The Royal Institution Grammar School. It's a good school.'

'Yes, it must be.'

She was afraid he might ask her the same question, but he did not. She guessed that he assumed that, like most girls, she had been educated at home. He did not brag about his education, taking it for granted that most men in his position had had roughly the same; but as they got to know each other better she discovered that he knew Latin and Greek and history and geography as well as poetry.

James had to work on Wednesdays, so she had the afternoons to herself. Patty was now walking out with a young man from the stores department, so she was not available, and May found herself at a loose end.

Pondering the huge gulf between her education, or lack of it, and James's, she determined to try to remedy the situation. He had said that he was sure she could hold her own in any society, but she knew very well that she would be at a loss talking to any of his friends. She began to buy the current editions of Charles Dickens's magazine, *All the Year Round*, and read articles about politics and the latest scientific discoveries, as well as the short stories, but there was so much she did not understand that she almost gave up.

Nan, finding her sighing wearily over a page, said briskly, 'Well, don't just sit there moping. There are encyclopaedias and all sorts in the William Brown Library. Go and find out.'

The library had been built behind St George's Hall with funds from the philanthropist whose name it bore. May approached the grand building with some trepidation but found that once inside the librarians were happy to direct her to the information she wanted. She began to spend most of her Wednesday afternoons browsing through the shelves.

One day one of the librarians asked if she had ever read a book by Samuel Smiles called *Self-Help; with illustrations of Character and Conduct*. She borrowed it and discovered that, although much of it was so far from her daily experience that it was hard to follow, there were inspirational passages. She particularly liked his denunciation of 'the worship of power, wealth, success, and keeping up appearances'. It made her feel that her rejection of some of the ideas she had been brought up with – to 'know her place' and 'respect her betters' – was not as wicked as she had feared.

One Sunday she and James found their way to the botanical gardens at Wavertree and were fascinated by the orchids in one of the glasshouses. May always carried her sketchbook and was immediately absorbed in drawing them.

Looking over her shoulder, James said, 'You draw so well, and I know you love colour. I'm surprised you don't paint as well.'

May looked up from her sketchbook. Somehow the idea had never occurred to her. 'I wouldn't know where to begin.' But she realised as she spoke that she did know. She had not thought about it for a long time, but now she recalled sitting on the stairs she was supposed to be sweeping and listening to Mr Latimer instructing Isabella. She remembered, too, Isabella's inept attempts to follow his instructions. 'I suppose,' she said, 'I just never had any paints.'

The following Sunday he handed a package. 'A little birthday present.'

Inside was a box of watercolour paints and a selection of brushes.

May's evenings and Wednesday afternoons were given up from then on to experimenting with colour. It was frustrating and one Sunday she remarked to James that she never seemed quite to achieve what she was aiming for.

'Maybe it would help to look at some really fine examples, to get some inspiration,' he suggested.

'Where would I find those?' she queried.

'Oh, that's easy. You remember I told you I went to the Royal Institution School? It's just part of the institute itself, which was set up to give people a chance to learn about art and literature and science. They hold lectures and they have an art gallery. We could go and look.'

Another new world opened up for May. Many of the pictures on display were by members of what she learned was called the Pre-Raphaelite School. She did not know what that meant but the romanticism of many of the subjects awoke a similar response in her own soul.

She went back again the next Wednesday and stood rapt in front of first one and then another. She knew that with the simple watercolours at her disposal she could never achieve anything comparable, but that did not stop her trying. Flowers and leaves and fruits were her favourite subjects, entwined into the intricate designs she had always loved, and after a while she began to gain some satisfaction from the results.

The introduction to the Royal Institution had another benefit. James had casually mentioned that lectures were held there and in that May found an answer to some of the gaps in her education. Lectures on the romantic poets allowed her to share James's love for their work; and for the first time she began to have some grasp of history and the geography of the world. As the summer passed she began to feel that in time she might become the sort of woman he needed as a wife.

* * *

The SS *Royal Standard* docked in Melbourne towards the end of June. For Gus, the voyage had been a great deal more enjoyable than he expected. For one thing, as purser's assistant he was no longer liable to be kicked and cuffed by the officers; and the ship, steel-hulled and built to carry passengers rather than cargo, as had been the initial purpose of the wooden-hulled *Shenandoah*, was a good deal more comfortable and stable than his previous experience.

In addition, whereas the *Shenandoah* had avoided entering any port and relied on replenishing supplies from the prizes taken, the *Royal Standard* made regular stops for re-coaling and resupplying. So Gus was able to visit places like Cape Town and Singapore, which he had heard of from the reports of fellow crew members, but had never seen.

But it was the presence of Kitty on board that really made the difference. Whenever the weather was good enough for the passengers to be allowed on deck, and his duties permitted, Gus sought her out and they spent hours walking the decks or leaning on the rail gazing down at the sea.

He showed her dolphins and flying fish and once an albatross came gliding on huge outspread wings above the mast. It was not an unadulterated pleasure, however. Whenever they met it seemed there was always at least one other member of the family nearby. If they walked, her brother would always find it necessary to take some exercise too. If they stood at the rail, her mother or father would be settled in a seat not far away. They were usually out of earshot, so their conversation was uninhibited, but talking was as far as their relationship was allowed to progress.

He told her about his time on the *Shenandoah* and she talked about the life she had left behind in Ireland; and eventually he admitted to having grown up in the workhouse. She said she was glad he had known what it was to be poor, among the lowest of the low, because it placed them on an equal footing.

Shortly after leaving Cape Town they hit bad weather and the entire O'Dowd family were prostrated with sea-sickness – all except Kitty. Gus persuaded her to join him in a corner of the deck where the superstructure gave some shelter from the wind, and also from prying eyes, and under the pretext of keeping her warm, he put his arms round her. She did not object, but huddled close to him, and embold-ened he bent his head and tried to kiss her.

His first attempt was not a success. She moved her head and he found his lips pressed to her ear, but then she realigned herself and he found her lips. He half expected a slap, or that at the least she would insist on moving away. But instead he discovered he had a willing partner. His heart was pounding, and his body was responding in ways he would have been ashamed to admit, and after a few min-utes they drew apart, breathless and unsure what to do next.

The situation was resolved by an order from the bridge. 'All passengers below! Batten down the hatches.'

She pulled away. 'I'll have to go.'

'Yes,' he agreed. 'Come on, I'll take you.'

He escorted her to the head of the companionway that led down to the steerage level. Most of the other passengers were already below decks and as he watched her descend he wished he could save her from the noisome darkness that would ensue, once the hatches were secured, but he knew that to keep her out would only end with them both in trouble.

Luckily, the spell of bad weather did not last long and the passengers were once again given the freedom of the deck, but he felt a certain constraint had arisen between himself and Kitty. They had both been disturbed by the emotions they had aroused and he was beset by a kind of gallantry; he needed to protect her from the possible consequences of a repeat performance. Very soon her family recovered from their seasickness and they went back to the safety of their supervised conversations.

As they watched the skyline of Melbourne materialise out of the haze on the horizon, he said, 'We will see each other, when we're ashore, won't we?'

'I certainly hope so,' she replied. 'But where will you be?'

'I don't know yet. I have to find a job. Where will you be?'

'There's a lodging house where we can stay, until Dad finds a place to set up in business. I'm not sure of the address.'

'I have an idea,' he said. 'When I was here before I made friends with some people who own a hotel. I'm going to call on them as soon as I get ashore and they may help me to find work. But anyway, if you were to send a note to me there, I'm sure they would pass it on. It's called Croft's Hotel. Anyone will tell you where it is.'

She looked at him. 'I've really liked being with you, Gus, and the talks we've had. I'd like it to go on.'

'So would I,' he responded. 'We'll keep in touch and maybe, one day ...' He left the sentence unfinished.

'Yes, maybe ... one day,' she said and glanced behind her. Her mother was in conversation with another women and her father and brother were straining their eyes for the first glimpse of their new home. She leaned up and kissed him, quickly, on the lips and then moved away to join her mother.

He was busy from the time they docked and in the turmoil of passengers eager to get ashore he almost missed her. He caught sight of the family just as they were about to descend the gangplank and waved and called, 'Good luck!' She waved back and he shouted, 'Croft's Hotel, remember.'

'I won't forget,' she called back, and then she was swallowed up in the straining, pushing crowd.

As soon as he had completed the necessary paperwork for his discharge, Gus said goodbye to his shipmates and headed for Croft's Hotel. The streets of Melbourne felt comfortingly familiar and, although it was winter now, the sun was shining. His heart lifted. There was no knowing what lay in store for him, but it was going to be a new life and the possibilities were endless.

The first person he saw when he entered the foyer of the hotel was Victoria, stationed behind the reception desk. She had put her hair up and looked very grown up but he had no difficulty recognising her. He dropped his bag on the floor and went to the desk. She looked up from a ledger and he said, 'Good day! Remember me?'

'Gus! Of course I remember.' Her face lit up. 'How could I forget? It's lovely to see you again.'

'It's good to see you, too,' he said, feeling suddenly shy.

'What are you doing back in Melbourne? Have you just come off a ship?'

'Yes, I'm straight off the *Royal Standard*.'

'You've never emigrated!'

'Not exactly. I came over as a member of the crew. But I plan to stay.'

Mr Croft came down the stairs and Victoria called, 'Dad, come and see who's here. It's Gus Lavender. You remember him, don't you?'

'I certainly do,' her father replied. 'Welcome back, Gus.' They shook hands and Mr Croft looked him up and down. 'Well, you look a bit different from the scruffy kid you were last time around.'

'Isn't he smart?' Victoria said. 'He's off the *Royal Standard.*'

'Not as a cabin boy, this time, at a guess.'

'No. Purser's assistant.'

'Really? Well, that's a step up and no mistake. I always thought you were a bright kid. What have you been doing with yourself since the *Shenandoah* was here?'

'Oh, this and that. I've been back in Liverpool, working as a clerk for the White Star Line, until I decided to ship on the *Standard.*'

'So when do you sail? You must stay here until then, unless you've got somewhere better to go, that is.'

'No, I've got nowhere else. I'd be grateful to stay for a bit. I'm not planning to go back. I'm looking for a job.'

Mr Croft studied his face for a moment. 'Looking for a job, eh? Well, there's one here for you, if you fancy it.'

'Here? Doing what?'

'As a receptionist. Victoria's only filling in. Our last girl left to get married and I haven't filled the post yet, so if you want it it's yours.'

Gus looked from him to Victoria and she said, 'Do stay, Gus. I'll be glad to get out of the job.'

'Well, if you're sure. I'd be glad to take it on.'

'It'll give you a start, anyway,' Mr Croft said. 'You may want to look around for something with better prospects, but we'll be glad to have you while you do. The salary's nothing to write home about, but you'll have your bed and board. So if you're happy with that ...?'

'More than happy! I'm really grateful, sir.'

'No need. You're filling a gap in the staffing and it'll save me advertising.' He turned to his daughter. 'You'd better take Gus upstairs and show him his room. Then when you've unpacked I hope you'll join us for dinner.'

The room was small, but not as small as the box room he had occupied in Nan's house, and it had a view of the garden with its exotic trees and brilliantly coloured birds.

'I'll leave you to settle in,' Victoria said. 'I'm so glad you've come back, Gus.'

As the door closed behind her, he dumped his bag on the bed and stretched his arms. He had a room and a job and he was among friends. He could hardly believe his luck.

* * *

In Liverpool, as the summer weeks passed, May and James continued their explorations. They walked the tow-path along the Liverpool-to-Leeds canal and watched the barges, drawn by their slow-plodding horses, carrying coal to the city or cotton to the mills. They took the train as far as Southport and listened to band concerts in Birkenhead Park or New Brighton.

On each occasion they found a secluded spot to exchange kisses, but May never allowed them to develop into the frantic passion she had shared with Armando. It was not that she did not feel the same desire for James's caresses. If anything, it was stronger; but it was that very strength that made her hold back. She remembered very well with Armando how their mutual passion had exhausted them both, in the knowledge that it could not be satisfied for many years. Her love for James was too precious to allow that to happen; and besides, she was still unsure what future consummation it might have. James seemed to understand all this without it being spoken. At any rate, he was prepared to exercise the same restraint and patience.

As the summer drew to an end, a shadow fell over both their lives. James was becoming increasingly concerned about his mother's health. The pains which she had put down to indigestion had worsened, and no amount of bicarbonate of soda, or the various other nostrums she was advised to try by friends, seemed to help. A doctor was consulted and prescribed rest and a light diet, but there was no improvement.

May, in turn, was worried about Nan. She was drinking more and more and the effects were becoming more difficult to conceal. She often did not come home in the evening until May was in bed, and she would hear her bumping into the furniture and knocking things over, swearing to herself until she managed to find her way upstairs. It was increasingly difficult to rouse her in the morning and she came to work later and later; then she would go to the pub again at dinnertime and spend the rest of the afternoon asleep. May worked longer hours in an attempt to make good the work Nan should have done, and tried to keep her away from

customers or anyone in authority, but it was getting more
and more difficult.

* * *

Gus had settled happily into his new life. His work as receptionist was not demanding and he enjoyed the opportunity
to meet new people. They came from all over the world
and all areas of the surrounding countryside and from all
walks of life and, in the egalitarian ethos of Australia, they
were usually quite happy to chat about their work and the
places where they lived. It gave Gus the chance to develop
a perspective on how the colony was growing and the new
possibilities that were opening up. He recognised that he
was not going to be satisfied in the long term with the job
he was doing, but until something better presented itself he
was happy to jog along from day to day.

Mark, one of Victoria's brothers, was home from school,
learning the hotel business from his father, and they got
on well. Victoria herself reintroduced him to the circle of
friends he had met on his first visit and he joined in their
sports and games. With the arrival of spring, the cricket
season started again and Mark began to teach him how to
play. Another friend had a small yacht and Gus enjoyed
sailing round the bay and adapting what he had first learned
at the Industrial School under Captain Thomas to the new
technique. More than anything, it was having leisure time
to devote to sport – something he had only sampled briefly
in Sunday afternoon football games – that he relished.

Kitty and her brother came in one day to tell him that the
family was moving on. It seemed Melbourne was already

well supplied with cobblers so they were going to try their luck in the little town of Chiltern, which had sprung up in the wake of the gold rush. It was a disappointment, but Gus consoled himself with the knowledge that it was less than a day's journey and he would be able to visit when he had time off.

One morning he was in his usual place behind the reception desk when a thickset man in middle age, smartly dressed, came into the hotel and asked for a room. Gus handed over a set of keys and took up a pen.

'Your name, sir?'

'Lavender.'

Gus looked up sharply. How could this stranger know his name? 'No, sorry, sir. I meant your name.'

'That is my name. And I don't want any cracks about how sweet or otherwise I smell. What's the matter with you?'

Gus had dropped the pen and was leaning with both hands flat on the desk. 'I'm sorry.' The words forced themselves from a tightened throat. 'Your name is Lavender?'

'I just said so, didn't I?'

'That's my name, too.'

'Yours?'

They stared at each other across the desk and Gus saw that although the stranger's hair was thinning, his neatly trimmed beard and moustache were fiery red.

'I'm Gus,' he managed to say. 'Augustus Lavender.'

'Dear God!' The man was now leaning his hands on the desk for support. 'Where were you born?'

'Liverpool.'

'How old are you?'

'Almost fifteen.' He swallowed hard. 'I think you may be my father.'

'Great God in heaven! I think you're right.' Hands reached across the desk and gripped his arms. 'Gus! By all that's holy! I never thought I'd see you again.'

'I knew you weren't dead!' Gus gasped. 'I always said lost at sea didn't have to mean drowned. But I thought you would be in America somewhere. How did you get here?'

'I might ask you the same question,' his father said.

'Oh, I came on a ship. It's a long story. But I'm staying here now.'

His father relaxed his grip. 'Lost at sea, eh? So that's what they told you. How's your mother? Is she here with you?'

'No, she died.'

'I'm sorry to hear it. But you had a sister, too. What about her?'

'May, she's still at home in Liverpool.'

'She must be a grown woman now.'

'She's seventeen.'

'Seventeen! How the years go by!'

'But why are you here?' Gus was beginning to recover from the shock. 'Why didn't you come home?'

Mr Croft came into the foyer and, seeing them confronting each other across the desk, came over. 'Is there a problem here? Can I help?'

Gus broke the intense eye contact and turned his gaze to his employer. 'Sir, this is my father.'

'Your father? I thought you told me you were an orphan.'

'I thought I was.'

Mr Croft looked from one to the other. 'Well, I can see the resemblance.' He held out his hand. 'I don't know where you've sprung from, my friend, but you're very welcome.'

'Thank you. I guess I've got a lot of explaining to do.'

'Not to me, but Gus must have plenty of questions to ask. Gus, why don't you take your father up to his room so you can talk in private? I'll get Victoria to take care of the desk for the next hour or two.'

Gus showed his father the way up to the room on the first floor and set his case down on the bed.

For a moment they looked at each other in silence, then his father said. 'I owe you an explanation and an apology. Shall we sit down?'

They sat on the balcony and Mr Lavender drew a long breath. 'You were told I was lost at sea. I'm afraid it wasn't the truth. The fact is, I was transported.'

'Transported!'

'I was stupid enough to let a couple of mates persuade me to join them in a bit of smuggling. Nothing much, just a bit of rum and tobacco, but of course it all went wrong and we were caught. I was sentenced to be transported for ten years.'

'Ten years?' Gus was calculating. 'I was only a baby when Ma said you'd gone. The ten years must have been up – what four or five years ago. Why didn't you come home?'

His father sighed. 'Perhaps I should have. But I hadn't had any word from your mother in all that time. I reckoned she'd made a new life for herself, maybe married again. I didn't want to come back and spoil things for her – and you. Having an ex-convict for a father isn't the best start in life.'

'You didn't hear,' Gus said, swallowing back tears, 'because she was dead.'

'When did she die?'

'I was two years old. She got ill and died.'

'Two years old? So May would have been, what, four. Who took care of you?'

'No one. We were sent to the workhouse, with the other orphans.'

'The workhouse!' His father sat silent, his throat working. 'If I'd known ... But I had another seven or eight years to serve. I should have come back, as soon as I was free. I didn't realise ...'

'There's no reason why you should.'

'You said you never believed I was dead. Why?'

'I don't know. I just had that feeling. I always said one day I was going to sea to look for you.' He gave a laugh that was almost a sob. 'Looks like I found you in the end.'

'So what have you been doing with yourself, since you left the workhouse? Did you go to sea?'

As briefly as he could, Gus outlined the story of his adventures: how he had stowed away and found himself on board the *Shenandoah*; the year-long voyage and the return to Liverpool. He glossed over his time working on the docks and his narrow escape from a prison sentence and told instead how he had found a job with the White Star Line. 'I knew I didn't want to stay in that job for ever, and I'd liked the look of Melbourne when the *Shenandoah* was in port here, so I signed on as purser's assistant for the voyage out here. I'd met Mr Croft when I was here before, so I came to see him and he offered me a job. So here I am.'

'And your sister, May?'

'She's all right. She had to go into service, for a while, but then she got an apprenticeship as a milliner. She's really good at it. I reckon she'll have her own business one day.'

There was a knock at the door. The boot boy, who doubled as a messenger and general servant, was outside with two bottles of cold beer. 'Mr Croft said he reckoned you could both do with a drink – on the house.'

Gus thanked him and carried the beer out onto the balcony. They clinked the bottles together and his father said, 'Here's to healing the past and a bright future.'

Gus nodded and drank. 'You haven't said what you did after you were released. From the way you're dressed, I guess you've done all right.'

His father took a long pull at his beer. 'You might say that. You might well say that. It's quite a story …'

Sixteen

Nan's drinking was getting out of hand. One day May had to send someone to fetch her after she fell down on the way back from the pub and was taken into someone's house, more or less incapable.

Next morning she was sent for by Mr Freeman.

'May, it has been brought to my notice than Nan is drinking far too much. I realise that you have been concealing the problem for some time. I applaud your loyalty but you really should have spoken to me sooner.'

May dropped her eyes. 'I'm sorry. I suppose I should, have but I didn't want to see her getting the sack.'

'I understand that. But the fact is she has become a liability. One of our best customers heard what happened yesterday and reported it to me.'

'So what do you want me to do?'

'There's no need for you to do anything. I've already had a long talk with Nan and we have agreed that it is time for her to retire. I shall give her a small pension, in recognition of her years of good work. Did you know she has a married sister who lives on a farm in Wales?'

'She mentioned her once or twice. They don't get on.'

'Apparently there has been a reconciliation. As far as I understand it, the sister married a man Nan had hopes of for herself and that caused the breach, but the husband is now dead and they have decided to let bygones be bygones.'

'She did go away for a couple of days a few week-ends ago. She didn't say where. I suppose that's when it happened.'

'So it seems. She plans to go and live with her sister.'

'Oh!' The implications of what had been said were just beginning to come clear to May. 'So what happens now?'

'That is what I want to talk about. Strictly speaking, your apprenticeship still has almost a year to run, but you have shown that you are more than capable of fulfilling the demands of the job, so I propose to free you from it and make you a fully qualified milliner.'

'Thank you, sir!'

'Don't thank me yet. The next thing I have to say may not please you so well. In many ways, the logical thing for me to do is to put you in charge of the millinery depart-ment. Lord knows, you've been running it more or less single-handed for months. But there is a problem. It really needs two people. I can't bring in a new apprentice. You are only just qualified yourself, and that without serving out your time. I can't put an apprentice to work under you, and I can't ask a qualified milliner to accept you as head of the department. The only solution seems to be to bring in someone else to run the department with you as her assis-tant. I appreciate that that may not be the ideal answer as far as you are concerned. In a few years you will be more than qualified to run a department, either here or in another store – or to set up in business on your own account. But for now it has to be as I have outlined. I hope you are not too disappointed.'

May was struggling to assimilate what he had said. 'I … no. I mean, I never expected to run the department. I don't mind working with someone else. Who will it be?'

'I don't know yet. I shall have to advertise. I'll let you know when I've appointed someone. But there is another aspect to the situation that we need to discuss.'

'Oh?'

'As Nan is going to live with her sister she will need to sell her house. I know you have come to regard that as your home, but there it is. I don't want you living in some sleazy lodging house on your own. So I think the best solution is for you to move in with the other girls.'

'Oh!' This really was a blow. May knew from her friends that life in the accommodation provided by the store was much more restricted than her own had been. The housekeeper in charge saw it as her duty to guard the moral welfare of the girls, as well as to look after their physical needs, and that meant strict rules about what time they came in at night and probing enquiries about where they were going and who they were seeing in their free time. She was pretty sure her relationship with James would not be approved of, and would soon get back to Mr Freeman's ears.

'Sorry, May. I know you don't like the idea, but that's just the way it has to be, for the time being at any rate. I'm sure you'll soon get used to it – and you'll have friends of your own age around you.'

'How soon will I have to move?' May asked.

'That will depend on how quickly Nan can sell her house. Now, you'd better get back to work. I'll let you know when I have any more news.'

Events moved too quickly for May's comfort after that. Nan declared that she intended to move in with her sister straight away and that she felt it would be 'unsuitable' for May to remain in the house alone. At the end of the week she moved into the store. It meant exchanging her familiar bedroom for a dormitory shared with four others, and the cosy sitting room, which she had had to herself most evenings, for the noisy common room. If she tried to sketch she was constantly pestered by other girls wanting to know what she was doing and why; and there was no room to paint. In short there was no peace and very little privacy.

On Wednesday afternoons she was invited to join the others in various activities, most of which involved clandestine assignations with some of the occupants of the men's dormitory, and was thought 'stuck up' when she said she was going to a lecture at the Royal Institution. She was subjected to intense inquisitions, both from the housekeeper and the other girls, about who she was meeting on Sundays and was forced to invent a boyfriend who lived in Southport and came down by train. She had told James never to call for her at the store and they always said goodbye several streets away.

It was not long before she was summoned again to Mr Freeman's office. There was a woman with him.

'Ah, Miss Jones, this is May Lavender. As I told you, she has run the department almost single-handedly while our previous milliner was indisposed and done a very good job of it. She is a talented young lady and already has her own clientele. I'm sure you will find her a very able assistant.'

Miss Jones was, May judged, in her mid-thirties. She was a tall, spare woman, respectably dressed in black but of a fabric and a cut that proclaimed her familiarity with the latest fashion plates from Paris. She was handsome, rather than beautiful, with strongly pronounced features and hair so black that May doubted whether it could be entirely natural, and dressed in a style that might have been becoming on a younger, prettier girl but looked quite inappropriate to May.

In response to Mr Freeman's introduction she inclined her head unsmilingly and said, 'How do you do?'

May bobbed a small curtsy. 'Pleased to meet you, ma'am.'

'Miss Jones,' Mr Freeman went on, 'is a very experienced milliner. She and a partner have had their own business for several years in Warrington but her partner has retired and so Miss Jones has elected to find "fresh woods and pastures new".'

Miss Jones looked down her rather long nose at him as if he had said something very foolish. 'I am not aware of many woods in Liverpool.'

May, familiar with the quotation from James, smiled. 'I think Mr Freeman was quoting the poet Milton.'

Her reward from her employer was a raised eyebrow and the hint of a smile. From Miss Jones it earned a stony glare.

Freeman cleared his throat. 'Miss Jones will start work on Monday. I'm sure I can look forward to a millinery department that will be the envy of all other stores. Thank you, May. You had better get back to work. I'm sure there are ladies eager to acquire one of your latest creations.'

When May arrived for work on the Monday morning she found Miss Jones already standing in the middle of the workroom.

'Well!' she said. 'I have never seen a place in such a mess. You may be able to work in the middle of chaos, but I cannot. So you had better get started and tidy up.'

It was on the tip of May's tongue to protest that she had an urgent commission to finish for one of her regular customers, but she thought better of it. It was true, she had to admit, that Nan's lackadaisical attitude to tidiness had rubbed off on her. She knew exactly where to put her hand on things, but she could see it would not be easy for a newcomer.

As May moved around, putting things away, Miss Jones fell to examining the hats, in various stages of completion, which were on models around the room. She picked them up, turned them around and returned them with a small snort of disdain. Then she began to look through May's sketch pad, where she drew out her ideas for new designs. Eventually, she closed it and looked at May.

'I can see that there is a need for someone to take this department in hand. Were you seriously proposing to execute these designs?'

'Most of them,' May replied. 'But I always show them to the customer for her approval first.'

'And these half-finished hats. Have the designs for them been approved by customers?'

'Oh yes. In fact, the lady who ordered this one –' she picked up the one she had been intending to finish when she came in '– will be here at any minute and she wants it for a special occasion. So if you will allow me ...'

'I am truly amazed at the poor taste some of these ladies must have. These designs are months behind the times. I can see that there is a big task ahead of me to re-educate you and them about modern fashion.'

'Some of the leading ladies of Liverpool society come to me for their hats!' May exclaimed.

Miss Jones shook her head. 'Dear, dear. I feel sorry for them, having to subject themselves to the caprices of an inexperienced girl. Well, they can rest assured that they are in safe hands now.'

May was about to protest when a messenger boy came to the door. 'Pardon me, miss, but Lady Vickers is here.'

'That is the lady I was telling you about,' May said. 'I shall have to explain to her that the hat is not quite ready, but it will be finished by the end of the day.'

She was halfway to the door when Miss Jones's voice stopped her. 'Where do you think you are going?'

'I thought you heard the boy say that Lady Vickers is upstairs waiting for me.'

Miss Jones stalked past her. 'Let us have one thing quite clear, young lady. From now on I am in charge here, and I shall deal with all the customers. When we have agreed the style required, I shall tell you and you can start on the basic work. The finishing will be in my hands.' She turned to the boy. 'Pray tell Lady Vickers that I shall be with her directly. Now, where is the hat in question?'

May handed it over, biting her lip, and Miss Jones took it with a theatrical sigh and left the room.

Alone, May was on the verge of tears – but they were tears of rage. She knew that her designs were adaptations of the very latest fashions and that her loyal customers were always delighted with them. Now it seemed she was to be demoted to being a mere skivvy and not allowed to use her creative talents. It was so unfair!

When she had calmed down she told herself that perhaps these were teething troubles, that after a while Miss Jones would not feel it so necessary to assert her position; and that her own loyal customers would speak up for her and insist on having their hats made by her.

In the days that followed she learned that this was not going to be the case. What passed between Miss Jones and the customers she did not know, but she could only assume that they had been browbeaten into accepting that their ideas of high fashion were mistaken and that Miss Jones was to be trusted as the fount of all wisdom on the subject. Meanwhile, she found herself relegated to the most basic and mundane tasks and kept well away from the front of the shop, where she might have met the ladies she had once designed for.

Three weeks of this, together with the discomfort of her new living arrangements, was more than enough. One Sunday afternoon, sitting by James on a bench beside the canal with no one nearby except a fisherman intent on his rod twenty yards away, she burst into tears.

'May? What's wrong? Dearest, whatever is the matter?' James put his arm round her shoulders.

'I can't bear it!' she sobbed. 'Miss Jones is so hateful and she won't let me do anything but the basic shapes, and all my good customers have forsaken me and I'm not allowed to see them. And I hate living in the store, too. I was so happy before, when Nan was still with me, and now I don't know what to do. I can't bear to go on like this.'

James handed her a clean handkerchief. 'Don't cry, my love. There's a simple answer to all this.'

'There is? What?'

'Marry me.'

'Marry! When?'

'As soon as it can be arranged. Oh, I know you are thinking I'm not in a position to maintain a wife, but I am. I've been thinking about it ever since my birthday. I didn't know until then, but my father left a substantial sum invested, with the stipulation that I should have the income once I reached the age of twenty-one. I already own the house. It was left to me on the understanding that my mother can live there until … well, for the rest of her life. So you see, with the private income and my salary and a house, I am in a position to ask you to marry me. I was going to wait until … until my mother is feeling better; but now I see you so unhappy it seems cruel not to go ahead as soon as possible.' He turned her towards him and looked into her eyes. 'You do love me, May? I know I love you and I thought you felt the same.'

'I do!' she said. 'You know I do. And I would love to be married to you …'

'Then what are we waiting for?'

'I need to think.'

'What about?'

'Well, for one thing, I would be living in your house, with your mother. She doesn't like me, James.'

'Yes, she does.'

'No. She liked me well enough as the little girl who made her hats. But not as your wife. She thinks I'm not good enough for you.'

'We've been through all that. I have told her that as far as I am concerned you are good enough for any man and I am not going to give you up. She accepts that.'

'She accepts me as the girl you are walking out with. I'm sure she hopes that sooner or later you will get tired of me, or something will happen to change things. Me coming to live in her house as your wife is not something she has ever dreamed of, I'm sure. And while she is ill it would be cruel to inflict that on her.'

'Nonsense! It would give her the chance to get to know you properly, to see what a sweet, clever girl you are. You could be a comfort to her in her sickness.'

May looked away. 'I don't think so, but anyway …' Running through her head was the thought of the lie she had told him so casually when they first met. She had wrestled with the dilemma of whether she should tell him the truth once before, until his kiss had put it out of her mind. Since then, it had been easier not to think about it. She had worked to make herself a suitable wife for him, without ever really believing that the dream could come true. Now she was faced with the reality, the question of her upbringing had to be resolved, one way or the other.

She got up. 'James, I need time to think. I'm sorry, but it isn't something I can decide on the spot. Give me a few days.'

She could see that he was hurt. He had expected her to agree immediately. But he said, 'Very well. I suppose I have rather sprung the idea on you out of the blue. But please don't make me wait another week. I couldn't bear that.'

'All right,' she responded. 'Can you meet me on Wednesday afternoon?'

'I should be able to get away early, if I can get all my work up to date. I'll tell them I need to get some medicine for my mother. About four o'clock?'

'I'll be here at four.'

'And then you will give me an answer?'

'I ... I will try. That's all I can promise. We'd better say goodnight now.'

'Goodnight.' He was looking at her with pain and confusion in his eyes and she nearly lost her resolve. To prevent that, she turned and walked quickly away.

On Wednesday, he was waiting at the appointed place when she arrived. Autumn had come and a chilly wind was blowing dead leaves along the tow path. He jumped up and grabbed her hands.

'Well, my darling? Have you decided? Please say yes and put me out of my misery.'

She lowered herself onto the bench and drew him down beside her. 'Before I say yes, there is something you have to know. It may change the way you feel about me.'

'How could it? How could anything change the way I feel?'

'Let me explain. Just listen a minute and don't say anything.'

'All right. Go on.'

'I told you my father was a sea captain. He wasn't. He was an ordinary sailor. We were poor. I was born in a courtyard house. You must have seen places like that. Tiny, poky places round a muddy yard with two privies between twenty people. When I was two, and Gus had just been born, we heard that he had been lost at sea. We never found out what happened, just that. My mother coped as best she could, but when I was five and Gus was three she fell ill and died.'

'Dear God! Who took care of you then?'

'No one. We were sent to the workhouse. That's what you need to know. I am a workhouse orphan, brought up and educated just enough to be a servant. When I was thirteen I was sent into service in the Freeman's house. For nearly a year I scrubbed and cleaned and opened the door to visitors. It was only because Mr Freeman saw some talent for drawing and design in me that he rescued me from that and made me Nan's apprentice. I owe everything to him.' She raised her eyes and looked at his face. 'So there it is. Now you know what you would be marrying.'

He did not reply, but after a moment he got up and stood gazing over the muddy waters of the canal. She sat silent, choking back sobs. It was over, then, just as she had feared.

After a long pause he came back and sat down beside her and took her hand. 'Dear May, what you have told me can't make any difference to the person you are, or the way I feel about you. I admire you for rising above all that and making yourself into the person you are now. It must have taken courage and determination.' She was breathing again. It was going to be all right after all. 'The trouble is,' he went on, 'it will make a difference to other people. My mother has reconciled herself to the idea of me marrying you when she believed you had had a respectable upbringing and had only had to work for a living when your mother died and you fell on hard times. I'm afraid knowing the truth would distress her deeply. I haven't told you, but her illness is more serious than we thought. The doctors are talking about a cancer and they say she may have only months to live. I can't inflict such a shock on her in her condition.'

'No, I understand that.' Her mind was racing. It would mean waiting, then. How long? Waiting for his mother to die? That would be terrible, for both of them.

'Unfortunately,' James continued, 'it isn't only my mother we have to consider. There is no doubt in my mind that if your background became generally known it could be detrimental to my career as a lawyer. It's a sad thing to say, but people are snobs and they do gossip.' May sank into herself on the hard bench. It was over, after all. 'So I have a suggestion,' he said. 'Let us keep what you have told me between ourselves. No one else need know and we can go on just as before.'

She lifted her eyes to his. 'You mean, marry and live with the lie?'

'Is that so difficult? You've lived with it for two years already.'

'But this is different. Suppose someone recognised me? As your wife I should have to entertain your friends, your fellow lawyers perhaps. Suppose one of the ladies I used to open the door to at the Freeman's house happened to meet your mother, or come across us at a gathering of some sort, and knew who I was.'

'That's very unlikely. In my experience, people see what they expect to see. Why should anyone associate the respectable, well-dressed wife of a professional man with a little girl they probably hardly looked at years earlier? And if anyone said anything, you could laugh it off. "How droll! Fancy confusing me with a girl like that! I wonder what her name was."'

'I'm not sure I could do that,' May said. 'And there are people who knew me in the workhouse. Patty, for instance. We grew up there together.'

'She wouldn't give you away, would she?'

'She wouldn't mean to, but she does gossip. She might tell someone, in confidence, and they might pass it on. And what about Mr Freeman? He knows my history, but he doesn't know we have been seeing each other. I don't think he would approve.'

'Why should that matter? I know you owe him a debt of gratitude, but that shouldn't rule your life.' May shook her head and sighed and he went on, 'If you are really worried, once I've completed my articles, we could move away. I could get a job somewhere else, where nobody knew us, Chester perhaps, or Manchester.'

'It's not just that,' May said. 'You say that it doesn't make any difference to the way you feel about me. But it does. You don't want to be married to a workhouse girl. You want me to be someone I'm not. I know you say I'm still the same person, but now that you know I've lied to you, you will never feel quite the same about me. If we marry, we shall always have that hanging over us.' She got up. 'We both need to think about this. When you wake up tomorrow you may find that you do feel differently. And I have to decide if I can ever live up to what you need in a wife. I think, perhaps, we should not see each other for a while, until we have both had time to work out what we really feel.'

He jumped up and caught her in his arms. 'Don't say that! Please, May. I can't live like this, not knowing. I do love you! Nothing can change that."

'You say that now,' she said, detaching herself from his hold, 'but I'm afraid you will regret it in the end.'

'No! Listen, we can't part like this. You must give me some hope. Say you'll meet me next Sunday.'

Her resistance was crumbling. 'All right. We can meet. But you must think really hard about the future and what it could mean. I'm going now. Goodbye.'

'Goodnight, not goodbye! Don't say goodbye!'

But she was already walking away from him.

Next morning, after a night during which she had hardly slept, a note for her was delivered to the store. It was signed by the agent who was in charge of selling Nan's house.

Dear Miss Lavender,

While visiting the property to make final arrangements I found a letter addressed to you. If you care to call at my office I shall be glad to hand it over to you.

May felt a slight lift in her spirits. There was only one person who might have written to her and that was Gus. Apart from a card sent from Cape Town, she had not heard from him since he sailed and it would be a relief and a distraction to learn how he was getting on.

At dinnertime she slipped out of the store and made her way to the address on the agent's notepaper. The letter was from Gus, as she knew it must be, and since the weather had improved, and there was a gleam of sunshine, she sat down on the steps of St George's Hall to read it.

Dear May,

I have some wonderful news. Our father is not dead but very much alive and living here in Australia. He walked into the hotel where I have found work out of the blue yesterday. What we were told, about him being 'lost at sea', was not the truth, though I can understand why our mother preferred that story. In fact, he was convicted of smuggling and sentenced to be transported for ten years. He served his sentence but when he was free, because he had not heard anything from mother, he assumed she did not want him to come back, so he stayed. Of course, he had no way of knowing that she was dead.

He decided to try his luck in the gold fields and he struck lucky! A good vein of gold ran right through his concession. He's a rich man, May! Very rich. Much richer than either of us could ever have imagined. But he hasn't just sat back and lived on the money. He has bought some land in the Rutherglen area, north of here, and planted vines. He is convinced Australia can make wine as good as anything you can buy in Europe. Of course, it's early days yet and you may ask what can our dad know about growing wine; but he has a partner, a Spaniard, who grew up on a vineyard in Spain and understands all the techniques.

Dad has built a house on the estate. I haven't seen it yet, of course, but it sounds very grand. The best bit of news is, he wants me to go and work with him. He'll make me a partner in the business and teach me all about it, with the idea that eventually I shall inherit it. And he wants you to come and join us. He has never married again, so you would be the lady of the house and never have to make a hat again, unless you wanted to. And so that you can come, I am enclosing a memorandum of a draft paid to the White Star company to pay for your fare. Not steerage, May. First class!

You must come! This is a wonderful country where no one cares who your parents were or where you grew up. No one worries about the fact that Dad is an ex-convict. It's what he is now that matters. You can have a new life here, in the sunshine, away from gloomy old Liverpool. And there are plenty of young men out here looking for a wife. You'll be able to take your pick.

Get a passage on the first ship, or maybe wait until you can come on the Royal Standard. *You'll be much more comfortable on her. Let us know as soon as you can when to expect you.*

Your loving brother,
Gus

May read the letter twice and found that her hands were shaking. All night she had wrestled with the problem of how to respond to James's proposal. She had no doubt that he was sincere when he said that he loved her and that her revelations about her upbringing had made no difference to his feelings; but at the same time a thought nagged at her. He wanted her to lie about her childhood.

He said it was because it would upset his mother and might affect his career; but did that not mean that in fact he was ashamed of her? He had fallen in love with the girl he thought she was. How long would it be before he had to admit that that girl did not exist? She knew that if she agreed to his proposal she would live in constant fear that one day, by some slip of her own or some casual remark from someone else, the illusion would be destroyed and he would realise that marrying her had been a mistake. Common sense told her that such a life would be insupportable.

Now, here was Gus offering her a way out. She reread again his words declaring that no one cared about where you grew up. Maybe it was true that out there a workhouse orphan could be accepted as 'the lady of the house', as he put it, without being afraid that revelations about her past could destroy her happiness. She felt a real, physical pain around the region of her heart at the thought that she would never see James again, but at the same time there was a kind of relief. It would be better for him not to be saddled with a wife he was ashamed of; and far, far better for her not to be forced to live a lie.

She looked down at the draft memorandum. It seemed she had only to present this to the offices of the White Star to be given a berth on the next ship. She got to her feet. Half her mind said that she should go back to the store; that Miss Jones would be furious with her for being late. The other half told her that it did not matter; that if she was leaving for Australia she need never go back to that workroom again. She drew a breath, straightened her shoulders and set off for the docks.

'You're in luck, miss,' the clerk said when she presented the draft. 'The *Royal Standard* is due to sail tomorrow on the morning tide and there's just one berth left in First Class.'

'Tomorrow! How long before the next ship?'

'That'll be another six weeks and a longer voyage. I'd advise you to take this one if you can possibly arrange it.'

Tomorrow! Tomorrow all her worries and conflicts could be behind her and a new life would open up. She would see Gus and the father she had never known and never have to sleep in a dormitory or submit to the jibes of the hateful Miss Jones. And James would be free to marry a girl from a good family who would make him a suitable wife.

'All right. I'll take the berth. Thank you.'

May returned to the store and went in, not by the staff entrance in the back alley, but through the main doors. She made her way to Mr Freeman's office and told his secretary that she needed to see him urgently. The woman looked worried.

'Oh dear! I hope it's not more trouble.'

'Not anything that Mr Freeman needs to be worried about, but I do need to talk to him.'

The secretary went in to Mr Freeman's room and came back to say, 'Mr Freeman can give you ten minutes.'

Mr Freeman leaned back in his chair and looked at her wearily. 'If you have come to tell me that things are not going well between you and Miss Jones, I already know. She was here twenty minutes ago complaining that you were late for work.'

'I'm sorry about that, sir, but you won't need to be troubled by that again. I'm leaving Freeman's.'

'Leaving!' he sat forward sharply. 'May, don't make a hasty decision. I admit that employing Miss Jones may have been a mistake. I should have trusted you to take care of the department. But give it a few months. I'll speak to Miss Jones. I'm sure we can resolve the situation satisfactorily.'

'It's not about Miss Jones,' May said. 'Or not really.'

'So what are you intending to do? Set up independently? We'll lose half our best customers.'

'It's not that, either,' she said and handed him Gus's letter. 'I think you had better read this.'

Mr Freeman scanned the letter and when he raised his eyes his expression was different. 'This is a most extraordinary turn of affairs. I thought you told me you were an orphan.'

'I thought so too, until I got this letter.'

'So what do you intend to do?'

'I'm going to Australia to join my father.'

'Of course. Of course.' He seemed at a loss for words. 'When do you plan to leave?'

'Tomorrow.'

'Tomorrow? So soon!'

'There's a ship leaving tomorrow and I've taken a berth on it.'

He sat back and looked at her. 'Well, I don't know what to say. I can see it is a wonderful opportunity for you. But I shall miss you, May. I think you know I've always had a greater interest in you than in most of my employees.'

May felt a lump rise in her throat. 'Please don't think I'm ungrateful. You saved me from a life of drudgery and you've given me a chance to learn a skill and opened up a whole new world of opportunities. Most girls from the workhouse never get that sort of chance. And I know I've given you trouble, more than once. I'll never forget how kind you have been to me.'

He got up and came round the desk. 'To be honest with you, I have felt towards you as I might have done if you were my own daughter. There have been times when I have wished that Isabella had half your talent and a quarter of your courage. I meant it when I said I shall miss you, but I wouldn't dream of standing in your way, even if I could. All I can do is wish you every possible success in your new life.'

'Thank you.' She could not hold back the tears, but she smiled through them.

He turned to the desk and wrote something on a piece of paper. 'Here. A little parting gift. It's an instruction to the staff to allow you to choose whatever you need to furnish you for your journey. A suitcase, for a start, and a new dress, something suitable for a warm climate, shoes and underwear – and a hat of course. You can choose one of your own creations.'

'Oh, that isn't necessary,' she murmured, 'but thank you. And thank you for all you've done for me.'

'Do you want me to inform Miss Jones?'

She hesitated, then nodded. 'Yes, I think that would be best.' There was a brief, awkward pause and then he leaned down and kissed her cheek. 'Take care of yourself, dear May.'

Later that evening, her new clothes and all her other possessions packed into a new suitcase, May found a quiet corner and took out paper and pen.

Dear James,

This letter will be a shock to you, but I am afraid there is nothing I can do to make it easier. I am leaving for Australia on the Royal Standard *at ten o'clock tomorrow morning. I have had a letter from my brother telling me that the father we thought was dead is alive and has struck gold. He is now a wealthy man and he wants me and Gus to live with him.*

I think this is the best solution for both of us. You know I love you, and I think you believe you love me, but I am afraid that that would not last when you are faced with the reality of having a wife whose background you are ashamed of. I could not live with the fear that that might happen. This way we shall both be free and I am sure that once I am out of sight and out of mind, you will find someone much more suitable to marry.

I know that this is going to cause you pain and, believe me, it hurts me almost beyond bearing, but I'm sure it is for the best. Please try to forget me and find your happiness elsewhere.

With my love,
May

She sealed the letter, put a stamp on it and carried it to the postbox. She told no one else about her plans. She could not bear the thought of explanations and tearful farewells; so no one came to see her off.

One of the messenger boys, detailed by Mr Freeman in a final act of kindness, carried her case down to the docks, and she was ushered on board and shown to her stateroom, which was equipped with a luxury she had never experienced before. She saw her case delivered and went up on deck. The ship felt familiar and she remembered that Gus had shown her round before he sailed on her. Final preparations were being made for departure and she heard the call of 'All ashore that's going ashore' and remembered how she had felt when she saw Gus off.

The friends and relatives of those travelling with her were saying goodbye, with tearful hugs and kisses, and she was glad that she had avoided that. The gangplank was raised and she heard the steamer's engines begin to throb. Ropes were cast off and the gap between the ship and the dock began to widen.

Suddenly James was there, on the dockside, waving desperately. His voice carried across the water to her.

'May, come back! I can't live without you. We'll tell everyone. I won't ask you to lie, ever. Come back and marry me!'

She felt a great sob rise in her chest, but the ship was already moving out into the channel. May filled her lungs and shouted back over the growing distance.

'I can't come back. If you really love me, catch the next boat!'

'I will! I will!' The promise came to her faintly across the water.

Also available from Ebury Press:

Flora's War
By Audrey Reimann

Dare she risk her reputation?

When the orphaned Flora MacDonald escapes from a
harsh reform school she falls – literally – into the arms
of Andrew Stewart, a handsome sailor on shore leave.
But their blossoming love is interrupted by the
outbreak of the Second World War.

With Andrew away fighting, Flora finds herself in an
impossible situation: alone and pregnant. Out of
desperation, she travels to Andrew's country estate,
but she doesn't know how kindly his well-to-do
family will welcome her in. Will she find a home
where she can raise a child?